The **Foundations** of **Kindness**

ESSENTIAL PROSE SERIES 175

Canadä

Guernica Editions Inc. acknowledges the support
of the Canada Council for the Arts and the Ontario Arts Council.
The Ontario Arts Council is an agency of the Government of Ontario.
We acknowledge the financial support of the Government of Canada.

Richard Vission

The **Foundations** of **Kindness**

GUERNICA
EDITIONS

TORONTO · BUFFALO · LANCASTER (U.K.)
2020

Copyright © 2020, Richard Vission and Guernica Editions Inc.
All rights reserved. The use of any part of this publication,
reproduced, transmitted in any form or by any means, electronic,
mechanical, photocopying, recording or otherwise stored
in a retrieval system, without the prior consent
of the publisher is an infringement of the copyright law.

Michael Mirolla, editor
Interior and cover design: Rafael Chimicatti
Cover art: *Connections II*, Irish Brooke
Guernica Editions Inc.
287 Templemead Drive, (ON), Canada L8W 2W4
2250 Military Road, Tonawanda, N.Y. 14150-6000 U.S.A.
www.guernicaeditions.com

Distributors:
Independent Publishers Group (IPG)
600 North Pulaski Road, Chicago IL 60624
University of Toronto Press Distribution,
5201 Dufferin Street, Toronto (ON), Canada M3H 5T8
Gazelle Book Services, White Cross Mills
High Town, Lancaster LA1 4XS U.K.

First edition.
Printed in Canada.

Legal Deposit—First Quarter
Library of Congress Catalog Card Number: 2019947054
Library and Archives Canada Cataloguing in Publication
Title: The foundations of kindness / Richard Vission.
Names: Vission, Richard, 1939- author.
Series: Essential prose series ; 175.
Description: Series statement: Essential prose series ; 175
Identifiers: Canadiana (print) 20190158344 | Canadiana (ebook)
20190158808 | ISBN 9781771834735
(softcover) | ISBN 9781771834742 (EPUB) | ISBN 9781771834759 (Kindle)
Classification: LCC PS8643.I885 F68 2020 | DDC C813/.6—dc23

Contents

You, who shall emerge from the flood
In which we are sinking,
Think –
When you speak of our weaknesses,
Also of the dark time
That brought them forth.
For we went, changing our country more often than our shoes,
In the class war, despairing
When there was only injustice and no resistance.

For we knew only too well:
Even the hatred of squalor
Makes the brow grow stern.
Even anger against injustice
Makes the voice grow harsh. Alas, we
Who wished to lay the foundations of kindness
Could not ourselves be kind.

But you, when at last it comes to pass
That man can help his fellow man,
Do not judge us
Too harshly.

> — From "To Posterity" by Bertolt Brecht

Only connect!

> — From *Howard's End* by E.M. Forster

When to the sessions of sour, noisy thought I summon up remembrances of things past, anger at things present, fear for things future ...

> — Not Quite Shakespeare, *Sonnet 30*

In memory of Fred Hampton,
assassinated by the FBI and the Chicago Police
December 4, 1969.

Prologue: The Maelstrom

Novelist: *We were kids on a raft we called The Movement, for we were moving constantly, tempest tossed on a raging sea of politics. We had heard rumours of a maelstrom but had little idea of what we were getting into and once into it, it, not we, determined how we would come out of it. If we would come out of it.*

Historian: *We talk different now that you and I are old and out of it. No fancy metaphors back then. Just uneducated kids (and a few educated ones) who thought we could change the world and got busted, beat and murdered for trying.*

Novelist: *We thought we could change the world because it so obviously needed changing. It still does, more than ever, but we're farther than ever from being able to do it.*

Historian: *That's why we need to dip back into your "it." It's time we learned from "it." Understanding the past gives hope for the future.*

Novelist: *How do you dip into a maelstrom? It grabs you, pulls you under, savages you, spins you around and spits you back out god knows where. No way I can understand it. But even after fifty years I cannot not feel it.*

Historian: *It's good, not bad, that you still feel it too. Just let time calm the waters a little. We didn't start the revolution and we won't finish it, but the better we communicate what we did and felt in the past and do and feel in the present, the farther we can advance in the future.*

Novelist: *Advance? We're going backwards. Time hasn't healed a damned (and damnable) thing. It's true that I don't think about what happened as often as I once did, but when I do, there's a new pain: knowing we blew it. This damned present is a result of that damnable past.*

Historian: *Then why did you write about it and show what you wrote to me? Writing what we did tells us what to do. Or at least what not to do. The way back is the way forward.*

Novelist: *For a historian maybe. I wrote about it to try to get it out of me and me out of it, but it didn't work: To write about it is to sink into it. Again.*

Historian: *Maybe you sank because you wrote for yourself, not for history.*

Novelist: *I like to think I wrote for art: politics for art's sake. I tried to get out of reality by getting into realism. Why should politics for history's sake work any better?*

Historian: *Politics, claim the politicians, is the art of the possible. I am a revolutionary, not a politician. In a world like this I like to think revolution is inevitable, but how to make the inevitable possible? We'll need politics* and *art to create history. Sounds very classical, like Thucydides or Sima Qian.*

Novelist: *Thucydides? For god's sake, we're still alive.*

Historian: *So we're making history.*

PART ONE

Late Winter, Early Spring 1975

1.

I DON'T KNOW IF I'M WRITING the story of Jazzman or myself, if it was Jazzman who made that year and a half so special or if that year and a half was so special it made Jazzman. I only know I'm so damn lucky to be able to write it that I must. You can't write in Chicago, you can't even think. You've got to do – whatever you can if only to cry to its millions of other prisoners: "I'm with you, suffering next door to you, struggling alongside of you; let's keep on keeping on; maybe it's not hopeless."

You can't tell the truth in Chicago. Chicago stifles truth by making it so stark or so ridiculous you can't believe it yourself. Even when you're busting a gut trying to tell the truth, your brain is screaming to get out so you can tell the real truth. Then your brain rationalizes staying but you know in your gut you have to get out. Five long years – after the year and a half – it took for my brain and gut to get it together. In the end I persuaded myself that I could help Chicago more by writing about it than by living in it and struggling against it. Probably that's not true, but in Chicago one settles for trite half-truths, and that one got me here. Here where the mountains that ring me sing of peace, a requiem for Fred Hampton and so many other victims of that flat, deadly city. I feel better and more honest than I've felt in many years. The mountains tell me not to worry about who made what or what made whom, just rejoice *(Gloria in excelsis!)* that at last I can tell the story and record the history behind the story.

The last time I ran from Chicago I felt the same exhilaration. It was 1970, almost the end of the siege of Lincoln Park. I had just managed to get out the last issue of *The Press*. I stacked most of the newspapers in the office and began delivering the rest to stores. After a few deliveries I suddenly gunned my hot rod, a fifteen-year-old Volkswagen which looked and sounded like it was about to fall apart and couldn't go over fifty miles an hour. I raced around the lake and headed north with the accelerator floored. At the first slightly green tollroad "oasis" I jumped out and rolled around for several minutes in what passed for grass. Then I gassed up and took off again, unable to stop until I was well into Canada and the night. I wrote a lot then too. Even more frenzied writing than this because that time I knew I would go back. I owed it to Fred. I owed it to the revolution I still wanted to make even if I no longer believed it was possible to make it. I looked at that notebook last night – I couldn't bear to open it in Chicago. My words are insane but honest, squalid and slimy but honest. Bile seethed up from inside me and I squeezed it into my pen then squeezed the words onto the page, covering every inch, the only small gaps presumably identifying pauses where I left off to sleep or pee or look out of the car at the world.

The afternoon of the third day I drove to a small town where I purchased food, the notebook and a flashlight that opened out into a sort of lantern and so enabled me to write at night. It was the only time in seven years I wrote anything resembling truth, not propaganda. I had to get out of Chicago to go crazy. Will it leave me less or more sane if I try to finish now what I began then? Playing with truth is playing with fire. The truth can drive you nuts …

A lesson Chicago taught me all too well. But why bother escaping if I let old Chicago fears shape my new mountain life? If I allow the sinking feeling I'm feeling to keep me from digging into the past, do I deserve the future I'm hoping to unearth here? … That special time was only sixteen months, not a year and a half. In Chicago I called it a year and a half. Here I can try to be accurate as well as honest.

After reading that old notebook last night I went out and waded through the snow. The stars were out, so the night would be cold. Come morning there would be a solid crust on the snow, but for now morning was as far away as summer. I sank in but slogged on, didn't think of anything, didn't dare, needed full concentration to keep from falling in the dark, just felt the mountains, the stars, the solitude and the night creatures and phantoms which sometimes closed around me. But when I woke up this morning I began writing as naturally as if I had blocked out several books and now merely had to fill in my outlines. Yet I don't know exactly which episodes I'm going to relate or how the hell I can tell my story. And I have no idea how to end what didn't. How can writing it settle what living it so unsettled?

I CANNOT COMPREHEND how both my recent lives can be real. Surely, I keep thinking, if all I learned and experienced in Lincoln Park was real, then this world of thick spring snows in the night, of hail blasting down from a bright sky which was sunny a minute ago and will be sunny again in ten minutes, of mountains which ascend into the sun and descend into clouds over the river, this magnificent last of winter world I walk in night and day trying to prove it is really there, cannot be real. Yet, amazingly, it was Jazzman, my symbol incarnate of the city, of the other reality, who led me to this world. And led me here without saying a word about it. I had to get out of Chicago to go crazy and I had to go crazy to get out of Chicago and I am just beginning to figure out that I might never have figured that out if Jazzman had not reappeared in my life.

JAZZMAN. THAT'S WHERE MY STORY BEGINS, four years after I thought it ended. It was 1974 and I was living on the southwest side of Chicago in the Marquette Park neighbourhood. Marquette Park was the antithesis of everything Lincoln Park had been, but it had one virtue: It was not about to be gentrified. Came a knock on my door. I opened and looked into blue eyes and a grin I hadn't ever expected to see again. Although (because?) I had worked hard not to think about Jazzman since leaving Lincoln Park, my eyes glazed and my knees wobbled. Jazzman's embrace had a practical aspect: to hold me up. I hugged him back hard and long, long to give me time to regather my wits. After a while Jazzman stepped back, mockingly returned my stare and asked if I was going to invite them in. Only then did I see the black haired, brown skinned girl holding the baby. Jazzman introduced her as Melba, his wife. Poor Lisa.

They came in. Melba sat quietly, absorbed in the baby but listening as Jazzman and I talked. We talked long, mainly about his plans. My thoughts were all about the past, but Jazzman always lived in the present for the future. He had escaped and returned, surfaced from underground and served his jail sentence so he could run for alderman in Lake View. Times and places had changed he told me when he saw my questioning look. I supposed his plan was a logical result of his practical, political nature, and although I loathed the idea of participating in a crooked Chicago election there was no way I could not agree to help his campaign. I did not ask him about his time in exile. It's not the kind of knowledge you want: Others may be hiding in the same place. Nevertheless, I had been listening to talk about the underground for years. Canada had provided an escape for me once, and earlier that very day I had heard a tale of the beautiful mountains in the interior of British Columbia and a mysterious valley populated by hippies who welcomed political refugees. The coincidence told me more than I needed to know, more than I would have let Jazzman himself tell me.

Jazzman seemed invigorated by his escape and his plans. The last time I had seen him he had been nodding, so this new spirit renewed my own. From that night on dreams of mountains mingled with my dreams of Lincoln Park as it had been. By the time of the aldermanic campaign I was dreaming of mountains during the day as well. My dreams I know now and suspected then – I had never seen a high mountain until shortly before this time – had little to do with the reality of these mountains I now live in and love. Wish fulfillment, Freud called dreams. My mind, my imagination was making the passage into a new life before my body could travel there. Back then I expected to be disappointed by real mountains, believed imagination always exceeded reality. In some ways it does: Even today I often find that new mountains don't look as high as my expectations and old mountains don't look as high as my recollections. But height is not all that makes mountains mountainous. No one who has lived only in flat prairies can conceive of the variety, the vastness and, most of all, the colours of the mountains.

I remember driving toward them for the first time, through one hundred five degree prairie days and nights too hot to sleep, knowing the Rockies were topped with snow year round and chuckling at my gullibility for believing such an absurdity. When they became visible, I thought for many miles they were simply white clouds in the distance, but when I finally figured out they were mountains, what impressed me was not the tops but the hazy purple swellings beneath the snow.

When I reached my first mountain lake, I threw myself down and refused to budge from it for three days, trying to understand the colours, closing and opening my eyes to see if the colours had changed, fearing that further mountains could only be anticlimactic. Of course they weren't: Those Montana mountains cannot compare to the Canadian Rockies, and much of the beauty goes beyond the eye or any other sense, lies in the extent of the mountains, in the world they create. A tourist is more than satisfied with colour and majesty, yet living among mountains one discovers they give much more, are spectacular even in winter shrouds of gray when the eye can see nothing fifty feet above the valley floor. The damp gray obscurity of mountain fogs is as much a part of this world as the gray city smogs which dampen the spirit yet fail to obscure the ugliness of Chicago.

Had I been able to write when I was dreaming of mountains in Chicago a year ago, I would now no doubt laugh at my old imaginings.

Nevertheless, those dreams gave me strength to work in an enterprise I didn't much believe in. In the election I carried my precinct for Jazzman, one of three he won in the ward and the only one in the east side, lakefront, honky area. I earned my passage, my right to leave. I escaped Chicago soon after the election and do not intend to return. It took some hard travelling to get here, but I had time and a legend to guide me.

I now live in the Slocan Valley in the interior of British Columbia, two thousand miles west and two thousand feet above Lincoln Park. Although the Sixties are long over, I am not the only stubborn fool who refuses to admit it. Beards and beads identify us. A stranger became a friend by producing a nickel bag of dynamite homegrown. When after a few puffs he invited me to help transform a hole in the ground into the Vallican Whole Community Centre, whatever that was, I knew with the all encompassing knowledge of the weed that I had discovered the unnamed valley whose far out legend had reached far off Chicago. So here I be, in love with my mountains and my valley, writing of the flat city I hate, writing to purge Chicago from my soul forever.

Yet still jumping up and down and around and showing off like I did in Chicago. Help me, mountains. You do not jump around. Steady me to tell my story somewhat consecutively. It is like you, solid yet prone to avalanche, full of peaks and chasms, storms and rainbows, scholarly fools who think they can conquer the heights by reading books about mountaineering and unread sages whose seemingly instinctive knowledge of the terrain comes from living in harmony with it.

I FIRST ENCOUNTERED JAZZMAN IN 1966. He knocked out my two front teeth. Nothing personal. I got in his way when I tried to break up a fight in front of George's hot dog stand at Halsted and Dickens. I succeeded in breaking up the fight: One punch did it for my teeth, and when I staggered up from the gutter with a tooth dangling at chest level from a strand of my gum and blood dripping from my mouth onto my sport coat, everyone scattered. I don't think I've worn a sport coat since. Neither Jazzman nor I figured out the other's role until a party three years later when Sal told the story. We laughed hard when Jazzman realized it was me he hit and I realized it was he who hit me. We didn't laugh long because later that night a cop shot into the party and killed Sal.

I actually met Jazzman right after the Democratic Convention, in August 1968. I was sleeping heavily, my first real sleep in six days, when

Meg, dear, damned Meg, ignoring Priscilla's protests just as I would have under the circumstances, burst into the room. Priscilla actually attempted to restrain her, and the two women seemed to dance in together, Meg leading, Priscilla clinging to Meg's shoulder, her body at an angle only a ballerina could manage, exactly between standing and falling. The position was so unnatural and I was so out of it that I assumed I was dreaming. Then Meg took one more step and Priscilla fell, Meg's shirt going with her with a rip which told me I was awake and going to stay awake. Meg's news was that the Puerto Ricans who hung out at Halsted and Dickens had been turned on by the Convention and wanted to stage their own protest march through the community.

I returned with Meg, who had put on one of Priscilla's blouses, to Halsted and Dickens. In the two years since I had lost my teeth, the action had shifted away from the southeast corner, where George's hot dog stand now stood boarded up awaiting the wreckers' ball. Fat Harry Berns, the mafia realtor, had opened a new hot dog stand on the southwest corner, but the guys who hung out at Halsted and Dickens avoided it out of loyalty to George and because the man who ran the place for Harry sometimes called the cops on them. They now hung out on the northwest corner outside a closed-down bar, beneath four stories of rusty fire escapes dangling down outside opaque-with-dust windows of dingy apartments where Mama Jane and others of the poorest families in the neighbourhood lived.

We sat on the sidewalk rapping with four or six guys while a dozen more dropped in and out of the discussion, walked around, called out to passers-by, sang, admired the few fancy cars which drove by, ridiculed the many jalopies, shot craps, played kick the can, whistled at girls, wandered off with groups of friends, returned alone or in pairs, hooted at cop cars and got ready to run. Cop cars passing the corner always slowed down so the occupants could stare, but none stopped this day. A week earlier, at a similar session to make posters for the Democratic Convention, a car had stopped and a cop had leaped out with drawn gun, lined all the males against the wall and patted us down. The incident stunned me, but the others had been prepared. After the cops drove off, Meg opened her purse and returned half a dozen knives, several sets of dice and a pea shooter belonging to someone's younger brother.

I don't recall much of what was said as we sat around. Probably a lot of it went over my head. The kids were showing off their newly acquired political rhetoric while Meg and I were showing off our newly acquired street lingo. Meg had acquired more of it than I. For an hour we engaged in a verbal ritual of greeting, a laboured effort to communicate to each other how hip we were without saying enough to prove what we all knew, that we were from different worlds. But we each craved some of the other world.

Sal, a tall, thin twenty-something-year-old hustler with black, slick hair, did most of the talking. He had picked up some radical jargon during the Convention week and rapped on about smashing the system and shoving the establishment up against the wall. I had seen him around; I did not recognize his friend, who said nothing to us but occasionally asked soft questions in Spanish of Sal and the others. The language and the respect the others showed him seemed out of place, for he was a small, blond haired, blue eyed, round red cheeked boy who looked years younger than anyone else in the crowd. When the street corner session broke up, Sal and the blond youngster walked Meg and me back to my place and came in for a beer. I was surprised to find that the stranger spoke good English. After a while he seemed to become more confident of us and Sal's loud talk stopped as if by a command although I detected no word or gesture.

The newcomer spoke quietly but freely. He said his name was Jose Morales but everyone called him Jazzman. He said he hadn't been around lately. He had been a junkie and a jailbird and was now a father. When he wasn't strung out or in jail, he had been in Aurora trying to make a family with his baby daughter and fourteen-year-old girlfriend. He had just got out of jail and came back to the "hood" to check out the action around the Convention.

In retrospect it seems strange, but I took in this story without a comment. I didn't say even to myself anything like: "Wow, and I thought my life was messy." That day I was too full of politics, rage and lack of sleep to pay much attention to the human side of his story. What I did pay attention to was that, as he and Sal were leaving, he went to my bookcase, questioned me about various books and asked to borrow a few. Among them was a book of selected writings of Marx and Engels and an anthology of twentieth century poetry.

A few days later he came back, books in arms, grinning like a child who just caught his first frog. I asked him what he liked best in the books, and his answer should have cured me of pedagogical zeal. He closed his eyes and rattled off a couple of pages of the *Communist Manifesto* verbatim. From then on I tried to let him ask the questions. He left my place with a new batch of books.

I thought that he was my student, that I was going to give a college education to an eighth grade dropout classified as "educable mentally handicapped" by an uneducable Chicago school system. It turned out that I was his student. Five years earlier I had completed coursework for a Ph.D. in English literature. At the end of a gruelling oral qualifying exam a professor asked me: "What is the key word in the penultimate chapter of Sir Thomas Browne's *Hydrotaphia or Urn Burial*?" I didn't know the answer, and although I passed the exam, brooding on the pettiness of that question revealed to me that I was on a wrong path, a path that led to a wasteland of dry as dust pedantry, a wasteland as barren as any made by the Department of Urban Renewal. Although I had qualified for the Ph.D., I never returned to the University of Chicago, never wrote a word of my planned dissertation, "Heterodox Mysticism in the Works of D.H. Lawrence and Aldous Huxley." Jazzman taught me to stop brooding, to laugh at the professor's question and my dissertation.

By the new year the Young Latins Organization, Jazzman Morales chairman, was front page news in Chicago and Jazzman had little time for reading, but in those last months of 1968 he continued a book education that had begun in jail.

▲ ▲ ▲

Historian: *We made history I feared was never going to be recorded or remembered. That's why I'm now a graduate student trying to do a history of the Young Lords with interviews and photos. Your book let me relive it from your point of view instead of my own.*
Novelist: *Good. It's supposed to be a realistic novel.*
Historian: *For me it's history. I can use it in my project.*
Novelist: *It's supposed to be a realistic historical novel, but it's still a novel.*
Historian: *You call it a novel. That's your thing. But every thing in it happened, so I can use it in my history project. That's my thing.*
Novelist: *Pure Sixties, everyone doing their own thing.*
Historian: *Right on. But your thing is better history than my thing because it's earlier, forty years earlier. When the rest of us were in despair and trying to forget, you wrote on. For a historian that's past tense for right*

on, old friend. This is the best history around of our Lincoln Park Move-
ment. But do you have to use fake names?

Novelist: *Not fake, fictitious. Like I keep telling you, this is a novel.*

Historian: *But like I told you, everything in it happened.*

Novelist: *That's because I didn't send you the conclusion.*

Historian: *There's more? There's a conclusion?*

Novelist: *There are three complete conclusions and several incomplete ones.*
The complete ones are about as long as the parts I sent you. They're pure
fiction and they all stink. I wrote a novel because I thought I could end
what didn't, but I couldn't. I'm an unimaginative novelist.

Historian: *But a hell of a historian. Novels end, history doesn't. In spite*
of the fools who say it does and the liars who try to change it. Some
people are trying to claim that the New York Young Lords were the
original ones.

Novelist: *Wow ... Shit ... I remember when those guys from New York*
came. They were sophisticated, educated, but they respected you. They
asked for advice, asked for permission to start a chapter ... Okay, I think
I can use real names for organizations but not for people. It might even
ground the novel, make it more realistic.

Historian: *Thanks, man. It's not the way I'd do it, but this is your thing.*
I hated to ask you to change your thing, but what you just agreed to do
is a big thing for me. And for history.

▲ ▲ ▲

A PRIEST HAD GIVEN JAZZMAN *The Seven Story Mountain*, the auto-
biography of a Trappist monk, mystic and pacifist, and the priest and the
Black Muslims had loaned the newly inquisitive jailbird other books.
I was going to say that Jazzman gave himself a college education, but the
jail's and my library were more limited than his curiosity, and his mind
was quite unlike a college graduate's. His mind perhaps was a preliter-
ate one, the sort that kept the words of Homer alive for the hundreds of
years between when Homer sang them and when the Greeks conceived
of writing and painfully devised a means and an alphabet that came close
to containing Homer. Or the sort of mind bred by alphabetless languages
when pictures become too complicated to be recognized as words, and
memory must be trained far more finely than in learners of languages
who only have to master a few letters to construct written words.

When Jazzman read something he liked, he learned it. Fully. Not only could he reel off whole pages word for word, but he could criticize and discuss the ideas, often brilliantly. He wanted to know all sorts of things and, to me more incredible, to apply them – in ways which would never occur to a college graduate or me. He could ask a question about the theory of relativity in the middle of a confrontation with the cops – then use the knowledge a little later to show up the police chief.

While wrecking balls and bulldozers were smashing and grinding much of our diverse neighbourhood to rubble, Jazzman's mind grew from the rubble the schools had made in his head and opened like a sunflower in a sunny summer. I watched this growth amid destruction, shouted out against the destruction but tried to keep my mouth shut about the growth. Nevertheless, my mouth often dropped open in amazement and kept jabbering out of habit. The addiction to teaching dies hard, but Jazzman's self education did much to help me kick my habit. Jazzman taught me that the mind must utilize all knowledge to grow, should never be ashamed of ideas, only of their use to hurt people or lead them astray.

Never again would I be ashamed of my own education though often I was ashamed of how most intellectuals used their education, and always I was furious at the thought of the many minds like Jazzman's starving and withering because our social and educational systems deny them nourishment. Jazzman taught me by example the lesson basic to all knowledge, the beauty and potential of every human mind. Perhaps someday I would be able to utilize even the key word in the penultimate chapter of Sir Thomas Browne's *Hydrotaphia or Urn Burial*.

Jazzman seldom talked much about himself, so I can only sketch his life before I met him. He grew up around Division and Clark Streets, *La Clark* he called it, a poor, tough area with a small Puerto Rican community. He spoke affectionately of that "hood," perhaps because it was the only place he ever lived in for more than a year or two. However, Mayor Daley had a plan for the city of Chicago, and poor folks living in *La Clark* and the rest of the city's core did not figure in this plan.

Jazzman sometimes reminisced bitterly that his people were tricked into leaving, told their tenements had to be torn down, urban renewed so good housing could be built, but that former residents would be given first choice of the new housing. When the new buildings went up, they were luxury apartments called the Carl Sandburg Village with rents triple what former residents could afford. (Sorry Carl, but Chicago has to use its native sons even if you weren't quite native. The People, No.)

So Jazzman's family and much of his community moved north to Old Town, arriving shortly before real estate speculators began turning that neighbourhood into Chicago's Greenwich Village, doubling and tripling rents. This time Jazzman and his young friends fought to stay in their new hood. Jazzman joined (and later became leader of) the Young Lords, a small gang which included Puerto Rican, black and poor white kids whose main activity was beating up the "beatniks" – as the Young Lords still called anyone with a beard in the early Sixties. These beatniks were moving in where the Young Lords' friends' families had been forced out. The gang never lost a fight in those days, but its battle was hopeless because it wasn't fighting the people who were really taking the neighbourhood. Soon coach lights, the symbol of the new, expensive way of life in Old Town, graced every doorway, and there were no poor people left, bearded or not.

Next Jazzman and most of his pals found themselves on Larrabee Street northwest of Old Town. They had arrived in Lincoln Park. The Department of Urban Renewal promptly moved in and tore down all the housing on Larrabee Street. Jazzman's family moved farther north and west, to Bissell and Dickens Streets. That's where he lived when I met him in 1968, but Elizabeth and Paul Swoop had already scooped up most of that block and were planning to evict the tenants, sandblast the bright paint and remodel the Victorian buildings into luxury townhouses. Today Jazzman and his community are located farther north, in northern Lake View and southern Uptown, where they are fighting the city's plan to urban renew that neighbourhood.

"Twenty one hundred Bissell," I muttered when Jazzman told me where he lived. My mind jumped back to a sunny spring afternoon in 1965 when I fell in love at first sight with a neighbourhood. I was still teaching at the University of Illinois, which had just moved from the warehouse at Navy Pier – a warehouse where, miraculously, education sometimes took place – into the new Circle Campus, another product of another urban renewal project, all stark concrete with narrow slits of windows tinted black lest sunlight ever disturb gray halls or brighten minds being trained to be drab. One of my few friends among my colleagues asked for a ride home, and I drove him to the 2100 block of Bissell.

What weird houses: gables protruding everywhere, odd angles and cockeyed cornices, clashing coloured pairs of buildings looking glued to one another and sharing a common porch. Later, after the people had been moved out, the buildings looked like Victorian haunted houses, but in 1965 they were brightly painted, red, blue, green, purple, yellow. Up close perhaps one noticed that some paint was peeling, but from the street it was the gayest looking block in the city. The sidewalks swarmed with children of all sizes and colours, brown, white, red, black. I had never seen so many children, so many people, in one block of two and three story buildings. Adults jammed the porches boozing, gambling, singing, dancing, arguing, loving, yelling advice and admonitions to the children who jammed the sidewalks eating, playing, crying, rolling, quarrelling, flirting, yelling back at the adults yelling at them.

I didn't have to brood about this revelation. It was life. The conviction was instant and unshakeable. I didn't doubt it then and never have since. Twenty one hundred Bissell, west Lincoln Park, life. Three years after I first saw the block, Jazzman told me he lived there and so confirmed my revelation, for something about this soft-spoken boy almost immediately told me he lived at the centre of real life.

Shortly after first sight I had moved into the neighbourhood, but I could not find an apartment on Bissell Street. I settled for Dayton Street, two blocks east. I was on the road. It wasn't quite Bissell Street, and it certainly was not Kerouac's road. It led away from the pedantry I was trying to escape, but what was it leading to? I had become friends with Jerry, a black hustler in a relationship with one of my female students. He was looking for a place to live, and since he represented another break with my middle class upbringing, I was eager to room with him. I had mocked the new Circle Campus in the school newspaper and my teaching contract was not being renewed; I planned to live by gambling and hustling.

I could more than hold my own in any bridge game in the city, and recently two friends and I had won a $5,000 twin double at Sportsman's Park and used the money to claim a pacer who was finishing in the money consistently. Jerry, my new roommate, had shown me how I could invest my winnings in dope and earn excellent profits. When I hesitated he turned me on to acid. Then his only task was convincing me I should buy the "cubes," which were still rare and expensive at that time, for five dollars and sell them for ten. I wanted to give them away so all people could discover themselves and change the world.

The road I was on in Lincoln Park was a very political one, but to find that out I had to get off it for nine months. After two years living with Jerry on the 2000 block of Dayton Street, I got a job teaching at a black university in western North Carolina. My first mountains though not very high ones. Just high enough to give me perspective, to begin letting me see the deeper changes our society needed. I found shelter and new life in a southern black community, became active in the civil rights movement and was arrested for the first time after integrating a "riot" following Dr. King's murder. My white lawyer advised me to get out and stay out of North Carolina, not even risk flying over it in an airplane.

When I returned to Lincoln Park, I moved into an old coach house with Priscilla. A year and a half earlier she had introduced herself: "My name is Priscilla; please don't call me Pris or Prissy," and I remember wondering whether Priscilla was the name of a witch or a wicked stepmother. But her nose, face and body were soft and rounded, not angular and sharp as a witch's or stepmother's should have been, so I had forgiven her her name. Besides, the coach house was cheap and genuine working class, which had become important to me. It was a miniature building behind the main house, built for servants, buggies and horses during the last century. For all we knew the ground floor, which was windowless, locked, never entered by anyone, may still have contained the coach. At least it did not contain a horse and, more important, did not sport a coach light.

The second floor contained a bathroom with a shower in an old fashioned tub so small I never attempted a bath, an eating area too small to be called a dining room and a tiny kitchen built to accommodate tiny people, the children who were expected to wash dishes in the low sink which gave me a backache, clean and sometimes cook while their parents were performing similar functions in the big house. The top floor consisted of two little bedrooms, one of which Priscilla used as a studio. The coach house was in the 2000 block of Fremont and so moved me one street closer to Bissell.

That's where I was when I met Jazzman and so finally made direct contact with the revelation which had led me first to move into the neighbourhood and then fight to save it. Sixteen months after this the Sixties were over, Jazzman was underground, his Bissell Street block was uninhabited and workers were putting the finishing touches on the remodelling. One of the workers was Jose Rodriguez, a member of the

Young Lords Organization, twenty, father of two children and attending high school at night. He had helped strip the paint and remove the porches from the buildings, including his leader's former home; he had helped install the coach lights which now modestly graced all entrances.

Suddenly one saw something that had been hidden by the gaudy paint and unadorned wood: Despite all their complicated Victorian architecture and strangely placed gables, the buildings all looked the same. The tacky paint and tacked on wood had been masking a Vickytickytorian assembly line subdivision. The night before I moved out of Lincoln Park I hurled a Molotov cocktail into Jazzman's former home.

Jazzman and I, from totally different backgrounds and directions, had crossed paths twice before we were introduced. These junctions mark the direction and fate of our community, Lincoln Park. Once we crossed in front of Greaser George's hot dog stand, which served the best hot dogs in Chicago and was later torn down by urban renewal shortly after Fat Harry Berns, mafia realtor, opened a new stand across the street; soon after this the land George's stand stood on became part of Chicago's People's Park. Once, in spirit at least, we crossed on the 2100 block of Bissell Street, my personal symbol of the life and centre of Lincoln Park, a block later remodelled and gentrified by Elizabeth and Paul Swoop, real estate speculators and pillars of the Lincoln Park Conservation Association, a group of wealthy property owners dedicated to getting wealthier by turning Lincoln Park into an upper middle class suburb in the heart of the city.

But most of that came later. Now it was late August, 1968, and an ex-bookworm in love with life he hadn't yet lived had just met an ex-convict in love with knowledge he hadn't yet learned.

2.

R AIN IS FALLING STEADILY. Clouds have shut down over the mountains I love. Occasionally as I look out a snow-capped peak bursts through a break in the clouds, but in a few seconds it is gone and the cloud cover is total again. My thoughts too, I now see, have been coming in bursts, in flashes of writing amid long daydreams. What I have written will seem disjointed to any reader though it is part of a beginningless, endless unity within me between my past and my mountains. Have I become part of these mountains? How astonishing that they, so opposite of Chicago, should control and illuminate life in that flat city. At least for me.

And there's the rub: How can such utterly personal reflections be intelligible to anyone else? My justification for leaving Chicago was to write about it for others, not myself. Yet my invisible mountains tell me I am as much a part of Chicago as of them, that my recollections and my present are part of one process even as the snows of last winter and the rains of today are part of the mountains. Somewhere up the mountain, rain and snow mingle in a crazy dance called the coming of spring. Somewhere behind the clouds, spring glistens, white above green below, one. So I write in spasms of a chaotic past and hope the calm oneness of all nature I feel or imagine now is somehow uniting what I write. And hope the spasms, past and present, inside and outside, give life to the calm.

THE POST-CONVENTION PROTEST MARCH came off more successfully than any of us foresaw. It had been publicized only by word of mouth and leaflets cranked by hand on our old mimeograph machine and distributed on the streets mainly by the Puerto Rican kids who had planned it, but after a week of tear gas the community was ready to celebrate just being able to be on the street and inhale deeply. At this time the neighbourhood was not accustomed to such demonstrations. We wanted to do something but didn't expect much. In Chicago one never does. Looking back now I can see how good our timing was.

That spring the black ghetto had risen to protest the assassination of Martin Luther King and had been violently repressed. In summer middle class students had tried to protest the Democratic Party Convention called to ratify the status quo; they too had been violently repressed. Even Chicago – dirty, dated, decadent Chicago – was ready for new things. Like spring rains in the mountains. They come when winter's white has become streaked with filth, when earth no longer needs the layer of snow which has protected it for months but is now holding down the life which must be born quickly if it is to mature in the short mountain summer. But the accumulated snows of a mountain winter are heavy, and earth and seedlings cannot be free until the skies come to their rescue. Warm rains wash away the dirty snow and enable life to kick its way out of its earthy womb.

In the same way life was ready to burst forth from Chicago. The ancient spirit of the city – the spirit of Haymarket and Pullman, the spirit clubbed, gassed and shot by the Chicago Police Department first in the black slums and then in the park east of our own neighbourhood – still lived and wanted out. Both the working class and the middle class of Lincoln Park had been gassed and beaten as fiercely as winter storms pummel the mountains. Both classes had endured the week of the Convention and now could cooperate like earth and sky in the mountain spring. The alliance could be no more permanent than the spring, but its time was now.

In machine-run Chicago even birth is an unnatural act, so instead of spring it was almost fall when a thousand neighbourhood people joined the hastily organized march planned by Puerto Rican street kids from Halsted and Dickens. Lincoln Park came together as it never before had. From the west came the poor, tired of seeing their communities destroyed, their friends disappear, their lives disrupted again and again. As the march passed simple but solid stone two and three flats – narrow, jammed together buildings with one apartment on each floor used to rebuild Lincoln Park after the wooden city Chicago had been burned to the ground in 1871 – people poured down shaky wood stairs into the street. From the east came the wealthy, the smell of gas still in their noses, on their lips stories of frightened "children" seeking sanctuary in their homes or brutally beaten on their steps. The rich forget easily troubles that are not their own, but on that day they still remembered.

A fifty-year-old woman proudly exhibited bloodstains on a dress that probably cost half a month's salary to a man in clean dungarees. She explained animatedly how her garment was bloodied when she tried to stop four policemen from clubbing a girl, even undid a button to show him a bruise on her shoulder. "Yes," he replied, "I too have received beatings from the police." "Was it Tuesday night?" she asked, perhaps sensing a coincidence in their lives. "No. Once summer before last, once in May. They broke down our door looking for my sons. It happens often where I live." The woman is silent, abstract. Is it the beginning of understanding or the beginning of forgetting? The two walk on. Occasionally their mouths seem to open, but nothing more is said. Yet they remain together.

The rally took place at Halsted and Armitage, the future sight of People's Park. The block was in the midst of demolition by the Department of Urban Renewal. Sal gave a long, impassioned, boring speech. He could use words like "establishment," "revolution" and "power structure" without worrying much about their meaning. Sal also introduced Jazzman and dragged him to the microphone. Jazzman stood there looking like a boy frightened by the mass of strange people. Sal kept urging him to speak.

Finally Jazzman pointed to a crane with a large wrecking ball and said softly: "They are tearing down our houses. Basta. Enough." The crowd had been waiting for something to yell. "Basta, basta, basta," it shouted. Kids pointed at cops and screamed "basta." Parents pointed at the kids and cried "basta" at the cops. Everyone pointed at the rubble all around and yelled "basta." Ministers, nuns, nurses, labourers, executives, pimps and prostitutes raised clenched fists toward the sky and chanted "basta." As the shouting continued and grew, Jazzman slipped back into the crowd.

THE YOUNG LORDS CLUB was the proud remnant of the gang that once protected Old Town from the beatniks. Its only function was to put on dances. In the early fall of 1968 it consisted of four Puerto Rican guys and five Anglo girls. It had not thrown a dance in almost a year. It occasionally met to plan one, but lack of volunteers to do the work usually broke up the meetings. Despite recriminations over who should or would work, the meetings always ended as they began, with a prolonged cheer which consisted of a rhythmic shouting of the name "Young Lords" accompanied by hand clapping and foot stomping. But now Jazzman, their leader, was back and conceived a grandiose plan: four consecutive Saturday night dances at a local Catholic church, a "Young Lords Month of Soul" featuring Latin and black teenaged bands from all over Chicago.

On one of his book borrowing expeditions Jazzman asked Priscilla and me to chaperone these dances. He was enthusiastic about the plans.

These dances would put the Young Lords on the level of the most important teenage gangs in the city. During his many stays in jail Jazzman had met most of the gang leaders and knew just what sort of bands each gang had. He rattled off an impressive list of names he could call and count on to get him bands, names I recognized because they were constantly kicked around the front pages of the daily newspapers as murderers, arsonists and terrorizers of their communities. Jazzman spoke of them as ordinary good Joes – or Joses – who wouldn't fail to help out an old buddy. The Black P Stone Nation had an out of sight Afro band with dancers; the Disciples also had an Afro band; the Vice Lords had several bands; the Latin Kings had a Latin rhythm band.

Not wanting to deflate Jazzman's excitement, I refrained from suggesting the Chicago Symphony Orchestra – and was rewarded in the next weeks by being allowed to drive Jazzman to the headquarters and homes of most of the city's most feared gangs and their leaders. In my new capacity as chauffeur I learned that I was welcome anywhere so long as I was in the company of this small, quiet, blond-haired, blue-eyed, red-cheeked boy. It was the first of many lessons in respect I was to receive from Jazzman and also one in a long series of lessons in disrespect for the news media and their distortions.

All the "murderers," "arsonists" and "terrorizers" I met seemed human and humane. I can't claim to have got to know them in any depth, but I suspected that they would probably do a better job of running their communities and our country than those presently so employed. Not that that is saying much.

When Jazzman first informed me of the dances, he stressed the importance of the chaperones. There would be booze, dope and weapons of all sorts at the dances; members of opposing gangs would try to provoke fights with one another; there would be attempted gate crashings, ripoffs and rapes. I doubted my ability to prevent all this, but Jazzman assured me the Young Lords would deal with security. The chaperones' job was to collect money and walk around looking distinguished, thus reassuring the priests and convincing the kids it was a respectable dance, not a place for street tactics.

This explanation of my role showed me how I looked in Jazzman's eyes: old and middle class. I was twenty-nine years old but "immature" according to a survey of my peers taken by the FBI. It did seem that as I grew older, my friends became younger. In my teaching days my friends were students, not other teachers. Jazzman had never seen me wear any clothes other than old jeans, tee shirts and sneakers, yet to him in the fall of 1968 I was some sort of venerable sage who for some strange, perhaps philanthropic, reason was encouraging him and his friends. I tried to sooth my wounded ego by thinking it was only natural that an eighteen-year-old ghetto kid would perceive college educated people as strange and respectable and would assume they were philanthropists if they treated him well. But damned if I would wear a sport coat.

I'd like to describe the dances. Unfortunately Jazzman's image of me was bang on: My world was too different for me to understand much. And it was awfully dark in the old church gymnasium. I couldn't help but hear the music, however, and much of it was surprisingly good. Two of the Afro bands played a sophisticated free jazz inspired by late Coltrane. In one of our first times together Priscilla and I had attended the all night funeral concert for Trane, so the music got us holding hands and reminiscing.

You couldn't dance to it – correction: I couldn't dance to it. The kids on the floor were gyrating, vibrating, shaking and moving in all sorts of wild ways to music I thought appropriate only to listen to, participate in mentally, as an audience, not physically. Watching them I thought ruefully: That's the difference between a thinker and a doer, an intellectual looking down at life and a partaker in the fray. Determined to be a doer for once, I pushed onto the dance floor. My performance lasted about fifteen seconds. Then I heard Priscilla's great guffaw and, as I always did, stopped what I was doing to laugh with her, at her. Alright, at myself.

The kids understood music directly. Later I was to witness, and eventually even participate in, several impromptu jam sessions in the church basement which would become the Young Lords' headquarters. The instruments were chairs, tables, pails, glasses, combs covered with paper, chunks of wood and metal and anything else anyone could get a noise out of. Such sessions might last an hour without a single melody, yet they were always music, not noise.

At the dances I spent my time collecting tickets and money, selling soft drinks (which were used mainly as mixers for the hip flasks which abounded) and generally looking like the respectable citizen Jazzman had me pegged as. I resisted all subsequent efforts to get me to dance after my initial attempt. The dances were financial and social successes and were without major incident although rumors of impending fights, shootings and destruction of the church circulated continuously and worried me greatly. I know a few knives and guns were removed, but those occasions were handled with enough diplomacy that few people saw them occur (though every kid there knew what had happened inside of five minutes) and no one was hurt. Those in attendance (other than priests and chaperones) apparently were quite used to rumours of disaster and enjoyed them as a staple of dance conversation, nothing more.

3.

THE RAIN HASN'T LET UP ALL DAY. It is washing away some of the snow and further dirtying what it leaves. In me too. Can anything wash me clean? Soon it will be spring here, green outside. But my green is inside, a seething bile I learned to see while wallowing in it at the end of my Lincoln Park days. It's still there. I must vomit it up to write my story. I am Dick, come back from Chicago to tell you all. I will tell you all – if I can puke it out of me. To hell with this rain which confines me. I have escaped. I shouldn't be confined any more.

Enough bluster. I'm not in Chicago. If seeing grayness and dirt drives me back there, I must do what I did at the dances, listen, not look. This rain has its own rhythm, loud on the tin roof yet gentle, its music more than mere percussion. In the Windy City rain is storm, a harsh clanging of prison doors. Here no wind punishes the world for being out, being wet. Raindrops fall through rising mists which will reach the sky and fall again. Water rubs against water, seems the world's sole element, prelude and coda, soft celli conjuring past and future to the dripping beat of a bleak present.

Yes, if I did not have to open my eyes to write, I could escape. But I must write. I try to recall the beauty of winter or anticipate the beauty of spring, look out my window once more at the featureless world with its gray snow streaked with black, fail to do either.

BETWEEN THE DANCES AND THE NEW YEAR: two coming together months, months which excited me at the time yet which I now hardly remember, so dull were they compared to the summer of 1968 or what was to come in 1969. However, we did do some planning during those months. We lacked time for such a luxury later.

One thing I can't forget was Meg, dear, damned Meg, unrolling a twenty foot roll of shelf paper decorated in five colours to show five different groups of happenings over the next year. Two days earlier about thirty people gathered in Jane Brewer's basement. Most were leading members of various radical or liberal community organizations, but they were present as individuals, not representatives of their organizations. Jazzman was there although he never said a word. Our purpose was to

35

develop coordinated plans for the Lincoln Park neighbourhood. At the end of the day-long meeting Meg volunteered to write up the plans we had discussed.

Two days later we met again. Only about two-thirds of the original participants showed up this time because there were numerous disagreements at the first meeting and most of those with minority opinions simply didn't return. Those who did were treated to a work of art. At the top of the roll of shelf paper the coming year was divided into months and weeks. On the first horizontal line, in red, was the number of recruits to the different organizations, which were to function as a loose coalition. This number was to mount gradually to several thousand (a thousand for Concerned Citizens of Lincoln Park) by the end of 1969.

On the second line, in blue, was traced the growth of alternative resources and institutions: the *Lincoln Park Press* coming out every month plus several special editions before major events; a community health organization which would operate a free seven day a week health clinic; a community legal organization which would run a legal clinic to defend movement people and offer free legal advice to poor people in the area; alternative schools; a free store; a secret group to sabotage urban renewal plans and machinery; a public organization in all sections directly threatened by urban renewal to oppose the plans; a people's architecture office; a people's Conservation Community Council; and so on.

The third line, in yellow, projected our effects on existing institutions: making the welfare office more human, forcing neighbourhood merchants to be ethical, making the hospitals accept poor people as patients and establish and expand clinics, destroying the city's Conservation Community Council, isolating the Lincoln Park Conservation Association.

The fourth line, in green, showed the growth of our own housing plans: blueprints for people's housing drawn up by architects on the basis of ordinary folks' visions expressed at open planning meetings, an alternate plan to replace the Department of Urban Renewal's Neighborhood Renewal Plan.

The bottom line, in purple, showed specific events which were to build the movement and accomplish the above purposes: meetings, rallies, marches, demonstrations, alliances, victories. Dates were given for each. Several months later there was a report of a confused conglomeration of cops outside DePaul University. Eventually Meg worked out that the pied plan had scheduled a demonstration for the date and place. Our plans had changed, but the police informer who had been present at the unfurling of the shelf paper had not been around to send corrections to the boss.

The informer had been right to worry. The pied plan had everything, from visionary sweep to intricacy of detail. As a means of saving our neighbourhood it was a work of art. In its artistry was its appeal – and its undoing. For its gaudy vision appealed only to artists and spies. To the practical minded present at its unrolling it seemed a cosmic daydream. Their own immediate tasks seemed more important than its abstract goals. Probably everyone shared those goals, but most either doubted the possibility of such great successes or feared that their own plans and ambitions would be overwhelmed by the plan. Most of all they were afraid that becoming part of the coalition envisioned in the plan meant relinquishing their own independence of action.

The artistically inclined revelled in the pied plan. They praised Meg, suggested subtle alterations, vowed fidelity – then went their independent artistic ways as they had all their lives. The plan appealed to just those who would not make it work while the practical minded who might have helped it succeed were little attracted.

As usual Chicago divided us among ourselves and within ourselves, opposed the artistic temperament to the practical temperament, destroyed hope of proceeding in a fully planned, tightly organized way. Twenty individuals who might have created real change together continued on separate paths, occasionally meeting about individual projects but seldom working together with the closeness and intensity needed to succeed. Many of the twenty present at the great unrolling eventually joined together in the Poor People's Coalition, but that was half a year later, too much later, and even then they joined too tenuously. Disjointed individuals and groups, however natural in our individualistic society, are not about to put a disjointed neighbourhood, city, society and world back together. So although many of the specific goals of the pied plan were actually implemented, the plan itself never had a chance of success. The Lincoln Park we all loved was doomed.

IT'S STILL RAINING, SO I'LL STAY INSIDE. I suppose I should be thankful for more time to do what I never could in Chicago, but the weather is too dull to write anything exciting or even interesting. Maybe some boring facts will help the reader.

Lincoln Park is a neighbourhood on Chicago's near north side. It is located west of the large lakefront park of the same name. It lies between Old Town to the south, Lake View to the north, the park and Lake Michigan to the east and the Chicago River to the west. The narrow strip of land bordering the park and overlooking the lake has always been part of Chicago's Gold Coast, the home of the wealthy, but the rest of the neighbourhood was long a mixed area both economically and ethnically. In the Sixties the neighbourhood contained five major institutions: three large hospitals (Children's Memorial, Grant and Augustana), DePaul University and McCormick Seminary (Presbyterian).

In the late Fifties and early Sixties these institutions, inspired by the University of Chicago's example in Hyde Park, gathered together the leading businesses and landowners in Lincoln Park to form the Lincoln Park Conservation Association (LPCA), met with city officials and had the community designated for urban renewal. Although almost none of the housing in Lincoln Park could have been called slum housing, the big landowners feared a decline in property values and stood to profit richly if the neighbourhood became predominantly upper middle class.

Urban renewal also provided the cheapest and easiest method for the institutions to expand. The city cooperated fully since Mayor Daley's Plan for the City of Chicago was to increase the tax base by driving poor people out (especially near the lakefront and the areas surrounding the downtown Loop) and luring back wealthy people, who had fled to the suburbs in the years following World War Two, by building fancy high rises, townhouses and gentrified apartments.

In Lincoln Park plans were drawn up to expropriate property near the major institutions (including the area's largest bank) for institutional expansion. A Conservation Community Council (CCC) composed entirely of white, male property owners and institutional representatives was recommended by the LPCA and appointed by Mayor Daley to rubberstamp these and other urban renewal plans. By the time opposition to these plans coalesced around a group of liberal and radical Protestant ministers, most of the plans had been approved and the first phase of demolition and remodelling (east of Halsted Street) was well under way.

Urban renewal was supported by federal, state and city funds. These paid for purchases and demolition and allowed developers to purchase

vacant land cheaply, usually at a loss to the city. Small property owners were forced to sell when their land was wanted because in urban
renewal zones the city could use its power of eminent domain to condemn any property.

The interval between demolition and new construction was almost
always lengthy. In Chicago the average was seven years. This forced
most of the old residents to relocate outside their community and gave
the anger generated by the destruction of people's homes a chance to
cool. Then luxury housing replaced rubble and the upper middle class
replaced the poor and working class. In areas adjacent to demolition,
property owners were encouraged to remodel in anticipation of new,
wealthier tenants arriving or were bought out by those who would
remodel. The mixed neighbourhood I had fallen in love with was already
entering its long transition period when I returned from North Carolina
to resume my life with Priscilla.

By 1968 Lincoln Park was already becoming the caricature of our
disjointed society it now is. Street by street diversity was becoming division. Larrabee Street, a striking plea for diversity, had been levelled. The
people who lived on the street had been approximately one-third black,
one-third Latin, one-third white. They had been factory workers and
small shopkeepers with a sprinkling of welfare recipients and professionals. There were members of almost every ethnic group in the city
on the six blocks between North Avenue and Webster Street. They lived
in tiny houses, two and three flats and in apartments above small shops.

Most important, the street was relatively stable in its diversity: It had
been diverse for many years though the exact mixture of its inhabitants
constantly changed. Although only two buildings could be classified as
slums, almost the entire three-quarters of a mile had to be destroyed
because the machine which ran Chicago could not tolerate what it represented: stable, working class integration. Department of Urban Renewal
plans called for construction of upper middle income townhouses and a
suburban type shopping mall on the grave of Larrabee Street. Only two
buildings remained: the Tap Root Pub, fighting to avoid demolition, and
the Department of Urban Renewal office, fighting to demolish the pub.

Like Lincoln Park the seasons here are changing. Where are the snows
of yesterday's winter? I am beginning to see bare ground. True, it is only
under evergreen trees where not much snow could accumulate, but it
is an omen of change. By 1968 the area east of Larrabee Street had also

changed. Once a solid working class neighbourhood, it was rapidly being remodelled to resemble Old Town to its south. Once every block had its own little gang, typically named after its street, like the Mohawk Boys. Now youths still living there were preparing to merge into CORP (short for Community of Repressed People or like the marine corps, depending on whom one asked: One branch of the gang eventually became somewhat political) because they were too few and scattered to fight each other anymore. Even the Gold Coast, east of this area, was changing. The low rise luxury apartment buildings and mansions, which had been the traditional dwellings of the Chicago's rich since the city began, were being torn down and replaced with huge glass and steel luxury high rises.

Everyone was being uprooted. In most of the eastern areas of Lincoln Park over eighty percent of the residents had changed in a few years. Small but often longstanding businesses had failed. School populations had declined drastically, by as much as fifty percent in some schools and at least ten percent in every public school in eastern Lincoln Park. Not only were working class people being pushed out, families were being replaced by individuals: single young executives and secretaries; newly graduated nurses and doctors; stewardesses and pilots; young teachers; call girls and other professionals sharing apartments as they climbed the social ladder; newlyweds planning to make a lot of money before considering children; middle aged couples, their children grown, moving back from the suburbs. People with money but no roots and little stake in the community.

And while Lincoln Park was the hottest real estate speculation area and had the fastest turnover of people in the United States, Chicago had a city wide vacancy rate of under two percent, and Lincoln Park's vacancy rate was practically nonexistent. There was no place for people, especially poor people, to move. Some of those who wanted to stay in Lincoln Park went west into hastily subdivided, overcrowded buildings which their owners planned to milk for a few years then remodel or tear down and reconstruct as luxury apartments. Or they moved in temporarily with relatives or friends and remained permanently – at least until they were again evicted along with the original occupants.

So the people of western Lincoln Park had to bear the burden of urban renewal to the east even as the Department of Urban Renewal and the real estate speculators moved into their neighbourhoods. The 2000 block of Dayton Street, where I lived with Jerry from 1965 to 1967, had been about two-thirds Latin when I moved in and about one-half Latin when I moved out. When I returned in June of 1968 the block was perhaps one-quarter Latin, and by the end of the year there were almost no Latins left.

Our own apartment on Dayton with its four tiny bedrooms had been rented by a large Puerto Rican family for $85.00 a month before the new owner, a Lincoln Park Conservation Association liberal who proclaimed his joy in being able to integrate the block, took over, repainted, and rented to Jerry and me for $125.00 a month. We were followed by four student nurses at $175.00 a month. In 1968 a black minister with four children tried to rent the apartment for the $225.00 being asked and was refused because he had too large a family. The Civil Rights Movement had taught middle class blacks what to do in such circumstances and court action forced the landlord to rent. He bitterly switched to the conservative faction of the LPCA because of the infringement of his free enterprise rights. By 1968 the area between Halsted, Sheffield, Armitage and McCormick Seminary was rapidly turning into an exclusively middle class section. Jazzman's Bissell Street, my true love, was one of the last to go.

Real estate speculation was incredible. A group of recent DePaul graduates formed a real estate company and bragged they made a four hundred percent profit in one year. One building they bought was a three flat in the 2200 block of Halsted (a busy commercial street poorly suited for residential living). They paid $18,000 for it in January, 1968, evicted the Puerto Rican and southern white tenants, spent $6,000 remodelling, re-rented the apartments and sold the building in June, 1968 for $36,000. Rents rose to $250 a month from $75.

By 1968 buildings were being remodelled all over Lincoln Park, still most actively in the east but now in the west as well. Almost every block sported a coach light or two. There was no law requiring remodelled buildings to display a coach light, but all of them did. The cover of the Lincoln Park Conservation Association's loose bound book detailing its plans for urban renewal was a full page picture of a coach light.

In most buildings the coach light simply indicated that the old tenants had been evicted, the apartments repainted and the rents doubled. When remodelling went much beyond a new coat of paint rents tripled. In cases of extensive remodelling the sky was the limit. In the Swoop development on Jazzman's old block rents were to go from $75.00 to

$425.00. Few of the old tenants had leases, so they had no legal grounds to refuse to get out. Human grounds, such as the length of time a tenant has lived in a place, the love for a community or the desire to provide a stable environment for children, are not admissible in eviction court, so few people wasted time going to court.

Our law belongs to the landlord as fully as it belonged to the master under slavery. In exceptional hardship cases (a serious illness or the like) a kindly judge might grant a tenant a thirty day extension, nothing more. Ownership comes before people. The rare tenants who did have leases gained nothing but a few months. They were evicted as soon as the leases expired. Most of those evicted moved quietly, but a few resisted. When they resisted as individuals, they were forcibly evicted by the sheriff's police, their possessions thrown out, often smashed, and piled on the sidewalk. We tried to aid such people and persuade them to allow us to move their belongings back in since the landlord had to procure a new court order and pay the police for each eviction. But the eviction process invariably broke the spirit along with the furniture, and no evictees let us risk arrest by moving them back in.

When people resisted eviction as a group, the end might come more slowly, but sometimes it came more spectacularly. Concerned Citizens of Lincoln Park helped form tenant unions. I was the organizer of one such union in the 2200 block of Clifton. The building had been converted from a twelve flat to twenty-four three room flats, and the owner, a wealthy suburban lawyer, had been milking it for several years. That is, he had done virtually no repairs, simply collected rent ($75 to $85 per apartment) and let the building decay.

In the summer of 1968 he decided there was more money to be made by remodelling and tried to evict the tenants, most of whom were Latin. When I came to canvas the building, they had just received eviction notices and were angry enough to accept my aid, organize themselves into a union and begin a rent strike. Because of numerous building code violations the owner had been in Building Court for years. Indeed, the eviction notices had been served only after the court made it clear that the owner could stall only a little longer before it began to levy fines for failing to make repairs.

This gave us some legal leverage; it was the only case I know of in which a judge did not automatically order the tenants' eviction. John Leeds' church agreed to act as receiver if the judge would place the building in receivership, and a six month legal battle was on. As winter came and the owner supplied less and less heat despite court orders to provide more, some tenants moved out, but at New Year's half still remained and remained determined to fight.

One night during a bitter cold spell with the temperature below zero Fahrenheit, the tenants saw the owner and another man enter and go to the top floor, which was mainly deserted. They heard clanking noises and shortly thereafter pipes burst in two empty top floor apartments. This flooded most apartments and forced the water and steam heat to be shut off. By the time I arrived to help people move out, there was thick ice in the lower apartments and all over the stairway. By the autumn of 1969 the building sported two coach lights and apartments were renting for $325 a month.

Aside from bitter lessons about powerlessness there was one positive result of the rent strike. I had brought a young Colombian artist to translate for me. He came from the upper classes of his country but was moved by the suffering and strength of the poor people in the Clifton building, especially one young mother of two babies. When the freezing waters flooded her apartment, she moved in with him, and so far as I know they are still together.

Other people in the building were less fortunate. They scattered all over. We helped a few move in with relatives; most simply vanished. Several years later I met a man from the Clifton building on the southwest side, where he and his family had moved. Their new living quarters were about to be torn down by urban renewal, and he was seeking yet another new dwelling place.

All this (and much more) was Lincoln Park at the time the Young Lords Organization was forming and fighting: a beautiful community being ravaged, rich speculators making new fortunes from poor people's suffering, a few organizers struggling despite knowing they had begun organizing too late, and wonderful people, surviving somehow, even falling in love.

By early 1970, when Jazzman went underground, most of these people had been pushed out and the new Lincoln Park had invaded: a disjointed cosmopolis of "sophisticated" liberals gushing with enthusiasm for their new neighbourhood with no knowledge of the history behind it and the deadly forces which had brought them to it plus cynical old-timers, who knew the forces only too well and had managed to work out a hustle to hunker down in the battleground from which their friends had been driven.

Jose Rodriguez, who loved Jazzman but worked remodelling his former home so Elizabeth Swoop could get richer and boast of how she enabled a twenty-year-old Puerto Rican school dropout to get his high school diploma. Vicky Saxon, one of nine members of the Young Lords Club before it became an organization, a call girl working out of a newly remodelled building with two coach lights at its entrance. Lovin' Charlie Green, a black swinger who the cops supplied with dynamite junk when he hung out with Jazzman and the Young Lords Organization, now barely supporting his habit pushing, usually nodding on a doorstep on Armitage. Cleo Conrad, Charlie's ex-girlfriend, whose imaginative accounts of "subversive gang activity in Lincoln Park" only the House Unamerican Activities Committee (HUAC) could believe, living with an LPCA speculator in eastern Lincoln Park, proud of going straight but afraid to venture very far west. Jane Jencks, whom the Young Lords named Mama Jane because she cleaned up after them, kept their headquarters presentable and was always around when they needed her, a neighbourhood character to whom people give food and spare change although she doesn't beg.

4.

WHEN WRITING WRINGS the dinginess of Chicago out from within me, I let it settle all around, then simply gaze out my window. Today sun reflecting off fresh snow blinds me. Winter does not give up easily in the mountains. Just yesterday I thought it was as good as over. Down here in the valley the snow is beginning to glisten with moisture. Up the mountain it is still brilliant white and glows against the perfect blue of the sky, which was purple this morning after the passing of the storm. As my eyes adjust to the light, the whiteness sorts itself into patterns: beneath the blue sky the blue whiteness of glacial ice, clear in one spot through the new whiteness of recent snow; hints of the deep green forest in a sequence of dark shapes descending the clean white mountain to a thread of thin, transparent crystal, a frozen waterfall sparkling through gray splotched, white hot rock. All this on a single peak laughing above the valley which had lost much of its snow before last night's new layer. Jazzman and Meg relaxed, happy, clowning together, a brief vision through the drunken confusion of a Lincoln Park surprise party on my thirtieth birthday.

My mountains enable me to write, but they do not allow me to record history or create living people. Mountains are too grand, the writing they inspire too heroic. Homer and his Greeks lived in the mountains. Today people are confined in flat Chicagos. Their lives are still heroic: Just to survive in such places requires heroes. But mere survival requires a quotidian heroism very different from that of Odysseus, who was raised on a rocky isle, one of the tops of an underwater mountain range rising above the Aegean.

I know the epic is long dead and that I should write of everyday life in Chicago, of ordinary folks who made something of their lives although their souls cried out for more. That is all Jazzman was, all any of us were. It is what our age demands we be. I resist; I cannot write as I am supposed to. To do so I would have to draw a curtain over my window. So I write of peaks, an epic fantasy, an unreal history, a tragedy whose cast would break up in laughter could its members but see how they are depicted.

If only it would happen. If only I could hear them laugh for more than an illusory second, only hear their voices, words, accents. I remember that the sounds thrilled me yet cannot remember the sounds themselves, sounds too different from the sounds I was raised on, too different from the heroic silence I have come to. Yet I write on, for when I write I can make the people I loved more than voices from the past. The pseudo epic I write may be neither accurate history nor believable art, but I write to fulfill my needs now. I need people in my beautiful, lonely mountains, so I summon them up in my mind's eye and write of them, to them, for myself, for my mountains, for the day when simple, prosaic people destroy the flat existence they now lead and assemble a new world where life is joyous and everyone has access to mountains.

Meg, dear, damned Meg, I need you again. How can I say anything good about flat Chicago and its lowly heroes here in these mountains? Once before when I left Chicago, that time for the miniature but lovely mountains of western North Carolina, you revived the love I felt when I first saw Bissell Street, then kicked and cajoled me into understanding that if I loved Lincoln Park I had to strive and fight to save it. Help me recreate the love which enabled us to work together although we clashed on all things except that love we shared for a community, for humanity.

Ah Meg, in what basement do you now sit poring over and over the works of Marx, waiting for the other members of your cell to arrive for tonight's meeting, waiting for the correct historical moment to climb into the daylight and strategically place the carefully constructed bombs that will summon the masses to the sacking of City Hall and the building of the barricades?

How can it have happened, Meg? For so long your love of Lincoln Park held my violence in check. For so long we argued, I for ringing denunciations of capitalism as embodied by the LPCA, you for common people who would not relate to that rhetoric; I for joining more fully with the antiwar and student movements, you for saying that poor people were too busy trying to survive to worry themselves with middle class intellectuals; I for "revolutionary action," you for reaching and talking to more people.

Now all your writing is anti-capitalist rhetoric; all your time is spent studying to be a communist intellectual; all your conversation is with the other four members of your cell. You have become a parody of what I would have become without you. Come to the mountains, Meg. Come for just a few days. Chicago is a disease. Too long a time there is death. I watched you try to cough your lungs into a toilet. I watched you go into the hospital with pneumonia every six months because as soon as you came out Chicago challenged you to subsist on cigarettes instead of food, to struggle without sleep until you were again too sick to continue. Still you struggle without sleep or breath of clean air. If only you could look out my window and clear your lungs and mind.

We loved the same thing, Meg, you and I who were so different. We loved, and Chicago turned your love to sickness, mine to hatred. Had I not come to the mountains, had I done the impossible and written this account in Chicago, I would not have been able to mention your name, you who enabled me to escape first by fighting my worst tendencies, finally by becoming what I would have become without you. Chicago drove us together violently and apart more violently.

Now I feel free to look back on it while you, who tried to leave first, remain imprisoned by it. Someday perhaps you will be able to leave again. Then you will forgive me for leaving, forgive me for trying to be free. Maybe you will even be able to thank me as I now thank you, who taught me that love without struggle is worthless, then that struggle without love is destructive. In a society built on avarice and hatred we must not love in peace but must use what love we can muster to fight until the foundations of greed crumble so all may love.

I do continue the struggle, Meg. Although I ran away, although I am two thousand miles away, the love I feel in these mountains is an outgrowth of the love I felt for Priscilla and you and Jazzman and Sancho and Jill and John and Mama Jane and Jose and Marta and for Lincoln Park. By combining my loves and struggling with words maybe I can show the world what it means to live in a city and country where love is a commodity sold on cosmetic shelves in bottles, tubes and aerosol sprays, where people are pawns to be pushed from one place to another so realtors can profit, where communities are Monopoly boards where politicians play at increasing tax bases so they can grease inhuman patronage machines whose moving parts are human beings.

▲ ▲ ▲

Historian: I didn't know what happened after she went underground. I was saddened to read this.

Novelist: Don't be. So far as I know, it's not true. I have no idea what she did after she escaped Chicago or after she returned.

Historian: Why say it then?

Novelist: Remember, this is a novel. The guy she ran off with felt dogmatic and secretive to me so it might have happened. And I'm free to invent what I don't know. Here I used the fictional Meg to beef up the character of the fictional narrator.

Historian: Who we both know is you. So you sacrificed truth to make yourself look good.

Novelist: I keep telling you it's a novel. The fictional is usually personal, and the personal is political.

Historian: When the historical gets personal and the personal is political, politics can turn into a fucking mess because it turns fucking into a political mess. I shouldn't have messed with her. She and you were like gods to me. You two had the education I didn't. But sex was my junk when I wasn't on junk. I think I drove her underground. One of the last times she saw me she saw me nodding. She took after Lovin' Charlie with a two by four. He told me she had murder in her eyes. He said he never ran so fast in his life. I wish I saw it. Charlie inspired the song about moving slowly, slowly.

Novelist: Junk pissed the hell out of her, and it scared the hell out of me. But she had a rather different philosophy from you. She messed with you because you were like a god to her – to me too for that matter. You had the street smarts and instincts we lacked. When junk came on the scene, I tried to pretend I didn't notice. She never pretended. She knew you wouldn't be very godlike on junk.

Historian: She was right. Once a junkie always a junkie. But I was always only a user. I was never a pusher. I've been clean now for over twenty five years, but I know I'm still a junkie. I don't think I'm very godlike.

Novelist: Gods don't grow old.

▲ ▲ ▲

I MET MEG IN 1966, shortly after she moved to Lincoln Park. She was short but big-boned, as if her body had never been given time to catch up with rapid internal growth, a dark-haired, small-eyed, big-hearted Irish Catholic. But she was tough. And needy. How could anyone so tough be so needy? How could anyone so needy be so tough? And how could anyone so tough and so needy hide both the toughness and the need so well?

For to all appearances Meg was a plain, pleasant, ordinary girl. You had to see her in the midst of a political struggle to see – and, wow, admire – the toughness. When I met her, she lived across Dayton Street from Jerry and me in an apartment shared by a group active in radical Catholic student politics. Her need soon made her one of Jerry's many lovers. He was the one who dubbed her "dear, damned Meg." Jerry was a blatant endearer of woman, so the first time he met Meg he called her "dear" and she almost bit his head off. "Damned if I'll let you or anyone else dear me," she snapped. This won Jerry's heart and from then on he always called her "dear, damned Meg," though never in her presence of course.

I never guessed her need until we began working together and she once thought I might be able to satisfy it. Wow again: She must have been damned needy. I didn't satisfy her, and we only tried once. Then we went back simply to working together, neither dear nor damned, but knowing each other better and working as a team despite frequent disagreements. We may have had very different needs and approaches, but we always knew we were dedicated to the same goals and ideals. Trying to live in "the city on the make" made all of us needy, desperate even. But you had to get out to learn it about yourself. We clung to each other, but our clinging ripped us apart or smothered the love we needed.

When I returned from North Carolina to see Priscilla during my Christmas, 1967 break, Meg told me of her new job with Concerned Citizens of Lincoln Park. At that time the organization was composed of church people and middle class liberals who wanted to keep Lincoln Park a diversified community, not let it become a fancy suburb within the city, but it included none of the poor people who were being moved out so the rich could move in. While I was back in North Carolina, Meg began changing that, and by June, 1968, when I returned to Chicago, the *Lincoln Park News* had become the *Lincoln Park Press* and its format altered from a newsletter for professionals to a bilingual newspaper which she was distributing free in western Lincoln Park. She was actively recruiting common folks, especially Latins, to the cause and had grand plans for a summer blitz in which students would canvas the entire neighbourhood to sound the depths of feeling against urban renewal and enlist new members. Concerned Citizens of Lincoln Park operated out of a small storefront office provided by the church of its founder and president, Pastor John Leeds, and the contributions of wealthy local liberals.

Most important Concerned Citizens had a cause: saving a community loved by all who lived in it.

For Lincoln Park was unlike any other neighbourhood in segregated Chicago. Waves of immigration had washed over it without levelling it. Every wave had left a deposit, so the community boasted a rich diversity unlike the rest of the city's rigidly ethnic areas. Canvassing was like a global tour. I remember two adjoining three flats on Halsted Street. On the ground floor of the first lived a Japanese Buddhist, above him an interracial family (black man, white woman, two children), and on the third floor was a Hungarian DP family in which the parents spoke almost no English and their children translated for them. In the building next door lived an old Italian couple who spoke in a rich accent I thought existed only in movies, a large Puerto Rican family and a large Colombian family.

That sort of mixture was typical. One also found Appalachian and Southern whites, blacks, many varieties of Asians, Germans, Irish, over half of Chicago's Gypsies and many other Europeans. St. Mary's Catholic Church was predominantly Latin while St. Joseph's Catholic Church, two blocks to the north, was Irish, but some Latins attended St. Joseph's and some Irish St. Mary's. St. John's Lutheran Church still conducted one of its two services in German while St. George's Lutheran, four blocks to the east, was thoroughly Americanized and had a program to help and house runaways and street people.

Commercial streets contained little stores specializing in German sausage, Italian lemonade and Puerto Rican plantains next to American supermarkets. If a customer in the Mexican restaurant wanted a drink, the proprietor ran next door to the Irish bar and procured one. It all worked: The different racial and ethnic groups befriended one another without losing their own identity. The various masses huddled together and breathed free. Folks did not worry about their neighbours' race, religion, ethnic background or social class and never felt obliged to conceal their own. No wonder the city of Chicago wanted to destroy this neighbourhood with under two percent slum housing: If other neighbourhoods got the idea, no one would move out when a person of another race or background moved in, and the real estate interests which ran Chicago and got rich from blockbusting would go broke.

THE EARLY SUMMER OF 1968 was the culmination of my romance with Lincoln Park which had begun on Bissell Street three years earlier. Later I was too busy trying to save the neighbourhood to savour it. Earlier I had known only its appearance. My friends had mainly been young, white, hip kids who appreciated the neighbourhood without penetrating it. They dug diversity and could rent a pad much cheaper than they could in nearby Old Town. But in the summer of 1968 I and several students Meg had recruited spent our evenings canvassing. I met the wonderfully varied ordinary people who made the heart of the neighbourhood beat.

They helped teach me a lesson I had only begun to learn in North Carolina, how to relate to human beings by being human myself. Before that people had been objects to be conquered: impressed by my intellect and wit, argued into agreement or silence, seduced, hustled. I played the games I had learned at universities. But now I learned to listen to just plain folks, heard and saw the tragedies they suffered because a sick society was built on their sound backs, observed the strength and beauty which had to be part of their character to enable them to hold up that society and still endure.

Mama Jane, I knocked on your door. You were younger than I yet looked twenty years older. Your clothes were others' castoffs and usually several sizes too large. Your life consisted of one disaster after another but you always smiled as you told of your latest catastrophe. Your two front teeth had been knocked out in a fight even as mine had, but you could not afford to replace yours, and the fist that knocked them out would never knock out others. The fist belonged to your husband Bob, who lay dying on the battered couch that first time I knocked.

You told me that doctors at Cook County Hospital had operated on Bob for the wrong thing and now wanted to operate again, but he refused to see them and pleaded with you never to take him to the hospital. Now he lay quiet, gathering strength for a new drinking bout. He used to drink every night but now could manage it no more than once a week. He didn't have many bouts left. His last one was to end with him staggering home and spitting blood all over the couch. He was too weak to resist when you put his arm around you and carried and dragged him half a mile to Grant Hospital. But the hospital respected his wishes, not yours: An emergency room nurse smelled the alcohol on him, insisted he was just drunk and refused your pleas to let him be seen by a doctor. So you dragged him home and sat up for two days feeding the two babies and watching your man die.

When I first met you only two-year-old Bobby called you "mama," but the next year you began cooking and cleaning for the Young Lords in their church basement headquarters. When I saw you there and called you Jane, you said: "Call me mama, everyone here does." It sure made you feel fine to be called "mama" by guys not much younger than yourself. Probably no one else but your son had ever called you anything endearing. I hope the pleasure was worth the pain you suffered, for it seemed as if every time I saw you there were new bruises and new stories of where they came from.

The gangs the Chicago police paid to harass the Young Lords were afraid to do much to the members, but you, who preferred the streets to any inside place and proudly wore a Young Lords Organization button at all times, were the perfect target for beatings, robberies and rapes. I don't know how, but you endured and smiled and spoke of the beatings as everyday occurrences that were your lot. Your late night walks were famous all over the neighbourhood. Most people thought you were crazy, for you greeted everyone and sang to your babies as you paraded them through the streets at all hours.

But to us who knew you, you were more famous for your kindness. You were always there to do small, necessary deeds in emergencies: begging bandages and medicine when someone was hurt, staying up just in case you were needed when the Young Lords were helping a junkie kick, scrubbing the walls when black paint was thrown on the murals outside the headquarters, waiting around for guys to be bailed out after a bust. Mama, you endured, endured insults and beatings, endured being used like a slave, endured a third baby born at home without medical assistance. I don't know how you did it. I am told you are still walking the streets of Lincoln Park, still smiling your gap-toothed smile. Keep walking, mama, we're marching behind you.

I KNOCKED ON YOUR DOOR, JILL AND JOHN. You were home, Jill. John was working overtime at the steel mill, and you were watching the nine children and waiting for the tenth. I still remember your initial suspicion of me: You were sure I was some kind of social worker. And I still regret you will not be able to read this because I never found time to keep my frequent promises to teach you to read. But I also still get joy from remembering the hours we spent just talking. No, not just talking, for children were running everywhere, climbing all over us and each other, demanding to be played with, disappearing and reappearing, laughing, leaping, fighting, mocking, loving.

You and John told me stories of bloody Harlan County, Kentucky, where you were born, and of Larrabee Street, from which you had been urban removed. You taught me to understand much about poverty, oppression and how to overcome them. One thing I couldn't understand, and cannot even now in these mountains which make so much else clear, was how a woman could have ten children by the age of thirty, raise them in a tiny three bedroom city apartment, not the farm you belonged on, yet never lose her exuberance for life. I know those children added to your exuberance instead of tiring you out, but I can't pretend to understand how you did it.

I'm afraid my middle class background is almost as far from yours as the pious churchman's, the one who asked you why poor people have so many children. He and twenty other churchmen will never forget you or ask that question again. You came into the office when they were getting my standard lecture on the neighbourhood ($25 honorarium from the Urban Training Center). I introduced you and mentioned your children, and the man asked his question without thought. Everyone saw the look on your face. They and I thought you were going to beat the heaven out of him, but when you reached him, you pulled up a few inches before his face, pointed your finger into his nose, and said in a voice which started as a shout but ended so quietly everyone was straining to hear: "Mister, you took everything we got. Our children are the only happiness left in our life. There ain't enough of you to try to take my kids away from me. Don't you ever try to tell a poor woman how many kids she can have."

You never lost your sense of justice either, Jill. When Steinberg at the furniture store talked Maria Sanchez, who spoke little English, into signing an unfair contract, you made so much noise and brought down so many local women that Steinberg not only tore up Maria's contract but agreed to tear up or revise several others and to buy an ad in the Lincoln Park *Press* to print an apology and statement of fair business practices. When a child was hurt – and that happened all the time because children had only streets, alleys and sidewalks to play on along Lincoln Avenue – it was you who patched the wound or carried the child to Children's

Memorial Hospital, usually trailing half a dozen of your own kids in your wake. When a family had no money you took them to the welfare office and insisted they be served. And you and John and your kids managed to lead every march we ever held.

Kids, country kids, eastern Kentucky kids, mountain kids. No matter that they had lived most of their lives in a flat city. How different your kids were from any I had known. How much they and you must have learned from the mountains. Middle class city parents bear their affordable children to inherit their fortunes and their names, to enter the family business or fulfill the dream they failed to attain.

Chicago is filled with kids who have run away or want to run away or should have run away to escape other people's dreams being imposed on them. You loved your children for themselves, not what they might become. Was it because mining company steam shovels had dug the land out from under your feet, land you and your people had lived on and loved for more than a hundred years? Did that teach you that nothing is solid but people, your own people, children? No, that's not it: These snowy B.C. mountains have not been dug up like that; they have resisted several onslaughts of miners and still stand tall to proclaim the same lesson, the majesty of nature and of people, who remain a precious part of nature whatever their size, for we are all children beside the mountains.

Chicago distorts, destroys what all nature knows, all people should feel. You taught me. You who could not read taught me who could not find the time to teach you. I didn't understand in Chicago. Now my mountains cry out that your teachers, your mountains, are right.

I almost didn't try to find you before I fled Chicago. I feared the city had defeated you, turned your fighting to frustrated flailing. You had seemed so discouraged and tired in the hospital. City doctors had performed a hysterectomy, supposedly to save your life, and I thought there could be no more babies. I found three, the grandchildren, their teenaged mothers and fathers as doting as their grandparents and child aunts and uncles. The dilapidated apartment was the same: kids still running all over, yelling, swiping dinner hours ahead of time, the babies being passed through it all, thrown, kissed, fed and loved by everyone, the circle, battered continuously by poverty and Chicago, still unbroken.

Perhaps I will understand when I see you all again in the mountains – mine or yours – not that stuffy apartment. Perhaps I do understand, seeing you again in my mind's eye as my body's eyes look out into the clear, cold mountain distance. You too endured it all, Jill: threats and propositions from cops and caseworkers, begging food from stores to feed hungry children (usually someone else's), the school's refusal to allow your sons to attend assemblies because they did not own white shirts and ties, the murder of your brother by a Kentucky deputy sheriff. All this, however much it hurt, made you fight harder. And you, John, never failed to support Jill, never stopped working except when you had to watch the kids when Jill had a mission to perform, proudly marched by her side.

I KNOCKED ON YOUR DOOR, JOSE AND MARTA. Jose, most gentle of men, you were awaiting trial for counterfeiting, armed robbery and aggravated assault. Never during the year you waited to be taken to Sandstone Penitentiary in cold Minnesota did I hear you worry about yourself, only about your wife and three children. Was it love of them which led you into "crime?" I never did understand what your crime was, only the great disparity between what you might have been capable of doing and what you were convicted of. The poor and uneducated are convicted of so much more than what they did, while the wealthy, the rare times they are brought to trial, are allowed to plead to so much less than what they did.

Where was the criminal when you played ball with kids on the block? Or when you risked an arrest that would have put you in real trouble to cool out some kids who were taunting the cops? Or when you took off work to translate for two elderly Latin women at the welfare office? Or when you sat patiently teaching Marta the English she would have to speak and read to survive when you were gone? Jose, you would not talk about yourself, but when you played with children or talked to teenagers, I could see in you a boy no one had had time to play with or talk to. And when you clowned with Bob on a march, I saw a boy who worked too hard to have much fun when he was young.

Are you out of jail yet? There are some people I can imagine in jail but not you. Your letters did not paint a bad picture of the penitentiary, but on my way to Canada I passed the bleak, gray walls. I cannot help you now, but I swear that someday all such walls all over the world will be blasted back into sand. That will be the people's urban renewal.

STAY WITH ME MAMA JANE, JILL, JOSE. Your time is coming, your roles in the drama, your pages in my chronicle of that time, that tragedy which had so many glorious scenes. A dreary drizzle is dripping outside my window. Let me keep using the rage I felt at your plight to write on. Lend me the light I found in all of you, for I am about to plunge into the heart of darkness. Or was it closer to a bad Disney fairy tale than the horror?

Let me tell you what I was doing during the days of the nights I was out canvassing and meeting you and many other friends. During those summer days I was in a world almost as different from yours as the one I am in now. Jan, a long legged student, and I were at City Hall researching property ownership in Lincoln Park. We wanted to find out exactly who owned our community, who was getting rich from urban renewal and real estate speculation. We had been told that property ownership was public information available at City Hall and that it was listed by address, so we didn't anticipate problems beyond hours of drudgery copying the information. We joked that we were heading into the heart of darkness or the belly of the beast, but what did we know? What we found was not particularly dark, and while we found lots of belly it was all too human. The heart of Chicago is a machine. City Hall houses the headquarters of the Democratic Party Machine, the Daley Machine, the machine whose moving parts are human beings, the patronage machine.

We gathered up our Bics and notebooks and took the el to the Loop. Soon we were forsaking the smog of downtown Chicago for the smoke of City Hall. We passed through imposing portals into vast, dimly lit catacombs where our footsteps clopped and every sound echoed. While our eyes were growing accustomed to the conspiratorial light, we thought we could hear the scratching of an army of drudges dwarfed by the cavernous halls and bent beneath overwhelming loads of bullshit. A large, gilt framed portrait of Mayor Daley looking young and svelte beamed down at us with fatherly love for all who come into his welcoming bosom. We shrank down to avoid the keen eyes which seemed to follow us as we ducked into the nearest room, where another copy of the same picture picked up the surveillance.

Here we found ourselves in a wide aisle beneath incredibly high ceilings and between shoulder high (to me, a six footer) parallel marble counters which slid into the murky distance. Behind the inner counter stood the desks of public servants who looked like gnomes in a giant's lair and were separated by stone from the public. The little servants drowsed at their desks until representatives of the public in business suits strolled in. We observed the servants bow to these representatives, reach under the counter and weightlift huge volumes for the representatives' perusal. Seeing such civic accord gave us the courage to approach a pleasant, motherly looking gnome and inquire timidly: "Can we see the book for north Halsted Street, please?" "What'dya want? Whatcha doin' here? Whatcha looking for? Who are ya? Whodya work for? What's duh legal number?" We stammered and looked as innocent as possible. "Ya gotta have duh legal number. Map room. Fourth floor." "We forgot," we muttered knowingly and retreated rapidly toward the exit. "No pens," she screeched at our backs.

"We're in the anteroom, trying to get into Kafka's Castle," I proclaimed to Jan as we rushed down the hall, feet thudding on the marble floor, and escaped into an elevator crammed with short, fat, fatherly men in suits. Everyone called out floor numbers, and a gnome on a stool cranked the barred gate closed and his machine into motion. A man behind me whose throat wheezed and belly jiggled, assaulting my kidneys every time he spoke, sang out "Hi ho, hi ho, it's off to work we go" and asked no one in particular: "Didja see duh Boss on duh tube last night?" A rapid discussion among the seven men ensued for the rest of the trip. In my mind's ear I can't hear the people I want to hear, but almost everyone in City Hall spoke the same way. "Yeah, it was great duh way he laid into dose damn hippies," a bass voice bellowed into my right ear. "Yuk, yuk. Hippies, yippies an' flippies, he called dem. Boyoboy, I love duh way duh Boss talks," exclaimed a fluty, perpetually amazed voice. "Yeah, he talks good enough to be a poet," chimed a cheerful tenor into my left ear. "He is a poet, boys, a veritable bard," an oily alto intoned. This guy didn't sound like all the others, and a jumble of congratulations greeted his profound observation. "Hey," (wheeze, poke, I was being goosed by a belly; the flab that looked so soft was impressively firm) "dat's right, Doc." "I never taut of dat." "Da Boss is great at anyting he does." "Yeah, an' he ain't takin' no more malarkey" (into my left ear).

"Second floor. Step up, please." "See ya around, Bashful" (from the flute). "So long, Sleepy" (wheeze, jab). "Don't take no wooden nickels" (into my left ear). "You neider, Happy," answered the slower moving of the two exiting dwarves from the other side of the clanging bars which had almost caught his coattails.

"It'll sure be great ta see dem damn hippies get what dey desoiv," shouted the bass into my right ear. "An' duh Boss" (an emphatic jab although I had tried to step forward into space vacated when the two men got off at the second floor) "is just duh very one ta give it ta dem, too." "Boy, if dey're smart dey won't cross duh Boss," piped the astonished flute. "Not after what dem niggers done on duh west side an' dat A-rab done in LA," the voice in my left ear slurped gleefully.

"Third floor. Just a minute, Mr. White, while I get duh elevator level." "Say, Doc, you let duh Boss know we're all behind him. Let's blow all dem bearded fairies right out of duh Windy City" (right ear). "Dat's right" (jab). "Yeah" (flute). "Second duh motion" (left ear). "The Boss knows where we all stand, boys. One reason he can take such a strong stand is because he knows the people of the great city of Chicago," sang the smooth one and exited with a flourish which shoved me into Jan. "Boyoboy. See ya around, Doc." "So long an' keep up duh good woik" (jab, wheeze). "Don't take no wooden nickels, Doc" (left ear). "Don't worry, Happy, I stick to the good old paper dollars," rang the oily voice from the other side of the still open barrier, which closed only after the little man turned ceremoniously away.

"Har, har, har." "Dere goes a real gentleman, Grumpy. An' he's duh Boss's right hand's right hand." However much room there was in the elevator, the tenor continued to speak directly into my left ear while the belly assaulted me from the rear. "Hey, Happy," wondered the flute after a brief lull, the first since the ride began, "why'dya tink dem white hippies is runnin' around actin' like niggers?" The syrup flowed into my left ear without hesitation: "It's da Rooshins, Dopey. Dey feed dem all dat dere dope, an' den dey gottem eatin' outta duh palm of dere hand." "So dat's it. Boy, dat maryjewanna must be powerful stuff. Can ya get any, Happy?"

"Fifth floor. Hizzoner's office. Step down." The bars opened, the belly behind me gave a final push, and I catapulted forward and stumbled out of the cell.

Jan and I stared at each other. When we were alone descending the wide, echoing marble staircase, I asked: "Were they putting us on?"

"They didn't even notice our existence. Even the operator went past our floor. I didn't know Walt Disney made the movie version of Kafka's Castle."

On the fourth floor we consulted the floor directory: no map room listed. Around and around we walked, trying to dodge Daley's omnipresent eyes and step softly so our shoes did not echo too loudly. We said "excuse me" to two other pedestrians, but they didn't seem to see or hear us. We went into an office and asked. "Fourth floor, County Building," a man snapped and turned away. "Huh?" "Dis is City Hall. Ya gotta go ta duh County Building," he snarled at the opposite wall and kept pacing toward the inevitable portrait of the mayor as if he planned to take comfort in the welcoming bosom. "Where's the County Building?" we asked an elevator operator. "Udder side." The doors clanged closed. We walked down the corridor and tried an office on its other side. The man in it took one look at us, trudged into an inner office and closed the door. We crept down the stairs to the main floor.

"Do we look funny?" I asked Jan. I thought I could have passed for an FBI recruit: In those days I was clean shaven, clean cut, crew cut. "I borrowed a pair of genuine slacks and dug my loafers out of my trunk." We decided Jan should try the next office alone and act helpless. "And if that doesn't work, I'll offer to clean up and cook their meals," she called back over her shoulder and plunged into a vast cave labelled "Recorder of Deeds." A few minutes later she emerged with the information that the County Building was the other half of the edifice we were in. Our knowledge was accumulating. Where long, high, dark corridors crossed in the centre of the building was a sign. Sure enough, an arrow proclaiming "City Hall" pointed down the cavern from which we had emerged, and another arrow labelled "County Building" pointed down the opposite cavern. This gave us confidence to risk another elevator. We carefully selected one with passengers of both sexes and a variety in their dress and appearance and made it to the fourth floor in a jumble of chatter about the weather.

The map room did not contain a single picture of the mayor: The county was an improvement over the city. The room featured another high, long marble counter, this one L shaped. Behind it were rows of desks with telephones on them and bored looking bureaucrats behind them. Several wore green eyeshades which made them look like bookies. In fact the room might have passed for a huge wire room if it contained more and busier people. A lone sign read, "Legal Descriptions 55c each, pencils 10c each." An industrious looking man in a suit stood on our side of the counter. Jan and I tried to look casual as we watched him consult a map in a book at least two feet square. He scribbled some numbers and letters on a pad and walked out hurriedly. We checked several such books lying on the counter. In addition to much unintelligible gibberish they all contained maps of city blocks divided into small rectangles with numbers in each box. None of the numbers appeared to be addresses. We tried all the books on the counter, but none were from Lincoln Park.

We stood around looking perplexed and stage whispering, "Where are the maps of Lincoln Park?" but no one noticed our existence. Finally I asked the nearest non-looker, "Can we get the book for Lincoln Park?" "Get duh number from duh map on duh wall," he mumbled to his desk without looking up.

On the wall we found a map full of red outlined boxes and numbers and letters. Eventually we worked out that the boxes represented books. Voila: We drew up a list of numbers covering the Lincoln Park area. Confidently we strode back to the counter on the other side of which a short, fat, bald man was wearily removing books and stashing them beneath the counter. "Can we have number …" "4:30, closing time." The clock on the wall read 4:15. We pointed that out. "No books after 4:15. Closing time." A man in a dark silk suit hurried in. "43A, Sleepy." "Right-cha are, Mr Grimm," said the man behind the counter and handed him a book. "Hey," we objected. "Didn't I tell youse it's closing time? Ya want I should call security? Jeez!" The improvement of county over city was only decorative.

The next morning we were back bright and early (10:30 in Chicago). We obtained one of the large map books. After an hour of studying the book, sneaking glances at what other people were writing, and listening to what employees told those who paid, we had it figured out. Each property had a legal description which bore no relation to its address. A typical one might be "31-12-14d in the southwest section of Wicked Witch's subsection of Snow White's section of Prince Charming's division of Chicago, 1882." We were ready at last. We began copying legal numbers into our notebooks. "Hey," a man behind the counter squealed, rushing to us. It was the first time in two days anyone behind the counter had shown life. "No pens allowed." After some discussion we purchased the stubbiest of pencil stubs for a dime. Then we returned with the numbers we had jotted down to the first office we had been in, the City Tax Assessor's Office.

Now that we were onto the system, we had no trouble. We gave a number and were presented with a wide book which listed the taxpayers for all properties by legal number. We didn't even need the stuff about sections and subsections. Since the numbers in the book were in order, we could get owners for all properties along a street. We still didn't know exact addresses (except when the taxpayer lived at the address), but we rapidly collected a long list of owners. We quickly observed a pattern:

Two-thirds of the property was owned by Lincoln Park Federal Savings and Loan. "Aha," we gasped, raced back to the map room and got legal numbers for properties scattered all over Lincoln Park. The pattern held.

We rushed back to Meg with our news. She too became excited and began phoning people. When she hung up she announced: "It doesn't mean anything. Lincoln Park Federal pays the taxes because they hold the mortgage. They don't necessarily own any of the property. You have to go to something called a tract book to find the owner."

So the next day we were back at City Hall. Eventually we located the tract book room. We could help ourselves to the fat, ancient volumes, but they were arranged (in some mysterious order we never quite figured out) according to division, section, subsection etc. We had to go back to the map room to get this information since we had stopped copying it once we learned we did not need it in the assessor's office. Then we returned to the tract books. There were thousands of them, and to find the one you wanted was a Herculean task, but in them every property in the city was listed – and by street address! Each address had one or more pages which listed every legal transaction which had ever taken place for that property.

It was a fascinating way to learn the history of a building or piece of land; however, it was less useful for contemporary needs, especially in an area changing as fast as Lincoln Park. The books were a year or more out of date, and they still failed to supply the owner's name, only a lengthy list of documents. To find the owner we had to copy the latest document number (in pencil, of course), take it down to an underground vault and hand it to an attendant who would then sign out a roll of microfilm to us. Somewhere on that film would be (in theory) a copy of the mortgage, deed or whatever we were seeking. On that document would be the owner's name – unless the ownership was in a trust, in which case there would only be a trust number and it was impossible to find the owner's name. The big owners, we soon learned, usually used trusts.

Jan and I spent most of our summer going through this rigmarole. We actually became fairly proficient at it, and Concerned Citizens of Lincoln Park wound up with a file, a year out of date, on a sizeable chunk of the property in Lincoln Park. By no means a complete job, but pretty good for Chicago. Probably I should describe some of the beautiful summer days we spent in the vault under City Hall, but I can write no more.

The sun is out, the warm sun of spring to complete the work of a week of intermittent rain and misty drizzle. The ugly snow is melting fast. Large areas of wet brown sod have emerged beneath the trees and are advancing on the house, exposing rotting corpses of last year's weeds, corpses which in the act of dying have already disgorged seeds into the newly awakened, hungry earth and are now, weeds and seeds in turn, being consumed by flocks of hopping, squawking stellar jays. Because the earth has had no time to digest its feast, there is still no sign of green on the ground, but the conifers are green and glowing in the sun. They seem to be giving off the faintest of hazes as if they were breathing for the first time in months. Or is the sun causing the haze by sucking great quantities of evaporating snow into the sky? Green me too, sweet sun of spring. Suck me into the fresh mountain air. This is no time to be in the bowels of the earth. Thank the heavens.

PART TWO

Winter 1975-1976

5.

I AM WRITING AGAIN. It comes as a surprise. Last March, when I finally got to the mountains, I wrote in reaction against Chicago. It was a way of justifying my escape. I didn't know how to write what I wanted to write. I didn't even know what I was seeing when I looked out my window. There are no glaciers or waterfalls visible from my house, but that didn't prevent me from seeing them. Snow on mountain peaks became glaciers; shafts of sunlight reflecting off snow became frozen waterfalls. At least I knew something about Chicago, so I wrote about that. Then spring came to the mountains and I began clearing land and building a garden and orchard. I had neither time nor desire to write.

I never thought about writing any more until just now. It took me half an hour to locate my notebook and pen, but since the weather was telling me to write, I searched until I found them. During the summer I occasionally wondered what I would do in the winter. I looked forward to things like cross country skiing and snowshoeing through the woods. Yet as soon as I looked out at the snow this morning, I knew what else I would be doing: Writing is the winter phase of the mountain living cycle.

It is inconceivable but wonderful that I have become a part of this beauty, so much a part of it that I have not wanted to write of Chicago and my great escape in months, maybe not since the last time it snowed like this, in early spring. Then it seemed as if this beauty, utterly opposite of Chicago, was the perfect medium to bring out my memories of the city. But that was when I was an admiring outsider, before I became a part of this world. Now the beauty this mountain country is has become a lover who demands that a flat city boy embrace her, feel her constantly, dig in her soil with his hands, plant life in her womb, help her children grow, mulch their roots before the coming of winter. So I have worked for her, with her, in her. And on Thanksgiving eve – the holiday comes in October here in Canada – she sent a sign of her approval, a symbol and a sacrifice. A grouse flew into my newly washed plate glass window, broke its neck and tasted great for Thanksgiving dinner.

I feel peaceful, content. The snow is falling more thickly now. Everything is much whiter than it was just a few minutes ago. The big ponderosa tinged with too white snow looks like a giant reality of little toy

Christmas trees lined up on a shelf in some city dime store. City boy me never before knew enough about trees to realize the toys were ponderosas (or at least pines), but seeing the wonder of the real thing explains why the toys are modelled after it. The snow tips the needles so they are both white and green. On the cedars and spruces snow accumulates much more heavily on the boughs, lies atop the green instead of blending with it as on the ponderosa. It is lovely weather but only for looking out the window, for remembering, dreaming, writing. One advantage of living in a place with distinct seasons is that the weather tells you what it is time to do. So I must write again. But how different anything I write now will be from what I wrote last winter and early spring. Even when memories carry me into the fire of Chicago politics, a glimpse out the window will cool them, put them back into their place, into the background, the third dimension whose proper function is to illuminate the gray screen between me and Chicago, between my two selves, to provide a diffused aura of light which makes my new world even more beautiful.

Once it snowed like this for two days in Chicago, the big snow of January, 1967. Over two feet of it. Everything stopped. People abandoned cars in the middle of main streets. CTA bus drivers kept motors running for warmth and slept in their stuck vehicles. No machines moved. It was thirteen days before Dayton Street was plowed, thirteen days without a single car polluting our street, thirteen days in which parked cars were barely noticeable lumps beneath the blanket of white. Schools and workplaces closed. And people became human. On the streets slow-walking strangers greeted each other gaily, stopped and chatted about the snow. New friendships developed on the spot. Jerry and I brought a big pot of his chilli to the girls we had been wanting to meet in the next building. I went for a walk with one of them, the little redhead with a slight limp and pronounced drawl, and fell in love.

Now I can understand why that was the one time in my life Chicago became beautiful. Not that Chicago didn't give me other happy times, not even that Chicago couldn't be beautiful anytime one walked to Lake Michigan and looked east, but the big snow was the only time the entire city and everything and everyone in it became beautiful. Even Mayor Daley would have looked beautiful under two feet of snow. For a few days Chicago became a part of nature instead of an insult to it, a robust tree glorying in the weather's bounty instead of a bully coercing nature and destroying beauty and joy.

If ever there was a time to fall in love in Chicago it was during the big snow. Priscilla and I could never have done it any other time. We were too different even to get together, had been staring and waving at one another for months without meeting. Three young women lived in the three flat next to ours, but it was Priscilla I most often saw and fantasized about. The two buildings were so close that the only way you could see the sky was by sticking your head out the window. I had no inclination to do that. Priscilla's bedroom and mine were opposite each other. Her bedroom window was slightly to the left and three feet below my bedroom window, and her smile and wave as she looked up at me before lowering her shade had become almost a nightly ritual for both of us.

She did it with a flair that led me to imagine her as brash and knowing. In fact, it was a remnant from the theatre she loved – she did costuming for Goodman Theatre, a bit of acting which disguised what she really was, a shy, repressed, unintellectual girl trying to escape the too real world of Waco, Texas in the too unreal world of the Art Institute of Chicago. I was still an intellectual despite all my gambling but searching to find some of the reality I had glimpsed on Bissell Street. Almost any reality other than the middle of white Texas would have done; eight months later black North Carolina certainly did.

I know exactly when I fell in love with Priscilla and see now that even at that transcendent moment I misunderstood her. We had been swishing gaily through the snow for an hour and had already exchanged a we will fuck glance; I was already congratulating myself on my conquest as we stood laughing at a bus driver slumped over his steering wheel. As I looked down at Priscilla, a large snowflake landed on her left eyelash. She sensed my gaze and looked up at me with big, moist eyes very different from the earlier glance or the ones we exchanged across the gap between our bedrooms. These snowstruck eyes asked for a tenderness I was a long way from being able to give. So I interpreted her eyes' question as a simple request to accept what she offered. I was touched and resolved to give her more than she in her simplicity expected.

I remembered that look and might have understood my mistake the next morning when I, gloating at my prowess, asked how she felt and she seemed not to want to reply, then admitted haltingly that her breasts ached from the violence of my lovemaking. But I just assumed she hesitated because she was overwhelmed and not very verbal; later I conceded to myself that her hesitation might have been from fear of piercing my vanity; now my mountains tell me she was weighing her loneliness against what she could foresee she would have to endure with me. During our relationship I gave her lesson after lesson, never noticing that she taught me feelings fragile as that snowflake gently melting on her eyelash.

I wonder if Priscilla and I would fall back in love here, where winters are always as Chicago was for those few days. I like to think so though this is the first time in what – six years? – when I could imagine such a possibility. After the big snow melted, I turned Priscilla on to D.H. Lawrence, a leftover passion from my university days, and Lawrence's ideas provided a basis for our love and arguments even after I turned away from Lawrence for socialism. Priscilla embraced Lawrence after I left for North Carolina, where I rejected his ideas. She wasn't much of a reader so must have read deeply as a way of holding on to me during my absence. The means she chose couldn't have been more inappropriate, for while her fantasies were of the two of us building our own world around our relationship, my fantasies were of rebuilding this world, and it didn't occur to me that personal relationships mattered much in that work.

So by the time we got back together in June of 1968, we had this new difference to add to all the differences of background and personality: She hoped to recreate in me the lover who would carry her out of this dirty world into a private universe of love while I hoped to create of her, Pygmalion style, a strong woman to fight by my side for change in this dirty world. I had returned to Chicago because nowhere was the world dirtier. Poor Priscilla. Because she had been trained in the best southern tradition to obey her man, she tried to follow my way.

Only after our relationship shattered along with the rest of my world in Lincoln Park could I begin to understand what these mountains teach me, that I had willed destruction for her by asking her to forsake every dream she ever had, the old, artistic ones which got her out of LBJ's stark Texas and the new ones I gave her to get her out of stark Chicago whose Art Institute was proving more unreal than Lyndon's idea of Texas. I look into the white world outside my window through tears of compassion, compassion I knew I should feel but never could in Chicago. If Priscilla were here she would understand and console me.

She isn't here except in the gifts she gave me. By the time my present story began, by the time I met Jazzman, our love was past its peak. My chronicle inevitably will include the decline of the relationship, so here let me pay belated tribute by naming some of the things she gave me, some few of many, like trying to describe two or three of the snow-flakes falling. Only then can I return to the whole scene, the snowy sky and landscape outside my window, the times she and I lived together in Lincoln Park while so far apart.

I skip over the most precious thing, the love relationship itself, the first lasting one of my life, the one that taught me love could and should be more than a roll in the hay. I did appreciate that at the time, appreci-ated it so much I tried to keep living with her out of gratitude (and desire for a few more rolls in the hay) after I had conspired with Chicago to destroy the best parts of that relationship. I learned many lesser things from Priscilla, things I could never comprehend while I lived with her. Must such learning be in retrospect? Can we never show gratitude at the time our teachers need it? How much more bearable a few words of thanks might have made Priscilla's sacrifice. I give them freely now, years too late.

Priscilla's gifts were of the senses. Taste: She was a marvellous cook and taught me to enjoy, not merely eat, food. By watching her I even learned how to cook, now one of my life's little pleasures. Only after we split up did I dare try, but I wouldn't have known to make the attempt without her. Sight: a better ability to see natural and human patterns, to see art in life. That too developed mainly after we were apart, when I got into acid, but acid could not have done it had not Priscilla prepared me. I had dropped acid before I met Priscilla with exciting but different results. Probably I would miss half the things I now see in the mountains (as well as all the things I think I see but don't) had it not been for Priscilla.

Sound was not Priscilla's medium – except for her laughs. She had two of them, a tiny, tinny tinkle and a great wheezing bellows laugh during which she inhaled when she should have been exhaling. She told me she developed this laugh, which caused neighbours to peer out their win-dows and wonder why the foghorns were blowing, when she decided not to be a giggly teenager and to stifle every giggle by sucking it in.

Priscilla's greatest gift was touch. That's why she made wall hangings and costumes, preferring fabric to paint for her art. Could I enjoy the textures found digging through the soil, the tenacity of couchgrass rhi-zomes tested from beneath, the melting of finished compost between the fingers, the raw readiness of a well dug plot ready for planting, had not Priscilla made me feel the many materials she worked with but most of all herself? My whole body feeling her whole body, stomach sweating, sliding with her stomach, toes tangled in her toes, feeling their tightness and playfulness, then untangling so our legs could rub together up and down and sideways, she moving hers inside mine then back to the outside, our legs scissors cutting opposite ways yet velvet, velvet to the touch, and her hands softly playing over my body while mine explored hers, so soft.

I remember once stumbling out of the shower in the coach house on Fremont Street. I was not rushing so it must have been June or early July, shortly after I moved in with her, before I was spending most of my time working with Concerned Citizens of Lincoln Park. In the cramped coach house the bathroom door opened into a corner of the kitchen. I intended to turn left and mount the stairs to the bedroom, where my clothes were. But the sight of the kitchen caught my attention. Priscilla owned an enormous collection of bowls, pots and receptacles of every kind, acquired at the second hand shops she loved.

It seemed that every one of these was scattered about the tiny kitchen, covering the table, stove, sink, windowsill and even the floor: chaos, yet Priscilla's presence gave it pattern. She united the clashing reds, oranges, blues, yellows of her pots and pottery, dancing from one to another, adding a dash of this there, giving a quick stir here, upsetting a bowl and deftly sweeping its contents into a pot as if the action were part of the recipe, singing and humming to the rhythm of her work – she only sang while cooking, thank heavens – a bee flitting from flower to flower, transforming the chaotic kitchen into a "beauteous" (her favourite word) garden. I felt myself drawn forward, perhaps by the sight, more likely by a desire to taste, for everything Priscilla cooked tasted wonderful and the bigger the mess the greater the food.

Now Priscilla stirred the contents of several containers into a pot on the stove, and I took a step forward, then another. Then I stepped into a bowl. Priscilla tinkled a laugh, stirred vigorously, exclaimed "my clumsy darling," scraped the goop off my foot with a rubber spatula, zipped back to the stove to stir, emptied the bowl I had stepped in into another bowl, wiped my foot with a damp cloth as I hopped about then fell to the floor because it tickled, turned off the flame under her pot, gave it a final stir and covered it, then laughing her great bellows laugh fell upon me and let me feel the texture of the velour pants she was wearing even as she pulled them off to let me feel her smoother skin.

We alternated between tickling and kissing, her body dancing above mine as it had danced above the pots and bowls, stirring me, heating me, tasting me. Her breasts skimmed my skin as they moved up me, exciting my genitalia, loosening my tickled-tight stomach, circling my own breasts. One of her nipples slid up the side of my nose, then her shaking belly made me laugh harder until she plugged up my mouth. "May I have this dance?" her clit asked my tongue. The tempo increased, but before it reached crescendo she slid back down and kissed me wildly while her vagina caressed my penis, muscles contracting and expanding to stimulate us and I responding to her pressures to change rhythm and position, which brought me into contact with another bowl and started my laughter all over just as she came.

I was laughing so hard that even her incredible vibrations failed to bring me to orgasm, so we tried to roll over, limbs askelter, utterly clumsy now and both breaking up with laughter yet maintaining contact in the middle, her muscles straining not to let me slip out, then her back bumping a table leg, preventing us from completing our turn, forcing us to roll back, our entire bodies convulsing in laughter at our clumsiness yet exulting that the clumsiness could not separate us.

"My silly, cockeyed lover, I need the crazy joy you bring me, but my sauce won't keep forever," Priscilla panted between bellows laughs as she rose above me and massaged my nipples with tender fingertips, my legs with hard knees and soft thighs, my body with her body until I came, clinging to her my thanks, my exhausted body promising it would always do the same for her.

That scene has always been one of my most precious memories of Priscilla, yet I completed it only last spring. As a boy in Chicago I was plagued by a sinus condition. My nose was constantly corked and I could neither breathe nor smell through it. Although the worst of the condition vanished at puberty, I still breathe through my mouth. Last spring I dropped acid and was tripping about my new mountain home when something smacked me in the middle of my face. At first I staggered back, but gradually revelation led me forward across a small field to the source of the blow, a large lilac bush in full flower exuding the most potent of odours. Long, long I lay under that bush glorying in the smell. It was the first time in my life I could recall smelling anything more subtle than teargas.

The acid trip became a nose trip. I went from one thing to another revelling in the smell of each: flower after flower, trees, grass, weeds, later inside objects. I could detect odours in books different from each other and quite different from a recently run off sheet of ditto paper. I sniffed clothes in drawers, soaps, the compost bucket, spent a long time opening bottles of spices and smelling each, then several together. I popped popcorn, as I often do when tripping to watch and listen to the explosions then eat the fluff, but this trip I found myself more fascinated by the aroma of the cooking oil than of the popped corn and spent a long time sniffing before I ate a kernel.

The nose trip went on and on, a whole new world for me. Eventually I fell asleep. I awoke still on the nose trip but a new – or, rather, old – and even more wonderful one. I had dreamed myself back into the coach house on Fremont after my shower. I had admired the marvellous disorder of the kitchen, chuckled to myself over Priscilla's awful singing and was turning to ascend the stairs when Priscilla stirred ingredients from a small bowl, a pan and a pot into her double boiler and a sharp fragrance of lemon filled the air and drew me towards it, lured me into the kitchen and love.

Seven years after the event I was able to understand it and appreciate for the first time the sense of smell Priscilla had also given me. I luxuriated long and longingly in the scene, then leaped out of bed, looked up a recipe for hollandaise sauce and recreated the delectable concoction Priscilla had been cooking that day, evoking the full memory at last, for as the same lemony odour filled my nostrils, I fell to another floor and re-experienced the feelings as they had really been, adding the smells of Priscilla and her kitchen to my other sensual memories.

Sex on the floor was not unusual for Priscilla and me in the early days of our love although it seldom was the kitchen floor and usually we came together, a single singing, wordless, toneless, moaning duet of total tension leading into total relaxation into one another, sensual love. Sometimes we came without fucking, fully clothed, so suddenly together we had no time to undress but kissed and hugged and rubbed and touched until we both trembled to orgasm. Only then could we remove our sticky clothing and lie together in wonderment – until we made love more conventionally. There seemed no need to speak at such times, but occasionally Priscilla may have whispered to herself. Once in a doze after lovemaking I heard such a whisper but couldn't make out whether she said: "Take me." Or asked: "Where are you taking me?" before I fell back into blissful slumber.

Priscilla liberated my senses, senses so dead from years of Chicago that only after we were apart and I noticed that I felt, felt deeply, wanted to see, touch, taste things and people, not just think about them or debate with them, only when I cried and did not know why at the loss of a woman whom I blamed for making me a creature of habit who could no longer live alone as I had most of my adult life before her; only then did I begin to understand that I had to get out of Chicago to savour the world she had opened up to me.

During most of the time she was bestowing her magnificent gifts, I seldom saw her except to eat and sleep with her, and when we did spend time together I often spent it complaining of her niggling ways, her concern with unimportant matters like dress and pots and pans, her prodigious waste of time cooking as I gulped down delicious dinners so I could race off to the evening meeting, eventually even her desire for the fullness of sex. For time seemed so valuable that I came to resent spending hours on what could be accomplished in minutes. Chicago was robbing me even as the most wonderful of gifts were being tendered.

Even now when I can smell, when I can appreciate and utilize Priscilla's gifts among my mountains, in my garden, in different relationships with people and in the ability to describe the hell of Chicago which taught me so much, even now I often slight Priscilla by thanking Jazzman for my mountains. For Jazzman somehow led me to this beautiful northern Porto Reco (the name of a long defunct mine near the Slocan Valley) which I might never have found had he not found me on the southwest side. Yet I could never have loved it well were it not for Priscilla, who has never been here.

6.

THE SUN HAS JUST POKED over the mountains, and I am just back from a walk on the snow, not in it. We had a thaw and for several days it rained more than snowed. The snow on the ground shrank, compressed more than melted, became heavy and crystalline rather than light and powdery. The sky cleared yesterday afternoon; then it froze quickly and hard last night. Today the ground has a hard, bright crust you can walk on spangled with shiny crystals and small gray pockmarks, depressions shaded by the white ground blocking the low sun. The trees are all touched with frost. On the evergreens this is a translucent white sheen which makes the greens lighter and brighter. On the bare trees it is a film of ice, ephemeral but lovely, the tiny tamarack branchlets like pure white feathers in the new sun.

In our hearts all of us with Concerned Citizens of Lincoln Park guessed that the struggle to save our community would be brief and futile. When the sun glares on the trees' frost, the ice flares up more beautiful than ever – before burning out and melting. We knew that once urban renewal began its destruction and removal, only a miracle could save the neighbourhood. We should have begun fighting years earlier. The problem is that during the planning stages only a few upper middle class men understand what is about to happen. By the time the rest of the community catches on, the bulldozers are already there and it is too late.

Sabotage of the sort Mick Finnigan advocated – draining crankcases of oil, dropping sand, sugar or, best of all, mothballs in gas tanks of the wrecking machines – can delay the process. Community organizing and mass protests are more effective delaying tactics. But as Fred Hampton reminded us in his every speech: "The only solution is revolution." We knew this, knew the best we could reasonably hope was to delay the destruction of our neighbourhood and alert other neighbourhoods so they could begin their struggle much earlier than we had. But we were young and the young are not always reasonable. The frost on the trees can be saved by a sudden clouding over of the sky, so we fought and hoped for a miracle in Lincoln Park. A miracle we must ourselves make.

The base for our fight was the Concerned Citizens of Lincoln Park office, a small storefront in the 2500 block of Lincoln Avenue. John Leeds' church rented it and used it as a church office, which meant their own desk and filing cabinet and use of that space to type and run off the church newsletter once a week. Otherwise the office was ours and we did a lot with it. To us it meant a phone, a mimeo, a broken down manual typewriter and a continually breaking down electric one, two desks and one table (salvaged from a building about to be demolished by urban renewal), two filing cabinets (same source) and folding chairs.

The most important of these was the mimeo, an old hand cranker which kept all our arms in shape because it operated almost constantly. We put out all kinds of literature: advertisements for dances sponsored by local gangs and our own rummage sales, a daily newsletter during the Democratic Convention, announcements of meetings and marches, political editorials, leaflets on anything of concern to the community. Our mimeo also served many other groups and individuals in Lincoln Park and sometimes other parts of the city. Putting out a newspaper was difficult and expensive – we never got out more than eight issues in a year although we tried to publish monthly – but it was easy to crank out a leaflet, and Jill's older kids and their friends were the best of distributors. We could get a leaflet into most mailboxes in the working class sections of Lincoln Park in less than two days. Occasionally the machine became temperamental and we couldn't crank out enough copies to keep our army of stuffers happy, but usually it managed to keep ahead of them.

Perhaps the most visible feature of the office was a clothes rack and pile of clothing. Clothing of all sorts was donated to us, and several large poor families were able to get for free better clothes than they could afford to buy. Several winos also patronized the pile. Presumably they could trade clothes for a drink. We generally withheld items from them which had not been checked out first by the families. Periodically the pile would reach proportions which threatened to drive us into the street. Then Jill, Liz and other neighbour women would sort it out while Meg solicited more items, and we would have a rummage sale.

It was the only time we ever sold anything. For two days I would be exiled to research at City Hall, and the office would swarm with hordes of bargain hunters. A rummage sale was almost always the harbinger of a new edition of the *Press*. Often it was the only way we could both raise enough money to print the paper and clear enough space in the office to lay it out.

For a while we also had boxes of fairly fresh produce and not quite fresh bread inside and outside the office. A group of college students collected it from supermarkets in wealthy areas. It was food normally thrown away although much of it was as good as the produce sold in stores in areas like ours. We never had to tell anyone it had arrived. People who could afford little fresh produce knew as soon as it came and snapped it up quickly. One day the students returned empty handed: Chain store higher ups had decreed that all food not sold must be disposed of as garbage.

We kept the office brightly painted: red floor, blue walls. But the paint never completely covered a shabbiness I and many people who came for help or conversation found comfortable. The big plate glass window was continually being broken by enemy rocks and replaced, and each time it was replaced, dear, damned Meg painted our name and symbol, an eagle with a pig bleeding in its talons, a little larger. By the end of our era the lettering and artwork covered most of the window.

Below the window, to the right of the door, which had the church name printed in small letters, sat our sofa. It was merely a long wood box with a removable top and a built up back, all covered with cheap vinyl cushions patched with coloured mystic tape. Inside the box were supplies, mainly coloured bond paper used for leafleting. Few people sat on the couch – the folding chairs were more comfortable and more centrally located – but it was often used for sleeping: by us when we were laying out a newspaper or just dropping from lack of sleep, by street kids temporarily without a place to stay or too spaced out to get home, by an old man evicted from his apartment of more than thirty years by real estate speculators, by fugitives on their way to consultation with a lawyer or the underground railroad.

The desks and chairs were arranged in various ways at different times. Only the church desk with the telephone remained stationary in a rear corner of the long, narrow room, next to the back door and mimeo, across from a partitioned area with a sink, toilet and more shelves of paper. However the desks were arranged, there was always empty floor space except when the clothes pile had reached rummage sale proportions or the folding chairs were all set up for a meeting. The floor space was excellent for impromptu dances when we received good news: Jazzman or another friend released from jail, Jill with a new baby, Nuncio (a cop who shot a local teenager in the back and watched him bleed to death before taking him to the hospital) convicted of murder. The empty floor space was also useful for pacing when the news was less happy and for setting up a long table borrowed from the church for laying out the newspaper. Otherwise it just looked as if a large, essential object had been removed and not yet replaced.

Days at the office were usually as hectic as a robin's nest with a squirrel trying to get at the chicks. Even when we weren't attempting to get out an issue of the *Press* or draw up, run off and distribute a leaflet, we were kept busy by a flow of folks. Most were working class neighbours with problems. When one entered, Meg invariably found me paperwork to do so she could deal with the problem. After she had talked a while, she would call me over to meet the person, explain the problem and her suggested solution, and ask for my opinion or assistance.

Meg was a born social worker: She empathized completely with such people and loved to help them solve their problems. I think she feared my approach would be more detached and therefore wanted to make the initial sympathetic contact herself. She need not have feared: Most of the people had been so obviously screwed by the Department of Urban Renewal, the Welfare Department, a merchant or a landlord that no one could have been unsympathetic. Though I must admit that perhaps Meg did handle the problems better than I.

I remember Marie, a woman of French descent in her eighties, so skinny I could have placed my thumb and finger around her calf. She always came in near the end of the month, when she was near starvation. She received $67 a month social security and paid $55 a month rent. The extra $12 had to pay for utilities and food. Of course there was no way she could manage, but she refused to apply for welfare. Meg always bought her a meal at the corner restaurant. Marie would eat it ravenously, weep, then thank Meg profusely, bless us and disappear until the end of the next month. We asked where she lived, but she begged us not to inquire after her or accompany her home.

Once she came in when Meg was out of the office. I was determined to solve her problems rationally. I had her wait in the front of the office while I called the Welfare Department and spoke to a somewhat sympathetic intake worker. I explained the problem and the worker agreed to set up assistance with a minimum of hassle. Then I told Marie I had a friend who could help her, bundled her into my car, and headed for the Wicker Park Welfare Office. In the car her gratitude was overwhelming, but when we arrived and she realized where I was taking her, she screamed, broke away from me, and ran off down Milwaukee Avenue with unbelievable strength and speed. When I finally caught up with her, she raged, then cried and begged me not to take her there. She was so frail I expected the energy she was expending to kill her. I could do nothing but take her to a restaurant, then drive her back to Lincoln Avenue. When she did not return to our office the next month, I accused myself of killing her, but the following month she appeared again, skinnier and prouder than ever.

The other large group of people who came in were students and movement people. Meg's reaction to them was to busy herself with paperwork and ignore them. I dealt with them and she refused even to be consulted unless they were volunteering to work with us, in which case she cross examined them until she was persuaded they were sincere. Once that happened she again became the warm person she usually was and overflowed with stories of the plight of poor people in Lincoln Park.

Groups were also my responsibility. Mostly they were church groups from the Urban Training Center. They were brought to the office and for a $25 honorarium I would discuss the problems of people in our neighbourhood for much of an afternoon. For $35 they got a few more hours plus a tour of the community. For $50 they got a full day including an ethnic dinner (rice and beans cooked in the church by Jill and Priscilla). It was our only source of income other than donations and rummage sales since we believed that all services, including the newspaper, should be free to poor and working class people.

There were many exciting times at the office. Once Meg and I barricaded the door against a swarm of cops in hot pursuit of Jazzman while he phoned a lawyer. Twice the cops practiced raids: They sealed off Lincoln Avenue, stopping all traffic between Fullerton and Wrightwood. Then half a dozen squad cars would screech to a halt in front of our office (the same thing would be happening in front of the other centres of radicalism on Lincoln Avenue, Alice's Restaurant, the *Seed* office, and the Wobbly Hall), and two dozen cops would pile out with guns drawn, rush to our door, then turn around, pile back into their cars and speed off. The entire exercise was done in about two minutes. It was good practice for the boys and had the unsettling effect it was planned to have on us.

The day in the office I remember best was Jill's first visit. I had met her and her family canvassing. She lived in a tenement above a bar across the street from our office. At the time I canvassed the plaster had just dropped out of her entire kitchen ceiling. There were gaping holes in the walls and ceilings of most of the rooms as well as other hazardous building code violations. Jill allowed me to take photos for the newspaper.

A few weeks later an issue of the *Press* hit the streets, and within an hour Jill, her mother and her friend Liz stormed through our door, backed Meg, me and Mary, the church secretary, into a corner and bawled the hell out of us. Jill handled most of the dressing down: She claimed we had made her look terrible in front of the whole neighbourhood, made it look like she couldn't look after her own living place. She accused us of only liking Puerto Ricans, of being anti-hillbilly. Then she put on an exhibition of swearing and threatening to beat the shit out of us one at a time or all together which awed me. First she challenged me, then Meg, then Mary. Poor Mary was a naïve eighteen-year-old who had just been hired by the church.

When Jill offered to do to her several things she did not know were anatomically possible, she broke into tears. Jill's fury instantly changed to sympathy. She took Mary in her arms and comforted her with all the experience of a woman raising nine children and big with her tenth. Soon Mary felt better and the women were ready to listen to us. We read them the article which accompanied the photos (all three women were illiterate) and explained that we had printed the pictures only to help pressure the landlord to repair Jill's apartment, that it was the landlord's legal responsibility to make the repairs, that we were only against the landlord and wanted to help Jill, her friends and all poor people in Lincoln Park whether they were black, Latin, hillbilly or anything else. After an hour or more they seemed to forgive us and left. We felt relieved and pretty good: If we could befriend these women we would have some real fighters on our side.

After they left Priscilla called. She was about to make a soufflé and wanted to be sure I would be home on time. I told her things were quiet in the office and I would come right home. As I was leaving, in stalked the three women plus Jill's father and her husband John. We read the story again, again explained our position and listened to them. The problem was that they didn't trust strangers. Outsiders had screwed them all their lives. Strangers had driven them off the beautiful Kentucky land their people had owned for over a century and then destroyed it. Strangers had put them to work in the coal mines, then took away their jobs because strip mining was more efficient. Strangers had torn down their new homes in our northern city. And now strangers were printing pictures which made it look like they lived like hogs.

We talked and talked and slowly became friendly. After an hour John slapped me on the back and invited us to have a beer at the bar. It was an honour and a pleasure. Before the evening was over, I was in love with the whole bunch of them (the bunch had grown to about twenty in the bar), and they were our friends. It was after midnight when I dropped Meg at her place, kissed her in jubilation and went home.

As I entered my door the soufflé came flying at my head, dish and all. It just missed me and smashed against the wall. Priscilla threw all the other dishes she could reach into the pile for flavouring, told me to eat it, and ran up to the bedroom. It took at least half a minute to break all those dishes, and I watched her face throughout. She had obviously waited with the soufflé for a long time, building up in her mind the pleasure she would derive from watching it hit my face. I don't think she threw it with all her force: It was partly a gesture, partly an attempt to make me look silly, but not an attempt to maim me. It was planned as theatre and her planning had gone no further. Had the casserole hit me and I cried out, she might have been satisfied.

Missing me was the great disappointment. Throwing the rest of the dishes was an expression of frustration at the miss and an attempt to elicit the reaction her original gesture had failed to draw from me. Each crash of a dish seemed to increase her frustration and my fascination. I considered words to describe her emotions, changing words with each change of her expression, but I said nothing. My lack of reaction must have been the worst blow to her. She stared at me waiting for me to say something. Only when she was sure I wasn't going to react did her face lose some of its rigidity, her mouth open to curse me. Then everything went slack and she ran upstairs crying in shame, shame at her terrible emotions and my lack of emotion.

I didn't lack all emotion. I had been high on beer and very different emotions, and the alcohol seemed to slow my ability to adjust without diminishing my understanding. A drunk is the most understanding of creatures. I knew Priscilla was right, but surely a little food was not worth such anguish. In my desire to befriend Jill and John and their friends and my delirium at doing so I had totally forgotten Priscilla and her labour in preparing dinner. That was what really hurt her, for she had put as much energy into the dinner as I had into the hillbillies, but my energy seemed to me to be over important matters while hers was over trivial ones.

I had watched her face and understood her, yet the intensity of her feelings and their utter dissimilarity to my own stunned me, frightened me, froze me. It was a long time before she would let me get near her. Finally she let me hug her chilled, shuddering body. Her intensity still scared me. I tried to explain, to justify my actions.

IT IS COLD AND PERFECTLY CLEAR. As the sun climbs higher in the sky, it illuminates tiny dust specks of frost in the air, specks it seems to draw from the ground and trees, certainly not from the sky. They turn a rainbow of colours, like microscopic soap bubbles, and seem to dance, first toward the north, away from the light, then, as if fear has softened into wonder or the band leader has commenced a new melody, toward the south and the sun which will melt them. The trees are light with a thin film of these frost particles. All the trees seem to shimmer and shimmy into the dance in the bright, cold air above the sparkling, frozen snow. The world is in motion, yet every detail is sharp. Even on the third mountain over, the tall one that vaults from the shoulders of the shorter ones in front of it, I can see each individual tree outlined against the blue sky.

At the time of the dish smashing I thought I had persuaded Priscilla. What little drunken understanding I had felt as I watched her face as she was throwing the dishes, listened to her sobs, held her breaking body next to mine, disappeared as soon as I began to speak. I talked of myself, explained why it meant so much to me to make friends with the Lincoln Avenue hillbillies. Oh, I apologized for not coming to dinner, called myself a miserable egotist not even to phone, but Priscilla saw that night that my emotions were no longer for her. I would have denied it, Priscilla couldn't have said it then – she did later, after over a year of trying to join me in my new life had failed to bring us closer – but that night marked the end of what we had found together in the big snow.

We went on living together, making love, sometimes beautiful love, but it was from habit. I tried to phone her when I couldn't get home for dinner, and our arguments became fewer and less violent. But that was partly because we had little time, what with my working all day at the office and going to meetings almost every night, partly because I had murdered the old love and spirit in Priscilla.

7.

THE IDYLL WHICH WAS THE SUMMER OF 1968 – knocking on the doors of strangers who quickly became friends, renewing my romance with Lincoln Park, traipsing around the fairy tale world of City Hall, returning to the coach house early enough to maintain my romance with Priscilla – ended with the Democratic Convention of late August. Delegates to the Democratic Convention gathered in Chicago to pay tribute to Richard J. Daley and nominate Hubert H. Humphrey in an eloquent statement of their faith in Amerika and everything it had come to stand for: murdering people fighting for freedom in Viet Nam and mutilating their land, ordering police to shoot to kill blacks seeking freedom in its own ghettoes, propping up every corrupt police state that would kiss its ass and calling it "the free world."

Police and National Guard troops gathered to show the world Amerika had the capacity to be as repressive as any of the police states it sponsored and would become a police state itself any time enough of its citizens wanted to change it. Demonstrators gathered for a mass regurgitation of all this that Amerika had come to represent. The place they chose to gather was our park, Lincoln Park.

Although it was located many miles from the site of the Convention, our community became a police camp several days before the Convention began and remained one until it ended. I had a total of eleven guns pointed at me (as an individual, not part of a crowd) by various cops during that time although my primary activities were driving injured people to hospitals (mainly Billings Hospital on the other side of town because injured young people were being arrested on suspicion or principle at north side hospitals) and helping put out a daily newssheet for distribution in the community. For over a week anyone braving the fog of tear gas to walk the streets of Lincoln Park at night was likely to be put up against a wall by policemen pointing guns. Even well to do people glimpsed what it was like to live in a police state or a ghetto.

At the beginning of the Democratic Convention I was still naïve. Two days earlier a black cop drew a gun on a bunch of us who were making posters on the corner of Halsted and Dickens. I insisted we seek the cop out instead of filing a complaint. Meg, Jan and I eventually tracked him down at the temporary police headquarters in the park. It was opening day of the Convention, and about a thousand cops were lined up receiving a last minute pep talk over a loudspeaker.

Why we were allowed in I don't know. We didn't look like hippies, I guess. We confidently and innocently approached a captain, told him we wanted to speak to Officer So and So of the Eighteenth District, and were directed in. We talked to the officer for about ten minutes, politely explaining that pointing guns wasn't nice but that we wouldn't tell his superiors this time if he promised to be a good boy in the future. He clearly didn't know what to make of it all but must have figured we were important since we were allowed into the private police pep rally. I was still fresh from the South, where blacks, even black cops, can look in the mirror and know which side they are on. I well remember this cop's astonished look at the end of our conversation when I called him "brother" and gave him the black power handshake.

Our entire conversation with the cop was held to the accompaniment of a bellowing voice on the loudspeaker. I had been too wrapped up in my own mission of converting the black cop to hear it all, but Meg and Jan did and filled me in on what I missed. Rumours of a blood bath had been circulating for months, but I had believed they were being circulated purely to scare people and cut down the number of protestors. Now the shouting voice called demonstrators "pigs," "copkillers" and numerous four letter and longer curse words.

The assembled protectors of the city were informed that intelligence (sic) reports indicated that demonstrators were heavily armed and planned to shoot to kill policemen, that one report claimed they might attempt to set up machine gun posts in the trees of the park, so at all costs they must not be allowed in the park at night to do their dirty work under cover of darkness. Police were repeatedly urged to show demonstrators no mercy. These orders were well carried out during the following days. The brutality of the police was documented by reporters and photographers (many of whom were beaten and had notes and film confiscated), TV coverage and eye witness accounts.

Most Chicagoans (who have been so exposed to lying by the media that they expect little else) and many Americans still don't believe that what occurred occurred or was unjustified. Almost all Americans, including many of the reporters who were beaten, believe that the brutality that did occur resulted from individual cops going berserk and disobeying orders. Of this charge I can absolve all Chicago police: They are fine family men who do not disobey orders; during the Convention they were good Germans following commands which came from above. I heard some of those commands.

THE FIRST NIGHT OF THE CONVENTION WAS CLEAR; although you couldn't see stars or badges on Chicago cops' uniforms, you could see the occasional star in the Chicago sky. It was the kind of warm summer night Priscilla and I liked to take an old blanket to the park and make love all night. But Priscilla had refused to go to the park even during the day. It was full of freaks foreign to the city and the rich traditions of the Chicago Police Department. Not as many freaks had come as the organizers of the "Festival of Life" (to contrast with the Convention of death the Democrats were holding down in Daley's distant neighbourhood far to the south) had hoped, but more were present than most members of Chicago's hip community, which had been loudly advising people to stay away through underground presses around the country, would have preferred.

Despite having heard the bloodthirsty pep talk that afternoon, I must have been the only person in Chicago not expecting violence. I still managed to believe that all the bluster was intended only to scare demonstrators away and that even Mayor Daley would not be pigheaded enough to provoke riots with half the reporters and camerapeople in the country in attendance. As a matter of form Priscilla asked me not to go and eventually settled on a good-bye kiss like one bestowed on a soldier unlikely to return alive and a warning to "be careful, dear."

I chuckled to myself over Priscilla's fears as I drove to the park. I knew my city. The "city on the make" didn't waste time on hippie protestors. As a teenager I had spent many a happy night in Bughouse Square listening to soapbox orators slam city, nation, system. No one cared. What was happening now? Just Bughouse Square on a larger scale. The protest had been organized by non-Chicagoans who didn't know where to go and had wound up in the wrong park. Daley would toss them a few soapboxes and ignore them. Why make a fuss about kids declaring out loud their intentions to sleep in a park that lovers and strollers used and slept in every nice night of summer? So long as the kids stayed cool, didn't flaunt their dope and didn't tear anything up, it would all blow over. I had forgotten all about their machine gun posts. Nevertheless, I remembered Priscilla's warning and parked my car a few blocks west of the park.

As I entered the park at North and Clark, a single file line of perhaps a hundred people was snaking rapidly around the grass and periodically splitting into smaller groups at the command of a guy shouting into a bullhorn which distorted his voice so badly I seemed to be hearing a foreign language. Maybe I was: As I stood watching and wondering what sort of a dance this was, someone tapped my shoulder and spat a spiel at the side of my neck: "Dig it, man, dig it. We're practicing Japanese police control techniques. Dig? The pigs ain't gonna make us run this time. We're gonna deal with them. Dig? Choose an affinity group, join in and rumble. We gotta be ready, and this is some ride on shit, man." I mumbled something and crept away slowly, scratching my head and wiping my neck, trying to look as if I were seeking an affinity group.

Further up Clark, still on the fringe of the park, a black man was standing on a bench haranguing a crowd about freeing Huey Newton and a bus boycott. At least that's what I thought he was talking about. I walked by slowly but didn't stop to avoid being singled out again. "Free Huey" and "ride on" this, "ride on" that were the only words I was sure I heard. In retrospect I suspect the man standing on the bench was Bobby Seale, who was later indicted for his part in the Convention protests. At the time I had never heard of Bobby Seale or heard the expression "right on." This was not yet my affinity group.

Deeper into the park the next group I saw was gathered around Allen Ginsberg, the first celebrity I recognized. I considered staying because I knew no one would bother me here and I wondered how long people could continue chanting "ommmmmmmmm," but up ahead I saw a cop with a crowd forming around him. He was a burly, balding giant in his fifties who wore police pants and shirt but no jacket or hat. He supported a bicycle which his size made look like a toy. As I approached he was telling of his mission.

"They sent me out as a scout," he reported, pointing at a line of cops in the distance. He spoke with Irish in his voice, an impish smile on his face and wrinkles on his forehead and right up his scalp. The wrinkles made his eyes small and bright. "I was the only pig (a big, sheepish grin at this word) they could find who liked ye. I told them I would na learn nothing, that ye are just like any other folks, some good, some bad. Ah, ye can be sure they donna believe it." He winked. "They want to see if ye kill me or beat me or rip off me weapon or at least pelt me with rotten eggs."

"How come you wear a gun if you like people so much?" a sceptic inquired. "Departmental rules. Never used the bloody thing in me life, but if I'm caught without it on or off duty I'll be chucked off the farce – I mean force."

"How come you don't quit?" a girl asked. "Ah, now ye'll be sounding like me young daughter. She's out here in the park with ye. Me heart keeps getting younger and saying to resign, but me belly (he patted the bulge affectionately) is old and spoilt. It keeps saying I've only got a few years to go for me pension."

"Are those guys going to attack us tonight?" asked another girl. "Niver trust a pig, lass, especially in the dark. If I were ye now, sure I'd clear out of this place before eleven o'clock. Na more questions now. I have to do some scouting or they'll not let me volunteer for this job tomorrow and I'll have to spend me time listening to bloody pig stories. Keep the faith now." And with a wink and a wave he mounted the spindly bike and wobbled off over the grass, heading deeper into the park.

I felt better and ambled about for some time enjoying strangers and hunting for friends. Eventually I found John Leeds. It was the first time I ever saw him in his minister's collar. "The North Side Cooperative Ministry has decided to add dignity to these proceedings," he told me. "We're all here mingling in full costume. But you can't put anything over on the Chicago Police Department. Burt Jackson told me a cop accused him of being a fake and told him his collar wouldn't help him after eleven."

"Do you really think they'll attack?"

"I'm afraid so."

I launched into my thesis: "I can't believe they'd be so dumb. I know Chicago. I've lived here all my life. Daley doesn't go looking for trouble. He'll make sure none of these demonstrators disturb his precious Convention. That's all. Letting them stay here miles away from the Convention is the best thing he could ask for."

"You were out of town this spring," John replied. "Chicago has changed. Something happened to Daley during the riots after King's murder. He treated the riots as a personal insult, and he's still offended. He ordered his cops to shoot to kill rioters – voters, overwhelmingly Democratic voters at that. This is worse. Daley's idea has always been that Chicagoans are devoted to him and his party. One reason the riots got to him was that he couldn't find any outside agitators to blame, but now he's got a park full of them. They don't live or vote in Chicago. They're here to pervert the democratic process – that's both upper and lower case 'd.' If you don't think Daley is going to enjoy watching his boys in blue take out their and his frustrations on all these shaggy heads, you're a bigger dreamer than I thought."

"So you think it will happen too. In front of all these cameras and reporters." Ahead of us a camera crew had floodlights on and was grinding away.

"Have you noticed what they're filming? They took a lot of footage of the martial arts training, and they're great at drawing the wilder looking kids into wild statements. That kind of stuff will be used to justify whatever happens. It will show the people in the park as aggressive and crazy. Their antics will be juxtaposed with interviews of sober police officials who will say they didn't want a confrontation but had to enforce the law. They will explain how they pleaded with unreasonable people to leave the park, gave warning after warning and tried to move them out gently but met with violent resistance. Besides, at night most of the camera crews will be down at the Convention, and it's dark here and tough to get good pictures once the action starts. No, the media will make the demonstrators look bad, not good. They'll help the nation believe that anything the cops do is justified. If Rennie Davis and Abbie Hoffman have any brains, they'll get these kids out of the park and lead a peaceful march downtown in the daylight. I know Dick Gregory is planning that. That's got some chance of getting fair publicity. What's happening here has none – unless the cops mistake some reporters as well as ministers for demonstrators. That's why the worst violence will take place right here."

"What are *you* doing here if it's all so hopeless?" I cried out.

John paused and laughed softly. "Good question. I always thought I didn't share the martyr complex a lot of clergymen have. It's an occupational disease." He paused again. I wanted to tell him that it was all right, that we needed people like him, that the presence of so many priests and nuns and ministers would give the demonstrations more respectability in the eyes of the public. But he spoke first. His voice grew slower, softer, less certain. "For a lot of my friends being here is a matter of faith, Dick. It's something between them and their God. It's not that for me. The god I believe in – I suspect it can't even be called a god anymore – doesn't interfere with this life and scorns those who act in order to gain points toward going to heaven. Sometimes I doubt that I act on my own at all. I feel that

I'm in the grip of some life force. Yet mostly I don't believe in that anymore either. I do believe in free will. I've chosen sides. Lincoln Park has forced me to. I started out in the LPCA thinking we were all people of good will who could work out their differences. It isn't true. There are differences far greater than good will can resolve. I don't see how our side can win. The others have the money and the power, but that's no reason not to choose any more than it was when Christians were being thrown to the lions. One consequence of the choice I made in our neighbourhood is that I have to be here too. I suppose I'm a bit of a dreamer myself ... And I ought to take this damn collar and toss it in the lagoon." The last sentence, which seemed an afterthought, came out more vigorously than the rest.

I clasped the hand that was rising toward his neck in both my hands. Before we could speak, people came dashing by. The last one stopped. "The pigs are busting people trying to get into the park. We need your help, Father. And yours too, Dick," gasped a dark haired Latin girl in a neat white blouse and blue jeans. As she turned to lead us away, I noticed that the back of her jeans was stained with grass and dirt. I followed, trying to place her face and failing.

It was approaching eleven o'clock, and the cops were preparing to clear the park. City officials had unearthed an obscure, never before enforced law closing city parks at eleven. Chicago is full of such ancient statutes waiting to have the dust blown off them so they can be trotted out and used against opponents of the Democratic Machine. Similar laws were later dug out of similar dusty file drawers to thwart groups attempting to open day care centres and build low rent housing.

The rest of that night is a haze, a fog which clouded the mind, but only stung the eyes. I didn't know what the hell I was doing or why the hell I was doing it, but I saw more than I wanted to see and the hell of it is I remember a lot. In the mountains fog forms when a body of water (or wet ground) is warmer than the air. Usually the fog remains low and can be viewed from above. I often marvel at it when I run. My house is a little above the river. When I run up the hill on a foggy morning, before I reach the top the air clears and I can look down on the fog above the river. Or a distant fog is visible as a cloud cuddled at the breast of a mountain whose sunlit head seems to glow with pleasure as if a baby were sucking. Or curdled at the foot of a mountain above the clear whey of a lake. The milky mists are sweet and sustaining. They feed the senses and inspire the mind to seek heights of clarity.

The fog which enveloped Lincoln Park during the Democratic Convention was bitter to all the senses: It teared the eyes, gagged the mouth, numbed the nose, hissed in the ears and grimed the touch. When the cops began firing tear gas canisters shortly after eleven o'clock, demonstrators were grabbing the missiles and flinging them back at the police; the wind too blew the fumes away from us. We enjoyed a few minutes of laughter as it seemed only the boys in blue would be gassed. Then out came heavy machinery which sprayed clouds so thick that no one could remain in the park. Heaven only knows what happened to the squirrels.

Daley and his cops' purpose all sublime was to make their punishment fit our crime. Since our crime was simply being who we were and even the city of Chicago could not dredge up a law against that, their punishment was to beat us with clubs considerably larger and heavier than standard issue police nightsticks, not arrest us and have to put us on trial. To beat us conveniently they had to drive us out of the park, which was too big for their purpose, too dark and too full of places to hide or set up machine gun posts.

In that stinking fog people ceased to be human and emotions turned to frenzy: Frenzied demonstrators fled like crazed cattle west toward Clark, LaSalle and Wells Streets followed by herds of frenzied cops bellowing, oinking and swinging their clubs. Maria, the Latin woman – she turned out to be twenty-three years old, not a teenager as I first thought – stayed at my side throughout the night. Whether she stayed to protect me or because she thought I could protect her I never discovered. The mutual frenzy of stampeding animals held us together, holding hands, running from one slaughter to another.

Everywhere droves of demonstrators were running frantically, milling briefly to taunt cops, then running again as the cops charged. Everywhere clusters of cops were singling out stragglers, rushing at them and flailing away. After each charge a few bleating bodies staggered back into the pack and both cattle and swine regrouped. The police were not attempting to arrest people, just to bloody as many heads as possible.

Near the corner of Clark and Eugenie a huge cop outdistanced the rest of his squad and bore down on a boy and girl who were so scared they huddled together under a streetlight instead of fleeing. Just as the cop reached his victims, a little priest from Lake View dashed between hunter and prey. The cop halted, lowered his baton, raised it again, thought better of things, turned and waddled off trying to look casual. The priest followed, berating him mercilessly, never noticing the grateful looks and words of the couple he had saved.

Maria and I ran from one block to another, sometimes alone, sometimes in a crowd that I hope was not an affinity group. We ran heedlessly as did every other demonstrator. We did not consider leaving the area. For what seemed like hours we were caught in the insanity of Chicago, were incapable of rational thought or action. It was Maria who spotted the medics and pulled me over to them. A dozen or more medics in conspicuous whites with large red crosses had been in the park all evening. At North and Clark two of them were trying to bandage several bloody people and simultaneously calling out for someone to drive the injured to a hospital. They attempted to flag down cars on North Avenue, but the drivers rolled up their windows and sped past.

I told the medics I had a car and knew where hospitals were. They sent three bloody kids with me and begged me to return quickly. Maria and I supported two who had trouble walking as we struggled west on North toward my car. The guy I had my arm around was moaning softly; the girl Maria aided was crying; the unsupported girl was swearing loudly. As we reached Wells Street, two dozen freaks raced around the corner with half a dozen cops in pursuit. The girl who had been cursing screamed and took off after the kids. The boy I was supporting stiffened, but I held him. The four of us huddled in a doorway with two other bystanders. Fortunately we were not observed, and when the coast was clear, we moved on as quickly as possible.

My white Volkswagen had a big splotch of blood on its roof, a stain which did not completely wash off until the next spring. The stains inside on the back seat remained as long as I kept the car. At the Augustana Hospital Emergency Entrance two squad cars were parked, but that is a common sight at a hospital. We let the kids off and hurried back for more. When we located the medics, they asked us about cops at the hospital and said they had word that cops were busting people who came for treatment at all local hospitals. They instructed us to take another boy, who had a broken arm as well as the usual bloody head, to Billings Hospital, far on the south side. All the way there the boy whined about the Chicago cops and compared them to the gentle men who patrolled his home town. He kept asking us if we thought he would be arrested at the hospital. He was terrified at the prospect of falling into the hands of the cops again. At Billings a squad car was parked near the emergency entrance. I parked a block away and told the boy to stay put while I checked things out, but before I reached the door Maria ran up to tell me the boy had fled into the night.

We drove around Hyde Park looking for the boy. I felt desperate to get him to my house at least so he could sleep. But the night had swallowed him. Finally we drove back north without a word. I had no heart to return to the park and drove Maria home. "Home" turned out to be an unused basement on Sheffield Street. Maria stored a bag of clothes and two blankets there. She showed me the grassy place where she spread her blankets and slept when it wasn't raining.

Although we had been holding hands all night, I had hardly looked at Maria. I did now. She had the smooth olive skin, straight black hair and small black eyes of the Latina. Needless to say after all she had been through, she looked wild. And beautiful. Suddenly we were rolling on the blankets, kissing and tearing at one another. In silent violence which was but a continuation of what we had shared all night we ripped each other's clothes off and bit, scratched and kissed each other madly. "So this is Latin loving," I remember thinking as, trembling and sweating, I rolled on top of her while she scratched furiously at my back and bit my shoulders and neck. But as I began to penetrate her, she stiffened and prated wildly about sin and god. I came instantly; we shuddered and relaxed, spent and ashamed. The gray city dawn sneered down at us. We pulled a blanket over our bodies and awkwardly redressed. Maria had tears in her eyes. I mumbled apologies and left.

At home Priscilla dryly informed me that Meg had already phoned twice. I changed clothes, ate a piece of bread and jam and walked to the office, where Meg and Jan were putting out a special edition of the Lincoln Park *Press*. I sat in the corner and wrote a violent denunciation of the violence in and around the park. As I wrote Meg typed copy on our ancient manual typewriter and urged me to hurry while Jan cranked the mimeo. When I finished I handed my article to Meg to type. Jan read it over Meg's shoulder and hugged me her congratulations, but Meg automatically deleted two sentences and softened the language so as not to offend local people. We ran off several hundred copies of a three page newsletter about what happened in our park and community, then zoomed to the Fullerton and Armitage el stations to distribute them to neighbourhood people going to work during the rush hour.

I SELDOM DREAM OF CHICAGO, thank heaven, but it influences my dreams. Yesterday I read something about New Zealand, and last night I dreamed there was a huge mirror in the sky above the equator. Mountain air is so clear that I was standing on a mountain top in British Columbia, and by looking out into the mirror I could clearly see the mountains of New Zealand. A pall lives above Chicago. No wind can blow it away. Chicago air is a pall. The city gives off its own stench. It rises from rotting ideals, the ideals of the Haymarket martyrs and of the governor who freed the survivors of their legal lynching, of the victims of strikes at International Harvester, Pullman, Republic Steel and many sweatshops, of millions of brave, nameless folk who fought Chicago's bosses for over a century. Usually the stench is strongest in the air around the Chicago *Tribune* Building, where the acid of printers' ink has decomposed so much beauty and strength, whose pages called for the blood of Albert and Lucy Parsons, of Spies, Fischer, Engel and Ling, of Debs and Goldman, and, later, of Fred Hampton and Jazzman Morales.

Most of the time the stench is merely one component of Chicago's smog, but during the Democratic Convention it drifted north, away even from the *Tribune,* many of whose reporters told the truth for several days, denounced police violence because they, like other newspeople, had been beaten by Chicago cops driven to frenzy by police bosses. But it didn't take long for the press bosses to get together with those police bosses and the political bosses. Then our free press quit pretending it really was one and so summoned back the atmosphere which hung thick over Lincoln Park, a visible pall, a putrid odour, a grimy presence.

Meg, Jan and I no longer noticed the gas. My ill functioning nose finally was of use. Besides, the gas had been part of our lives for several days. That night we breathed it during the nightly melee in the park and the streets of Old Town. It waited outside for us for hours as we wrote, typed and ran off our accounts of sadism, stupidity, bloodshed and bravery we had witnessed. It greased our skin as we drove home before dawn to get an hour or two of sleep before distributing our newssheets at bus and el stops during the morning rush hour. We had been conditioned not to notice the essence of our city and were too tired anyway to notice it poised above us until, as we drove east on Armitage approaching Dayton, Chicago materialized from the gas above it. A flash of lights, a gust of wind, a roar of motors, a screech of brakes. Two police squad cars landed at the curb opposite us, and four rifle bearing cops leapt from one and vaulted three steps at a time up the stairs of the three flat next to Armitage Avenue Methodist Church.

We parked directly across the street and waited to see what was happening. Soon the doors of the other squad car opened and four more rifle toting cops jumped out. These trotted to our car, pointed their big guns at us, ordered us out of the car and against the wall. Two of them kept us covered while the other two first frisked all of us roughly then searched Jan's car, ripping seats and smashing anything smashable they came across. They looked over our identification and swore at us for a while, jabbing us in the bellies with their rifle barrels as they did so. Then they engaged us in conversation as scintillating as the Chicago air: "What are you doing on the streets at this hour?" "What are *you* doing on the streets at this hour?" "Aw right, we'll ask the questions here (a jab in Jan's stomach). What are you doing here?" "We live here. This is our community. What are you doing here?" "I said we'll ask the questions here (a jab in Meg's stomach). What are you doing here?" "Watching you." "Oh, a wise guy, huh?" (sharp pain in my stomach).

Worse was surely coming. The officers' faces seemed to be glowing red. Whether it was their anger, my imagination or the sun trying to rise and penetrate the layer of gas above us I'm not sure, but their faces seemed to be turning into incarnations of the devil before my sleep deprived eyes. I blinked and turned away. When I did so, divine aid: Burt Jackson in his minister's collar loping across Armitage from his church. I was never so happy to see anyone. The cops did not become more polite, but they were distracted from us. Then the other four cops came out of the building, and all eight charged back into their cars and peeled off into the gas. During the Convention almost no Chicago police wore nameplates as they are required to do, but one of our four had his on, and we noted his name as well as the numbers of the two squad cars. I remember staring at the nameplate and the cop inviting me to take a closer look, simultaneously jamming his rifle into my gut. I declined the invitation, but Jan sang out: "See you around Officer Buck," as they departed.

Once the squad cars pulled away, a guy came cautiously out of the three flat and across to us. He said he was from SDS in Connecticut and that he and several others in a "media collective" were staying in the apartment of a friend in the building. He said the cops had kicked in their door, forced everyone to lie on the floor, ransacked the apartment and stolen wallets, money and expensive cameras and photographic equipment. He said they had exposed all film including many rolls of police actions in the park. He assumed their mission was to get that film. As he spoke the same two squad cars pulled up on our side of the street and the four cops we hadn't seen jumped out, jabbed their rifles (M-16s, the same gun used in Viet Nam, the SDSer later claimed) hard in our bellies, ordered us off the street, threatened to shoot us if we were still around in five minutes, swarmed back into their car and sped off. The kid from Connecticut was shaking and Burt offered him sanctuary in the church. The rest of us walked home to nurse our stomach aches.

After the Convention a lawyer took Meg, Jan and me to see two different Assistant State's Attorneys with our story. Both refused to listen and told us they could only investigate after a complaint had been filed with the Police Department's Internal Investigation Division. We went to the IID, signed sworn affidavits and were individually grilled on what happened. We heard nothing for six months, then each received a form postcard stating that our complaint had been dismissed for lack of evidence. One needs considerably more witnesses than four (including a minister) to have evidence of wrongdoing by a Chicago cop. Campbell Borst, police commander of the Eighteenth District (now in jail himself on corruption charges) assured us and several public meetings where we told our story that he had investigated thoroughly and that the incident never took place although he admitted that the officer we named and the squad cars whose numbers we gave were all assigned to his district.

THE SNOW HAS STOPPED. It fell for twenty-four hours, fine flaked but thick, over a foot accumulation. The sky is uniformly overcast and the air is still, but the visibility has lifted and the temperature is rising. The earth is white and the air is dotted with white, the snow on distant trees. The dots grow smaller as I look higher up the mountain, but they continue until the mountain merges with the gray sky. Every few seconds I hear a thud and look around to see a miniature snow flurry in the conifers. Big clumps of snow sag off the higher boughs and smash into the boughs below, where they are broken back into flakes which dust the air before they fall to the ground. By the river these belated baby snowstorms will soon cover the prints of the animals who crept out for a drink when the snow ceased. By the time the next storm comes, the boughs will be green again, ready to accept a new burden.

8.

W HAT I EXPERIENCED during the Democratic Convention completed my transformation. By the end of the Convention I was ready to join the affinity group I had rejected when I walked past Bobby Seale at the beginning of the Convention. And Jazzman was there to induct me. I ceased to be a reformer who believed things wrong with my city and country were mistakes which could be corrected by making them clear to those in power or by electing a few new politicians. I became a revolutionary convinced things were terribly wrong not because of mistakes but because of a social order which must be demolished and replaced by a humane one. Human, not urban, renewal; urban slum, not human, removal.

The Convention changed others too. People living elsewhere in Chicago and the United States may have doubted reports of the violence. People in Lincoln Park saw it, and I know of no eyewitness (other than cops and city officials, whose livelihoods were at stake) who did not condemn the police. In the weeks following the Convention a number of "town meetings" were held in eastern Lincoln Park, the area closest to the park. Hundreds of people attended and all were outraged by what they had seen.

These eastsiders were neither poor nor radical. They were successful businesspeople, lawyers, doctors, people to whom the system had always been kind. Until the Chicago Police set up camp in their neighbourhood, they assumed the system worked for most people and always would. Few changed their minds permanently: Their minds had been too well made up, and they stood to lose too much by changing them. But at the time all these people were angry at what they had seen and most were puzzled by it because it had no place in anything they were prepared to believe. Eventually most of them swallowed excuses about "bad apples," individual excesses by individual cops, but not until the vividness of what they had witnessed faded. Until then their temporary outrage and confusion became a part of Lincoln Park. It gave them sympathy for protests against the status quo; it added to the unsettled atmosphere pumped in by urban renewal and changed it as a dry gust of wind lifts snow off winter trees and briefly blows clear air into white dust of snow or, if the wind lasts long enough, into an actual storm.

In about a year most of the upper middle class residents forgot or stopped worrying about their anger and confusion, saw their pocket-books were at risk and ceased to oppose the Lincoln Park Conservation Association's efforts to halt protests and make the neighbourhood comfortably bourgeois and safe for speculators. But for that year a fugitive breeze in the windy city roused the complacent and battered old conceptions. The slogan in the air of Lincoln Park turned from "poor people go" to "anything goes."

The ghetto kids in the west and south of Lincoln Park were also changed by the Convention. They went to the park singly (as Jazzman, fresh from jail, had) or in groups. A few joined the fighting, most only watched, but all came back impressed by the fact that pigs were treating white kids as brutally as they treated blacks and Latinos and that many white kids were fighting back. This gave them more confidence in whites who supported them and more willingness both to join new struggles for change and to call for white support in their own struggles. Kids like the Puerto Ricans who hung out at Halsted and Dickens, almost all of whom spent a lot of time in the park during the Convention, became activists for change in Lincoln Park. They formed the nucleus of the Young Lords Organization.

To me the Young Lords appeared like a blizzard in the night. You wake up one morning, look out the window and see a foot of new snow. We had announced the formation of the organization in late September, but the members were the same few kids we knew from Halsted and Dickens. Better than nothing I thought, but nothing to storm the Bastille with. A couple days after Christmas Jazzman held a meeting. Almost forty street kids showed up at our office. "Where did all the kids come from?" I asked him at a New Year's Eve party at Meg's.

Jazzman had a quality of innocence which often left him amazed at other people's innocence. He looked at me, perplexed: "If you don't know, man, who does?" Only in retrospect can I see that his question was a compliment: He had assumed I was as observant as he was. One had to be quick to notice Jazzman's innocence because he learned so fast. "You wasted all your time looking at the pretty girls at our dances," he said.

"It was too dark for me to see anything at those dances," I said.

"Everyone in the hood was at those dances. I made almost all my contacts there. Same way *I'm* being contacted here. Who's that old dude in the corner, and why is he so anxious to feed me bread?" A glance at me told Jazzman I didn't know. "Ask around, Dick. I'll wait outside."

A discreet enquiry revealed that the old dude was a Communist Party cadre. Jazzman laughed knowingly at my information. "So that's how they operate. I'll remember. Walk with me, man. I'm going to another party, but I want you to tell me about some other dudes at this one."

As we walked Jazzman shot question after question at me. I tried to keep up but didn't always succeed. Perhaps Jazzman was already into the speed I know he used later to maintain the pace 1969 was to demand. But I have no good reason to believe this. Jazzman's mind simply worked much faster than mine, speed or no speed. He read people as well as he read books. He borrowed many books from me in the old year. By the new year he didn't need to. At Meg's party he had noticed that one young radical's southern accent was fake, that someone else spoke more slowly to him than to Anglos, that Priscilla took herself elsewhere when I talked to him or Meg.

At the Puerto Rican party I got quietly stoned. Jazzman had told me he wanted me to guide some of his friends back to Meg's party. I sat in a corner and enjoyed my high and the high energy of everyone else until Jazzman reappeared from a back room with six guys and sent me on my mission. I was being used, yet I felt happy. Jazzman affected people that way. He was like mountains: powerful yet so beautiful you loved his power instead of resenting it.

Maybe that's it. Maybe that's the element I never understood. Maybe Jazzman had something like these mountains in him. Maybe knowing him began to teach me to appreciate these mountains. Jazzman exerted a force over me and others, but he was not charismatic like Fred Hampton. Fiery sentences did not spring naturally to his lips nor bold gestures to his body. In private conversation he was quiet and thoughtful (unless he wanted specific information; then he could become relentless); in public he was fearful. His first public speech was one sentence. His second didn't come off because he ran from the room. His third was even more concise and direct than his first. He told a rally of DePaul University students who had been sterilely debating whether or not their school, which was located in a Puerto Rican neighbourhood and had fewer than ten Latinos in a student body of thousands, was racist: "Kiss my ass, motherfuckers," and stalked out.

Jazzman occasionally suffered soft fools, never loud ones. As he gained experience and confidence, he became an adequate public speaker, seldom more, although the short speech he improvised at the Eighteenth District Police-Community Workshop showed that he might have become more. He was, however, a participant who worked actively and hard on any project he favoured, whether he knew anything about the work or not. People followed his example, not his orders. When political education classes were conducted for the Young Lords, Jazzman was a student along with the rest; when leaflets had to be run off, Jazzman pecked at the typewriter with two fingers and turned the crank of the old mimeo; if bricks were to be thrown through the windows of a merchant who was fleecing the community or the Urban Renewal Office, Jazzman was one of the throwers; when fat Harry, the mafia realtor, pulled his submachine gun, it was Jazzman who calmly looked down the barrel; when lumber was needed to construct a day care centre, Jazzman went to the lumber yards asking for donations; and when no wood could be begged, he refused to let anyone else rip it off and was caught with twenty-three dollars worth of stolen lumber and eventually sentenced to a year in jail, the only conviction of his political career despite almost twenty arrests in a year.

This willingness to work accounted for some of the fierce loyalty his followers felt for him. He did not ask them to do things he did not do. He got work out of those around him because he never stopped working himself. But being a hard worker does not make one a leader. In fact, the combination of quietness and hard work is usually thought of as belonging to the faithful followers. No, there was something more which set Jazzman apart, something strong, simple and solitary, like the mountains.

Jazzman retreated into himself when he needed strength. No doubt he did it even as a child, but the time spent in prison perfected this ability as the monastery perfects it in a monk. (Interestingly, the book which turned Jazzman on to reading in prison was *The Seven Story Mountain*, the memoir of a man who became a Trappist monk.) Jazzman's silent courage and refusal to be bullied made him hated by guards and prison officials. Lawson Wilton, the huge warden of Cook County Jail, threatened to kill him several times, but Jazzman didn't back down from

Wilton or anyone else. For this reason everyone who had known him in prison respected him. It is also why he did most of his time in the hole, solitary confinement. When one must spend weeks at a time alone – teenaged Jazzman did stints in the hole of up to forty-five days, one either breaks down or builds self-control into the solitary strength of a mountain. The way out is in. Jazzman never said that and I never thought it. Then. But I must have begun to see it, for writing about it now, in my mountains, it seems clear.

Jazzman shared with the mountains the quality of making things clear. Just as here in the mountains I can see through the smog of complexities which is Chicago, so I could often see individual issues clearly in Jazzman's presence. "Simplify, simplify," might have been his motto as it was Thoreau's. He was never indecisive about an important matter, and his directness could be as crisp as a clear winter night. Perhaps the rare combination of the intellectual's thoughtfulness and the simple person's decisiveness made him what he was. Most likely he is like the mountains, can only be described (and that inadequately), not analyzed. It is the right image: Jazzman, mountain stuff, the very opposite of the flat city where he lived out his life. No wonder he stood out; no wonder he inspired in me so many of the powerful emotions I feel here and now.

▲ ▲ ▲

Historian: *Maybe you should stuff this "mountain stuff" bit. It's not true. I've lived almost all my life in the flat Midwest. I guess I've flown over a few mountains, but I've never really seen a real mountain in my life.*

Novelist: *I had never seen high mountains until about two years before I began living in them. It was love at first sight when I saw the Rockies. I spent two years dreaming about mountains before I moved into them.*

Historian: *That's you. But here you're saying it's me too.*

Novelist: *In fact it's not you, it's Jazzman. Because this is a novel, characters don't have to be true in detail to what they are in life. In one of my failed attempts to conclude this novel I wrote a long section on how Jazzman gets to British Columbia. He crosses into Canada on a canoe through the Boundary Waters between Minnesota and Manitoba.*

Historian: *Stuffing me into a canoe is even less likely than stuffing me into the mountains.*

Novelist: *Exactly my point. When I wrote this, I didn't know where you had been underground. I knew a lot of radicals had been underground in the Slocan Valley.*

Historian: *I was underground in a farmhouse near Tomah, Wisconsin.*

Novelist: *I know that now. I didn't when I was writing.*

Historian: *But you can still change a small thing like that, can't you? I want to use your novel in my history project.*

Novelist: *I can. But I won't. This is a young man's novel. The old man I am today can't mess with its spirit that way. Besides, Jazzman insisted he had been here.*

Historian: *You talk to your characters?*

Novelist: *Usually they talk to me, but I always listen and sometimes I have to talk back. If characters aren't alive, they aren't much good. Having lived in the mountains is an important part of Jazzman's character. It's one of the things that makes him alive.*

Historian: *There's a big difference between fiction and history. When I was in Tomah, I used to talk to Fred, but that didn't make him alive.*

Novelist: *The two of you talked under the stars, I bet.*

Historian: *Right on. It takes a novelist to know how to make that kind of history.*

Novelist: *Talking to Fred must have made you more alive. We were all pretty dead after Fred's murder. Hearing this makes you a better person in my eyes – or, rather, ears.*

Historian: *That better person is what you're hearing when you talk to Jazzman. In your novel you're doing to me what you did to the woman we knew as Pat. Only you made Meg worse and through Jazzman you're making me better.*

Novelist: *Not better or worse – different. Believe it or not even the narrator is often not me. That's what I love about writing novels, the freedom. And its lack when the characters take over. The novel rules. What works in the novel goes into the novel. Anything goes so long as it makes sense for the reader. It's the kind of freedom you don't get in real life.*

Historian: *So your freedom is more important than truth.*

Novelist: *"Beauty is truth, truth beauty – that is all you know on earth, and all you need to know."*

9.

THE LINCOLN PARK CONSERVATION Community Council was a select group: Its members had been selected first by the Lincoln Park Conservation Association, then by Mayor Daley himself. They were all white; they were all Anglo; they were all male; they were all established businessmen or professionals; they were all active Lincoln Park Conservation Association members; they all owned property in Lincoln Park or represented institutions which owned property; they were all selfless men who were not paid a cent to sit on the Council but served from love of their community. They all shared a vision: One day in the golden future Lincoln Park would no longer be the ragtag mixture of mainly poor and working class people of mixed up races and ethnic groups it had long been; owing to their devotion and planning Lincoln Park would become as lovely as Forest Park or Scarsdale, New York, a beautiful upper class white suburb in the very heart of Chicago.

This blessed vision had inspired all Conservation Community Council members since their appointment in 1960 and most of them since 1955, when DePaul University, McCormick Seminary and Children's Memorial Hospital had organized the institutions, businessmen and large property owners into the Lincoln Park Conservation Association for the purpose of obtaining Urban Renewal funds to make the vision a reality. The vision of the tax base they would create had inspired Mayor Daley and the Democratic Party of Chicago for even longer.

The years through 1967 had been pleasant ones for the Lincoln Park Conservation Community Council. The Council members understood and enjoyed their mandate to plan and preside over the improvement of their neighbourhood. They well understood the generals who bombed Hue in order to save it. In cooperation with the Chicago Department of Urban Renewal they quietly developed a plan which called for the razing of many parts of Lincoln Park and the remodelling of the rest. Only thus, they comprehended, could they conserve their community. Again in cooperation with the Department of Urban Renewal, they printed their plan in a lovely loose bound book entitled *Lincoln Park General Neighborhood Renewal Plan* available *gratis* at the Lincoln Park Department of Urban Renewal Office for the edification of all. The book's preface proudly affirmed the unity of purpose of the city and neighbourhood:

> The Lincoln Park General Neighborhood Renewal Plan represents the culmination of at least seven years of activity by the community through its overall community organization (the LPCA), and through seven local neighbourhood organizations (the seven local branches of the LPCA), all working in the closest relationship with the Department of Urban Renewal … of the City of Chicago. The concepts presented in the plan and discussed in the pages that follow, reflect a high order of compatibility between the goals and objectives as enumerated in a series of memoranda prepared by the community and neighbourhood organizations, and the city with its consultants who assisted in the preparation of this plan.

THIS WAS THE BOOK whose cover was entirely taken up by a picture of a mass-produced coach light, the symbol of the Conservation Community Council's vision. So powerful was that symbol that all remodelled buildings in Lincoln Park were decorated by at least one coach light. Even buildings whose interiors had nothing more elaborate done to them than the application of a new coat of paint always displayed a coach light on their exterior. The coach light made new buildings look antique and old buildings look modern. It proclaimed to all that the edifice it graced combined the taste of the horse and buggy days with the convenience of the present and that those who dwelt therein paid exorbitant rents.

The concrete form of the Conservation Community Council's vision was embodied in the General Neighborhood Renewal Plan. This plan was presented to the community not only in the book but also at open meetings always attended by a few other middle class businessmen and professionals who listened and nodded and occasionally demurred slightly and politely to show the Council they supported its efforts and were trying as hard as it to brighten the neighbourhood with more and more coach lights and fewer and fewer poor people and children.

Then in 1968 non-professionals began to get wind of the Council's plan and even attend the open meetings. Mama Jane and Jill and John and Jose and Marta began asking: "What about our children?" It was embarrassing for the Council, almost demeaning, trying to explain the vision and its plan to such people, people who could never understand anyhow, selfish, uneducated people who kept asking about their children no matter how much one tried to tell them about the new neighbourhood being created and how much better it would be for everyone, grownups and children, who lived there. How could humble Council members guarantee that any one person or group would still be living there? That wasn't their job. Why couldn't these people understand? They couldn't even seem to understand the sacrifice of time and effort Council members gave freely as a labour of love for the community. Still the Council was confident that its love was stronger than all the shortsighted protests, and it persevered.

1968 had been a trying year for the Conservation Community Council. The Concerned Citizens of Lincoln Park had turned out enough angry people to tie up three or four meetings and prevent additional plans from being approved. In fact the only vote taken during the last half of the year was a vote to delay demolition of the Orchard-Willow-Vine area. After an organizing campaign by Concerned Citizens of Lincoln Park fifty residents of that area, most of them senior citizens, had braved a November storm to plead for their homes. That had been the first Council meeting at which the middle class had been outnumbered. Still, the Council hoped that with the Orchard-Willow-Vine residents' request granted business as usual could resume. Perhaps 1969 would be less trying than 1968.

It was not to be. More and more poor and working class people of Lincoln Park were outraged and ready to fight. Jazzman had been reading and talking, learning and organizing for four months. At Meg's New Year's Party he had declared that things had been quiet for too long and that soon the shit would hit the fan.

The first Conservation Community Council meeting of 1969 failed to come off for lack of a quorum. A quorum was present briefly, but two Council members left after viewing the audience. The audience was large, close to two hundred people, and few of them wore the suits, ties and fancy dresses which in the past had made the Council comfortable. No, these were the other residents of the neighbourhood, the people who were being moved out so the people in business suits could always feel comfortable and turn a good profit.

Outstanding in this new audience were about twenty proudly purple bereted Young Lords and another twenty unbereted Young Lords who hadn't yet been able to procure a headpiece. The organization was too new and poor to have organized all the material symbols which were important to its members. But that same newness contributed to a spirit unimaginable to those who did not experience it directly and unforgettable to those who did.

Every member and follower of the Young Lords Organization had met an hour before the meeting was scheduled, and they had marched in force from Armitage and Halsted to the Department of Urban Renewal Office at Armitage and Larrabee. They found the isolated building, the only structure around not levelled by the bulldozers, almost deserted. Entering the front door of the building, they swarmed down a long corridor, barely pausing to ridicule the proclamations, pictures and plastic scale models of the future Lincoln Park. They charged through the rear entrance to the auditorium and sized up the turf. There were side doors at both front and rear of the hall, but the front door simply led into a large room of desks for bureaucrats. The rear door had the only convenient access to an exit. They were in enemy territory so their first consideration was maintaining an escape route. Therefore, they took over the rear of the hall and plastered the walls with posters calling for an end to urban renewal. Tape for this purpose was graciously supplied by a very nervous looking Department of Urban Renewal functionary. Command headquarters were established in the john, also at the rear of the hall.

At first a party atmosphere prevailed. It was the first public appearance of the Young Lords Organization, an occasion worth celebrating. The odour of dope wafted from the john, which had been decorated with every slogan fertile young minds could think of, from "urban renewal is people removal" to "revolution now" to "fuck you." As middle class people arrived they were greeted with laughter, catcalls and comments like: "Hey man, the funeral parlour is down Armitage Street." And: "How did all those monkeys escape the zoo?" And: "How many Puerto Ricans did your husband kick out to buy you that coat?"

A few of those so addressed left, but most walked with strained dignity to the front of the auditorium and took places on the stage or in the first rows. "Let's put rollers on their noses and paint the ceiling," someone suggested. A few middle class males joined in the light-hearted repartee but quickly retreated when the responses showed it was not light-hearted repartee.

I led Jazzman to the front of the room and introduced him to Jack Seal, the Department of Urban Renewal's project director for Lincoln Park. Jack was always frank and so sure of his views he would gladly expound them to anyone on the assumption that truth would quickly convert the unenlightened. Jack glanced at Jazzman as they shook hands, saw nothing of interest and never looked at him again. He spoke only to me, whom he was always happy to convert. I asked him to elaborate on a statement he had made at a previous meeting to the effect that it was impossible to build a viable community composed of poor people.

"Now don't misinterpret me," he replied. "I didn't say no poor people. A few poor people are useful: In the right proportions they add diversity to a neighbourhood. At most twenty percent. Fewer would be better. Ten percent is probably a good figure. If you have too many poor people there's no capital and you can't get any in from outside the community either. Where's the profit for a businessman? You can't squeeze milk from a stone. On the other hand, it is obviously good for poor people to remain in an upper middle class area. It automatically raises their standard of living, improves their schools, and gives them concrete goals, something to strive for that they can see all around them. So it's great for them, but that's paradoxical because there just can't be many of them for social as well as economic reasons. Look at this audience tonight. They're not interacting at all. Now if there were half a dozen of your people here instead of a hundred, they (indicating the carefully dressed, rigidly perpendicular people seated at the front) would enjoy standing around talking, explaining things. They might even learn something themselves. Everyone would profit. What good can come of this situation? None. They don't even want to start their meeting and it's already late. I'd better get them moving." And Jack hurried off to get the meeting started.

While Jack was talking to me, I was watching Jazzman. He studied Jack without showing emotion. I kept waiting for him to get mad, maybe even punch Jack, but he remained calm. After Jack left, Jazzman nodded reflectively. "Interesting dude. I didn't believe anyone could really talk like that." Just then Father Vechter, DePaul's representative on the Council, shambled up. He seemed to know Jazzman, who had received a very Catholic upbringing, and held out his hand limply. Jazzman stepped back in disgust. "Keep your dirty hands away from me. Liar, hypocrite. All you bastards with collars around your assholes have ever done is sell my people out. Get the hell away from me." The priest jumped back as if he had been hit, practically ran to the platform, said a few words to Council Chairman Henry Larcen, and vanished out the front door. The quorum vanished with him.

It was now well after meeting time and the crowd was impatient. Cheering, booing, stamping, whistling and other noises arose from the rear of the room. Every conference or movement on the stage was met with cheers and comments. The local dignitaries were not about to be ruffled by a bunch of unruly kids, but somehow they did look a little uncertain of themselves. I'm sure this didn't occur to the dignitaries, but the kids were unruly mainly because they too were nervous: They were in a strange place amid unfamiliar people and procedures, and many of them had spent hours preparing speeches, real speeches, their first ever. They were expecting to deliver those speeches, which detailed indignities they and their families had suffered at the hands of urban renewal, and ask the Council to end urban renewal. Most of them were not that different from Jack Seal and thought their speeches would show others, the Council members, the error of their ways and convince them to end a bad program. I doubt if one of them knew what a quorum was.

Henry Larcen stepped to the microphone and announced the meeting was cancelled owing to lack of a quorum. A roar from the rear. Jazzman forgot his fear of public speaking in his fury. He ran to the stage and demanded the meeting be held. No one seemed to hear so he leaped to the microphone. The clamour from the rear subsided, but the mike had already been turned off.

"You moved my family six times. You're going to listen to me now," he shouted to the backs of the well dressed crowd already turning toward the front exit. When no one paid any attention, Jazzman swung his fist at the microphone, knocking it to the floor. The gesture of frustration acted as a signal for the noise from the rear to resume. Swearing, threats and challenges were yelled and ignored as the middle class swarmed for the front door. None of them used the main exit in the rear, and except for Jazzman none of the poor people moved toward the front. It was as if there were a rigid barrier dividing the two groups as, in life, there was. Seeing there would be no meeting, most of the older poor people filed out the rear door muttering.

At first the Young Lords remained, chanting, demanding a meeting, talking about holding their own meeting. Then someone ran in and said cops were coming. This added to the anger, but no one wanted to be trapped on unfamiliar turf. Everyone grabbed a coat and headed out the auditorium door, down the corridor to the exit. No one else was around since none of the respectable people had dared come to the rear of the hall. As the kids left they smashed the display cases containing models of the Lincoln Park of the future, the Lincoln Park with no place for them. The first one to reach the glass door to the street kicked it out. Windows around it were also quickly broken. Two squad cars were parked in front of the door. The cops stayed inside their cars with the doors and windows tightly closed. Several kids yelled that there were bricks in the surrounding empty lots, but the older leaders organized a hasty but orderly march west down Armitage. So the Young Lords Organization left its first public appearance as it had come, marching and chanting slogans: "Down with urban renewal," "Free Puerto Rico now," "All power to the people."

Back at the Urban Renewal Office several knots of people in coats stood around in the breezy entranceway and corridor. With his foot Jack Seal feebly nudged the shattered debris that had been the model of the new Lincoln Park. John Leeds could not resist commenting: "It looks like you've been urban renewed, Jack. Now you know how *they* feel."

"I knew it had to happen," Jack said. "I'm just surprised it took so long. Now you can see the folly of arousing people's emotions. Planning a community is a hard job even for the best professionals. It becomes impossible if you let all sorts of people with an emotional investment or stake in the status quo barge in on the process. This is the result," indicating the wreckage around him. He walked over to talk to the police captain, to whom Henry Larcen was ranting: "Nine years I've slaved for this community without a cent of pay. And now these punks want to smash it all. You've got to find them and arrest them all. There won't be peace in this community until they're all behind bars."

"Any warrants, Mr. Seal?' the captain asked. "Nope, it was just one of those things, sergeant. An accident and a mistake. On everybody's part." His voice trailed off into thought. "Call George and tell him to get a clean up crew over here as soon as possible," he directed an assistant, then bent down to pick a few unbroken model homes out of the wreckage.

I raced out with the news there would be no attempt at arrest and caught up with the marchers as they approached Halsted Street, the start of their turf. I felt exuberant although I was not sure what had happened was good. At least it's clear we're not going to take any more without fighting back, I told myself. I reported my news and wanted to explain to the marchers that they had made their point far more effectively than speeches could have, but it was not the time for lessons, which left me out of place and wishing I weren't. As Halsted Street was crossed, the mood changed instantly from anger to jubilation. "Did you see those cases blow, baby, blow?" "Nice job on that door, man." "You handled that window pretty good yourself." "Wait 'til they try to use the john." "Party at my place. Get some wine."

I ran back to the Urban Renewal Office. By now twenty or more squad cars had converged on the scene and the men in blue were running around frustrated that there was no one left to arrest. As I approached the building, some cops grabbed me from behind, but a black cop at the door shouted that I was okay and ordered me inside, where I was obviously headed anyway. Later Chuck and Bob, two active Concerned Citizens, told me they had been saved from arrest even more dramatically by the same black cop, who told them a whole story about how he tried to work for the people from inside the Police Department.

Inside the cold office Henry Larcen buttonholed me immediately. He had experienced conversion from liberal do-gooder to conservative law-and-order advocate and was proclaiming his revelation to the world. I listened to all I could stand then turned my back and joined a group consisting of Meg, John Leeds, Burt Jackson and several Lincoln Park Conservation Association stalwarts. John was protesting. "How many years did I try to work within the LPCA to prevent this? How many times did I tell you this was bound to happen unless you began planning for people, not just buildings? How many times did I say that you can't keep kicking people out of their homes without inciting violence? You're reaping what you have sown."

"No," Milt Moore, past president of the Lincoln Park Conservation Association, replied. "We're reaping what you sowed. Don't tell me that gang just appeared out of the woodwork. You're behind this whole thing."

John laughed. "You really think an old fogey like me can control those kids?"

"You and your pals here," indicating Meg and me with a sneer in his voice.

That made Meg furious. "Of course it's impossible for poor people, especially black and brown people, to act on their own. Some middle class white man must be pulling the strings. Well, let me tell you, poor people are sick of being screwed and manipulated by the likes of you and they're not going to be controlled by anyone anymore. They're making their own decisions now, and you're going to be unhappy about a lot of things they decide."

"Now I'll tell you something, young lady," said Dick Steale, Council member and an actor who played staid, aristocratic males in TV commercials. For some years he had been quietly purchasing and remodelling buildings in the Ranch Triangle neighbourhood, then selling them to other wealthy, middle aged homosexuals. His voice was quiet, his tone ice, but his small gray eyes locked into Meg's and blazed. "There are people who have invested their wealth, their time and their spirit in making this neighbourhood a place where they can live their lives in peace among friends and decent people. They are not going to let a bunch of radicals and hoodlums bully them out of what they have worked to build. Especially now when their dreams are beginning to take concrete shape. When you play with people's lives and dreams, you play with fire, and when you play with fire you get burned – badly."

Meg tried to return the stare, but the hatred in Steale's eyes was too intense even for her. She looked down and I thought she was preparing to kick Steale in the shins when Burt Jackson stepped towards them and placated: "Let's stay cool. I don't think we need to go to war over a little broken glass. If the meeting had been held as scheduled, none of this would have happened."

"I'm not so sure of that, but I am sure it better not happen again. That's all I'll say for now," Steale said.

"Instead of arguing and threatening, why don't we use the occasion," John Leeds said. "Tonight's meeting – non-meeting I should say – should prove to all of us, wherever we stand, that the Project One plan is unworkable and can only lead to violence and tearing the community apart. The question now is whether we're going to let that happen or change the plan."

"That plan is the product of years of hard work by many people," Moore said.

"That plan has already driven four thousand poor people out of their homes and calls for a grand total of eighteen units of low income housing to replace what was torn down and remodelled," Meg said, stamping the foot which had been vibrating since Steale's stare.

"Wait a minute. There's nothing sacred about the Project One plan." The speaker was Frank Pender, an architect and one of the founders of the Lincoln Park Conservation Association. "The number of low income units in the plan can be increased without doing much harm. The purpose of the plan is to upgrade the community, not to be vindictive.

Everyone wants a mix, poor and middle income people as well as wealthier ones. Lincoln Park has always been a mixed neighbourhood, and I, for one, and everyone else who developed the plan, want to preserve that. What we've needed all along is input from the representatives of the lower class community. How many low income units would you consider fair?"

Meg looked like she wanted to stamp on Pender, but John Leeds stepped between them. Meg stalked away and I followed. We were both mad. However, we could not stay that way long: It had been a good night. Not that the physical damage was significant or useful. Jack Seal was already philosophical about that and even made a joke to us about it. What seemed important was that people had expressed their outrage, had begun to fight back. A new stage had been reached. Our conversation with the LPCA members showed that they too realized this. Before tonight, when we had only objected verbally, we were treated as nuisances not to be taken seriously. We were ignored, not spoken to. Tonight we were treated as serious enemies, argued with, even threatened.

As we were leaving John Leeds overtook us and apologized for pushing us off. He said he thought the earlier conversation had been too important to let it turn into an argument and told us more of what had been said.

"It might not mean anything," he said, "but it was the first split in their ranks. The way he made his offer was demeaning, but Pender's statement was the first time I've seen any willingness from any of these guys to concede anything but platitudes to poor people. Another fifty or a hundred units of low income housing may be just a drop in the bucket to poor people, but it's a red rag to a bull for someone like Steale. He wants a solidly upper middle class community, a place where he and his friends can live comfortably. His goal is to be able to walk the streets without even a hint of the seamier side of life. Poor people mean big families to him. He hates children. They might taunt him and even if they don't they're noisy and unrestrained. He's after dignity, restraint, urbanity.

"That's why he was so riled up tonight. He can't stand the kind of passion those kids showed. He'd be glad to murder the lot of you. At least he would if he could do it with a clean, quick-acting poison. He wouldn't want bloodshed. I couldn't get him to argue with Pender, but you could see he was angry, and the more I got Pender to expand on his offer the madder Steale got. I'd love to hear the private conversation those guys are having now.

"Pender is an important person. He may not have an official position, but he does the technical work of the LPCA planning committee. If he works to get changes in the Project One plan, that will make plenty of waves within the LPCA. And I think he will do it. He's a sincere guy and was upset over what happened tonight. He really believed the plan was benefiting everyone. But tonight he saw how much some people are hurting, and while he's just not the sort of person to get beyond technical alterations, he'll go all the way on those. I suspect there will be a revised plan if Pender has to draw it up himself, and that revised plan may create a real division in the LPCA."

"It just seems ridiculous that these guys can be fighting and quibbling over a few lousy units of housing when more people than they're considering building for are being driven out of their homes every week," I said.

"But those bastards don't think about people. If they did they wouldn't have started the whole urban renewal process or made their inhuman plan," Meg said.

"Right," John Leeds said. "And if you can't get them to think in human terms – and God knows I've tried everything I could to get to them without an iota of success – you can at least make them doubt their mechanics enough to slow them down and give us more time to organize more humans to fight them."

I silenced my inclination to argue. Leeds' theory sounded impressive, and I was quite willing to let him use it to handle Pender and company. So long as I didn't have to deal with them. I suddenly realized I would prefer to slug Pender or Steale, not dispute them. The thought surprised me because I thought I had resolved such ideas in favour of nonviolence. Was my association with Jazzman and the Young Lords changing me? Or was it seeing the way those with power reacted to them? Or was nonviolence the product of a different way of life than I was now leading?

Mick Finnigan, whose Larrabee Street bar the Department of Urban Renewal was trying to tear down and who had just had his liquor license revoked, interrupted my metaphysical meditations. He wanted to celebrate, so he slipped me a ten and told me to buy all the beer I could and bring it down the street to his pub, which was now functioning as a restaurant. Mick and Meg and I and Chuck and Bob and a few others stayed talking a long time after closing. Everyone thought it was a miracle no one had been busted and had a story of a near bust to tell.

Four months later, when it had become apparent that the Young Lords were a real force, Jazzman was indicted for mob action at the meeting. In retrospect it is obvious no one was busted only because the authorities were caught off guard and hoped what happened was an accident that would lead to nothing else if no big fuss was made of it.

But it was no accident. It was the public beginning of a new organization, one which, in emulation, would soon spring up in Puerto Rican communities from coast to coast, the Puerto Rican equivalent of the Black Panther Party. It was also the end of the old Conservation Community Council. Never again would that body be able to act as a local rubber stamp for City Hall's Urban Renewal plans. For most of 1969 the CCC was afraid to call a meeting. Those it did call were shouted down by angry audiences demanding a representative council. An attempt to placate opponents by appointing two blacks and two Latins to the council (along with eleven whites and still no women) accomplished nothing.

In fact it led to a small scale riot when one of the black appointees argued with Henry Larcen over possession of the microphone. An orderly meeting was held after, but the entire proceedings were occupied by a debate about the presence of two hundred gun toting, uniformed policemen to maintain order. No new urban renewal plans were approved by the Conservation Community Council from mid 1968 until February 1970, when the Council was allowed to meet to approve the Poor Peoples Coalition Housing Plan.

10.

THIS MORNING THE WEATHER, for once, is uninteresting, but the sky is startling. After weeks of alternating heavy snow and clear, cold brilliance, the weather seems to be resting. The snow has compacted, but over three feet of it covers the ground. Around the house it mounts so high from what slides off the tin roof that I must shovel the mountains in front of the windows and doors or else it will be impossible to see in and out, let alone get in and out. The temperature remains steady a few degrees below freezing with a thin layer of cloud which seems to presage neither snow nor sun. The sky has put its energy into colour rather than weather.

Up the valley to the north there are blue breaks and the clouds are pure white. Above me the breaks are smaller and less blue, the clouds grayish white. To the west the clouds gradually lower and thicken, shading into an unbroken dull gray. But to the south and east the clouds both blacken and brighten; their colour deepens until at the horizons, which today hide the mountains at the lower end of the valley, the sky erupts into a deep, bright purple. The glory of that purple obscured the logic behind it. Long I feasted my eyes, but only later did I conclude that the purple was the sum of all the sky's colours illuminated by the unseen rising sun. Or perhaps all the colour was concentrated in that one layer of purple, and the sun behind it projected a varying patchwork onto the rest of the sky.

THE JANUARY, 1969 Conservation Community Council meeting began the most hectic period of my life. No wonder I don't know how to write it. Even now, as I look back with my head utterly clear – I think – I cannot sort out the happenings of the next year. Portions of meetings, marches, murders, arrests, celebrations flash through my mind. I sense a pattern, but mostly I cannot fit the pieces together, cannot remember chronology. Oh, to have had the time, the luxury to do what I do now, keep a journal. But part of the frenzy of those days was the conviction that we were too busy making history to record it. After the revolution there would be time.

It was Chicago polluting our minds, refusing to permit thinking and understanding. I did not even save any of the old activity calendars Meg faithfully made and distributed and do not have a single copy of the Lincoln Park *Press* or the Chicago *Seed* to refer to. All I can do now is recall individual events and trust an unseen sun or an innate muse to order and illuminate my memories.

One picture is clear although it was taken by an untrained kid with a cheap camera. Meg, I and several others spent an hour around Meg's hospital bed ogling the picture and debating how large a portion of the front page of the *Press* it should cover. It showed fat Harry, the mafia realtor, his huge bare belly hanging way out of his too short shirt, pointing a big semi-automatic tommy gun at Jazzman's face. Jazzman looks perfectly calm as, from all accounts, he was at the time. Several other photographs, which we scattered over the inside pages of the newspaper, show Harry waving that gun and a revolver and pointing them at Jazzman and other Young Lords. Certainly these were the most dramatic photos we ever managed to obtain.

I don't know that Harry was in the mafia, but everyone claimed he was, and Mick Finnigan, who grew up in the neighbourhood with Harry, insisted not only that Harry was part of "the outfit" but that he was so mean and rotten that "the outfit" used him for the dirtiest of its dirty work. In grade school, according to Mick, Harry took great pleasure in torturing younger and smaller kids and more than once broke bones of kids half his size. Mick bad mouthed the Department of Urban Renewal and land speculators louder and more passionately than anyone else around. He wasn't afraid of anybody – except Harry. He encouraged us in Concerned Citizens of Lincoln Park, even goaded us into taking on anyone, but he always told us not to mess with Harry: "He's crazy. He's as likely to kill you as scratch his ass." Mick later would swear it had to have been Harry who murdered Burt and Eve Jackson.

All that is speculation, as was Harry's business. He bought up real estate, held it awhile, then sold it to other speculators to remodel. Usually he did the dirty work of kicking out residents himself. Whether this was part of the deal with the buyer or whether Harry did it for pleasure I don't know. Jazzman knew several people who had been threatened and evicted at gunpoint by Harry. And now Harry was trying to close down the San Juan Club, one of the best known Puerto Rican bars in the city. The rumour, probably false since it never happened, was that he planned to convert the San Juan Club into a pizza parlour. The week after the CCC non-meeting the Young Lords decided to picket Harry's Realty.

It was an all Latin picket because, said Jazzman, it was a Puerto Rican problem and Puerto Ricans in the hood had to see there was a Puerto Rican organization that would help them. Everybody present agreed it was a very spirited picket line. It had to be because the temperature was below zero Fahrenheit. Little wonder when Fat Harry began waving his gun and threatening to shoot anyone who stepped on his property, everyone followed Jazzman into the office. The picketers had tropical ancestry and disliked removing their winter coats until temperatures neared eighty. To challenge them to come inside on such a day was ludicrous. They had all had guns pointed at them before; the cold inspired considerably more fear. Probably even the police who eventually turned up were welcomed in on the theory the more bodies the more warmth.

Jazzman laughed at how solicitous the cops were of Harry: "He had been pointing a machine gun at my head for ten minutes and they're going to spend their time just asking him if we did any damage and what does he want them to do and not even pay enough attention to me to tell me to shut up when I keep telling them he was threatening me with an illegal gun which is still in plain sight. Man, if it wasn't so cold outside I'd have gone down to picket the pigpen too."

So the Young Lords had fun that cold day, and that night Mick Finnigan swore it was a miracle Harry hadn't wiped out the whole bunch. Also that night the windows of first the San Juan Club and, an hour later, Harry's Realty were broken out by unknown vandals.

The Conservation Community Council protest and the picket of Fat Harry's office accomplished nothing concrete. But they had been well planned and had been brought off without anyone getting hurt or arrested. This alone generated phenomenal enthusiasm in the Young Lords and in every young Latin in the area. "Beats gangbanging all to hell," proclaimed one old gang member at a party the day after the picket. When that statement went unchallenged, I knew some measure of victory had already been achieved. Gangbanging – fights between local groups – had been the best excitement, almost the only pleasure in most of these kids' lives.

Their parents were working too hard at surviving to pay them much attention; the schools, cops and other authorities did little except punish them and tell them how stupid they were; local merchants refused to let them into their shops or followed them around trying to catch them shoplifting. Many of them spent most of their lives playing the fool because it was expected of them and was the best way they knew to avoid being berated, belted or busted by their elders. Only during their brief turf wars with other gangs could they feel they had a say in the outcome of their lives. Only then could they act as if they were free, strive for success with equals in a world controlled by their own rules, not those imposed on them by people with more experience, more weapons, more power.

"This discipline stuff is hard work," Sancho said. "But I think it's going to be worth it. I think we're going to win." Sancho, stocky and incredibly strong, cheerful and fearless. Sancho, happy and cool even when surrounded by cops but sweating and straining mightily as he sounded out syllables from the *Little Red Book* to an Anglo college girl trying to teach him to read. Sancho, the faithful, struggling ox of the Young Lords, representative of the best, if most simple, characteristics of the group. What did it mean to Sancho to "win"? Revolution? An end to urban renewal? An end to oppression? Power to the people?

Eventually Sancho learned to toss around such big words and phrases, but there always seemed to be a wink in his voice as if to say: "Well, if we need this stuff, I'm for it – so long as there's action and I'm in on it." Freedom, to Sancho, meant being around friends, lots of people, different kinds of people, so long as they all joked with him and fought alongside him. Freedom did mean the end of oppression to Sancho. Oppression was a boss always telling him exactly what to do and how to do it, complaining as soon as he paused to make a joke or take it easy. Freedom didn't mean not working, for learning to read was harder work than anything he had done before in his life; it did mean working among friends, among equals he could laugh with. Perhaps most of all it meant things were never dull.

In exuberance Sancho seemed the youngest of the Young Lords, but he looked older and was in his mid twenties, half a dozen years older than most of the others. He had a wife and three small children with whom he spent little time during the height of Young Lords Organization activity but moved back in with later. He had been a gangbanger most of his life. (Although it was hard to imagine him mad enough to hurt anyone badly. His great strength probably made it unnecessary to hurt anyone because opponents generally backed down.)

After Jazzman went underground and the action died down, he joined a motorcycle gang and quickly rose to leadership under the name Hercules. He seemed to get almost as much pleasure from his blue jean jacket cluttered with chains, medals and patches as he had from his purple beret, and he acted as cheerful as ever although he privately confided to me that he missed the good old days and wished Jazzman would return. Indeed, when Jazzman wrote from exile that he was returning, Sancho brought the whole motorcycle gang to address and stuff envelopes to announce the return and ask for assistance.

Sancho usually seemed the most cosmopolitan of the Young Lords. He was not afraid to talk to anyone and joked with white radical intellectuals as easily as with Latin street kids. Priscilla, who often felt uncertain among the Young Lords, liked him very much. Everyone did. Even the cops seldom bothered Sancho. He often appeared on television because he looked approachable even at militant demonstrations. His interviews always amused him when he heard them, and he would scratch his head and ponder the meaning of what he had said along with everyone else.

Eventually the organization decided to appoint official spokespeople at demonstrations, and Sancho's friendly but inscrutable utterances passed from the public domain. Yet this same Sancho could never be induced to speak to a crowd. And this fearless warrior lost out on a trip to Cuba because he lacked courage to take an el downtown to apply for a passport. Too late I cornered him and got him to admit that he, who had lived all his life in Chicago, had never been on an el and never been downtown. He had been ashamed to tell his comrades he was afraid to go alone.

By summer, when repression was coming down, Sancho had become the veteran, the unmovable, the constant source of strength in the organization when Jazzman and other leaders were in jail or hiding. But it must have been different in January of 1969. After all, Sancho had grown up in the same neighbourhoods as had Jazzman and was older. He had seen his new leader when Jazzman was a punk kid leading a gang of twelve year olds, when he was a street fighter whose enthusiasm was often greater than his skill, when he was a junkie.

Little Jazzman's determination to overcome insuperable odds must have seemed perplexing, perhaps insane, to someone of Sancho's strength and temperament. Yet in January, 1969 Sancho's devotion to Jazzman was as total as that of the younger Young Lords. Jazzman had turned a bunch of street kids no one cared about into a political force the entire city government would have to reckon with. That was enough to insure the love of every one of those kids. For Sancho, who had survived by never worrying about people and forces he couldn't see but battling like hell against visible enemies, watching Jazzman deal with troublemakers at a dance without starting a brawl, with the leaders of the Blackstone Rangers or Black Panthers, with sloppy Fat Harry and the fancy dressed, fancy talking urban renewal dudes, with ordinary folks in the community and in the organization, was a convincing education.

Sancho knew he would never go out of his way to take on a guy with two pieces just because the guy was threatening to close someone else's bar, to take on slick talking big shots because their policies were threatening to move unknown people from crummy apartments, to seek out the toughest gangbangers and revolutionaries in the city and make alliances with them while at the same time caring for plain, meek everyday people enough to risk his life for them. His thoughts and actions simply didn't range that far from himself and the concrete reality he lived in, but watching Jazzman do such things showed Sancho that Jazzman was indeed his leader and that his leader needed Sancho's level head and strength as much as Sancho needed Jazzman's passionate intelligence.

Without thinking of such matters Sancho knew he could help Jazzman win the crazy fights Jazzman would pick, and that winning, or even trying to win those fights, would be more exciting than the rest of his life combined. How Sancho must later have wished to be back in January, 1969, at the beginning of those hectic times in which little physical fighting took place, instead of leading his motorcycle gang into the wildest of brawls. I spent the time he was in his motorcycle gang and Jazzman was underground wishing the same thing.

And for Sancho there was more. More than the love of excitement which had always been the main part of his life and more than the new love of Jazzman, the crazy kid who was always right and for whom he would be willing to die. There was the discovery of himself and the world. He was suddenly learning he was a complex human being living in a complex world. It was no longer sufficient simply to get enough food, enough booze, enough fun. Others were asking him to read, to think, to understand. No one had ever before suggested he might be able to do such things, yet now everybody around him was assuming he could and would do them.

He found himself believing the others, believing in himself. And the more he believed in himself and thought about the world, the more he both wanted to change it and wanted to be a part of more of it. That contradiction puzzled him on the occasions when he thought about both aspects. Like when Priscilla took over the college students' task of teaching him to read. He carried Mao's *Little Red Book* in his back pocket because that was how millions of people learned to read in China. He was proud to tell people he was learning to read: What an organization was the Young Lords, what feats could it not accomplish if it could teach him to read?

So there he was, sounding out syllables about proletarians and bourgeoisie, taking pride in being a proletarian, being listened to and helped by a very bourgeois woman with a broad Texas accent, an incomprehensible yet fascinating woman. Did the triumph of the proletarians mean the end of such creatures as Priscilla? Perhaps he had better get to know her now, before the revolution. Was that a counterrevolutionary desire? Such situations and problems were very new, very strange, very perplexing, very enjoyable. He hoped such problems would increase as he understood more and wondered if learning to think and read would help him solve them.

He astonished old friends by becoming philosophical when drunk. He astonished himself by dreaming dreams in which he spent half of his time fighting in the front lines of the revolution and the other half protecting girls like Priscilla from the revolutionary forces. It was very confusing and he wanted more of it.

I remember him getting very excited about "developing human potential." It was a few months later – May? June? – during the takeover of McCormick Seminary. Some professors and seminarians were giving talks as a part of a political education program, and one spoke about "developing human potential." It turned Sancho on. He talked to me passionately about how children in the ghetto could be educated, how the Young Lords Organization could set up schools to reach them and teach them to read and add and make a revolution and develop their human potential.

Certainly *his* human potential was developing rapidly. I had watched Jazzman's mind open up and bloom under the influence of new books and ideas in the fall of 1968. By January, 1969 Sancho's mind too was blooming. Nothing like Jazzman's, for he never learned to read well and wasn't made to aspire to the intellectual heights which could excite Jazzman. Yet he was becoming a bigger person mentally: His mind had been so confined previously that he had understood nothing beyond his own streets and pals; he had always avoided anything beyond this either by fighting its representatives or ducking it. Now he was being brought face-to-face with this beyond and learning he could both participate in it and change it. He tried to do both and by trying made himself a new man, one he liked because for all his new knowledge he was not stuck up and was always willing to talk things over with the old Sancho.

The Young Lords Organization was teaching him the lesson schools and environment had kept from him all his life: that he was a beautiful, complicated and interesting person living in a large, complicated and interesting world. Of course he was turned on. Of course he was loyal to the organization which showed all that to him. Of course he shouted: "All Power to the People" with new pride in his own personhood and race. Of course he was willing to make any sacrifice for the Young Lords Organization and for the people. Right on, Sancho. Right on, Young Lords Organization, composed of many young people learning many such lessons in many different ways.

11.

WINTER ON THE GALENA-SHELTER BAY FERRY. The ferries are free (hurray!) in the interior of British Columbia. They extend the highways across the large lakes which occupy the whole of some valleys. Slocan Lake doesn't have a ferry. As a result the west side of the lake, the Valhalla Range, is a roadless virgin wilderness accessible mainly by small boat. The ferry across Kootenay Lake is a forty minute ride. The Galena-Shelter Bay ferry is only half that but gives a magnificent view of Upper Arrow Lake, a widening of the Columbia River.

Although the temperature is below freezing, I cannot sit in my car. A strong wind off the water simultaneously chills me and fires my imagination as I stand on deck viewing the flux of a white, watery world. I look out at miles of deep green, white-capped water edged by quiet strips of white shoreline. The lake seems to narrow in the distance although I know that it and Lower Arrow Lake comprise an unbroken expanse of water over a hundred miles long. Mountains rise from both shores to join the clouds, the pure white of the mountain tops exactly the colour of the clouds today.

Far off no distinction between snow and cloud is observable, but nearby texture distinguishes them. The clouds are smooth, the snow fine and grained like wood where the wind winnows it into vertical lines. Up high, where the snow lies untouched by trees or thaws, it resembles billions of individual spores, as if each snow dot is independent, fluid, alive. I sense continuous movement as if the dots realign themselves constantly, individual granules congregating and recongregating on a whim of the wind. Near the top of the treeline the snow dusts the trees.

Half way down the mountain there is a line below which the trees become green, the snow on the ground a deeper white. This is a thaw line, where snow has fallen off the trees and fused on the ground into a thick mass instead of a shifting powder. Yet even amid this lower forest there are countless rivers of white, slight remains of numerous miniature slides now unmoving yet appearing to plunge down the steep slopes toward inland oceans of unbroken, ungrained white. These last are places which have been clearcut logged. In summer they are ugly – like Larrabee Street or the corner of Armitage and Halsted after the bulldozers finished their devastation – but in the mountain winter they present another distinct body of snow, a contrast which ebbs into the winter waterscape. Here nature can turn human destruction back into beauty. Will that always be so, or is it so now only because there are still few people here, only sporadic exploitation of the land? What will these mountains look like after the implementation of the Upper Arrow Lakes Rural Renewal and Improvement Plan?

I wrote the above paragraphs going on a trip soon after I arrived in British Columbia. A woman I encountered returning home on the same ferry filled me in on some history. I thought I had been joking at the end. The joke was on me: The "Upper Arrow Lakes Rural Renewal and Improvement Plan" had already been implemented. The widening of the Columbia River which is Arrow Lakes was a good deal narrower just seven years before I described it. A dam at the foot of the lakes widened them and flooded their valley. Water backed up by the dam inundated many small towns and farm properties along what had been the lake and was now a reservoir, no longer an ecologically functioning lake. Not only that, the purpose of the dam was not to generate power for Canada but simply to control the flow of water for the Grand Coulee Dam in the United States.

At the same time the United States government was funding urban removal in Lincoln Park, it was funding rural removal in the Kootenays of British Columbia. When I was admiring the beauty of the waterscape, I was floating over the graves of the communities murdered to create it just as the people living in Lincoln Park today live on the grave of the community murdered to create their landscape and lifestyle and Chicago's tax base. We who don't know history are doomed to repeat it. Which seems an excellent reason to write what I write.

Yet the more I write the more I realize that this history is not what I intended to write. It is not a history. There is little order to my memories of 1969 – and less concern for the lack. The events that took place have some importance, the movement of which they were part more importance, the people who participated in them the most importance. Chronology has little importance. Hopefully the movement the events of Lincoln Park sprang from and added to will someday abolish cautious academic histories which spend pages establishing whether A blew his nose before or after B scratched his belly.

Suffice it to say that during 1969 far more was occurring than I could keep careful track of, and seven years later it is impossible to remember accurately most of the meetings, marches, pickets, busts, escapes, arguments, alliances and dalliances. I worked from ten in the morning until after midnight most days – though I didn't think of it as work then and still don't. I was caught up in a flood of events and let myself be carried along. Whenever possible I exerted myself to aid others similarly caught or splashed around in the hope I might somehow affect the course of the flow, but mainly I was carried along and did what I had to do to survive. I well remember the jumble of feelings aroused by the events which carried me along. In the middle of the current a snag would loom, perhaps placed by the LPCA or the cops, perhaps a product of our own blunders. I would give all my attention to avoiding it. Until that snag was dodged, my thoughts were of nothing else, and as soon as one obstacle floated by, another floated up. So I seldom thought of anything other than events and wrote nothing except descriptions of and reactions to events for our newspaper and announcements of coming events for leaflets.

The motto of the Lincoln Park *Press* was "People First," yet it contained little space for news about people, so bursting were its columns with events: a demonstration, a frame up, a meeting, an eviction, an informer exposed, a mass arrest, a new alternative institution, a new instance of institutional racism or oppression, a boycott, a murder and more and more and more. Here in the Kootenays our floods are of water, not events. I know few people and my relationships are mainly with nature. Yet when I write of Chicago in what I thought would be a chronicle of historic and historical events, I find myself remembering people. The events which so engulfed me at the time now seem merely watered down, the goals of our movement shrouded in fog. Only the people remain vivid. Am I making up for the unfulfilled promise on our newspaper's masthead?

MEG HAD TREMENDOUS SPIRIT AND DRIVE. It seemed part of her character and her philosophy to push her body past the limits of her endurance. Outwardly she and Jazzman were similar in this, but where Jazzman's drive drove others to emulate him, Meg's often drove them away. Perhaps the punishment she inflicted on her frail frame showed too much whereas on Jazzman it seemed natural. Certainly I felt she understood what she was doing to her body while Jazzman usually didn't. She lit a cigarette when she got up in the morning and never used a match thereafter, lighting each new cigarette from the old butt. It saved on matches, but was tough on her weak lungs.

We all smoked excessively back then; it offered some release from the continual tension. My own smoking tripled during the period I worked with Concerned Citizens of Lincoln Park. I smoked my last pack waiting for the jury to return in my trial. Still I stayed healthy, probably due to the good food Priscilla was feeding me. Meg hated to waste time cooking or eating. Once in a while she sent someone across the street to buy her a hot dog and fries. Once or twice a week I dragged her home for dinner, usually over her protests. She always appreciated Priscilla's meals once she began eating. John Leeds and several other people also took her home to make sure she didn't starve.

She didn't starve, but she did catch pneumonia twice a year. She and everyone around her knew when the pneumonia was coming on: Her smoker's hack became a serious cough, her cheeks got red and hollow looking, she shivered even when the weather was warm. The disease always hit when she was working extra hard, putting out the *Press* or preparing for a demonstration. Her response was always the same, work harder. Eventually the pain became great enough that, in a moment of weakness, she would allow herself to be dragged to the doctor, who would immediately hospitalize her.

At least she could not smoke there. In theory. In the hospital she was at her dearest. And her damnedest. She charmed the nurses and turned her bed into an office – sometimes more. She looked and was weak, but she refused to remain unless she was well supplied with work to do in bed. So we would bring her stacks of books, newspapers, congressional records, census tracts. Except for City Hall records, researching which was my job, all of Concerned Citizens of Lincoln Park's extensive files resulted from Meg's stays in Grant Hospital. Two editions of the *Press* were also laid out at her bedside. Dear Meg would somehow bewitch the night nurse, and a bunch of us would come up two at a time bringing the layout sheets, pizza and beer during evening visiting hours, then stay with damned Meg much of the night.

The first time we did it was shortly after the January CCC non-meeting and picket of Fat Harry's realty. Repression had not yet hit, and we had that magnificently funny roll of photos of Fat Harry, his belly and tommy gun pointed at Jazzman and other Young Lords. At first there were six of us with Meg in the hospital room (her roommate must have been drugged; she slept through everything): Linda, slight, wispy except for a thick, blond Afro, quiet, a divorced mother of a ten-year-old boy, full time secretary and part time student, who somehow also volunteered to do much of the typing for Concerned Citizens of Lincoln Park; Chuck, broad shouldered with short, wiry hair, tough enough looking to be out of a gangster film, but soft spoken and gentle, a forty-year-old ex-longshore-man and disciple of Harry Bridges who had lived in Cuba for five years and was full of great stories about the good old days; Bob, roly poly with straight shoulder length hair, our only member who looked like a hippie (the first meeting he showed up at he gave a fiery speech which prompted Jazzman to say: "Maybe we should have checked out some of those hip-pies before we beat them up in the old days"), fifteen years younger than Chuck but his friend and fellow taxicab driver, an impetuous, fun-loving working class guy who had eloped with a rich girl only to have her lawyer parents steal her back, confine her in a mental institution and annul the marriage; Sal, our translator; Priscilla, whom I had persuaded to work more with us; and me. Before long Linda was sent home to type one last article and Priscilla left, as she always did when she thought Meg was overextending herself. I told her I would try to be home by midnight.

Sal had smoked some reefer before coming and was in a quiet, relaxed mood. He said little and spent the time he was not writing up transla-tions rubbing Meg's aching back. Chuck and Bob, on the other hand, were conducting a competition to see who could come up with the most outrageous story about the fares they had picked up in their taxis. After each story Meg would start to laugh and end up coughing and choking, whereupon we would all join Sal and pound her back until she was able to reprimand Chuck and Bob for not working on the newspaper and trying to kill her by making her laugh.

About every half hour the night nurse would tiptoe in to remind us to hold down the noise, then ask questions about the newspaper and tell us how Grant Hospital messed over its employees and patients. By her third visit we decided she had given us a story, so we sat her down and I took notes while Meg plied her with beer, pizza and questions and tried not to glance at Bob and Chuck, who were behind the nurse doing pantomime in which Bob reached and tried madly to clutch the nurse's body while Chuck restrained him. When the nurse left, I began writing furiously on the article with Sal peering over my shoulder trying to translate as I wrote. Meg directed Chuck and Bob in the juggling of the big layout sheets, which were spread all over her bed and the floor as she searched for space into which to squeeze the article. Finally she announced: "We'll have to take out all the slogans, but I've got fourteen and a half column inches."

"I'm sure I'm already over that," I said.

"Well, cut it down. You always use too many adjectives anyway. I'll see if I can squeeze out a few more inches." So she reshuffled the sheets while I began crossing out sentences and paragraphs.

"Hey man, you can't cut that one out," Sal said. "It took me ten minutes to figure out how to translate it and it sounds real nice in Spanish now."

"That's just what we need, a goddamned poet in our midst," I replied.

"It's okay. I got us six more column inches by cutting way down on the headshop's ad," Meg said from behind a stack of layout sheets.

"Hey, I made up that ad and sold it to the headshop. It's the only revenue the whole edition is going to bring in," Bob said. We hissed and booed him into submission.

"I didn't eliminate the ad, just cut the size in half," Meg said. "Now why don't you grab some presstype and lay it down on a smaller scale so we don't have to pay the printer to shoot it down? It'll fit quite well if you get rid of your doodlings."

"Oh, forgive me Pablo, wherever you are."

"Who's Pablo?"

"Picasso, you philistine."

"Quiet," Meg said, sitting up suddenly. "Someone open the fire escape door."

Sal ran to open the door. "What's happening?" Jazzman greeted us, hugging Sal. "A guy could freeze out there before you communists open the door for him."

It was almost 2 a.m. "You were supposed to be here by midnight," Meg said.

"You were supposed to have the newspaper finished by midnight," Jazzman said.

"Dick and Sal, take the hospital article over to Linda's for typing. You can glue it in with the other article she's typing in the morning, before you drive the sheets to the printer. I've marked where they both go including the continuations. Tell Linda she's got exactly twenty and a half column inches. Bob and Chuck, you might as well go too. The printer can shoot the ad down to the right size."

"I'll redo it out here. You can pull the curtain round your bed," Bob said.

"Yeah, stay a while," Jazzman said. "You can help teach me how to lay out a newspaper. The Young Lords are going to have their own soon." Bob and Chuck were still scratching out presstype and Meg was carefully running down how to lay out a newspaper to Jazzman when Sal and I left to wake up Linda.

It was after three o'clock when I arrived home. Priscilla was sitting in bed crying. "Am I late for dinner? A good woman should have the dinner hot when her man comes home from work. The last time I was late you had a whole soufflé waiting for me."

My attempt at humour was as successful as it always was: Priscilla cried harder. "I'm sorry to be so late, Priscilla, but I'm also exhausted. Can't we wait until morning to talk about it?" I began undressing. Priscilla screamed and threw a clock at me. I ducked and turned to watch it crash into the wall. She jumped at me and began pummelling me with her fists. She had learned that violence was her best method to make me treat her seriously; otherwise I made fun of her or talked down to her as if she were a child. I blocked most of her blows and waited for her anger to subside, which it did fairly quickly. When she collapsed onto the floor in new tears, I finished undressing, then carried her back to the bed and got us under the covers. It was cold in our bedroom, which lacked a space heater. I hugged Priscilla and tried to be consoling. I explained about the nurse and the new story on the hospital and apologized more sincerely for being so late.

"You've got as much consideration for others as a preying mantis," she said, sobbing.

"I said I'm sorry. You know how it is when we're trying to get the newspaper out. You should have gone to sleep."

"And as much sensitivity as a cockroach. I don't give a damn about your stupid newspaper or what time you come home. You come home late every night. I'm used to that. It's you and your phony idealism I'm crying about: You're going to save the world, but you don't care how many of your friends you kill to do it."

"Poor Priscilla, she's being sacrificed on the altar of world revolution."

"That's just what I mean. You're so blinded by your world revolution you can't even see what I'm talking about. Can't you at least shut up a minute and listen to what I've got to say?" She looked directly at me for the first time to see if I would keep quiet. When I did she continued: "Meg is your friend and mine. She's very sick. She doesn't care whether or not she kills herself, but you might. This is just what she needs when she's in the hospital and the doctor says she should have complete rest. He won't even let her out of bed to go to the bathroom, but you have to keep her up all night working on the damn newspaper and sneak beer and cigarettes in to her too. That's exactly what put her in the hospital in the first place. As if your newspaper can't wait until tomorrow."

"It's got to be at the printer's before noon. If we don't get it there on time, they won't run it until next week."

"And of course you incompetent males couldn't possibly lay it out yourselves."

"We could. It wouldn't be as good a job, but we could do it. The problem is that Meg wouldn't let us do it. If we had tried to lay out that newspaper ourselves, Meg would have walked out of the hospital, climbed down the fire escape in her hospital gown if necessary, and come to the office to help. You know that's true."

"Maybe so, but you still don't have to help her kill herself."

"Finding accomplices, especially male accomplices, is not Meg's problem. She even arranged for Jazzman to drop in after the newspaper was supposed to be finished."

"Let Jazzman kill her. You don't have to do it."

"Meg is Meg. She's not going to change no matter what I say or do. Do you remember how we decided last summer that four of us would share the work at Citizens? Jan went back to school and Joan left because Meg either insisted they kill themselves working or did so much of their work they didn't feel like they belonged.

"Sure, I could leave too, and Meg would hardly notice. There are plenty of groups which would love to have me working with them and would appreciate me more than Meg ever will. But I love Lincoln Park and this is the best way I know to help it. I love Meg too, and I know damn well that if I wasn't around to pick up some of the load, she would kill herself sooner and surer than she will with me around."

Priscilla protested a little more, but I had won the argument. I always won our arguments. Soon we were making love and it was good. The newspaper even reached the printer in time.

12.

I'M WRITING IN A CUBBYHOLE amid unwanted rooms used as an "alternative school" in Trail. I can look out a dirty window towards smelter hill with its huge smokestacks farting out the remains of some of the mountains I love. Trail is visible for miles as a pall of smoke squatting between mountains which rise on either side of the Columbia River, whose power turns Trail's light into dusk. The pollution shat upon the town and pissed into the river is monumental although the residents claim to be happy because there is so much less than there used to be. Twenty years ago nothing could grow and the land was black for miles in every direction.

Despite the claims of improvement the atmosphere affects the dropout kids I can hear in the next room in many of the same ways the polluted atmosphere of Chicago affected the Young Lords Organization kids: They are nervous, out of place without quite knowing why, and full of bravado to conceal how they feel. I guess kids all over love words. Someday when corporations no longer exist and people are important, educators will educate rather than shape children to fit the moulds our society demands, in the case of a mill town like Trail the need for a surplus labour pool. Then a decent educational system might be developed around the youthful love of words. Meanwhile, I listen to all the fine words going to waste here and think I might as well be in the storefront church office on Lincoln Avenue a few days before the February, 1969 meeting of the Eighteenth District Police-Community Relations Council.

The Eighteenth District Police Station at Chicago Avenue and Clark Street was a jolly place. Its officers lived well, for both Rush Street and Old Town, Chicago's busiest nightlife areas were within its precinct, and many an officer's main activity was collecting payoffs from bar and nightclub owners, pimps and other business people. Many of the payoffs took place in a local Sicilian restaurant which seemed always to have at least one cop car parked in the no parking zone in front of it. Campbell Borst, the district commander, later was the highest ranking Chicago cop convicted in the shakedown scandals of the early Seventies.

The fun and bar loving nature of the Eighteenth District cops never prevented them from harassing folks opposed to city plans, and I spent many a lovely hour inside their cozy lockup and outside it bailing out friends. So it was pleasant to be able to harass them a bit, and the monthly police-community relations meetings were a good place to do it. Like all such meetings in Chicago these were intended to serve no function beyond propaganda, "public relations." They existed purely so the police could say they existed, could say the Chicago Police Department was attempting to reach out to the community for responses and suggestions. Just how far they were trying to reach was shown by the fact that in the Eighteenth District the meetings were held in the police station itself, in the courtroom upstairs.

I had begun attending police-community relations meetings after the Democratic Convention because many Gold Coast residents, horrified by what they saw the police do in front of their homes, wanted to object and decided that speaking up at these meetings was the proper way to do so. In the Eighteenth District there had actually been a debate over the resolution commending the Chicago Police Dept. for its handling of the events surrounding the Convention, a resolution introduced and passed in every district meeting in the city. Commander Borst, the only cop with a brain I ever encountered in Chicago, had been able to handle the pack of east Lincoln Park college graduates despite the occasional embarrassing moment, but neither he nor anyone else at the station was ready for the February, 1969 meeting.

Jazzman wanted to take our protests (against police harassment in the ghetto as well as urban renewal) to the police. His reasons were not those of the Gold Coast liberals. They were the same reasons the Black Panthers always called the cops pigs and were not easy for whites to understand. One had to experience the presence of police in a minority community to understand why hatred of them was natural and, therefore, a prime organizing tool. To the kids in the Young Lords Organization the cops were the cause of most of the mistreatment they and their friends received.

Jazzman understood that the police were servants, symbols of authority rather than real authorities, but he was a poet of action who knew just how to use a symbol. So we were forever at police stations protesting a bust or a beating or a shooting by a cop. Jazzman wanted to confront Borst in person, and Meg and I suggested the police-community relations meeting as one time we could be sure of doing so and one time the cops would have to deal with us openly. They couldn't refuse to talk to the very community they were supposed to be holding a meeting to communicate with.

Everybody who heard the idea derived great glee from it, and preparations for the meeting were festive. All the Young Lords had their own slogans to make into a poster or banner. They bragged endlessly among themselves of how they were going to tell the cops off:

"Man, I'm going to tell all those people how that pig Esposito beat the shit out of me in the back of the paddy wagon when I was handcuffed and couldn't fight back."

"Hell, what about what McMillan did to me?"

"And Czonka."

"Don't forget Carter and Jones."

"Let's make a list and tell the people about every bad pig in the district."

"There ain't no good ones."

"Fuck that list shit, man. I'm gonna go right up to the pigs and tell them if they don't lay off the Young Lords, we're gonna off 'em one by one."

"The hell with that one-by-one shit. Let's blow up the whole pigpen."

"Fuck talking to the baby pigs. I'm going right up to Borst and tell him he's a bore because a boar ain't nothing but a big pig."

"I'm gonna tell Borst that me and my piece is gonna hold him responsible for anything his pigs do. And if he don't smile when I tell him, I'm gonna kick him in the ass until he does."

The reality wasn't nearly as dramatic as the kids' plans, but I was satisfied. Priscilla, Meg, John Leeds and I arrived early. The hall was packed because a lot of people from both sides of Lincoln Park knew what was supposed to happen even if the cops didn't. The meeting was called to order and still no Young Lords. I was nervous: None of them liked to leave their own turf, especially in winter. But a few minutes after the meeting began, sounds of a commotion swelled up in the stairway, and then a cop ran into the room followed by twenty purple-bereted street kids chanting: "Young Lords, Young Lords, Young Lords," then half a dozen more cops and finally a trickle of hatless street kids who had trailed along to catch the action.

The meeting halted while the lead cop, now flanked by the others, conferred with Borst. He whispered, but his face and gestures indicated he wanted to clear the hall of the troublemakers. His commander replied audibly that it was an open meeting and that anyone from the community was welcome. Borst was speaking to the audience, not his own men. Meanwhile, the Young Lords were busily taping posters all over the back and side walls of the room. A big banner proclaimed "Young Lords Organization" and showed a fist gripping a rifle rising from a map of Puerto Rico. Posters declared such slogans as "Community Control of Police," "Pigs Out of the Puerto Rican Community," "Free Huey," "Hands off Jazzman," "Free Puerto Rico Now" and "Off the Pig." Most contained little hand drawn pictures, usually of pigs. As the posters went up, the artists were arguing with cops who were threatening to tear down the posters and bust the kids. The cops kept looking to Borst for orders. Finally the commander stated that the posters would be allowed providing those who posted them cleaned up later. He had to repeat the last half of his statement several times before it could be heard above the cheers.

Now Commander Borst tried to get the chairperson to resume the meeting, and when demands to be heard from the back of the hall made this impossible, he told the Young Lords that they were attending a regular meeting of the police and community and that the meeting had an agenda, which he read accompanied by boos and groans. The agenda included a guest speaker (a police detective) and would have taken an hour and a half before the "new business" section, which Borst explained was the proper time for the kids to speak. John Leeds quickly made a motion to suspend the agenda, the chair tried to rule it out of order, and after a long debate about parliamentary procedure Borst, ignoring the frightened businessman who was supposed to be chairing the meeting, permitted a vote. The motion carried to loud cheers, Borst declared the meeting would have to be orderly, and we were off.

There followed a lengthy and bloody catalogue of complaints of police brutality. The first complaints were made by Young Lords Organization members, but soon non-members spoke up as witnesses and to describe incidents that had happened to them. After each complaint Borst declared his indignation at the act of brutality and his sympathy for the speaker. Then he promised a full investigation and asked for very specific details of time, place, order of occurrence, badge and car numbers, etc. When the speaker was unable to provide all this information, Borst apologetically replied he could not investigate without it and made a new speech about order when jeers and catcalls filled the room.

Middle class people, including Meg and me, then stood up and said they had supplied such details about incidents during the Democratic Convention (except badge numbers since almost no cops wore badges during the Convention), and that an investigation either never took place or was a total whitewash. Borst pledged new investigations and investigations of the investigations. He kept his cool except for two carefully staged, controlled bursts of anger ostensibly directed at excess noise but obviously intended to show his men and supporters in the audience that he was in charge.

After nearly two hours of this Jazzman stood up and everyone else quieted down. Without notes but with astonishing accuracy he summarized almost every complaint that had been made – there must have been over twenty – and Borst's response, pointing out how the response was no response, gave no satisfaction, punished no cop and promised no different treatment in the future.

"Do you refuse to investigate a murder because the murderer failed to leave his name, address, phone number and social security number?" Jazzman asked. "Do you refuse to investigate a mugging or a robbery because it happened on a dark night and the victim didn't get a good view of the criminal's face or the getaway car's license number?" Jazzman's summaries brought out injustices more sharply than most of the original speakers had, and his dissection of Borst's answers was so deadly that the commander's supporters at first winced but soon could not suppress smiles. Borst interrupted occasionally to object that Jazzman was misinterpreting or distorting his words, but soon he too fell silent before a virtuoso performance of memory and analysis.

I sat as awed as everyone else although I of all people should not have been surprised since I had seen Jazzman do the same thing with books he had borrowed from me. Yet it had never occurred to me that he could speak so clearly under circumstances so different from sitting on the sofa in my living room or that the same powers he used to understand books could be applied in everyday life. Partway through Jazzman's analysis I began cursing the Chicago school system, which had classified him mentally backward, but soon my curses turned inward. I had to admit that until now I had still considered Jazzman my student, a boy full of street knowledge but in need of my own greater education and intellectual capacity. Ha, this was the point I knew what I stated earlier, that I was his student, not he mine, and I was ashamed. Why had I refused to heed overwhelming evidence for all these months?

Jazzman talked for about fifteen minutes, but I hardly heard the last half so busy was I berating myself and trying to see reasons for my blindness. There was a colourful reason: racism. Had Jazzman not been Puerto Rican, had he not spoken with a slight accent, would I have underestimated him so vastly? Many times I had uttered platitudes about the all embracing racism of our society, but, typically, I had never really believed it could embrace me. Had I not lived nine months as the only white in a black North Carolina ghetto? Alas, the pervasive influence of our racist society hung on despite both intellectual criticism and powerful real life experience. Could it never be eradicated? (I look out at my mountains for a sign, but they stand stony. And white.)

There was a social reason: class prejudice. My middle class upbringing blinded me. Because I knew Jazzman had not the advantages of my upbringing, I unthinkingly assumed he could never be my equal. (For this even my mountains mock me: They too lacked the advantages of my upbringing.) And an intellectual reason. I hated intellectual snobbery, quit my graduate studies in protest against it, had even been branded anti-intellectual, yet despite my loathing, years in universities had prevented me from seeing real intellect in someone without formal education, someone who didn't use his brains to show off, only to make practical progress for himself and his people. (Ah mountains, monumental without thought, lovely without logic, eternal without sophistry, how high above us you reach, how you dwarf our petty lives and reasons.)

So my reverie (now as well as then) proceeded until I was roused by laughter. Jazzman's final summation of Borst's non-replies had made even the commander's supporters laugh, and I looked up in time to see the commander himself smile briefly in appreciation of a job well done. Then he seemed to inhale and puff out his thin frame for a reply. Jazzman waited a few seconds while the laughter died down and the commander puffed up. Then, "We've listened to enough of your phony answers and promises. When you're ready to talk seriously, come to Armitage Street. All power to the people! *Viva Puerto Rico Libre!*"

He turned and walked up the aisle, out of the courtroom and down the stairs followed by the rest of the Young Lords cheering, stomping and chanting. The remainder of the audience followed them. As I was leaving, several cops began to rip down the posters which decorated the hall, but they were acting out of frustration while we were leaving in jubilation. On the sidewalk outside Young Lords and community people were doing an impromptu dance in the slush. Jill hugged me and pulled me into the dance yelling: "Wasn't Jazzman great?" Sancho was hugging Priscilla, Sal was hugging Meg, Mama Jane had hold of Pastor Leeds, and everyone was dancing, much to the amazement of two cops and the herd of drunks they were escorting into night quarters.

Jazzman didn't join the dance. He looked nervously at the cop-shop, pulled Burt Jackson away from a heavy Puerto Rican *madre*, conferred briefly with him, then shouted: "Everybody meet at the church at Armitage and Dayton." As we left several cops came out to hurl four letter words and racist epithets at our backs.

It was the first community meeting in the basement which would later become the "Young Lords Organization National Headquarters." It wasn't really a meeting, more an expression of joy and emotion. Close to a hundred people, perhaps half of those who attended the workshop, milled about, danced to the accompaniment of spoons banging glasses, feet stomping, chairs banging the floor, hands clapping and people singing. When people began leaving, Jazzman stood on a chair, thanked everyone for coming to the police-community relations meeting, said a few words about how we could save our community if we all stuck together and told the police plainclothesmen, two of whom Burt Jackson had ushered out earlier, to thank Commander Borst for his hospitality. He ended: "They're not going to be nice much longer. Now they know we're for real. The repression is going to start coming down."

He was right as usual. The next night I received the first of many late night phone calls. Five Young Lords had been busted at Halsted and Dickens for loitering and disorderly conduct. Jazzman wanted to know if I could raise $125 bail. It was the first of over $10,000 in bail money Concerned Citizens of Lincoln Park raised in the next year or so.

13.

IN EARLY MAY THERE WAS another demonstration at the Eighteenth District Police Station. There were far more people and the weather was good enough so we could parade all the way from Lincoln Park, a distance of over two miles, but the joy was gone: Sal Ramirez had been shot and killed by an off-duty Chicago pig.

The murder was one of the few key events in this chronicle I did not witness and which took place well away from Lincoln Park. It happened in Bridgeport, Mayor Daley's neighbourhood, Miguel Dominguez's neighbourhood. Miguel was one of the original Young Lords, one of four left from the old gang days still active in the social club Jazzman found when he returned to the hood from jail in the summer of 1968. The others were Sal Ramirez, Angel Silva and Jose Santamaria.

Miguel's family had been urban removed from Larrabee Street and then evicted from an apartment being remodelled. After searching Lincoln Park in vain he had found a job and a cheap apartment in Bridgeport. He often talked about moving back to Lincoln Park. He told me that he was sometimes insulted and threatened on the streets of Bridgeport. But the job had enabled him to get an old junk of a car, and the car enabled him to drive to work although the gas station where he was employed was only three blocks from his home. The only time he felt safe outside in that neighbourhood was inside his car with all the doors locked. However, he knew he couldn't move. Where, he asked with a grin, would he find four rooms for fifty bucks a month in Lincoln Park?

To celebrate his twenty-first birthday Miguel threw a party at his place. Priscilla and I left early to drive Jazzman to meet Fred Hampton at the Black Panther Party office. After dropping him off we decided to go home instead of returning to the party. At first when we were awakened by a loud banging on the door, I wished we had returned to the party. I felt certain that only the cops would make so much noise so late at night and gave Priscilla hurried instructions on whom to call and what to say and orders not to stir unless I called her. Then I put on a robe and struggled down to the door, where the banging had never let up. It was Angel in his undershirt, excited, mad, sad but coherent. His shirt had been ripped escaping and he had discarded it to avoid being identified, but as he always seemed to do, he had squirmed free. Everyone else at the party had been busted or detained, he thought. Despite his excitement Angel told his story in detail, but essentially it was a simple one.

The party was noisy – in Lincoln Park the noise probably would not have attracted undue attention but these were Puerto Rican kids in Bridgeport – and an off duty cop, who was across the street painting his mother's house, pounded on the door and told people to shut up. Some of the kids at the party taunted and jeered the guy in the paint stained t-shirt claiming to be a cop, and an argument ensued. One of the kids had the inevitable Saturday night special and it got passed around, "as a hint," Angel insisted. It was not used or even pointed. They all thought they were playing a game with a guy no one believed was a pig until he proved his identity by stepping back, dropping to one knee and firing into the crowd.

He might have killed them all if he hadn't been so close that Roberto, an ex-marine recently returned from Nam, could leap from the porch and grab his arm so the third shot went wild. Angel and three other Young Lords quickly piled on and together they wrestled the gun from the cop's hand and kicked it away. Sal was shot in the head, and Juan Martos, another Young Lord, was shot through the neck, the bullet narrowly missing his windpipe. When on-duty cops arrived in force four of the kids who grabbed the killer were arrested (and later charged with aggravated assault of a police officer), but Angel got away.

▲ ▲ ▲

Historian: *I'm confused. I thought Sal was Raphael.*
Novelist: *He was and Raphael was only wounded, not killed. There were two problems here, one personal, one literary. I didn't know Manuel Ramos. I had seen him around, but I never talked to him. I don't think I ever heard him say anything, so I had no idea how to depict him. The second problem was worse. Since he had never appeared as a character, his being killed has no impact. I had two choices: I could create a fictional character with his name earlier in the book or I could let someone my readers know be the one killed, and Sal was almost killed. Also Sal was prominent early on, but after he was shot he pretty much dropped out of the action. Since he wasn't going to be around anyhow, it seemed easiest for him to be the one killed.*

Historian: *That's a major change.*

Novelist: *Only to us. It's a change that only people who knew the guys can notice.*

Historian: *It's a big twist of truth, and to me it seems unnecessary. I'm beginning to understand why you couldn't use people's real names.*

Novelist: *Call it what it is to you, a lie. It's true in the context of the novel. There the truth would be clumsy, the novel read poorly. For me reality is a prison, fiction is the art of freedom.*

Historian: *How can I use this in my project? It's fiction to you, but it's history to me. Maybe a footnote.*

Novelist: *Go for it. You're the scholar now. I quit being one more than half a century ago.*

▲ ▲ ▲

ANGEL FINISHED HIS STORY then said he would get Gloria. "Who's Gloria?" I asked. "Sal's wife." "Sal has a wife?" I exclaimed in surprise. "Sure, and two kids. I may have to stay with them when Gloria comes here."

After Angel left the phone rang and Jim Dennis, a Waller High School teacher who had been at the party, confirmed everything. He said that Juan was alive but that he had seen Sal's body and thought he must be dead. The cops had released Jim (he being white, middle class and Irish), and he was on his way to Mercy Hospital. I told him to find out for sure and call me right back.

Gloria arrived alone and frantic. Angel had told her Sal was hurt but not how badly. I told Gloria what I knew, omitting that Sal was probably dead, and Priscilla and I tried, not very successfully, to comfort her. Then Jim called back and said Sal was dead and Juan critical. I had to tell Gloria but didn't know how. I stared at her unable to speak. She had always stayed home and out of politics like a good Latin wife. She was tiny and fragile looking, neat despite being dragged out of bed at three in the morning, pure black waves of hair around a small, smooth olive face with black eyes that looked to me big with fear and knowledge. She knows, I thought. My face has told her. I said the words: "He's dead." She hadn't known. I had been sudden, brutal. She screamed and fainted but Priscilla caught her. I began dialling a doctor, but she revived and insisted she did not want a doctor; she wanted to know what happened, not be sedated.

Her frail body had a reserve of strength which was to make her a symbol and a leader to the women of the Young Lords and the community. She led the fight to bring free day care to the community, a fight which resulted in Jazzman's one criminal conviction, the one which sent him first underground, later to prison. Priscilla and I stayed with the twenty-year-old widow that terrible night and most of the next sad day. During the night she alternated between hysterical weeping and rage, but by dawn these were replaced by a profound sadness. She called for her babies (two and not quite one year of age), held them and tried to explain that they would never see their father again. After an hour she allowed a friend to take them away and sat trying to talk to us and some of her friends but lapsing into long silences which ended in convulsive crying. I felt rage, which I controlled lest it lead to more hysteria in Gloria.

Only after I left her with Priscilla did I fully feel the sadness, silence and fear which vibrated from Gloria. In the afternoon I accompanied a male lawyer and a female law student to Miguel's apartment. When the shots had been fired a dozen or more people were jammed into a four by four foot vestibule sunk a few inches below the front doorstep. Nothing had been cleaned, and now that vestibule was filled with congealed blood, thick, deep red, with a dull sheen which was probably a film of dust deposited by Chicago's air.

I had never seen anyone faint before Gloria did it, but the technique need not be studied. The law student caught me and got me into a chair. I revived but my stomach was tight, all my fears concentrated there until we escaped that ghastly house and neighbourhood. The human body has so much blood, so much life in it. I wouldn't have believed it held so much, and seeing it concentrated in one place sickened me, yet my stomach was too knotted in fear to respond to the nausea I felt. That little lake of blood haunted my dreams for years. The lawyer and student dug deep into the ceiling to retrieve the third bullet, a big flattened forty-five shell. Then they tape recorded extensive notes on the physical layout while I laboured not to look at the blood puddle.

When we opened the back door and stepped onto the porch, a man came to the screen door of the next apartment. "You dirty spics," he shouted at us, three middle class whites. "Didn't you learn your lesson last night? This is a peaceful neighbourhood. We don't want your kind. They should have killed the whole lot of you. You quit snooping and get the hell out of here. I'm calling the police right now." We got the hell out of there. My stomach didn't begin to relax until we were back in Lincoln Park. Years later, when I moved out of Lincoln Park to the southwest side, just south of Bridgeport, the man at the screen door with his horrible, irrational hatred joined the lake of blood in my nightmares.

THE NEXT NIGHT WE MARCHED on the police station in Bridgeport, where Sal's murderer was stationed. There were only several hundred of us because Bridgeport was a long way and we had to jam people into every available car to get them there. There were probably as many people from the rest of the city as from Lincoln Park: Fred Hampton and a large contingent of Black Panthers plus numerous white radicals, both old and new left. As I drove off the Dan Ryan Expressway past White Sox Park, I saw that one section of the parking lot housed an army in blue and white squad cars, paddy wagons and mobile jails, huge police vans used to arrest large numbers of people at demonstrations. There might have been as many as a hundred police vehicles. The police were present in force to protect their leader. What none of us from Lincoln Park knew but every cop and reporter in the city did was that the Bridgeport Police Station was located on the same block as Mayor Daley's house. The police and media had all been told we were planning to storm the mayor's house.

Our protest must have been very disappointing to the police and reporters. The reporters kept asking questions about the mayor. It took a long time to persuade them we were marching to the police station, not Hizzoner's house, and when they were convinced, most left and the story got little play in the newspapers. That made me mad since I had wasted my time trying to explain to a group of reporters that a man, a father of two young children, was dead and twenty people could identify his killer, yet the authorities had no intention of placing the killer on trial and letting our incomparable system of justice determine his guilt or innocence. No, they were only going to try four people who risked their lives to prevent more bloodshed. We asked only for a pretence of justice.

No one reading any of the Chicago daily newspapers could have determined that this was the simple reason for all our marches and protests after the murder of Sal Ramirez. Not only was the legal system protecting the killer and prosecuting the innocent, it was also making it impossible to present our side of the story. The police fed the media story after story which the media presented verbatim, never mentioning that today's "news" contradicted yesterday's. One story had the assault of the arrested four occurring before the shooting; another claimed Sal had threatened his killer with a gun; another said that people at the party had shot at residents before the cop arrived.

A day or two after the incident the police claimed to find a gun supposedly used by Sal. "That's funny," a Young Lord told me, "the piece we had is at my crib." Apparently Angel was not the only one who escaped. As usual the "drop gun" had a rough handle and no fingerprints. I doubt if we could have got our side of the story printed; certainly no reporter seemed interested in getting it. But we could not tell it anyhow: Our lawyers forbade public statements by witnesses. Anything said now might be used against the four at their trial. Even a slight difference in an account presented now and one presented at the trial could be used to impugn a witness. (After almost two years of legal wrangling the assault charges were dropped without a trial. Whether the contradictory public statements by the police hurt the prosecutor's case I do not know. I like to think charges were dropped because there never was a case against the four. Charges were laid as a smokescreen to the public, to prevent us from telling our story, and to tie up valuable bail money. The plot succeeded in these aims although no Young Lords went to jail.)

I was about to write that the march itself resembled a funeral march, but that isn't correct. The funeral march the next day was a powerful event, a sad but strong and united people laying a hero to rest before resuming the struggle which would vindicate him. The few cops in sight had to muster all their courage to drive by that march in closed squad cars. But in Bridgeport it felt as if there were more cops than marchers. The cops marched in single file lines on both sides of us, taunting, glowering, waiting impatiently for a chance to use their clubs on our heads. And I kept thinking of the army of reinforcements lurking in the parking lot. I had to recall Gloria's face after I told her Sal was dead in order to make myself mad enough or brave enough to join the marchers' half-hearted chants and songs. At other demonstrations the shouting and singing expressed people's feelings; at this one they were an attempt to hide our feelings, our fear.

At the station itself more police and barricades behind a solid line of cops to prevent anyone from venturing down the street toward the mayor's house. We paraded around a while and requested an audience with the commander, who duly appeared, argued a minute or two with

Jazzman, then announced over a bullhorn that we had ten minutes to disperse. I was more than ready to go, but Jazzman came over with a grin on his face, asked me some questions about the theory of relativity, then invited me to talk some more with the commander. "It won't do much good, but I doubt if it will get us killed."

If I hadn't been so scared, I could reproduce the conversation better, but basically Jazzman explained the theory of relativity to the incredulous cop. "Physical laws are the same for all coordinate systems moving uniformly relative to one another," he quoted. Then he showed how the commander was following one set of laws based on a coordinate system running parallel to Mayor Daley's house while we were operating in a nonparallel system, one which demanded an entirely different set of laws and actions from him. "In other words," he concluded, "we never came to bug the mayor and we'll promise not to go near the mayor's crib if you negotiate seriously with us about your cop who shot our friend Sal."

The commander's expression was worth the terrible trip. After he got over being stunned, he glowered and said: "Kid ..." Then he broke into a laugh and asked: "Kid, how would you like to be a cop?" When Jazzman declined, he said: "If you ever change your mind, come see me. Now get your friends out of here and don't go near Lowe Street (where the mayor's house was). No one will get hurt or arrested. If you want an indictment, you've got to go to the States Attorney."

The commander turned and conferred with some of his subordinates while we in the crowd milled around a little longer to show we weren't afraid, then left because we were. Once again I felt relieved as soon as I was back in Lincoln Park. It was my turf as much as it was the Young Lords'. Mental laws were not the same in other coordinate systems.

THE NEXT DAY WAS THE FUNERAL. St. Mary's Church was packed. It was Lincoln Park's poor Roman Catholic Church, the one mostly attended by Latins, and not large as Catholic churches go. Still it had pews for hundreds of people, and every seat was full and the aisles as well. In death Sal Ramirez became the inspiration he never quite was in life. At his funeral a movement mourned. Black Panthers and white radicals filed into the church along with the Puerto Rican community of Lincoln Park. Two rival motorcycle gangs arrived together, black armbands over their blue jean jackets, parked their bikes behind the hearse and trooped side by side into the church. Every minister in the North Side Cooperative Ministry was there as was almost every shop-keeper on Armitage. Police in street clothes from the Black Patrolmen's League defied their superiors and attended as mourners. A minister and a priest from Bridgeport brought a few of their parishioners to show that some people from that neighbourhood cared. Ordinary folks from the Cabrini-Green projects, Wicker Park, Lakeview and Uptown joined their sisters and brothers from Lincoln Park.

The service was one of silences. What could be said? During the pauses we could hear Gloria's sobs and softer echoes from all over the sanctuary. The procession to the cemetery was a mile long, a mile of clenched fists. The bikers behind the funeral cars began it. As they revved their motors, each of them raised a fist. Behind them every car window opened and fists challenged the skies and the cops (almost none of whom were visible) all the way to the cemetery. Our sadness only intensified our hope. It was spring and we were young and as together as the fingers of our clenched fists. They might murder some of us, but our movement would continue to grow. We knew that by murdering Sal the police had made us angrier, and making us angrier simply hastened the coming of their downfall.

In the crowd at the cemetery I noticed Mama Jane. At that time I just called her Jane. She wore a fancy black dress several sizes too large for her. She was pulling the older baby by the hand and carrying the younger. I had met Jane the previous summer when I was canvassing and had occasionally seen her on the streets since then. She was utterly poor and uneducated with so many of her own problems I would never have expected her to have time to worry about others. I went over to her out of curiosity. This was a movement funeral. She knew nothing of politics. Why should she care about a Puerto Rican youth?

"When my husband died," she told me, "I thought I would never get mad again. But when I heard about that poor boy getting shot for no rea-son and him the father of two babies just like my Bob, I got more angry than I ever did over Bob. I'm glad I come to the funeral and see all these people as mad as me. Before I felt like I was a sister to that poor girl who was his wife because she's a widow now like me. Now I feel hope. All of us here are like sisters and brothers, and together we're going to change things so when our babies grow up they won't have to be afraid their hus-bands are going to get killed just because they're poor or Puerto Rican."

NEXT CAME ANOTHER MARCH to another police-community relations meeting at the Eighteenth District Police Station. State's Attorney Hanrahan, the man who would soon become so notorious for planning the murder of Fred Hampton that even the Democratic Machine could not re-nominate him, was scheduled to speak. Our demand of him was simple: indict the cop who shot Sal. Three months of repression and a murder had made a big difference in the number of people supporting us and their mood. There were close to two thousand protesters by the time we reached Chicago Avenue. Although there had been little time for advance publicity, the march snaked through Lincoln Park, then the Cabrini-Green black housing project, and people flocked from their homes to march. We were serious, angry. No more laughter or dancing. It felt good to see people pour out of their houses to join us, but we could not feel happy.

The confrontation was not what anyone expected. As the front of the march neared the police station, Mama Jane came running up holding her bleeding head. With her was Jill, a baby in each arm and several children running after her. Mama Jane cried while Jill panted out the news: The rear of the march was being attacked by black kids in red berets. Mama Jane had been hit by a rock. I couldn't figure out any reason for the attack, but the Young Lords knew. As the word reached them at the head of the march, they began filtering toward the rear.

"Cobrastones, let's go," shouted Sancho as he passed me trying to wipe the blood off Mama Jane. The march was stopping because the front had reached the police barricades guarding the station. Later Priscilla and others told me how the police had threatened and jostled the demonstrators there and how the police-community relations meeting was cancelled due to the arrival of the community and the failure to arrive of the State's Attorney. But I was at the rear, where the action was.

The Cobrastones were proud of being the baddest, maddest kids on the near north side of Chicago. They were part of the Black P Stone Nation. Cabrini-Green was their turf and we had marched right through it. Jazzman had contacted several groups in Cabrini-Green who were supporting the march, but the Cobrastones fought the other groups inside their community. So not only did they refuse to join the march but now they were defending their turf from both their black enemies and the mass of brown and white invaders from the north.

The scene at Chicago Avenue and LaSalle Street might have been believable if it had not been happening at Chicago and LaSalle, one of a big city's busier intersections. Out in a field with opposing armies dug into trenches it would have seemed appropriate. Yet somehow the city felt like a field: There seemed to be no cars and lots of space although tall buildings blocked out most of the darkening sky and two thousand people were jammed in just to the east. At the west end of that conglomeration of people the crowd was sparse and consisted almost entirely of young males. Most wore purple berets, and several purple bereted soldiers patrolled an invisible line that stretched between buildings across Chicago Avenue and its sidewalks. They were warning people to stay back, not to cross the invisible line.

Beyond them, to the west, lay a no man's land perhaps thirty feet wide and then, behind another patrolled invisible line, another army, this one clad in red berets. A continuous barrage of taunts sailed back and forth across the empty no man's land. Occasionally a taunt was accompanied by a rock or other missile from the Cobrastone lines. General Jazzman kept his army under control, constantly urging them to stay cool and not throw anything under any circumstances. Many of his troops grumbled to be so restrained but all obeyed orders.

Jazzman also kept calling out to the enemy for a truce, and finally, through some mysterious channel, a truce was arranged and Jazzman, flanked by Sancho and another lieutenant, advanced to the middle of no man's land to parlay with three Cobrastones. As they came together, one of the Cobrastones snatched a purple beret from the second lieutenant's head and fled back to his own lines followed by his two comrades. A cheer rose up from the other side. The purple beret was tossed back and forth and up and down among the enemy; their insults became more cutting and increased in number and volume.

On our side Jazzman no longer calmed the faction favouring all out war. Sancho was organizing an expedition. Both sides accepted the stolen hat as an unquestioned symbol of a Cobrastone victory, and the Young Lords were not about to give it up without a battle. A bonfire appeared on the other side and the whooping and dancing increased as the beret sailed back and forth across the flames. The fervour to save the cap mounted on our side. Then a lone figure moved into the no man's land.

Juanita Rilco was a Mexican woman married to a white radical. She wore a purple beret and was the toughest looking four-foot-ten inch, forty-year-old grandmother in the world. As she strode slowly across the open space there was utter silence. As she approached the fire, the leader of the Cobrastones, who must have been a foot and a half taller than Juanita, held the beret over his head. Juanita walked up to him, said: "Give me my brother's hat," stretched out an arm which had to be four feet long to overcome the physical distance, snatched the cap, turned and strode slowly back to our side. The silence on both sides remained unbroken.

Then someone ran up to announce that Hanrahan hadn't shown and the meeting was cancelled. After some confusion the Young Lords at the rear led the marchers back towards Lincoln Park. The Cobrastones who had blocked the way moments before had vanished. But later I saw several of them off to the side of the marchers talking to Jazzman. A few weeks later, when we took over McCormick Seminary, the Cobrastones were with us.

14.

McCORMICK WAS A PRESBYTERIAN SEMINARY. It was like a small clearcut in a large forest or, to use a more accurate image, like a gated suburb within the heart of Lincoln Park. It occupied two square blocks between Halsted and Sheffield, Fullerton and Belden and included classroom buildings, a large well-stocked library, dormitories for students, spacious single-family houses for faculty, a daycare centre and playground for staff and students' children only, and a huge new administration building constructed on a donation of over a million dollars from W. Clement Stone, a Chicago insurance tycoon who was also the biggest single donor to Nixon's 1968 campaign fund. This village within our community was enclosed behind a tall, black wrought-iron fence. It lacked only stores to make it self-sufficient, and supermarkets, clothing stores, a bank and numerous small shops were less than a block away on Lincoln, Halsted or Fullerton Streets. So those within the seminary's fence seldom needed to look at, let alone interact with, the neighbourhood they were in.

Nevertheless, the seminary did interact with the neighbourhood. Its spokespeople often proclaimed its sympathy with Lincoln Park and the struggles of the populace. Simultaneous with these loud proclamations of sympathy McCormick was quietly strengthening its fences. Since the Fifties a debate had gone on among the seminary's administrators and trustees. They saw that Lincoln Park was becoming less middle class. To them this meant it was becoming less safe for their institution: Good fences don't necessarily make downtrodden people good neighbours; sometimes fences make them wonder what is being concealed; sometimes they get angry at finding themselves fenced out of their own community. Besides, as the neighbourhood became less middle class, the property value of the seminary's land would decrease. Something had to be done.

One faction of McCormick's directors favoured selling out and moving to a safe suburb; another favoured "upgrading" Lincoln Park. The upgraders prevailed at first. (However, eventually the movers won out, and in the mid-Seventies McCormick sold its land and buildings to DePaul University and moved to the suburbs.) In 1955 McCormick was one of the main forces behind the founding of the Lincoln Park

Conservation Association, which promptly asked the city to designate Lincoln Park for urban renewal. The seminary also signed a secret agreement with the other two major institutions in Lincoln Park, DePaul University and Children's Memorial Hospital, to remain in the area and "improve" it, to move out poor people rather than move out themselves.

Early in 1969 a McCormick faculty member unburdened his conscience by showing Meg a copy of the 1955 secret agreement. The Lincoln Park *Press* began pointing to McCormick's hypocrisy and campaigning for it to back its liberal rhetoric with support for programs to keep poor people in Lincoln Park and give them control over their lives. This campaign culminated in a list of ten demands made by a Poor People's Coalition formed for the purpose. The main demand was for seed money to create a corporation to build resident-controlled, low rent housing. Other demands included funds to set up a community-controlled legal office, a community-controlled day care centre, a community-controlled free medical clinic, a Puerto Rican cultural centre and other alternative institutions to be run for and by poor people in Lincoln Park.

McCormick was not expected to give all this money, simply to use its name and resources to help us raise it. After all, it had recently raised millions of dollars for its own expansion. Our demands were paltry next to this and next to the millions of urban renewal-land speculation dollars McCormick had helped bring in to destroy our community. One demand was non-monetary: We asked the seminary to remove its fence.

Although we demanded instead of begging, our demands were negotiable. The Poor People's Coalition was formed to negotiate them. Its core was Concerned Citizens of Lincoln Park, the Young Lords Organization and the Latin American Defense Organization (LADO), a militant community organization from the West Division Street (Wicker Park) Puerto Rican ghetto. Because everything we demanded would benefit the entire community, several traditional organizations and church groups were drawn towards the coalition. At first they dared not join. They accepted our priorities, even agreed that McCormick should raise the funds. But we were demanding, not requesting, and prepared to act to enforce our demands. This frightened them.

After McCormick agreed to our demands, however, they were anxious to join and participated in the community planning that went into such projects as the Poor People's Coalition Housing Development and the Free People's Health Center. On the other hand, several groups of street kids, especially the Cobrastones and the Black Action Group (BAG), two traditional rivals from southern Lincoln Park and Cabrini-Green, had little interest in our programs but joined the coalition because they wanted to be in on the action. When the occupation of McCormick ended, they dropped away from the coalition although we sometimes mentioned their names when McCormick acted too slowly to fulfill its bargain.

During the spring of 1969 we negotiated with McCormick and received assurances of the seminary's love for us and vague promises to study ways of helping us. Nothing more. After Sal's murder we felt great frustration at being unable to bring his murderer to any semblance of justice. One afternoon Mick Finnigan phoned the office and reported that the pig that shot Sal was in an Old Town bar, drunk, showing off the murder weapon and bragging of the deed. Meg, Jazzman, Sancho, I and a few other good sized Young Lords rushed to the bar, but the killer was gone. That evening we met with McCormick. They talked and stalled. We gave them an ultimatum and walked out.

Meg always did her homework. She included a date in the ultimatum. The date was in late May, the day before the opening of a national Presbyterian conference in San Antonio, Texas. The head of LADO was planning to attend that conference to try to get Presbyterian support for his organization. He would represent the Poor People's Coalition as well. The night before the conference was to begin a group of sympathetic seminarians opened the gates of McCormick and the doors of its new administration building, and Jazzman and a few other Young Lords walked in. By morning about thirty members of the Young Lords Organization and Concerned Citizens of Lincoln Park were occupying the building while the students patrolled the gates and grounds. About fifty more people, primarily from the Cobrastones, BAG and the Latin Princes, a neighbourhood gang the Young Lords were trying to politicize, joined us by afternoon.

Our six day holiday in the plush Sal Ramirez Memorial Hotel, as we quickly renamed the W. Clement Stone Building and proclaimed to the world in gaudy banners hung from the windows, gave me my best opportunity to observe the Young Lords Organization in action. The YLO ran the show, and their show ran in an environment as spectacularly artificial as my mountains are natural. Sixty or seventy or eighty or more people, mostly between eighteen and twenty-five and from several groups, some traditional enemies, were living in a luxurious building but one built for administering, not living. The kids were usually too cool to say anything or act impressed, but if you watched closely the first time they saw the place, you could often catch "the wow look in their eyes."

The artificial environment created situations which could never have arisen otherwise and intensified problems which might have been insignificant under more normal conditions. The most obvious and funny situations arose from dropping kids who had experienced nothing but poverty into what to them was the lap of luxury. The lack of beds and kitchen facilities wasn't even noticed, for most of these kids had often slept on floors considerably harder than the rugs they could sleep on here and seldom done any cooking during their lives. Besides, there were plenty of soft couches and armchairs, and supporters in the community cooked up big, delicious meals and brought them in.

What was noticed were lush rugs, drapery, furniture, office equipment, mechanical gadgets, etc. Kids who had never seen a rug that was much more than an oversized towel got down on hands and knees to examine the two inch pile. Dollar signs lit up eyes of young burglars when they gazed upon electric typewriters, dictaphones and vending machines. As word spread, more and more youthful visitors dropped in and received full tours from friends inside. The high point of the tour was always the president's suite, the most lavish part of the building. It evoked rhapsodies from the tourists and comments from the guides like: "These chumps want us to believe they don't have the bread to meet our demands. Shit man, I could make enough money to build an apartment building by fencing the stuff in this room."

Several people tried to walk out carrying electric typewriters. When told there was to be no ripping off, they looked puzzled, but when it was explained that we were trying to get hundreds of thousands of dollars for the community and needed to hold the seminary's property for ransom, they usually nodded knowingly and returned the machines. Security, originally established at dances to keep weapons and unwanted people out, soon found its main job to be searching all those leaving – Jazzman made sure he was searched every time he left the building to set the example – for souvenirs, a pile of which was always sitting on the security tables to be taken back where they belonged. The most difficult task the leaders faced during the entire occupation was persuading their followers to leave after the seminary agreed to meet our demands. It was the best life these kids had ever had, and they didn't want to give it up.

Not that they had no social consciousness or awareness of why they were there. Even those who came to the seminary on a lark could not stay long and avoid the continuous political education – both semi-formal classes and informal rap sessions and conversations – in the air. A radical lecture circuit formed spontaneously. Radical university professors, labour organizers, lawyers and other professionals did classes on economics, government, the third world, Marxism and law; seminarians lectured on the role of McCormick in the exploitation of the community and the world through its ownership of stock in multinational corporations, including many with large investments in South Africa; community people came in to talk informally about community problems. It was as if time itself had been temporarily liberated. Everybody knew there would not be another chance for all those gathered in McCormick to be together inside again, except perhaps inside jail. Everywhere there was an eagerness to use the precious time to learn as well as enjoy.

Jazzman was as impressed by the new surroundings as any of the other ghetto kids although he had been to the suburbs on fund raising expeditions and knew what luxury looked like. Also he had been shown around the Ramirez Memorial Hotel by friendly students a few days before we took it over. Indeed it was at that time that Jazzman renamed the place. But a few hours after the takeover I came upon him leaving the president's suite.

"Dick," he said, his tired eyes almost twinkling, "keep reminding me that we're in here for the community, not to enjoy ourselves, because every time I get near this damn office, I want to lock myself in there and stretch out on that huge, soft sofa for a few weeks. At the least I want to make my headquarters in there even though I know it would set a bad example to the guys."

So I did begin to remind him. I spoke of our strategy meeting and the decision not to use any of the fancy offices to make sure the place was in as good condition as possible when we returned it. He looked annoyed, then laughed, patted me on the head and said: "Don't worry, little Dick" (I was half a head taller than he), "I won't let crass personal desires interfere with the revolution." Then off he dashed. It was the first time he had ever chided me in that way, and it left me feeling like a jilted lover. We were both tired, and I had lectured him like a child, so no doubt I had earned some scorn, but that knowledge couldn't sooth me. The incident started me thinking about some things I had been trying to avoid.

I hadn't talked seriously with Jazzman in months. I knew that the phenomenal growth I had witnessed during the last part of 1968 had not stopped, could see Jazzman gaining self-confidence, decisiveness, strength. But his jest forced me to admit I did not know what he was growing into. Suddenly I feared he may have grown away from me or grown too fast for me to keep up with him. I had been involved in every public political decision he had made, liked to think I was as much a part of the decision making as he, had even participated in his private life by driving him to meet his girlfriend, Lisa, and his baby daughter several times. Yet I knew I was not aware of his intimate thoughts and feelings as I had been before January.

I had persuaded myself that events were moving too fast to allow the leisurely discussions of bygone days; still I pined for deep discussions and suspected that Jazzman had been avoiding them. Several times I had driven him around and so spent half an hour with him in the car, but our conversation had been superficial. I might have pushed for something more, but I did not like to push a friend and with Jazzman it had never before been necessary. Now Jazzman's jibe made me determined to use some of our time together in McCormick to speak privately and either revitalize our friendship or discover what new paths my friend had taken so I could choose whether or not to try to follow.

The next time I was able to speak with him was with Meg. The three of us were preparing a statement on the occupation. I had written a draft which mentioned "socialism;" Meg disapproved of the word. It was a debate Meg and I had often: Meg claimed that most people were not ready for discussions of socialism and that the word automatically turned them off; I contended that they would never be ready if we did not begin discussing it and that it would be dishonest to hide our convictions. In the *Press* the word appeared in my articles but not in Meg's. Here Jazzman would have to resolve the dispute.

"It's a problem," he admitted. "We've all been brought up with this supernatural fear of socialism and communism; they're like the devil. So Meg is right: The word 'socialism' turns people off. But," Jazzman continued, ignoring my half-hearted attempt to interrupt, "we also have to say that we don't support what gets called 'democracy' because we desire real democracy, not capitalist democracy. We can't use the word 'democracy' either. The capitalists have urban renewed that one. If only we could get away from all the 'issys' and 'isms' and just talk about everyday dudes, just plain people. That's what I like about dealing with my people: They're poor and humble and want solutions to their problems but not solutions imposed on them. They don't give a damn about names. They only want the power to work out their own solutions. You can talk to them as ordinary folks and don't have to make speeches and mass appeals. The word gets around pretty quick. That's why I don't write much or make public speeches. If I have to use an 'ism,' I say 'people-ism.'"

"Populism." I blurted out the correction.

"No, 'people-ism.' Populism's something old and phony. It's something that has never worked and no one understands. It's a name that gets thrown around by politicians who talk slower than other politicians but whose program is the same as the fast talking politicians: to get elected. 'People-ism' is awkward to say. There's nothing intellectual sounding about it. Educated people like you even think it's a mistake when they first hear it, but ordinary folks know it means them so they like it."

I had said the wrong thing again, but Jazzman was right. I would never be able to say or write "people-ism." Still I admired the feeling behind the word and the thought which had gone into its invention. Hearing Jazzman's explanation made me desire a private talk with him more than ever. But other issues, some drab as the weather outside my window, arose and had to be settled first.

Since Jazzman returned to Lincoln Park, Lisa and the baby had been living with Lisa's mother in Wicker Park. The mother was a fervent Pentecostal who spent most of her time praying and reminding her daughter of sin in general and the particular sin represented by the baby. Now Lisa always seemed to be at McCormick during the day. Sometimes she brought the baby, sometimes not. Whether her strict mother was relaxing the restrictions she imposed or whether Lisa could always get out when she really wanted to, I do not know. I suspect the latter, for Lisa had a style to her wheedling which could only have developed through much practice and frequent success. Probably she could get around her mother in all but the older woman's most resolute stances.

Before the occupation Lisa had preferred not to come to Lincoln Park and only did so when she could see Jazzman no other way. When Jazzman came to Wicker Park, he came without buddies and so gave full attention to Lisa. In Lincoln Park there were many people and things to distract Jazzman from her and few places she could feel comfortable. This was especially bad because relaxing was almost impossible for Lisa under the best of circumstances. It seemed as if every time she came to Lincoln Park, she ended up pacing the streets laboriously lugging the baby, who would have preferred to toddle, her face exhausted yet almost blissful in martyrdom.

The seminary was good for Lisa. There was plenty of room, places to sit down, people who would talk to her (something Young Lords seldom did) and watch the baby. She often seemed almost at ease, even joined in political discussions. Lisa's everyday family life gave her almost no chance to get away from herself, her problems, her guilt; McCormick did. She formulated a new plan: to return to Puerto Rico with Jazzman and set up a day care centre for women there. Every time she saw me at McCormick, she spoke of the poverty and oppression of Puerto Rican women on their island, how their husbands have to work long hours and are rarely home and when they are they expect to be served all the time, do no housework and beat their wives.

Her indignation against injustice, usually reserved for her own suffering, became almost eloquent rather than whining; her fantasies, usually pure self indulgence, became almost altruistic; her developing religious fanaticism was replaced by social and political fanaticism. In the seminary she began to conceive of herself jailed instead of crucified. Perhaps during the months after the occupation, when she tried to hang on to her new-found political ideals, she conceived of jail as a place with the warmth of comradeship she briefly felt at McCormick. If she had to be martyred – and to her the one thing Jazzman and her mother seemed to agree on was that she did – why not suffer among friends? Fifteen-year-olds lack the dedication and sophistication of more experienced martyrs.

Lisa and Jazzman stood outside a doorway, the baby, Donna, behind her mother. An artist would have revelled in the angles they made, none approaching the perpendicular: Donna, tilting sideways toward open space, clung to her mother's pantleg, which was the only thing preventing her from bolting down the corridor; Lisa leaned the other way, toward Jazzman, her hands clasped tightly as if each were straining to prevent the other from grabbing the man; Jazzman's hand gripped the knob of the closed door, and his body seemed poised in the act of passing through it. But his face and conversation were serious, patient, seemed to belie a body bent on escape.

As I approached, Jazzman was explaining something to Lisa, who was either misunderstanding or disagreeing. It was their usual too tense attitude, so I made my usual attempt to lighten the atmosphere. I snatched Donna and threw her into the air. She suffered my excesses with stoicism, but when I pretended to run off with her she reached for Lisa. I threw her to Jazzman, who caught her, ruffled her curly hair, kissed her and set her down. She promptly reattached herself to her mother's pantleg.

"Dick, can Lisa and Donna stay with Priscilla tonight? She wants to sleep over, but I'm afraid of a bust." Scarcely an hour went by during the occupation without a new rumour of an impending police raid.

"Why can't I just leave the baby with Priscilla?"

Poor Priscilla. At least she liked babies. "I can't volunteer her. Call her up and ask if you like. Or wait a while. She'll be over this afternoon with dinner."

That night Lisa and Donna stayed with Priscilla. The next day Priscilla was upset: "Dick, you've got to do something. Lisa's mother is going to throw her out and Jazzman doesn't want her and the baby to move in with him."

"Has her mother actually thrown her out?"

"No, but she's so sure it's going to happen she's afraid to go back home at all."

"So she wants to move in with Jazzman right now?"

"Yes, she took most of her things and Donna's things in a suitcase when she left her mother's place."

"And what am I supposed to do about all this?"

"You've got to talk to Jazzman."

"I've been wanting to talk to Jazzman for months. There's too much going on, too little time. Why do you think he doesn't want her staying with him? He doesn't even have his own place, just stays with various friends. Half the time he doesn't even sleep at night."

"That's what Lisa says too. She's very worried about him. She wants to make a stable home for him."

"I refuse to meddle in this. Jazzman doesn't need a mother, and apparently he doesn't want a wife right now."

"But what about Lisa?"

"Why didn't she think about any of this before she packed up and left her mother's? How can someone move out with a baby and no place to go?"

"For god's sake, Dick, she's still a child. She's barely sixteen." She must have added a year for Priscilla's sake.

"And you want Jazzman, who is not only working day and night in Lincoln Park and Chicago but also trying to organize a national Puerto Rican movement, who already hardly sleeps at all as far as I can tell, you want him to look after a child and her baby as well?" Young Puerto Ricans from New York had recently visited Chicago to discuss forming a New York chapter of the Young Lords Organization. Jazzman was planning a trip there and to other cities with sizeable Puerto Rican populations.

"What do you want Lisa to do, curl up and die?"

"Go back home to mama." My god, was I really saying this?

Anger had been mounting in both of us. Now Priscilla's southern rage exploded: "Hooray for the great liberator, the great freedom fighter, the supporter of women's liberation, the encourager of independent adolescents, the man who says even children should be free to run their own lives. Just let his precious Jazzman into the discussion and watch his ideals fly out the window. Let freedom or independence inconvenience Jazzman and see what happens."

"Do you have a better solution?" I shouted. Suddenly my anger vanished and I groaned inwardly. The better solution was all too obvious: We even had an extra bedroom that Priscilla used as a studio.

Priscilla had the idea at the same time. We stared at each other for a long time until Priscilla shook her head. "I'm sorry. I guess I'm not ready for that."

"I hate myself for saying so, but I'm awfully glad," I admitted.

We embraced each other with tears in our eyes. I tried to break the spell by quoting Brecht: "Alas, we who wished to lay the foundations of kindness could not ourselves be kind."

Later I talked to Juanita Rilko, by far the most mature mind associated with the Young Lords. Her primary concern was the same as mine, that Lisa's petulant possessiveness would hinder Jazzman's work. Just as I did not suggest that Juanita might take Lisa into her apartment, so she did not suggest that I might take her into mine. Although we both knew that Lisa was not yet capable of caring for herself and her daughter and both knew we could help, neither of us was willing to accept such a burden.

No doubt Lisa would have taken up much of our time just as she would have taken up Jazzman's and no doubt that would have made it more difficult to organize for the revolution. So Lisa and Donna were sacrificed for the cause: Juanita and I spoke to her, persuaded her that she could talk her mother into taking her back and that she could help her people more by raising a strong child than she could in the middle of the struggle. I drove her back to Wicker Park. Within a year she was beseeching us to repent, for the Judgment Day was nigh. And by then it looked as if she might be right.

DID THIS UNIFORMLY GREY WEATHER bring Lisa back to my mind? I know the weather here affects my writing about Chicago. Had I subconsciously hoped to exclude Lisa from this chronicle? The days crowd together, all alike, some with a little more snow, some a little less. Only the feet of the mountains are visible. There is no sun during the brief day, no stars at night. The only breaks in the gray-white world are patches of green and brown in the woods and the filthy snow banks, taller than I am, piled on both sides of the road by the snowplough. Lisa is a woman now. Is she standing on some dirty street corner passing out tracts? Does she furtively send Donna to put the holy papers into the hands of people studiously trying to ignore her at bus stops? Is any good for any number of people worth the waste of a single human soul? The uncountable trees, bowed by their burden of gray snow like the backs of every humanitarian the world has known, are silent. I can conceive of revolution no more than I can conceive of the sun.

I DID GET TO TALK TO JAZZMAN at the seminary. I came upon him sitting half asleep in a comfortable lounge, the other side of which was being used for card games. When he saw me he got up as if to leave, then sat down again. It was the next to last day of the occupation, and he seemed relaxed with Lisa gone, no sign of the police, and high ranking Presbyterians from all over the nation pressuring McCormick to grant our demands. The seminary was stalling, but I felt confident and assumed Jazzman shared my feelings. Hoping for a personal conversation, I asked if he did much reading anymore. He pulled an abridgement of Marx's *Capital* from his pocket and sighed: "I try, but there isn't much time. Maybe that's why our political education classes never seem to get very far. The guys see me marching and rapping and working, but they don't see me reading so they don't read themselves. I wish I could be a better example for them."

"The day is only twenty-four hours long. No one expects you to do everything."

"Yes, someone does."

"Who?"

"Me."

I couldn't find a reply that would not have been another platitude, so I tried to change the subject. "Do you ever think about last fall when you used to come to my pad to borrow books?"

"That was the Garden of Eden. Everything was new and possible. I was Adam, just created. It's hard to believe that was only six months ago."

"But surely more things are possible now." Although I argued, inside I was in agreement.

"With the money and commitments we're going to get from McCormick we can bring real changes to Lincoln Park. If we keep struggling, we can turn this community into a liberated zone like the ones Mao created in China during the Thirties." The creation of liberated zones was a mantra of the day. It was why all the young radicals in the city were trying to move to Lincoln Park, never noticing whose housing they were usurping and what speculators were reaping the profits, never minding that they were leaving the rest of Chicago to the Daley Machine and the right wing.

Jazzman snorted: "You're still trying to live in the Garden of Eden, huh. Don't you ever think about what's going to happen when all these liberated people get together? They're going to fight among themselves. In China the basic situation was simple, two sided and mainly military. If it comes to a real battle here, we don't even know who we'll be fighting: The cops? The National Guard? The army? The Ku Klux Klan? Middle class vigilante groups? Some of our own people bought off by money and media propaganda? Even among us there are almost as many sides as there are people. Look at what's going on here, man. Josie and Cleo are running around telling everyone in sight they were raped by the Cobra-stones. Our so-called supporters in the student body are running out to report every time a piece of chalk gets broken. The blacks are boycotting the political education classes because the instructor is white. Half the Young Lords are spending their time on the street finding chicks they can bring in here and put the make on. When we let some student radicals in yesterday to help us go through the seminary's files, they spent so much time arguing about what to do with the information that we barely got started on the files. And wait 'til you see what happens when we have to leave this place."

Instead of responding I defended myself. What else? Wasn't I in Chicago? Here the mountains do not respect human egos, and I like to think I have learned to control mine a little. At McCormick, for once, my egotism had a good consequence. "Perhaps I do live in the Garden of Eden," I said, ignoring the substance of Jazzman's rap. "But I also spent a lot of my life gambling and know a little about getting out of tough spots. When a good bridge player is in what seems to be a hopeless contract, do you know what he does? He figures out the only distribution of the opponents' cards that will give him a chance, then assumes that distribution exists and plays accordingly, at least until he's forced to cut his losses. It's the same in politics: We have to assume the enemy, the system, is vulnerable and make our plans based on that. If we're wrong … Well, if we're wrong it probably doesn't matter anyhow. The criminals running this country will kill and jail us all. Or they'll blow up the world. Or they'll reduce the human race to idiots and automatons and we'll either become automatons ourselves or go crazy. No doubt the odds are against us, but we have to assume we can beat those odds. If not we might as well commit suicide or become junkies."

"Leave the junkies out of this. We may need them." I suddenly remembered that Jazzman had once been a junkie. I thought he was remembering that too because he paused. Then he looked at me in a way that made me realize he hadn't looked at me seriously for a long time. "Priscilla once told me you used to be a gambler. I never could see you as one. Tell me more about playing cards."

I wound up trying to explain the game of bridge. We borrowed a deck of cards from one of the card tables. They were playing whist, the ancestor of bridge, and Jazzman knew how to play it, which made my task a little easier. I introduced the basic mechanics of bridge and Jazzman surprised me as usual. When I explained what a dummy was, he immediately saw how this added an element of skill lacking in whist. After many questions from him and explanations and illustrations with the cards by me, I laid out a hand in which I could only make a slam if one opponent held no more than one card in a side suit, in which case I could strip him of that card, throw him into the lead, and force him to play away from a key honour in another suit. It was a hand I once played in a national championship, a hand it should have taken a bridge expert to understand. I played it out slowly, card by card, and Jazzman understood.

"But what if he has more than one spade?" he asked. The right question.

"He plays it and I'm defeated an extra trick, but the additional penalty is tiny compared to the bonus for making the contract. Besides, on many hands like this a good player can postpone the final decision, count out the opponents' distribution and cut the losses at the last minute if it is impossible the hoped for distribution exists. And with me, even if I couldn't count out the hands, I usually knew. Against any but the best players in the world and sometimes against them too I knew. I could feel what the situation was and usually make the right play based on my feelings."

Jazzman made me play the hand several times, sometimes changing the opponents' cards to obtain different results. When he understood – I don't see how someone who knew nothing of bridge could have understood, but Jazzman seemed to, just as he always grasped new ideas from books – he smiled in the childlike manner he used to back in the Garden of Eden. "They say Mao learned revolutionary strategy from the game of *Go*. Maybe I just learned something from bridge. It's a cockeyed world. We never know for sure what's happening, but we damn well know we've got some things going for us, and we've got to play to win. Even if we lose, by the time one game's over we're into the next one and can look for ways to win it. There's hope. You can keep going. Of course if you win you're into the next game too. Does it ever end?"

"For a gambler I suppose not."

"So it's just a new kind of junk."

"Only if you let it control you and become the only way to view and do things."

"Well, it's a nice idea anyhow. It's good to be in the Garden again, even for a little while." He put his arm around my shoulder, and I felt like a thirteen-year-old boy who has just been kissed by his first true love. "Come on," he said, "let's get this occupation over."

▲ ▲ ▲

Historian: *I remember our talking and I remember the way it ended, but I don't remember the bridge game.*

Novelist: *I don't remember many things after all these years, but I think I remember this. I think I wrote it the way I planned it at McCormick. I had a plan all worked out, even the bridge hand I was going to show you. I set out to lead you and ended up following you. You never got the benefit of my full plan. You didn't need it. That hardly surprised me at the time: It was just the sort of thing you did. But six years later, when I tried to write it up, I couldn't. Writing it the way it happened either made it too simple if I skipped my own plans and expectations or too complicated if I didn't. I took the self-indulgent way out and wrote it the way I had wanted it to happen.*

Historian: *You wrote it better than the way it did happen. The bridge game was fiction to make our talk more dramatic, right?*

Novelist: *In fact the reality was more dramatic, but that drama was all in my mind because only I knew what I was expecting. Everything happened too fast. I planned to get a deck of cards, but I didn't have to. I did much less than I intended, but much more than I hoped for happened.*

Historian: *But the bridge game makes Jazzman smarter than I ever was. You do that in other places too.*

Novelist: *I didn't make Jazzman smarter. I made him slower, less instinctive, maybe more thorough sometimes, certainly more comprehensible, more …*

Historian: *Contemplative?*

Novelist: *Yes, that's a good word.*

Historian: *For me too. I wonder if the more contemplative Jazzman would have been able to do what I didn't when the going got tough after Fred's murder.*

Novelist: *It's useless to speculate on things like that.*

Historian: *But he wouldn't have got into junk, would he?*

Novelist: *Right. Jazzman is not a junkie. I guess that's a difference I needed.*

Historian: *Let's contemplate that difference.*

Novelist: *Jazzman did all the things you did, but he's not you. You were quicker. Readers wouldn't have been able to conceive how quick. The bridge hand is there to help them. I did mention bridge and what a good declarer does in a tight contract, but I didn't have to get a deck to show you. You got my point before I fully made it and acted before I knew it.*

Historian: *Anyone who didn't know me and reads your novel will think I was a genius. My professors today would be glad to set you straight. Now that we're both old, we know that neither of us is as smart as we thought we were back then.*

Novelist: *Don't diminish yourself. How many eighth grade dropouts end up in graduate school? If I were a good novelist, I would have created a fictional reality in which you didn't have to end up where you are.*
Historian: *I could have ended up in a lot worse places.*

▲ ▲ ▲

JAZZMAN QUICKLY GATHERED UP SANCHO, Miguel, the biggest, blackest dude he could find, and a seminarian who supported us. We went out into the late afternoon sun and over to the library. Inside we strolled around conspicuously examining rooms, doors and windows. Students were studying all over. A few greeted us, most pretended to be too busy studying to notice us but followed our every move out of the corners of their eyes. Jazzman spoke only Spanish, and Sancho and Miguel replied in Spanish; the rest of us tried to look knowing. After about fifteen minutes we left. Outside Jazzman laughed and predicted we would soon hear from the administration.

When the occupation began, the seminary administration had issued a press release saying there would be no negotiations while we occupied their property, but our timing had been perfect. Our representative at the national Presbyterian conference in San Antonio had lobbied well. He even organized the San Antonio Mexican-American community to demonstrate in support of us. As a result the conference passed several resolutions in favour of funding indigenous community groups and insisted that McCormick negotiate amicably with us. There had already been two negotiating sessions. At the first McCormick accepted two of our ten demands and promised to research the others; at the second they agreed to five of the ten but said they couldn't offer more and that this was their final offer.

Since that session, almost two days before the library tour, we had heard nothing from them. It seemed apparent that their strategy was to let us sit and hope we got bored and accepted their offer. To the administrators an administration building seemed like a poor place to live. They had no conception of the love the street kids were developing for their humble three million dollar surroundings. Every day spent in that luxury made leaving more difficult. Some of the Cobrastones wanted to demand a large cash payment for leaving peaceably.

On our library tour the Puerto Ricans had discussed in Spanish possible plans for occupying the library. Many students understood Spanish and within minutes the campus was abuzz with rumours of new takeovers, of hordes of gang kids who wanted to get in on the fun, burn books, sack dormitories, rape seminarians and god knows what else. An hour later the administration requested a negotiating session that evening and issued a press release stating that attempts to occupy other campus buildings would be met with force.

At the negotiating session they agreed to nine of our ten demands: They agreed to raise up to $600,000 seed money for a Poor People's Coalition low rent housing plan (our key demand, the one on which our hopes for a future Lincoln Park which included poor people depended and the one which until now they had insisted was impossible to meet); agreed to donate $25,000 to open a people's law office (which, six years later, still exists and serves the movement all over the city); they would raise the money – sums of thousands of dollars were specified – for all the other community projects as well.

The only demand they refused to meet was to tear down the fence which divided the seminary from the community. We had included that one at the urging of students who wanted to humanize the seminary by making it less isolated from the life surrounding it. It was the only demand that would not have cost the seminary money: We promised to provide volunteers for the work. But theologians are people of principle: The sanctity of private property meant more than money. We saw the humour and symbolism of their refusal and did not insist. Our lawyers drew up a formal agreement in which they met our nine demands and we agreed to vacate the premises the next day. When they signed, the eight of us who had negotiated for the coalition cheered and embraced.

For the most part McCormick acted in good faith on its promises. Once, a few months after the occupation, when we detected foot dragging, Meg, Jazzman and I called on the seminary's urbane president, Dr. Craig. He went with us to talk in a meeting room in the Ramirez Building. He explained sympathetically how things took time and asked for our patience. As he spoke the room slowly filled up with community people. Soon there were perhaps fifty of them, and Sancho had quietly seated himself on one side of Dr. Craig while Sam Jones, a two hundred fifty pound black, who was later appointed to the CCC, sat down on his other side. When this occurred Dr. Craig's speech became less suave. He seemed to stumble over words. He assured us that the $25,000 for the legal office would be forthcoming next week, as soon as the head of the board of trustees returned from a Colorado vacation, and that other cheques would follow.

People continued to trickle in and sat silently staring at Dr. Craig. Someone remarked that there were more people present than during the occupation. Dr. Craig stuttered that he might make some long distance phone calls, so Sancho, Sam and Jazzman accompanied him to his suite. After a few phone calls he signed a $25,000 cheque to our legal committee. We had no further trouble with McCormick, but the president resigned his position later in the year for reasons of health. Everybody regretted losing so distinguished a leader.

I THOUGHT THE SIEGE OF McCORMICK Seminary over and victory won when we signed the agreement. I had overlooked some details. The first was one I could help with, cleanup. Eighty people, mostly teen-aged males, living in a building not designed for living in can create an incredible mess. While there had been few violations of rules against damaging seminary property, there had been little effort to keep things clean. As a typical male I had not even noticed what a colossal mess the Ramirez Building was until I looked around after the agreement. The next twelve hours comprised the most concentrated cleanup I ever hope to participate in.

I was proud to see that most of the Young Lords stayed up all night working. As word of our victory leaked out, community people came in to help. Jill came bringing her two oldest daughters and assorted friends and relations. John and Linda Leeds, Eve and Burt Jackson and assorted clergyfolks came. Priscilla brought a couple of our friends. A large group of Latin women arrived early in the morning. It was hard work, but we managed to get the place fairly clean because the spirit of the workers was great. Especially at first.

As the time to leave approached, rumours began circulating: The two black groups were refusing to go, a number of Latin and white street kids who had drifted in were also refusing to go, even many of the Young Lords were reluctant to leave. I was working with Sancho cleaning rugs, fifteen and twenty foot runner strips along the corridors. They had to be swept then carried outside and shaken since we had no machines. It was one of the most rewarding jobs I ever did, not because of the work, which was difficult and tedious, but because of Sancho, who was lecturing me about "developing human potential." He had trouble pronouncing it, but the phrase had been used in one of the political education classes and he had been inspired by it.

He explained it to me as we worked: "People ain't born stupid. Babies are all born undeveloped. That means they don't know much, but they can learn. I never even thought about it, but babies learn lots of things like how to talk and walk and even how to eat food 'cause all they can do is suck when they're born. Even I learned all that stuff when I was a baby. I was a sucker, but I developed. But after a while kids need to get taught so they can develop more. Like learning to read and write. All of them can learn. Only some of them don't get taught, the ones that go to bad schools like all us guys in the Lords. And the black dudes too. The rich white kids go to real good schools that learn them real good so they can get good jobs and make lots of money when they grow up.

"But we don't learn nothing on purpose. And do you know why? Not like I always thought, 'cause we're suckers. Everyone was that. It's 'cause we're exploited. That means we have to work real hard, but we don't get paid shit 'cause the boss is making all the bread. The reason he can do it is 'cause we ain't learned nothing. The schools keep us stupid so we don't figure out we're exploited. And that's why we got such lousy schools and our human potential ain't developed. We all think we're stupid suckers, but really we're not. We got born with as much human potential as anyone else. It's the lousy schools. We ain't stupid, even me."

"Now here's the good part," he continued as we came back in after shaking out another runner. "If we catch on and make a revolution instead of letting us be exploited, we can still develop our human potential. Do you know that in Cuba and China everyone knows how to read, even though most of them didn't know how before the revolution? After the revolution the first thing they done was send thousands of teachers all over to teach people how to read. Even old people. Everyone was developed. But there weren't enough regular teachers 'cause before the revolution there were so many people who were being exploited and didn't know how to read. So you know who else went? Soldiers. Thousands of soldiers from the Red Army 'cause all the soldiers knew how to read 'cause they taught them in the Red Army. They had schools for the soldiers right in the army. Even when they went on long marches, they had school 'cause there were teachers in the army who were revolutionaries, and they marched too. And they were good teachers so all the soldiers learned to read and write.

"Then when the fighting was over and they needed more teachers for all the people who didn't know how to read and write, the soldiers knew how so they became like teachers. And some of the students from the rich schools who were revolutionaries too. Everyone who knew how to read and write went out and teached everyone who didn't, and now everyone knows how. Their human potential is developed so now they can't be exploited.

"And here's the best part. The Young Lords are going to have our own school, just like the Red Army. And all us guys are going to learn to read and write real good. Even me. This dude from the Chicago University is coming down to teach us. And some other real smart dudes too. And do you know what I'm gonna do when I learn how? I'm gonna go back home and teach my kids."

"What kids?" It was the first I had ever heard of kids from Sancho.

"Yeah, didn't you know I got a wife and three kids? I just don't go home much 'cause I don't have bread, and if I hang round my pad the welfare will hassle me and cut my wife off. But when I learn to read and write, I'm gonna go home anyway. Fuck the welfare. I'm gonna develop my kids' human potential. The schools sure ain't gonna do it 'cause they want kids like mine to be exploited. And do you know what else we're gonna do? The Young Lords? We're gonna set up day cares so all the Puerto Rican kids in the whole hood can come and learn to read and write and develop their human potential and not hassle their mothers all the time. And you watch, I'm gonna help teach those little kids. You just watch me. We ain't gonna let any of those poor kids not get their human potential developed. That's what it means to be a revolutionary."

"Come on, Sancho. Let's take this rug out and shake it." I turned away from him not because I was interested in the rug but because I knew that if I didn't divert myself I would cry. We had been working all night, and in my exhausted state I wasn't up to resisting the lesson Sancho was teaching the way I might have on a good night's sleep. I'm not sure what I would have done or said if we were not interrupted by Angel, who ran up and told Sancho he was needed right away in the vending machine room down the hall. I had heard crashes from that direction while Sancho was talking but assumed they were part of the cleanup. Sancho probably would have drawn the right conclusions if he had not been so absorbed in spreading his new ideas.

The Cobrastones were refusing to leave the seminary and threatening to trash the place. Jazzman was already on the scene. I wanted to go, but Angel said emphatically that Jazzman only wanted Young Lords. So Sancho headed toward the vending machine room, a large student lounge, while I went the other way in search of someone else to help me shake the rug.

During the next hour I spent as much time pacing by the closed door to the lounge as I did cleaning up. The Ramirez Hilton was actually resembling the Stone Building it had once been. I couldn't say that was good, but I could say it was a whole lot cleaner and that the cleanup squad had performed wonders. The question now was whether the work would be wasted, for after close to an hour of arguing – I could hear raised voices every time I passed the door – loud noises of furniture moving began coming from the lounge.

After a few minutes of this the door opened and Angel emerged and instructed me to round up everybody in the building: We were marching out in five minutes. I started to protest that that was a half hour before the scheduled press conference. "Just get everybody," Angel said. "We've got to get those dudes out while we can. Who knows what will happen in another half hour. Go, man." Angel's voice sounded very tired. It was not a voice that tolerated debate.

THE SUN EXISTS! It has broken through. It seems like months since I last saw it. Everywhere the heavy snow sparkles. The cedar and spruce boughs hang almost vertical beneath their lovely loads. Even the ponderosa pine glitters with big clumps of white. The fogs are gone, the air clear. The pale blue of the sky seems reflected in every icicle, myriads of which descend from the outcroppings of rock on the rocky mountain face. Across the river, high above the snow spangled trees two ravens play, their blackness a jest for all the white world below them to enjoy. The thin whiteness of the last high clouds beckons, and they fly over the mountain in pursuit.

WHEN THE OCCUPATION ENDED, we who marched out knew two things: We were a power that could not be ignored, and we were terribly disunited despite our agreement in purpose. Living together for six days had taught us both these things. We had achieved more than any-one dared hope: Our demands had been met and we had learned much about each other, sometimes more than we wanted to know.

We had also learned where we stood in the community. The evening after McCormick had offered to meet five of our demands we held an open meeting to decide whether to accept their offer. Many of our supporters and sympathizers from the community came. During the first part of the meeting a series of community leaders spoke. Liberal ministers, lawyers and businessmen unanimously and verbosely urged us to accept the seminary's generous offer and leave before the police were called.

Meg, who was sitting next to me, vacillated between fury and dismay. The housing demand had not been accepted, and that was the big one. Then John Leeds stood up: "I came to listen, not speak, because I think those taking the chances should make the decision. But since other people who didn't risk their necks have been giving advice, I may as well too. There isn't a single unreasonable demand on your list. McCormick can and should meet every one of them. It should have done all those things and more years ago. You'd be crazy to leave. This building is the only power you've got and the only power you're likely to get in this community without the support of a major institution like McCormick. Use the power you've got right now to force them to choose sides. By being here you are asking McCormick if it supports poor people or the city government and all the wealthy developers and others who are profiting from the misery of poor people. Make McCormick answer your question decisively before you leave."

"Right on, stay," seconded Burt Jackson.

The whole room broke into applause and shouts of approval. Everybody except the ten or twelve middle class "leaders" who had spoken earlier seemed to be on their feet telling us to stay. After the applause ended, person after person stood up to voice support. No speeches, just brief statements of support. I liked Jill's best: "I'll move every damn Hatfield, Thomas and Calder in Chicago in here and call the ones who aren't here up from Kentucky. Then let the fuckers try to put us out." The next morning she came down with all ten kids, her friend Liz (whose husband was a cop) and her five children, and Maria, the Puerto Rican woman next door and her two children. They all stayed until dinner time, and Jill returned after dinner to help clean up.

15.

LAST SUMMER WHEN I FIGURED OUT there are no glaciers visible from my window, it came as a great disappointment. In my mind as I yearned for escape from Chicago, glaciers had come to epitomize all Chicago was not, eternal whiteness, eternal ice and snow, eternal beauty, the peaks of the mountains I sought. When I discovered that the snow I could see out my window was melting even on the highest peaks, that one day there would be no snow visible from my window, I set off in search of glaciers. The nearest one was Kokanee Glacier, thirty miles north but a fifty mile drive to get there. It was the centre of a provincial park with a trail that led to a cabin at the foot of the glacier.

I didn't even get to see the glacier the first time I tried. It was early July. The trailhead was clear although just reaching it involved a half hour drive up a winding, steep dirt road. But as I hiked upward I encountered more and more snow until I was wallowing in it up to my waist. Without special equipment glaciers, even in the south of Canada, are accessible only at the height of summer. Even fully equipped skiers die attempting glaciers in winter. A month later the path was clear and I did hike up to the glacier, even walked on it near the toe, carefully avoiding the higher part with its deep, deadly crevasses. Beauty is power and power is danger.

The Black Panthers were the Chicago movement's equivalent of glaciers. In Chicago, where everything is unnatural, it seems fitting that the peaks should be black, that black, not white, is beautiful, often inaccessible, dangerous. And that the special equipment which made the Panthers accessible to us should turn out to be our primitive, out of date mimeograph. Of course we had seen much of the Panthers. Like glaciers they were eminently visible and everyone in the Chicago movement looked up to them. When they called a rally we all attended and Fred Hampton's spirit held us in awe, his speeches remembered and quoted, his one-liners shouted. "I AM A REVOLUTIONARY." We shouted it loudly and proudly. "YOU CAN KILL A REVOLUTIONARY, BUT YOU CAN'T KILL THE REVOLUTION."

It sounded great. If only it were true. The Panthers had even marched to support us, once to the Wicker Park Welfare Office on a snowy March day, once in Bridgeport, though we in the Concerned Citizens of Lincoln

Park knew that the support was mainly for Jazzman and the Young Lords. In my mind's eye and a desk drawer I cherish a picture of Jazzman and Fred Hampton laughing together as big snowflakes fell in Wicker Park.

Jazzman knew Fred and the Panthers, but although I had shaken Fred's hand at the Wicker Park march, I certainly did not. Until the day the Panthers called and asked if they could run off material on our mimeo; their much more modern machine had broken down. We quickly cleaned and inked our machine and spiffed up the office, hanging some additional posters I fetched from Meg's place.

Several hours after the call Clytie showed up with a shopping bag of stencils and paper. Clytie looked like a Panther should, big, black and tough. She was from Haiti and spoke with a thick, unfamiliar accent which accentuated her toughness. At first she said little, as seemed fitting for a panther dealing with us alleycats, but the respect with which we all treated her broke down her reserve, and soon she was talking and joking with us, asking questions about our organization, suggesting closer ties with the Panthers. It wouldn't be accurate to say she won our hearts, for they had been won before she walked in, but she was so earthy I would have liked her even if she had not been a Panther. By dinnertime she was nowhere near finished with the material she had to run off and obviously would have to return the next day. When I realized she intended to go home by bus, I offered to drive her. I called Priscilla and told her I would be late for dinner. I liked to think I was becoming very considerate.

Clytie lived in Wicker Park, a Latin rather than a black neighbourhood, and not a long drive. When we reached her apartment, she asked me if I liked hot, spicy food, which I do, and invited me up for a Haitian dinner. I did not hesitate.

Her apartment was a single room. I washed a sink of dirty dishes while she cooked the dinner. I don't think she was a great cook – certainly she didn't put the effort into cooking that Priscilla did – but the food was so hot I couldn't be sure. After dinner I started to wash the dishes. Priscilla would have been impressed, but Clytie wasn't. She told me to leave them in the sink. We stood by the sink looking at each other. She laughed. "You is bashful, mon," she declared and kissed me. Then I knew what to do.

With Priscilla lovemaking was a cooperate endeavour. With Clytie it was a competitive sport, and she always won the competition, for she had muscles I did not know existed and gyrated and vibrated them in ways

I did not think possible. She rose above me singing. Singing! A song I did not recognize but knew in a language I did not know but recognized. In tune to her victory song, I submitted, came, started to relax. But she kept going and guided other parts of me in ways that continued her pleasure. To please her I worked harder than I ever had before. We worked most of the night and when I awoke at dawn her leg sprawled over me. Even in sleep her strong leg pinned me down.

She was the most demanding lover I have ever known yet not hard to satisfy because she guided me in exactly what she wanted. I only had to follow her lead. She was older than I, in her mid or late thirties, I guessed. But I didn't ask. During rest breaks we talked about Haiti, which she loved despite its poverty and violence. Perhaps because of its violence. I could sense her violence during the sex act and was glad I was satisfying her. If I failed, I suspected, I might have been in trouble. She also talked about the Panthers. Or, rather, Fred Hampton. Her love was obviously for him, much more than the organization. She told story after story about how beautiful he was. I don't think her feelings for him were particularly sexual – she would have been fifteen or more years older and, I heard first from her, another Panther woman shared his bed and was carrying his child. On the other hand, as I was rapidly learning, sex was life to this woman and most of her feelings were connected with sex.

In the early morning I woke wondering if I should creep out and return to Priscilla, but I couldn't have done that even if I wanted to, which I didn't, for Clytie's strong leg lay sprawled across me. I stayed put, surreptitiously stroking her leg, touching other parts of her body with great care. I dared not move most of my body for fear of waking her. For what seemed like an hour I lay beneath that powerful leg. As soon as I dozed off, she woke, laughed happily and mounted me again. I had run out of sperm but remained hard enough to allow her to climax, which she did sitting high and mighty and digging her nails into my back.

"Very peaceful," she said a few minutes later, still on top of me.

"Yes," I agreed although it was not. It was the most violent lovemaking I had ever experienced.

We went back to the office to complete her work. Priscilla phoned in the late morning and I told her I was still working with the Panthers and that I might not be home until the next day. She offered to come and help, but I pointed out that there was not much she could do, that it was simply a matter of changing stencils and cranking the mimeo.

I suggested she finish the wall hanging she was working on. She did not sound happy when she hung up.

When Clytie's mimeographing was finished, I drove her and it to the Panther office on Madison Street in the heart of the west side ghetto. Although I had driven Jazzman to the office several times, I had never been inside. She took me in. I couldn't help wondering if she thought of me as a headhunter thinks of a head dangling from her belt, but I was happy to be taken in and proud to have helped the Panthers. It wasn't easy to get in: Security clanked at every door and oozed from walls and ceilings. Inside she handed her voluminous material to a man at the desk. He looked at a clock, and I felt her bristle at the suggestion she had been dawdling. I tried to explain how slow our machine was. There were only two other people, one man and one woman, in the office and the air felt tense.

Until Fred Hampton walked in from an inner office. Clytie brightened like a sun worshipper whose dance has produced a rent in the clouds through which her god was streaming. She introduced me and told him I had done much of the work. Fred didn't bother shaking my hand, he hugged me. Wow! I was floating. Had Fred lifted me off the ground? I had to shuffle my feet to prove I was still in contact with the earth. We talked for a few minutes, but I remember nothing we said, only that I felt great, light, proud to have won this man's approval. I knew why Clytie and the rest of the Panthers loved him. After his murder it became obvious that the organization in Chicago had been held together largely by his embraces. As we left the Panther office, Clytie, who knew what had happened, said simply: "He does that, doesn't he." It was not a question.

Back in her bed that night I asked Clytie why she left Haiti.

"Ah cut my mon, so Ah had to split." I didn't understand. "My mon, mon, my husband. Ah caught him with another woman, so Ah cut him. He bled like a pig. Ah got out of there quick. Ah had a friend with a boat and he got me off the island."

"Did you kill him?" I asked, awed.

"Ah don't know. Ah got out too fast and never went back, but Ah kept the blade." She lifted her pillow and there was a small curved knife and a gun. "If it wasn't for Fred, Ah'd cut _____." She named the Panther who had given her trouble earlier.

"Is the gun loaded?" I ventured.

"Sure, mon. Ah'm a Panther. You never know when the pigs are gonna come down. But Ah'd only use the piece against a pig. When Ah fight, mon, Ah want my blade. Ah want to feel who Ah'm cutting." She looked over at me and laughed. "Don't sweat it, mon. Ah wouldn't cut you. You're so sweet you'd bleed honey."

It was another long night. When I left after breakfast, she told me: "Ah know you got a white girl, mon, but you can come back here any time."

I never did. The sex may have been good, but she scared the hell out of me. The only time I saw her again was at the memorial service for Fred Hampton, but half a year after that two of our lawyers showed me transcripts of testimony of an unidentified informer and asked me if I thought it was Clytie. The underlying violence, the threats of cutting, the love of Fred Hampton left no doubt in my mind. Without Fred, Clytie had quarrelled with other Panthers and, when arrested on a minor charge, turned state's evidence in return for being let off her charge. The Clytie I knew – for two days and two nights – would have died before she betrayed her comrades. But it was Fred Hampton she loved, not the Panthers.

Seeing her testimony made me very sad, but in a way it made me proud too. I had revealed a lot of things to her, about myself and the movement in Lincoln Park. I had to: She was a Panther and I had to prove to her that I was a genuine revolutionary. She could have betrayed me and us in Lincoln Park too – the cops always tried to get every scrap of information an informer could give – but she didn't. She must have still considered the boy who bled honey, not blood, a comrade.

I raise rabbits here in the Kootenays. When shopping for a knife with which to kill and butcher the poor things, I came across one with a familiar curved shape. It does the job well. In my mind I call it "Clytemnestra."

I went home. I needed to see if I still had a home. But Priscilla took the whole thing uncannily well. She was still in bed, which made it difficult for her to throw anything at me. "Have the Panthers released you, or is this just a furlough?" she asked when she saw me.

"Honourable discharge," I replied. "They worked me pretty hard though. Would it be all right if I lie down?"

"Suit yourself," she said getting up. But when she saw my mauled back she whistled and said: "Panther claws are too sharp. I'll stick to the Young Lords, thank you." And she tinkled her little laugh. I fell asleep marvelling at my good fortune and Priscilla's tolerance.

16.

AFTER McCormick, repression. What can I write about repression among my mountains? The sun is smiling on the winter's snow, melting it gently in a dazzle of white. Clouds are skidding in from the west. If they build up before sunset it may not freeze tonight. A premature spring is attempting to sing in the trees, which dance gaily in one of the valley's rare winter breezes. Everything is beautiful and I feel utterly free. I know that somewhere to the east and south of me a flat, dark, rank sterility named Chicago ("stinking onion" in the native language its name was taken from) still exists.

I look to the east and south and see the tallest mountains in the vicinity pointing jocularly at the clouds scudding above them, the mountains whiter than those white clouds, brilliant in the bright sunlight. Intellectually I am as knowledgeable of repression as once I was ignorant when I called "brother" to a black cop who had pulled a gun on me. Emotionally my soul is filled with laughter from trying to contemplate repression here. Can the clouds repress the mountains or the mountains the clouds? When I was a youth in Chicago, I knew nothing of repression, yet my soul never laughed.

The United States usually lacks poetry, but there repression is a fine art. It can be as gentle as a strange cop saying "Hi Dick" at a demonstration or on the street. It can be as brutal as the murder of Fred Hampton. The gentle methods and the brutal methods are connected. The cop who greets you by name lets you know you are under surveillance. This would not be much to worry about if you didn't know what the police can do to those they know and watch. Before the murder of Fred Hampton I was often harassed by the police; nevertheless, I frequently chided people in our movement for being paranoid. After Fred's death all I could muster was an occasional warning to try not to let our paranoia interfere too much with our work. After my trial, when I knew the police were after me personally, the gentle pressure of surveillance added to other, greater pressures to drive me crazy.

Repression is like asparagus beetles. Asparagus beetles are small bugs, orange with black spots. They resemble ladybugs, and since ladybugs are beneficial insects, the beetles look innocent as well as pretty. They appear in midsummer, when the asparagus plants have branched into small, green, ferny trees. One beetle or a few seem laughable: What damage can so tiny a creature do to a five foot plant? Defense seems a cinch: They show up so plainly they can easily be picked off by hand. Then one day an entire asparagus plant is stripped clean of foliage and hundreds of the little buggers are laughing at you.

So with repression. Individual incidents are often hard to take seriously, but taken together they can be deadly. Complaining about one incident is like pointing to a single beetle and warning of danger. In itself it isn't dangerous, and any listener would be justified in ridiculing your fear. And if the listener has been trained, as all American schoolchildren are, to observe only individual events, never to clump them into a pattern, never to see the whole as a poet does, then your complaints and warnings can never be taken seriously until you – or Fred Hampton – are dead.

FESTIVAL! 26TH OF JULY, 1969! Celebrate the Cuban Revolution! Dayton Street barricaded in front of the church which houses the Young Lords Organization headquarters. Priscilla supervising the burial of two whole baby pigs in hot ashes in the rubble at Armitage and Halsted which would one day become People's Park. Latin music. Dancing in the street. Apprehension in the air because the alderman has refused to grant a routine permit for the festival.

Studs Terkel, cackling his signature cackle, interviewing everyone he can waylay with his tape recorder. Does Studs have a microphone concealed in that cigar? Jose Gonzales, his prison term to begin in a few days, riding Bob's back, pretending to whip him, shouting: "Yankee, go home!" Burt Jackson with his pipe in his mouth upside down. Julio, the youngest of the Young Lords, with his arm around Laura, the oldest of Jill's daughters. Jill shouting at me to dance with her. Priscilla shouting at Sancho to dance with her. Gilberto, blackest and hippest of the Young Lords, passing joints, Miguel trying to persuade him to cool it. Lisa without the baby, looking lost, searching for Jazzman. Jazzman hidden from view, surveying the scene from the church belfry.

Most of what he sees pleases him: the street all mass and energy; people crammed together rebounding in pulses of colour, bare flesh and hair of every human and many chemical shades flashing in the sun amid cloth of every imaginable colour, weaving wonderful patterns on sidewalk, curb and asphalt; people rubbing together, whirling alone, sliding past, prancing apart, linking arms in sudden circles, breaking off into speeding snakes; people gaping, gasping, grasping, gambolling, galloping, gallivanting, gumshoeing. The cops don't please him: too many, too hot in their heavy uniforms, too heavy in their hot hatred of people having fun which they cannot join, playing in ways which make work for them.

Jazzman goes down to speak to the aldermen, Crower from our ward, the 43rd, Krier from the 44th. Soon he has the spirited independent from the neighbouring ward berating the slow-thinking Machine Alderman Crower for inciting possible violence by refusing to grant a permit, causing all these policemen to waste their time and taxpayers' money watching a party, provoking people by their presence where they are not wanted, not needed. Jazzman smiles. Will it help? he wonders. Will it confuse the cops, make them doubt their role? He looks over the blue crew scowling the same scowl as Crower, at Dick Steale instructing the watch commander who gives these cops their orders, and feels pessimism return.

He leaves the aldermen to their altercation and wanders over to Steale and the cop. As he banters with the commander about his white hat, he suddenly, as if on impulse, reaches his hand through the hatred emanating from Steale and pats his shoulder. The actor jumps back, his face a mask of disgust, and stares at Jazzman, who returns the look until he thinks he detects something other than hate in it. Jazzman winks and instantly knows he has overplayed his part. Steale turns and strides off rapidly. Jazzman shrugs his shoulders and winks at the cop. The TV reporters are arriving. Jazzman re-enters the church.

There is nothing more inflammatory at a scene of potential conflict than television cameras. It's part of their job to inflame; if no conflict develops the TV crews have wasted time since there is little news value in a peaceful party. Even when there is no deliberate provocation by the crews, the cameras lead to incidents: People are inspired to show off, or a cop makes a crack to a youth or vice versa; instantly the cameras are there, grinding away. Suddenly the cop or kid who backs down stands to lose face before a million eyes. Once fighting begins innocent bystanders invariably get arrested, clubbed or even killed. Chalk up another victory for our mass, macho culture.

Studs Terkel, his tape recorder and cigar had been at the festival all day; he made a prize-winning documentary without provoking anyone.

Studs was a participant. He was there enjoying himself, meeting and talking to people of all different views, cackling his raucous laughter, jumping around to music in the street, sitting on the sidewalk chatting with giggling teenagers and bemused old timers. Studs and his recording equipment were there because Studs liked people, not because some boss was paying him to crank out sensational footage for the five o'clock news. Within half an hour of the arrival of TV crews action began.

Late afternoon. Alderman Krier is still sincerely but ineffectually trying to persuade the cops to leave. Occasionally he is joined by an irate taxpayer objecting to the waste of tax monies to pay fifty policemen to stand around all day doing nothing but provoke trouble. The crowd is at its largest and happiest, perhaps five hundred dancing, singing, laughing folks. A huge tray sporting two perfectly browned and blackened whole pigs is bobbing up and down in the air, gradually approaching the church. Beneath the pigs is Priscilla, her body and arm obscured by the crush of people. She is shouting for everybody to make way.

A huge cheer goes up from the multitude, then as the noise diminishes somewhat solo voices become audible amid a chorus of barnyard oinking: "Off the pigs." "Can you fit some larger pigs on that platter?" "Why aren't those pigs wearing badges?" "Hey piggy, what a nice curly tail you got." "Here's an apple for your mouth, pig." The said apple sails through the air, lands at the feet of one of Chicago's finest and shatters so completely as to suggest a rotten tomato rather than an apple.

"Hey, who threw that?" the officer asks profoundly. Since there are several hundred people who might have launched the missile, the question is mainly a philosophical speculation, and the inquiry might have ended with it. But young Julio gaudily leaps from the crowd with Laura clinging to his arm, trying to hold him back. "What's the matter, pig? Don't you like a little fun at a festival?" For a second everyone moves toward Julio. The cop grips his club and takes two giant steps. The TV crews bludgeon forward with their heavy equipment, propelling several bystanders into the ring closing around the participants. Every cop shoves toward the action. Jill screams, tosses a baby at someone near her, dives into the crowd and surfaces behind Laura. Willie, Laura's older brother, flies over the crowd and lands between Julio and the cop.

In the next second the motion stops. Jazzman strides down the church steps yelling: "Hands off the Young Lords." Sancho appears at his side and a lane seems to open for them. The cops forget Julio, flail their clubs to make paths through the crowd, and converge on Jazzman. "Get Jazzman out of there," I scream, trying to push through the swarm of people between me and Jazzman. The cops have been waiting all day for a chance at Jazzman's blood. I hope Sancho will see the danger, but Sancho, grinning, is already flattening the lead cop.

Suddenly Jazzman vanishes. A figure emerges from the crowd behind him, snatches him off his feet and carries him back into the crowd toward the church. Seeing their prey disappear, the cops go wild, swing at everyone they can reach. People flee in all directions. Burt Jackson throws open the double church doors and hollers for people to come inside.

Inside the church a few minutes later Jazzman was receiving reports on what was happening outside and trying to avoid Lisa, who was trying to pull up one of his pant legs and frantically informing everyone that he was hurt and needed a doctor; Meg was washing blood from Mama Jane's head; John was holding down his son Willie, who was struggling to get loose and shouting: "Let me go. I'll kill that pig," while Jill, barefoot, was cleaning his scratches and bruises; Jose was supporting Bob, whose leg had been injured; several other people were nursing injuries, none of which looked serious.

A few minutes later Sancho sauntered in puffing and rubbing his knuckles. He reported to Jazzman that Julio and several neighbourhood kids not in the Young Lords had been beaten and arrested and that six pigs were chasing Angel down the alley. He had tried to follow but couldn't keep up. Several Young Lords volunteered to go to Angel's rescue, but Jazzman told them to remain in the sanctuary. "Right," Miguel said. "What pig is going to catch Angel in a footrace?" The Young Lords laughed and relaxed. (About half an hour later Angel did stroll into the church wearing different clothes than he had on earlier.) Jazzman asked me to get on the phone and raise bail money because the Young Lords Organization had to take responsibility for what occurred at its festival and bail out everyone, not just its own member.

I had been calling for some time when Priscilla and Bob entered the little office where the phone was. They brought succulent slices of roast pig and filled me in on what happened. It was Jose who saved Jazzman. Jose Gonzales, already sentenced to five years in a federal penitentiary, for whom an additional arrest might mean five or ten more years, had hoisted Jazzman from the path of the police and borne him to safety in the church. Jose had never met Jazzman; he risked several years of his life to save a stranger. No one could find him now. After aiding Bob and assuring himself his friend's leg was only twisted, he had disappeared.

Willie was okay. A cop had knocked him down and was about to club him when Jill attacked the cop with her shoe and drove him off. Meg had taken Mama Jane to the hospital, but even her wounds did not appear to be serious. No one knew if the arrested people had been hurt. Laura had bit a cop and been held briefly, then released. There were rumours that the cops were gathering reinforcements and were going to raid the church and other rumours that they were getting search warrants. John Leeds and other pastors had already arrived to help Burt Jackson keep them out. Studs Terkel was still interviewing inside the church, but the TV crews had remained outside with the cops.

That an environment like Chicago could produce a human being like Studs Terkel is a reason to hang on to hope for the future of the human race. Studs was an extraordinary man. He did a series of tapes of Appalachian migrants in Chicago in our office, so I got to watch his technique. He delighted in and delighted people of every variety, was always interested, indeed absorbed, in the person he was interviewing. He never turned on the tape recorder until he got the interviewee talking and established a rapport. I've never seen anyone else who could establish a rapport so well and so quickly. Jill, one of the Appalachians he interviewed – he met her at the festival, and she recruited most of the people for his series – loved him. His son, Paul, was a friend of Bob and an occasional member of the Citizens. Studs asked me about him once. When talking about Paul, Studs did not cackle; he scratched his head, as if his son was the one person in the world Studs could not understand, could not develop rapport with.

AFTER MCCORMICK REPRESSION, one bust after another, most of them preposterous, never brought to trial or quickly dismissed in court, but all of them costly: of time, money, effort, pride. Hardly a week went by when the phone didn't wake me in the middle of the night: "Jazzman is busted. We've got to raise $500 bail." Or "Four Young Lords busted. $100 bail each. Can you raise it?" Then it was my turn to wake people up, beg for bail money, pick it up, bring it to the jail and wait endlessly until the pigs brought their victim down.

I called them "pigs." We all did. Is it strange that people should hate those who are beating and killing their brothers and sisters, who make them fear walking down the street, who harass them so thoroughly they can never relax? I didn't always call them "pigs," and when the Black Panthers began using the word I objected: Cops were human; there were even good ones like those in the Black Patrolmen's League and an unknown cop who used to tip off Mick Finnigan when a raid on our office was planned. The Lincoln Park *Press* maintained a policy of not calling cops pigs except for specific ones who had done piggish deeds. For example, the pig who murdered Sal. But by June of 1969 Black Panthers were being shot all over the country, Sal was dead, and we in Lincoln Park were being busted and beaten as a matter of police policy.

I was busted six times in 1969. Once for walking down a sidewalk. At least I assume that was what I was busted for since it was what I was doing. I had just left the Three Penny Cinema and was strolling along Lincoln Avenue with a friend when a squad car pulled up and a cop demanded my identification. I showed it politely. He chortled: "I thought so. You're under arrest." He put cuffs on my wrists as tight as they could go, then put his nightstick between the cuffs and twisted. This was standard practice for all arrests, and it hurt like hell.

In the squad car he and his partner taunted me, but I knew I had to remain calm if I hoped to avoid a beating. Finally I learned the reason for my bust: "Garcia down at Gang Intelligence wants some colour photos of you." So they booked me for disorderly conduct and took six pictures of me from various angles. It took several hours and twenty-five dollars, raised by the friend who saw me busted, to get me out of jail. Then I had to waste most of a day sitting in court before the charge was dismissed. The pigs didn't waste their time coming to court.

Another time I was busted for walking through the open front door at the Armitage and Larrabee Urban Renewal Office. A student visiting from London, England had come to our office to learn about urban renewal. He wanted pamphlets and statistics available free to the public, so we went to the Urban Renewal Office to get them. We arrived just after 4:30, closing time, although I didn't know this. The door was propped open and every light in the place on, but when we entered the building seemed deserted. We went to the rack where the pamphlets were, took several and turned around. A security guard, his gun hand trembling, had us covered.

"Keep your hands away from your pockets," he said. "Now walk over to that desk, and don't make any sudden moves." We did as we were told.

He followed us cautiously, picked up the telephone receiver, laid it on the desk, dialled police headquarters and requested reinforcements, never taking his eyes or his gun off us. Only when four squad cars screeched up and eight cops raced in did he relax and put away his weapon.

The Englishman, after his initial terror subsided, waxed indignant and demanded his rights as a subject of the Queen. He wanted to know why he was being arrested and insisted that the British Consul and Ambassador be called. He may have been about to demand a call to the Prime Minister or even the Queen herself when I managed to whisper to him to cool it. He had long, kinky, freaky hair, was wearing battered blue jeans and carried no identification. The cops were conferring while staring at him with such hatred I assumed they were debating whether to shoot him or just work him over a bit. But his accent obviously identified him as not American and one of the cops must have been told not to beat foreigners, for we were simply busted for trespassing and bailed out after three hours.

The next morning Jack Seal, the local urban renewal coordinator, phoned me and apologized. The urban renewal office was justifiably unpopular and there had been attempts to bomb it. That's why the guard had been nervous. Jack assured me we would not be prosecuted and we weren't. But we had to waste another day waiting in court for the cops to fail to appear. Given all the time the Englishman and I had to spend together, we became good friends. Several years later he came to Chicago again and stayed with me for a few months when I was living on the southwest side. He still lacks appreciation of the fine family men on the Chicago police force.

Another time I was busted for failing to disperse. One cop gave the order to disperse to a group of us, but when we turned to do so another cop was pointing a shotgun at us and telling us not to move. So we failed to disperse.

My favourite bust wasn't even a real bust since I never actually was arrested. It was the case of the upside down license plate. One afternoon Priscilla and I met Sancho on the street and took him to our place. Priscilla liked Sancho and Sancho liked Priscilla, but he was scared to death of her. While Priscilla was helping Sancho read, as she often did, I tried to sneak away. I had just got into my Volkswagen when Sancho came running after me, saying he wanted to come. I told him to finish his reading lesson and tried to drive off, but there was no way he was going to stay alone with Priscilla. He lifted the rear end of the little car off the ground and left me spinning my wheels in the air. By now Priscilla was out and everyone was laughing, including me. I had to give up my escape plans. Sancho continued to mess around behind the car for a while. Then we all went back inside.

That evening I was driving Jazzman to a school-community meeting at Cooley High School, south of Lincoln Park in the black ghetto. Suddenly lights flashed behind us and a cop pulled us over. He was quickly joined by six or eight squad cars, some of them unmarked. The original cop told us that Eighteenth District Intelligence had radioed him to stop us. Jazzman was routinely followed by the cops wherever he went and I was often tailed too, but the cops who tailed us had never stopped us before. We figured we were in trouble when were ordered to get back in our car and follow the first cop car. All the others followed us.

We were not led to a dark country road, only to the Eighteenth District Station. Commander Borst himself met us and informed me that I was driving a vehicle with an upside down license plate. I denied knowledge of the crime. The commander proudly led me to the rear of my car and showed me the upside down plate. I continued to deny all knowledge. It was the only time I ever saw Jazzman bewildered: He seemed uncertain whether to laugh or keep his back to the wall so he couldn't be shot from behind. Finally he asked if he could leave since he could not be accused of this crime, but he was ordered to remain as an accomplice.

Then people began arriving. Someone had seen the bust, told the meeting, and over a hundred people came down to rescue us. Jazzman was an officer of the school-community group. After much confusion I was issued a traffic ticket and released, and everyone went back to begin the meeting. During all the confusion I noticed Sancho bent with laughter in a corner; he had turned the license plate upside down that afternoon. It was one rap I couldn't beat. I was convicted and had to pay a ten dollar fine. Sancho reminded me of the incident almost every time he saw me, and Jazzman was able to tell a television interviewer who asked what crimes he had been charged with that he had once been accused of being "an accomplice to upside down license plates."

Some of Jazzman's other busts were almost as ridiculous. He was charged with more offenses than any other person in Cook County. I believe the number reached seventeen. He was convicted of only one, and he was guilty of that. He had tried to take twenty-three dollars worth of lumber to complete the Young Lords' day care centre. For that he was sentenced to a year in jail. Of course with seventeen cases pending the cops had Jazzman spending half his days in court and so kept him from doing much useful work in the community.

I was present at many of Jazzman's busts. One was for sitting on city property, a fire hydrant. This occurred right before a march he was scheduled to lead and speak at. He wasn't released until the rally was over. Another was for aggravated assault: He stepped between a welfare supervisor and a woman the supervisor was threatening to strike for spilling coffee in the welfare office. "Hit me, not her, motherfucker," he said. This restored peace without anyone being touched. He was charged a few days later: $200 bail.

The January CCC meeting has already been described. Jazzman was the only person busted as a result of that meeting, and not until over four months afterwards: $500 bail. On two different occasions Jazzman was busted on juvenile warrants which had been cleared up over two years earlier. Both times were right before rallies. It got so Jazzman could predict: "There's a rally tomorrow afternoon. That means I'll be busted in the morning." Usually he was right.

Jazzman acknowledged no authority, accepted no infringement of freedom. He sought to avoid confrontations but never backed away from one. "Cross this line," a cop would dare. Jazzman would step forward.

Only once did Jazzman attempt to avoid arrest. It was when he was wanted for kidnapping his own daughter. Lisa phoned and asked to see him. I drove him to Wicker Park, picked up Lisa and Donna on a street corner and drove them all back to Lincoln Park for a few hours. It turned out that Lisa had had a fight with her mother and left the house without permission. The mother called the police, and they persuaded her to swear out a kidnapping warrant against Jazzman, which she could do because Lisa was a minor and Lisa's mother was the baby's legal guardian.

"Gang Leader Wanted for Kidnapping" screamed the front page headline of the *Tribune*. $2,500 would have been required for bail at a time when we had depleted most of our bail sources. It was a hectic period and Jazzman needed a rest anyhow. He set his lawyers to work clearing up the charge (which was not hard to do but took two days), and then I drove him to my parents' summer home in Nippersink, a summer resort area just over the Wisconsin state line, about sixty miles northwest of Chicago. Since it was winter the place was deserted. I left him plenty of books, told him to lie low and take it easy, then returned to the city and waited for the lawyers to finish their work.

When I picked him up two days later, it was nighttime and the house was dark. I thought he was asleep, but he wasn't. My parents' house borders the golf course and he had been lying low – on his back looking up at the stars or walking the golf course always looking up at the stars. He took me to see them. We didn't talk. We didn't have to. It was a clear, moonless night in an utterly dark place. The stars were magnificent. I knew those stars from my boyhood but had forgotten them. They were like nothing that could be seen in any city sky. Jazzman reopened my eyes although it took me a few months to make good use of them. I wanted to talk about other things.

In the car Jazzman continued to be silent, abstract, somewhere else. I suspected he had been on junk, but now I'm not sure of that. Eventually he commented: "That is one strange place." I guess it was strange to him, but we saved a lot of work and $250. (Ten percent of bail or one percent of bond, which was $25,000 in this kidnapping case, is not returned.) It was not long after Fred Hampton's murder, so it was a strange time, an awful time, as well as a strange place. Without Fred to lead us and moor us, we were rudderless boats adrift in a raging sea.

Jazzman was our best hope to lead us back to land, but Jazzman was drifting back into the junk he had steered clear of for over a year. I fought not to see, fought with myself not to push him, for I knew him well enough to know that pushing him was likely to push him deeper in. Whenever I suspected junk, I shut up, but shutting up now shut me in, locked me into imagining a place I would never want to be high in, an overly ornate summer shack in winter. Only years later can I see that Jazzman, high or low, had not gone where I went. After another silence he said: "Without the stars it would have been like being in the hole."

The first time I met him, he was just out of jail and talked about "the hole," solitary confinement. I remember him saying: "Some of the best conversations I ever had were with myself when I was in the hole." I remember a conversation in the car, a very good conversation, but I have always assumed I was simply talking to myself, trying to haul myself out of the storming sea.

17.

MOST OF OUR BUSTS seem ludicrous now, in retrospect. Like January rain in the British Columbia interior mountains. It's minus forty-four in Regina (straight east of here) and raining in the West Kootenays. Where does rain go when there's more than a meter of snow on the ground? Does it hollow out rivers, lakes, caves beneath the snow? Is there a hidden world known only to mice, moles, ice worms and other tunnelling creatures? Is some contented mouse now taking a break from gnawing on my fruit trees to shower under a sudden miniature waterfall or dip in a new-found pond? Don't get too sassy, little plunderer. When winter returns and all this water freezes, your snow world will become an ice world. I'll equip my cat with ice skates and send her gliding down the frozen channels after you. Perhaps I'll discard my skis and take up cross country ice skating.

EVEN AT THE TIME we had to laugh at most of our busts. After all, they were ridiculous. And we knew what would happen when we stopped laughing at them: Either we would rage so furiously we would lose contact with ordinary people – I could feel this happening to Jan, who, according to reliable sources, had joined the Weathermen – or we would become so demoralized by our impotence to defend ourselves we would collapse as a movement – which to a large extent was what eventually happened.

We knew what each bust cost. Time and money were the obvious prices. Every arrest meant the loss of at least four hours, usually a full day or several days, in jail for those busted and then at least one and often many days wasted in court. It also meant loss of time for the many people who had to raise bail and legal defense money, a task which became increasingly time consuming since our supporters eventually and inevitably ran low on cash or on willingness to throw more of it away, or at least our way. Finally it meant loss of time to our lawyers, another loss which inevitably mounted, as having few lawyers and many cases began to cause conflicts of court dates and the necessity of postponements, which meant some people had to spend several days in court just to have one absurd charge dropped.

Had our goal been to create a better world for our grandchildren, perhaps we could have accepted this loss of days philosophically, but we were too ardent. All of us hoped and most of us expected to live in the new world – and by "new world" I do not mean, alas, the new world of mountains I discovered – so we had no time to lose.

What hurt more was the way these losses led to petty quarrels. When people had to sit in jail longer than necessary, they suspected that those on the outside were not working hard enough to free them; when supporters considered well heeled refused us money or contributed only token amounts, they were insulted behind their backs and sometimes to their faces; when some of us felt forced to devote almost every waking hour to the struggle, it was hard not to resent those who worked less; too often we ended up competing with those we should have been cooperating with for the honour of being the hardest worker.

But the greatest price was the buildup of hate. Each senseless bust, each casual beating of one of us by a cop increased our hate – the hate of people originally so driven by love of humanity that they had to try to help it. We dared not take the busts too seriously or our hate would have made us unable to function.

So we laughed at jail, but death was another matter. We survived the murder of Sal Ramirez, even organized around his death and made ourselves stronger as a result. The murder of Burt and Eve Jackson threw us into confusion, and the murder of Fred Hampton effectively destroyed us. After those killings we in Lincoln Park were running on little but hate. No doubt it was a more realistically based hate than that of our enemies toward us, but that was because we lacked the power to injure them that they possessed over us. By the end of 1969 had our positions been reversed the police pigs, the realtor pigs, the politician pigs would have suffered as many or more injuries at our hands as we did at theirs. They would have deserved what they got, but hate, however justified, cannot long fuel a movement for beneficial social change, a movement that should be based on love.

IT'S HARD TO BELIEVE anyone hated Burt Jackson. He was a young minister who was often overshadowed by more experienced pastors like John Leeds because he didn't talk much. But he always smiled, not an easy task with a pipe stuck between his teeth and a ministry of street kids who were often busted, beaten, strung out or dead. He had a way of being around when he was needed. During the Democratic Convention when Meg, Jan and I were being prodded by pigs with M16s he managed to saunter up in his collar and save us. When cops wanted to bust kids for painting slogans on church walls, he was there to assure them the kids had his permission.

Who knows how much violence he prevented when he threw open the church doors at the festival? He spent almost as much time bailing kids out of jail as I did. Once when we were both sitting around the Eighteenth District Station waiting for someone to be bailed out, I asked in jest what a man of god was doing in a place like this. He assured me it was the only proper sort of place for a man of God to be.

Burt opened his church to the Young Lords Organization although this meant opposing most of his overcautious congregation. The organization was given offices on the second floor of the church and the entire basement in which to build a day care centre. Many of his old parishioners quit the congregation, but Burt was too happy with his new ones to worry much. A few days before he died he exulted to me that not only were several Young Lords attending church services, but that they were speaking out on social issues and giving the services a relevancy he had seldom experienced in church.

Actually Burt did not open the door of his church to the Young Lords. He just neglected to lock it. The Young Lords came in and took it. Because of this some people tried to claim there was bad blood between Burt and the Young Lords and hinted that they might have been responsible for his murder. Under those circumstances Burt would not want me to keep a pledge of secrecy I made at the time, and I will repeat the heart of a conversation between Burt and Jazzman before the takeover.

The history is that before Burt became pastor, excess space in the church, whose parish had declined, had been given to a city agency which ran youth programs which few kids used because they were considered part of the police spy network. Burt persuaded his parishioners not to renew the agency's lease, then wanted them to lease the space to the Young Lords Organization. However, a series of meetings failed to convince a majority of his small congregation, and the space remained idle.

After a second series of attempts, this time to rent the space to the Young Lords, failed Burt apologized to Jazzman and told him: "I'm a man of God, but my ministry is people, and most Sundays I'm lucky to get twenty of them to church. Meanwhile, the church has space hundreds of community people could use and it's going to waste because my twenty won't be Christian. I'm not asking of them what Christ does, to take what they have and give it to the poor, only to rent space they don't use anyhow to the poor. The Young Lords try to help the poor. They work for the community. In other words they lead Christian lives even if they don't come to church Sunday. Among those of my congregation who come to church every Sunday a lot are too prejudiced to lead Christian lives and most are too scared to. Still, they employ me; they own the church; they have the power; I can't choose to ignore their wishes."

"Suppose we liberated the church like we did McCormick?" Jazzman asked.

"I wouldn't blame you. It's your community more than mine. You have a right to control one institution in your own community."

"But what would you do, you yourself, man?"

"I'd try to convince the congregation and Board of Elders. I might have a better chance in the face of an accomplished fact."

"What if they still refused?"

"I'd probably resign."

"And let them call in the cops to throw us out?"

Burt thought a moment, then smiled broadly. "I guess if you liberated this church, you would become my congregation and my boss. You could accept my resignation or refuse it. The old congregation could join the new one or refuse to as individual members saw fit. No one could call the cops – except you, of course."

Jazzman and Burt embraced. "Your resignation is refused. See you soon, brother," Jazzman said happily.

Burt wasn't paranoid like most of us. Like the door of his church the door of his home was always unlocked. One early fall night someone came in who slashed him and his wife to death before the eyes of their two- and four-year-old children. The murderer has never been found.

Burt would have enjoyed his funeral. The memorial service was called "A Celebration of the Life of Burt and Eve Jackson" and featured colourful banners and balloons and joyous music. Loudspeakers had to be installed outside the church, and Dayton Street was once more closed to traffic, for there were far too many celebrants to fit inside the chapel. It was the most beautiful funeral I have ever attended, but no amount of beauty and forced joy could disguise the fact that another brother and sister were gone. At Sal's funeral we raged, at Burt and Eve's we celebrated; in neither case could we do a damn thing to stop the murder of our people.

It seemed as if all the same people who attended Sal's funeral came to Eve and Burt's. Neighbourhood people, movement people, church people, street people, even the two motorcycle gangs, although they didn't arrive together this time and one ended up inside, the other outside the church. At Sal's funeral mourners had been angry and united; now they were confused and scattered. Everyone knew who killed Sal, so there was an object for anger. No one knew who killed Burt and Eve or why, so wild speculation replaced directed anger. Some of the older parishioners claimed the Young Lords as a group killed Burt because he wasn't radical enough. Others thought maybe one of the Lords got drunk and did it.

The cops and their sympathizers nodded their heads sagely, licked their chops and said when a person took gang kids into his church and home, something like this was bound to happen. Those who knew the Young Lords and their love for Burt easily dismissed such nonsense, but their own theories had little more credibility. Some Young Lords thought the murderer was from CORPS or the Concerned Puerto Rican Youth, a group the authorities had set up to oppose the Young Lords. The Chicago Police, the FBI, the CIA or all three were accused. Some thought it was an old parishioner outraged at losing the church. Mick Finnigan was sure it was Fat Harry Berns "because Harry would get a real kick out of doing something that dirty." Meg suspected Dick Steale, who lived half a block from the church and hated the influence the Young Lords were having on "his neighbourhood."

Had the murder been a neat, professional assassination instead of a butchery, I might have agreed with Meg. Had there been any run in between Burt and Harry, I might have agreed with Mick. No one could answer the question: "Why Burt?" If the motives were political, there were many more prominent leaders. Even among ministers John Leeds was more active and influential. Nothing made sense then, and nothing makes sense now. Maybe the senselessness was deliberate; maybe the whole thing was a dreadful coincidence.

Everybody was stunned and bewildered. At the memorial service Mama Jane seemed more coherent than I. Her face was dirty as it usually was these days when she lived mainly at the church. Tears had washed long, clean tracks down her cheeks. Yet when I saw her she was laughing and chasing little Bobby, who was chasing a balloon.

"It's the most beautiful funeral I've ever seen," she told me. "Look at Bobby. He's collecting all the balloons. He and I have been laughing so, but then I think of those poor babies left all alone and I start to cry. I DON'T know what to think. It's so confusing. How can people celebrate when two lovely people are killed right in front of their babies? What are those children going to grow up like? I think they're going to be so mad they will become revolutionaries and make all the changes we can't."

THERE WAS A GAP OF OVER TWO MONTHS between the murder of Burt and Eve Jackson and the murder of Fred Hampton, but in my memory they follow consecutively. Although they did not come together, "the mind is its own place," and in my mind they go together.

The usual tactic of radicals dealing with the police, especially the Chicago police, was to bluster publicly and try to ignore them privately. No one would admit it, but most of us knew we were at their mercy. Some of us took karate lessons, bought guns and tried to learn to use them. For white radicals it was a feeble attempt to live up to our bluster and be worthy of association with the Black Panthers. Black pride was still a new sensation for most black people, and the Panthers could not sacrifice self-respect and esteem in their communities by accepting the indignities of police insults, unjust searches, beatings and arrests.

We whites laughed at these things partly because we suffered far less from them but mainly to keep ourselves from being driven into the corner the Panthers found themselves in. A few whites, notably the Weatherpeople, solved the problem by going underground. The Black Panthers neither laughed nor hid; they defended themselves. It was suicide. The cops could increase their firepower indefinitely.

In North Carolina I had seen tanks used to prevent black children from throwing bottles. The Chicago cops machine gunned Fred Hampton through his bedroom wall as he lay, drugged by an FBI infiltrator, in his bed, then shot him in the head at close range. It was the message of the FBI and the Chicago Police to tell blacks that they could not defend themselves. The Panthers got the message. In Chicago Fred's murder pretty well destroyed them. Nationally it destroyed them as a self-defense organization.

Recently the newspapers up here in Canada have detailed CIA attempts on the life of Fidel Castro. These were a continuation of an American tradition which has accounted for the assassinations of

Mossadech, Lumumba, Allende and other political leaders opposed to American capitalism. The plot against Fidel failed because the CIA could find no competent local dupe to commit the murder, and one rule the CIA and FBI seem to follow is never to do the dirty work themselves. One assumes Huey Newton and Bobby Seale are alive today because the local California dupes were either incompetent or not vicious enough. Of course that problem never arises in Chicago, so Fred Hampton is dead.

He was a beautiful man, the most exciting person I have known, always moving, always talking, always keyed up, always intelligent, a big man who moved like a small one, light, agile, his body reflecting the constant motion of his mind. No one could remain unmoved in his presence. I saw him first on a cold, snowy March 1969 march on our welfare office, which was located in Wicker Park. The Rainbow Coalition (Young Lords, Black Panthers, Young Patriots) had just come into being. Fred Hampton and a number of Panthers joined our march. Fred's spirit and jokes helped keep us warm.

Heat, fire: That's what I felt every time I saw him. On stage he was a natural orator but never a formal one, used no notes, never seemed to be making a speech, was extemporaneous, spontaneous. Combustion: "Come on baby, light my fire," Jose Feliciano sang. Fred did. He was the Molotov cocktail who ignited the entire Chicago movement. He lit all our fires, inspired our entire movement. He is six years dead, but I still feel his hug, feel his hug inspiring my words as his words continue to inspire me. I do not know if he spoke in meter, but I know I thought he did. He was a poet, a lover of words like my teenage idol, Dylan Thomas, was. On stage he sometimes reached up as if to pluck a word from the air, but the words must have all been inside him. Who knows what he could have become? He lived twenty one years. If I have a muse, let it be the spirit of Fred Hampton.

Fred visited Lincoln Park many times, but I visited him at the Black Panther headquarters on west Madison Street only twice, the last time the night of December 3rd, 1969. I was part of a delegation of white radicals chosen to meet with him to plan a demonstration protesting the rising police repression and brutality against the Panthers. Just the day before a south side Panther apartment had been raided by the police. It was a shoot-in, a rehearsal for what was to come, and two men and a pregnant woman were beaten and arrested. Three weeks before that another Panther, Jake Winters (for whom the Panthers named the free medical clinic they opened soon after) was shot and killed by the police.

Fred explained those incidents and helped us plan a demonstration. We had proposed it be held outside Cook County Jail, but Fred felt more people would attend if it was held indoors at a church on South Ashland Avenue where the Panthers often held rallies. Five hours after he shook our hands goodbye, he was shot dead in a drugged sleep (the drugs surely slipped into a drink provided by O'Neal, the FBI infiltrator) in a pre-dawn attack during which the police fired almost a hundred shots (many from a machine gun) into an apartment containing nine sleeping Panthers, including eight and a half month pregnant Deborah Johnson, who would give birth to Fred Hampton Jr. a few weeks later. The rally Fred helped plan became his memorial service – at the date, time and place he had chosen.

The frustration I felt after Fred's murder is indescribable. Chuck phoned and woke me at six in the morning. He was in his cab and heard that there had been another "shootout." The radio said that one of the dead may have been Chairman Fred. Hope made this report sound tentative enough so that I was relieved: If it were true surely someone would be asking me to get up and raise bail money. I told Chuck: "It can't be true; I was with him last night." What did I know of death? It kept shocking middle class me. Death was supposed to be something that happened to old people.

Young Fred was the most alive person I had ever met. How could someone who had been so alive so few hours ago be dead now? I went back to bed. Chuck called back at 7:30. I got up, went to the office, talked, fantasized. For weeks I dreamed of blowing up State's Attorney Hanrahan's office, crashing a kamikaze car loaded with explosives into his house, dynamiting the walls of Cook County Jail. Only years later did I begin to understand that even my fantasies had been misdirected, that Hanrahan was a dupe, that the operation that killed Fred had been planned much higher up, at the highest levels of the FBI, perhaps even higher.

I did nothing, not even raise money. I just attended the funeral and various rallies. Our lawyers exposed Hanrahan's lies, but no one else in the Chicago movement did much of anything either. No doubt action at this point would have been suicidal; the remaining local Panthers were right about that. That was what made it so terrible: our utter helplessness. Which inevitably led to hopelessness. Had Jan and her Weatherpeople friends, whom I had argued against most of that summer, been around, I would have joined the underground on the spot.

Before the funeral Mama Jane came to me and said she had heard Fred Hampton speak when he came to the Young Lords' church and thought he was a wonderful man. She told me she was very sad he would never get to see his baby, but that I should convey her regrets that she could not attend the funeral. She thought the cops might try to kill the whole crowd at the funeral, and she was afraid for her babies. She wanted me to tell people that was why she wasn't coming to the funeral, that she was sorry but she had to think of her babies. She said she was going to get an apartment and stay home with her babies more. She no longer felt safe on the streets or at the church.

By the end of 1969, the year which had begun with such promise and continued with such fervour, the political struggle in Lincoln Park was really over. None of us ever said so or admitted it to ourselves. We all stuck around and went through the motions of continuing the battle. Indeed, there were more solid achievements in the first half of 1970 than in 1969: Both the Young Lords and Concerned Citizens of Lincoln Park opened successful free medical clinics, the law office (which had opened late in 1969) began free legal clinics, the Poor People's Coalition put together a low rent housing plan that was so impressive that our old enemy, the Conservation Community Council, approved it overwhelmingly. Only Dick Steale opposed it vocally. There were almost no busts in 1970.

Yet before the middle of the year, Jazzman, Meg and I were all gone. Jazzman was in exile, I thought in my mountains; I was in exile on the southwest side of his city, and Meg was in California chasing a man she had fallen in love with and being converted to the secret cell conspiracy theory of communism. Chicago had broken us. Oh, Jazzman and I have patched our spirits a bit by repairing to the mountains; perhaps even Meg has recovered by now. I heard she was back in Chicago. But something is missing from all of us. We keep struggling, apart now, alone often, on smaller scales, never with the confidence and gusto we shared with each other and so many more in 1969.

We were right in 1969, and our cause may triumph yet, but now we have children and are making the revolution for them, not ourselves. Most likely they will be left to complete our task – if they decide it is worth completing. In 1969 I shouted with Fred Hampton: "I AM A REVOLUTIONARY." Now I think of a friend who named her daughter Revolutionary Hope, look out my window and try to be content.

18.

THE WEATHER IS COLD AND SUNNY. Today is an anniversary: Exactly one year ago I arrived in these mountains. This morning the road was clear enough for me to run on so long as I avoided the steep, slippery hill. In winter I'd rather cross country ski than run. There's nothing more beautiful than gliding through a forest blanketed in new snow, but now the snow is old, crusty, more like ice than snow. Yesterday I skied a hilly trail and returned bruised and shivering. The slopes were so icy and I fell so often that I soon forgot about looking anywhere but down, and the only beauty I could appreciate was that of a warm house. So today I ran, and running made it seem summer.

How glorious that first summer in the mountains. I was perpetually excited. I suppose I was perpetually excited in Lincoln Park too, but how different these excitements. In Lincoln Park, especially toward the end of my time there, excitement arose in reaction to Chicago: indignation, rage, frustration. Chicago pressed me down in bed, and I had to force myself out every morning, but as the day advanced, anger against the city mounted in me, usually reaching a climax during meetings I went to nearly every night. I would feel it build inside and grip my chair and clamp my teeth together to keep from shouting obscenities at well-meaning people who were not the real cause of my anger.

Occasionally I did shout out – good if it was a CCC meeting that needed to be shouted down, bad if it was a less adversarial meeting, in which case I generally paced the room until I could speak more calmly. Mountains have changed that tense pacing into exuberant running, into excitement which fulfills, relaxes. After those meetings in Lincoln Park I had to talk, drink and smoke myself into condition to sleep.

Often I would not have closed my eyes by the hour I was getting up every morning last summer. For I could not sleep mornings in the mountains: too many bird cries and too many wonderful odours streaming on cold air through the open window. My nose never functioned in the city. Does pollution impede the sense of smell, or are the odours so foul the brain must protect itself by reducing its sensitivity to all odour?

Whatever the case, I rediscovered my nose last spring and every summer morning followed it: out into the purple knapweed which besotted my motley lawn but was loud with bees during the day, into the dew-soaked garden to see how my vegetables had grown. Not that they could have grown much during the short night, but I was too excited to be objective: The poles of scarlet runner beans, which drew tiny humming-birds to hover and suck then disappear faster than the eye could follow, seemed to grow like Jack's fairy tale beanstalk.

It was all so full of wonder that I could not stand still, had to run. Up the hill, through the trees, across the meadow, around and down along the creek, five miles, eight miles, exulting at every bush and bird, startling grouse, deer and elk, once rounding a curve and practically colliding with a bear. (Fortunately wild animals are as fearful and faster reacting than we. The bear was crashing away into the forest before I even broke stride.) Finally charging down to and into the cold river to wash off the sweat, then back up to the garden, this time to work, wonderful work, hands in the soil, under the strong mesh of couchgrass roots.

How different from the long, hot Chicago summer of too many people too close together in the humid air, the feeling of riot, smashing, destroying instead of growing. But as summer in the country wears on and everything points to one end, the harvest, so the summer of '69 wore on through busts, murders, threats and parades, everything pointing toward one end, People's Park. The idea came from Berkeley, but the need was native Chicagoan.

ARMITAGE AND HALSTED had long been the symbol of "the hood" and what was happening to it. It was there that Jazzman made his first speech ("Basta!"), there that marches ended with a rally, there that was an integral part of all our festivals. In 1968 the wreckers had levelled the block east of Halsted between Armitage and Dickens, urban removing eleven hundred families of poor people, black, brown and white, and demolishing George's hot dog stand. The urban renewal plans had long been drawn up for the spot: a private tennis club, minimum annual membership fees of $1200, a playpalace for the plutocrats the city planned to lure to Lincoln Park.

This in an area where the housing shortage was desperate in an over-crowded city with one of the lowest vacancy rates in the country. For years the city and private developers had refused to build low rent housing: It wasn't profitable; if people couldn't afford the rents, let them move elsewhere. Daley's masterplan to increase his tax base by moving people with money back into Chicago from the suburbs depended upon the disappearance of poor people. Their housing would vanish and they along with it.

The same city government which refused to build housing was practically giving an entire block which used to house poor people to private developers to get rich on the pursuit by the wealthy of fashionable exercise. By summer many people in Lincoln Park were talking about exercise for the poor: clearing and claiming the land. It was a cause almost too popular. Even the daily press editorialized against Daley's plans. Mike Royko wrote a very funny, very bitter satire in the *Daily News*. He advised the mayor and his cohorts to practice their backhands. Did they really need more practice?

We had been on the defensive most of the summer of '69. After McCormick the city and its cops attacked us so fast we had to spend most of our time in jail, in court, raising bail money or at funerals. Every time we seemed ready to act on the Armitage-Halsted land, something else distracted us: another mass bust, a campaign by radical student organizations to support the Young Lords which resulted in much energy being diverted into student and international politics (the international aspect might have been beneficial if the student bickering didn't take up so much time that ought to have been spent on the community), the Concerned Puerto Rican Youth (a new group organized by an ex-gang-banger now being paid by the city and Dick Steale and his friends to oppose the Young Lords).

All this plus rapid growth, especially of hangers on craving glory without work, was causing internal problems in the Young Lords Organization. But we had to act: The city, through its Conservation Community Council, was preparing to dispose of the land formally at its next meeting.

One late summer morning Meg called, got me out of bed and told me to go to the Young Lords' headquarters to talk to Jazzman. It must have been before the murder of Burt Jackson; as usual my chronology is of feeling more than time. We had a tentative plan to clear the land as a park and hold it until we could get low rent housing erected. The CCC meeting was only a few weeks off. We could not allow the unrepresentative Council to decide the land's fate. It had to be presented with an accomplished fact.

I walked to the church, which was only half a block from the coach house. It was before ten o'clock and I did not expect Jazzman to be there.

All our hours usually began and ended late in those days. But Jazzman was there, alone and haggard looking. He usually looked clean and neat. He had little beard because he was so fair, but even in the dim church light his scraggly beard – for him it must have been two weeks growth – was evident. He looked tired and said he was, that he hadn't slept all night because he had stayed up helping a junkie kick.

The Young Lords had a standing offer to help any junkie who wanted to go cold turkey. One room in the basement was set up for this purpose. I knew normal procedure was to work this gruelling job in shifts, so I asked Jazzman why he had worked the entire night. He began to brush off my question but seemed too tired to do so and finally admitted there had been a party and that he and Sancho had volunteered to work all night so the others could party. Sancho had just left to get some sleep. I wanted to ask more questions about the incident – it certainly was no way to run an organization – but I knew that the Young Lords were having internal problems. That was none of my business, so I turned to the business I had come on.

Before I had finished explaining our plans, Jazzman broke in and said the Young Lords could not begin any outside projects right now: "There's some dynamite junk floating around. We've got to deal with it. And other problems too. I'm scheduling nothing but internal political education classes for the next two weeks."

I explained about the upcoming CCC meeting, told him we had to act quickly and that Concerned Citizens could not act alone on land that was so obviously Puerto Rican and Young Lord turf.

Again he interrupted: "Look, man, Meg laid all that shit on me and I told her there was no way we can help right now. Quit hassling me."

Meg had not mentioned that she had already talked to Jazzman although I should have known it was not like her to entrust such an important mission to me. I apologized to Jazzman, advised him to get some sleep, gave him a half-hearted hug which he did not return and strode to the office to confront Meg. It was not the first time she had put me in that sort of position.

Meg denied nothing. She said it was essential to act now and that we needed the Young Lords with us.

"But why didn't you tell me you had already tried and that Jazzman had refused?" I demanded.

"Because you wouldn't have gone if I told you that."

It was a typical argument between Meg and me. She was right: I wouldn't have gone. Jazzman didn't need things explained more than once to make a decision. I began to object, but she cut me short, saying: "We don't have time to argue. We've got to call an emergency meeting immediately." She turned away from me and began phoning people. As I stalked out, she called after me: "Don't pout too long. We've got to write up a position paper and set up for the meeting tonight."

At the meeting I tried to argue that we should not act until the Young Lords were ready. It was futile. The Citizens never opposed Meg when she really wanted something. Only Bob and Chuck gave me any support and abstained on the vote. After the meeting Meg took me aside and told me not to worry, that the Young Lords would join us once we began working.

On a fine sunny afternoon about a dozen of us carried two shovels and a pick to Armitage and Halsted and posted signs proclaiming "People's Park – *Playa de la Pueblo*" ("*playa*" means beach, but without the Young Lords our Spanish wasn't too good), and inviting everyone to help us clear the land, which was a mass of rubble and garbage. Soon Jazzman and most of the Young Lords were working alongside of us. By evening there were two hundred folks picking up garbage, forming long human chains to move rocks and bricks to a pile on one side, singing "We Shall Overcome" and "The Internationale."

My voice broke and my eyes filled all that evening at the spontaneous response of the community. Maybe I see more with my eyes full. Usually I'm awfully good at not noticing things. Priscilla used to joke that I only noticed a room had walls when I bumped into them, but I bumped into a wall in the wide open spaces of People's Park. I noticed Priscilla and Sancho laughing and joking together and suddenly understood her tolerance of my association with the Panthers. The people I was working with must have thought I had lost it, for suddenly I broke into uproarious laughter and raced toward Priscilla and Sancho. Priscilla understood immediately and broke into her great bellows laugh, but Sancho turned heel and ran off.

"Upside down license plates," I shouted at his retreating back. He looked back at us, and seeing Priscilla and me laughing returned sheepishly. Soon we three were embracing. That was the spirit of People's Park.

That was the spirit of our movement. People's Park summed up the best of our revolution, the personal side of our political revolution, the coming together of strangers to make community, the coming together of lovers to laugh at the jealousies of the past – and, alas, the future.

The next evenings as many as three hundred people helped clear the land. Soon it was flat and clean. Sancho got hold of a tent and moved in with several friends to guard our park. Local artists brought us posters and primitive sculptures. A local architect helped kids build a geodesic dome jungle gym. A New York architect volunteered to construct several large, far out playground pieces. Buckminster Fuller came to address us at the Young Lords Organization church and offer any service he could.

That was a moving day. "Bucky," as he asked us to call him, wanted to see the neighbourhood, so we borrowed a van and Meg, Jazzman, I and several others drove him around western Lincoln Park. Studs Terkel recorded a lot of it. Bucky told us he had lived here when he was young and poverty stricken, that his four-year-old daughter had died here, and that that had been a turning point in his life, had led him to try to help alleviate world poverty and its effects. Back at the unheated church he spoke with – not to – an audience of hundreds. He was one of us.

Although few people in the audience had much education, everyone understood what he said. He was never abstract. When he spoke about domes and buildings, he showed us with triangles and rectangles made of loosely bound sticks how much stronger the triangle was, how triangles could be used to construct domes which were structurally stronger than the boxes we now live in. When he talked of people, they were never masses or statistics but individual, living, loving human beings, some of whom lived in Lincoln Park while others dwelt in Africa or Asia. Without mentioning the word or speaking of politics he made the most eloquent plea for international socialism I have ever heard, a plea for a rational, sustainable, co-operative world, an end to selfishness, war and waste.

Bucky's visit was a downright sentimental occasion, perhaps the only one we ever managed in Lincoln Park, certainly the last. After Fred's murder there could be no more. The neighbourhood and its preservation were as important to Bucky as to us, and this created a bond of soft emotions which united different generations and methods of work. Most touching was the instant empathy between Bucky and Jazzman. In the van Fuller had begun talking about his own past and ended speaking quietly with Jazzman about the Young Lords and the problems of its members. At the end of that tour he wanted to walk around People's Park. He took Jazzman's arm and the two of them ambled off together.

His friends, who apparently always accompanied him to look after his health and make sure he ate all his meals and caught all his planes, declared they had never seen him "like this." I assume they meant both that he was very emotionally moved and that he was strongly attracted to Jazzman. At the end of his speech, as his friends attempted to hurry him off to the airport to catch his plane, he and Jazzman embraced. Both their eyes were brimming. Of course, flashbulbs popped and every paper in town carried a photo labelled: "Renowned Scientist Embraces Gang-leader" or some such nonsense.

Even I, writing in the *Press* and caught up in the general sentimentality, said: "The two men, so different in every other way, embraced because they shared a great love for humanity." No doubt the trite bit about love for humanity is true enough, but probably, except for a fifty-five year difference in age, Buckminster Fuller and Jazzman are remarkably similar and both of them recognized this immediately.

It would have been nice to know Bucky better, if only so I could write a detailed comparison of him and Jazzman. Looking out my window at my mountains, green in a sudden sun flashing on thick, snowless trees, I know I would find the two akin. Certainly both lead by influencing others with their simplicity and sympathy rather than with bombast and showmanship.

▲ ▲ ▲

Historian: *Did you move Bucky's visit for dramatic reasons?*
Novelist: *No, I kept this scene straight. It didn't need any dramatizing.*
Historian: *But Bucky came to People's Park after Fred's murder, not before.*
Novelist: *For once the historian has his facts confused. I'm not sure of the date. It was cold, so sometime in November I suppose, but certainly before Fred was murdered on December 4.*
Historian: *I think you're wrong. It's easy to check. All the newspapers carried the story... Bucky's visit was on December 14, 1969, ten days after Fred's murder. I've emailed you a link to a newspaper story about it.*
Novelist: *Obviously I was wrong, and I don't know now whether I made a mistake when I wrote this in 1975-6 or whether I deliberately changed the date then. My memory now still insists Fuller came before Fred's murder, but that may be because a change I made when I wrote it has*

become the reality in my aging memory. Bucky personified hope, but hope had died with Fred; therefore, Bucky – "beauteous Bucky," Priscilla called him – must have come before Fred's assassination.

Historian: *The danger of messing with history. The advantage of messing with history. History can be a dramatic art. We read the great historians less for the facts they tell us than for the order, drama and understanding they bring to events. You can be right even when your facts are wrong. Your novel makes sense as history and your history makes sense as art. It's like Bucky's speech in the cold church. We didn't notice our bodies were freezing because our heads and especially our hearts were warm. He never mentioned politics, but we all understood the connection. Everything he said was political. The order of your book is yours, the understanding ours. Even when it is historically inaccurate, it makes poetic sense. Like Bucky did.*

Novelist: *Bucky's visit should have been a visitation. The lovely, hopeful, hope filled day we spent with him in the cold, rain and mud should have proved to us that revolutionary hope cannot be killed; but even six years later, when I wrote this, the shock of Fred's murder prevented me from learning the lesson Bucky taught us, and I misplaced his visit in time.*

Historian: *And as a result your history frees the mind from the bind of time. The fire of the was heats the will be.*

Novelist: *Geez, you are in graduate school, aren't you? Maybe I made another mistake when I loaned you books of poetry.*

▲ ▲ ▲

SIX YEARS LATER IT SEEMS TO ME that we did not understand our own revolution. We did not think big enough, poetically enough. We failed to fully realize the power of our movement, fully exploit the spirit of People's Park. We should have kept Bucky on or called him back to help us construct a huge dome to cover the north two-thirds of People's Park, a dome big enough to house the community that came together to help clear the land. That dome might have spawned baby domes, one for George to open a new hot dog stand, one for handball courts, plebeian sport to mock the idea of the aristocratic tennis club. Etc., etc. No doubt the problems would have been insurmountable, but simply trying to surmount them might have made us much more than what we became.

ALTHOUGH THE TAKING OF PEOPLE'S PARK was the most popular move we made, it was not popular with everybody. The Lincoln Park Conservation Association, after all, was based on making money through property: If the city's urban renewal land could be seized by people with no title to the land, no speculator's property, no landlord's property, no property period, was safe. Dick Steale paid several visits to Commander Borst and then to Borst's superiors downtown demanding that the police use force to end the occupation.

But public opinion was behind us, so although cops were forever dropping by to provoke us and even made one or two arrests, when we greeted them with good spirits – the last good spirits we were to feel – they usually gave up and left. Members of the LPCA with softer backbones than Steale's knew we were too visible and too just in this cause for police force. They stayed at their own level and bent their efforts toward trying to make us look bad and assuring that their tool, the Conservation Community Council, made the final decision.

The newspapers were full of pious statements about morality, legality, reality, nationality, punctuality and metempsychosis. ("No doubt *they* pick up garbage, but so do vultures.") The Society sent a letter to every loyal member, businessman, conservative minister and professional in the area informing them that gangs of thugs (us) were determining the destiny of Lincoln Park (oh, that it were true) and blocking the orderly progress of urban renewal. The letter urged everyone to attend the next meeting of the CCC.

We did some publicity ourselves though few of our supporters ever missed a Council meeting. The result of all this was a CCC meeting with close to a thousand people in the audience plus TV crews and newspaper reporters. It had to be held in the Waller High School auditorium to accommodate the crowd. Even before the melee it made great copy: a very visual scene, easy to tell the players because both sides wore uniforms, half the audience in suits and dresses, the other half in blue jeans.

The Conservation Community Council had not made a decision in almost a year. We had long ago taken the simple position that since the Council represented only the tiny fraction of men who owned and controlled most of the houses, businesses, institutions and money in the area, it shouldn't be allowed to decide the fate of the majority of the people of Lincoln Park. To try to calm the outcry against the unrepresentative Council Mayor Daley had appointed two black and two Latin men to the Council earlier in the summer (to go with eleven middle class white men). Three of the four minority appointees wanted to refuse to serve as tokens, but Sam Jones, who had a voice even louder than mine and who used to sit on the opposite side of the audience from me and alternate with me in leading the shouting down of all attempts to conduct business by the Council, wanted his voice to be heard legally and so accepted, and the others went along with him.

Sam had prevented the two previous meetings from making any decisions simply by monopolizing the microphone. This seemed an adequate method of immobilizing the Council although it was less fun and less democratic than allowing the audience to do the job. We were no closer to having a representative CCC, but the city and the LPCA were no closer to getting the "community" rubberstamp approval of their plans which the CCC had been set up to provide.

Then came the People's Park meeting. There were new forces to be reckoned with. First women: At the Concerned Citizens of Lincoln Park meeting to discuss plans Jill had protested against the lack of a single woman on the Conservation Community Council. This was especially unfair, she argued, since it was housewives and children, who spent their time near home, who were most hurt by being forcibly uprooted. Jill knew. Since being forcibly uprooted from her native Kentucky by strip mines, she had been moved three times in two years by Chicago urban renewal.

Other women in our organization – and we had more active women than men – backed Jill up and voted that women alone were to prevent the Council from conducting business. They chose an initial tactic, to arrive early and fill up the stage, including councilmen's chairs, with women and kids; from there they would play it by ear. A second new force was Jim Krier, Lake View's new, independent, liberal alderman. His intentions were good: He wanted to prevent the giveaway to the tennis club. But being a politician his way of achieving this was to confer secretly with the council members and work out an under the table compromise. A third new force was a group of young, aggressive speculators and remodellers.

When Priscilla, Meg and I arrived at the high school, we were surprised by the number of people and TV cameras. The Conservation Community Council was, after all, but a local group without any real power (as we would discover spectacularly when we got them to approve our own housing plan). Yet as people walked in the outside door before the meeting, they found themselves in the glare of floodlights with microphones pushed in their faces. The TV crews were gathering background for a feature story.

I listened to these interviews for a while and was pleased: Our people knew the issues; few of our well dressed opponents even knew why they were there, muttered vaguely about law 'n' order and keeping the gangs from controlling Lincoln Park (which the *Tribune* had been screaming was happening); most didn't even know about the tennis club. When I entered the auditorium two young lawyers, protégés of Alderman Krier, were trying to persuade our women to quit the stage. When they failed these two men took folding chairs from a large stack and sat down with the women "to act as observers." Several other liberal males joined them, thus watering down the women's protest.

Since I had been ordered by the women not to interfere, I took an aisle seat next to Priscilla in the middle of the hall. A half dozen guys in their twenties wearing slacks, knit shirts and crewcuts sat in front of me. I thought they were plainclothes cops, but it turned out they were speculators. After a quarter hour of fruitless debate between the councilmen and the women on the stage, Henry Larcen attempted to call the meeting to order. There were about forty extra people sitting around the stage. Sam Jones called for the microphone. Henry refused to yield it. Sam rose. He was six foot three and weighed close to three hundred pounds.

"Let's get that nigger first," said one of the crewcuts in front of me. They headed for the aisle. I wanted to protect or at least alert our people up front without getting busted or beaten, so I tried to block the men's exit and asked them politely to remain in their seats. One of them quickly shoved me to the floor, and they stepped over me and headed for the stage, grabbing folding chairs on the way. By the time I regained my feet they were swinging chairs over their heads and trying to mount the stage. Before I could follow my instinct to move to the rescue, I saw Jill deliver a haymaker to the leader's jaw. I sat back down to watch the show.

The front rows of the audience were filled with street kids who loved a good fight and weren't about to let a bunch of women have all the fun. They charged the stage with bloodcurdling yells. But except for one crewcut with hair too short to scalp belonging to a speculator too stupid to run, the enemy retreated hastily. For a few minutes the stage was bedlam with kids yelling and leaping on and off tables, but except for the crewcut, who received some bruises, the only casualty seemed to be Mama Jane's four-year-old daughter, who was off to the side of the stage crying. I went to the child, took her in my arms and carried her to my seat. She was more frightened than hurt, and when the noise died down ran back to the stage and her mother.

The TV cameras recorded total pandemonium, and some photographers got exciting photos. A picture of suave looking, suited Henry Larcen on his knees being protected from an unseen assailant by the freakiest looking of freaks made the front page of one daily. But the camera people were too close. Certainly there was chaos and the cameras recorded this, but from my vantage point it was apparent that little more was happening than some kids pretending to be in a grade C western; no one was being injured. The Department of Urban Renewal later claimed there was almost seventeen dollars in property damage (mainly to the microphone stand), and Henry Larcen claimed his wrist had been hurt. That was it.

After about twenty minutes of sorting things out on stage a shaky Henry Larcen tried half-heartedly to reconvene the meeting, but now the audience was so noisy, with dignified ladies and gentlemen standing and screaming for the clearing of the stage, the arrest of everybody but themselves, and for blood, that he gave up and adjourned the meeting. Alderman Krier ran up and tried to get Henry to hold the meeting, but Henry was not cut out for heroics. He was so scared he resigned his position a few days later.

I walked out of the meeting arguing with Krier. He informed me he had arranged for the CCC to revoke the tennis club sale and that our violence was to blame for whatever happened now. It was a lengthy, futile argument which was later to keep me out of jail. The next day Mayor Daley tried to salvage a few political points by announcing the city would not let the Armitage and Halsted land be used for a tennis club. Victory!

MONTHS LATER I AND FIVE OTHERS were indicted for "mob action" at this meeting. It was the era of the "balanced indictment": when national guardsmen shot unarmed students, the prosecutor was supposed to indict equal numbers of guardsmen and students. In Chicago a "balanced indictment" meant that one leader from each of the five organizations leading the struggle against urban renewal in Lincoln Park plus one unaffiliated opponent of urban renewal were indicted. Further it meant that two Latins, two blacks and two whites were indicted. No women were indicted.

None of the speculators who started the fracas were indicted although the two liberal lawyers who acted as observers later told me they had testified to the State's Attorney and to the grand jury that the speculators had caused the commotion and thrown the chairs (at Sam Jones) that probably damaged the microphone stand. One of the lawyers had even managed to see the identification of the leader of the speculators and gave his name and address to the grand jury. It was a typical case of Chicago justice, but the cops blew one detail: In line with their policy before important events the cops had busted Jazzman on his way to the meeting, so he could not be indicted for causing the disturbance. I was chosen in his place.

Since the indictments were reported in the newspaper before we were arrested, Sam Jones, who was also indicted, and I decided to turn ourselves in. The indictments had been timed to come down the day before the Weatherpeople's "days of rage" demonstration. I had a pretty good idea of what was going to happen at that demonstration and had no intention of attending, but the cops, acting on their tired theory that all radical activity was one big conspiracy, intended to bust me right before the first march, on a Friday evening, and keep me in jail for the weekend of the demonstrations. Or perhaps they planned to use their warrant for me as a pretext to invade the first march and bust lots of heads.

The newspaper leak spoiled their plans, whatever those were. Sam and I each raised five hundred dollars cash bail, and our lawyers arranged for our arraignment and release on bail. We went to court Friday morning and the judge agreed to arraign and release us, but the State's Attorney had not brought the proper papers, so the judge told us to return after lunch. Then we made a mistake: We left the courtroom to get lunch.

When we reached the lobby of the courthouse, cops appeared from behind every pillar and surrounded us. One of our lawyers raced to get the State's Attorney while the other explained the situation to the fuzz (who knew exactly what the situation was). The State's Attorney arrived, declared us under his custody, ordered the cops to release us and sent our lawyer to summon the judge. This was enough for the cops: They dragged us into their waiting van and drove us from Twenty-sixth and California, the location of the courthouse and County Jail, to Eleventh and State, central police headquarters.

After a few hours our lawyers located us at Eleventh and State, so the cops loaded us into another van and zipped us back to Twenty-sixth and California. I knew the routine: Jazzman had once been kept incommunicado for forty-eight hours being switched from lockup to lockup. I guess when all hell broke loose without me that evening, Sam and I became small fry or the cops ran out of men and vehicles because Priscilla, who had dutifully pursued us with the thousand dollars, was allowed to bail Sam and me out. For months I gleefully related the story of how I had been kidnapped by cops from the clutches of the courts. Knowing I had done nothing illegal at the CCC meeting, I found it impossible to take my indictment seriously.

THERE WAS ANOTHER RESULT of that Conservation Community Council meeting: the next Conservation Community Council meeting. It was essential for the city, the Lincoln Park Conservation Association and the liberal forces led by Alderman Krier to have another meeting just to show that the forces of anarchy could not obstruct the democratic process. So another meeting had to be called, a meeting which marked a high point in the attainment of democracy, Chicago style, and the lowest point of my political career. The meeting was held perhaps a month later in the same auditorium with most of the same people present. Also present were several hundred cops. Outside their squad cars and paddy wagons filled the vicinity. Inside every wall and aisle was lined with blue uniforms, and the entire stage was surrounded by them.

From the time I entered the hall I was possessed by the kind of fury and frenzy I have experienced but one other time, at the Democratic Convention of 1968. It must be the state of mind induced by a police state, but it is not the best state of mind in which to oppose a police state. There was no effort to transact business at the meeting. Its purposes were to show us how disorder would be dealt with, to show middle class people they would be protected and to prove to all that under American democracy everybody has a right to speak freely (and be indicted freely: this was before my indictment). People from the audience were recognized by the chair (whom I did not recognize) and allowed to proceed through the police lines to the stage and speak. The supporters of democracy were prepared. I think Alderman Crower and Krier each spoke. Then Milt Moore was recognized and read a prepared speech. Then I was recognized.

I was totally unprepared to speak. I had often dreamed of the opportunity to address our foes, dreamed of persuading them, making them understand the rights, the humanity, the suffering of the people they were forcing out of Lincoln Park. But in the atmosphere of that meeting I could think of only one thing, to defy the alliance of swine and cash. I raised my fist high above my head and strode through the pigs shouting: "Power to the People" and "Off the Pigs," accompanied by a roar of support from our side.

For several minutes I shouted slogans, threats and curses into the microphone as half the audience cheered and the other half booed and screamed back at me. I did not lower my clenched fist until I reached my seat again and was pummelled with congratulations. Priscilla later told me that as I sat down I was trembling violently and soaked all over with sweat. I remember only the shame.

19.

PRISCILLA'S RESCUE OF ME AND SAM was the last good thing to happen between her and me. Somewhere between my indictment and trial we split up. I guess the actual breakup occurred some time after the murder of Fred Hampton. Christmas and New Year's must have intervened, but I didn't notice. Looking back I wonder why it took so long. We had been moving apart for so long that I had lost all recollection of the good times. How much rain must fall to melt a meter of snow?

The best thing about our relationship at the end was that we seldom saw each other. Work had become an obsession for me. It seemed like I had to keep up my earlier pace even though there was less to do. The People's Park melee at the Conservation Community Council seemed to mark the end of something. There was less to protest since the CCC did not attempt another business meeting for the rest of the year, People's Park was not to become a tennis club and McCormick was coming through on its promises. There were fewer protesters too. Sal Ramirez was dead; Burt Jackson was dead; Jose Santamaria was dead, senselessly beaten to death with baseball bats by a Polish gang as he got out of his car in a predominantly Polish section of Wicker Park. He had moved to Wicker Park after being evicted so his Lincoln Park apartment could be remodelled. More people were burning out than joining the movement. After the murder of Fred Hampton, the police flooded the hood with good junk and the Young Lords with pushers, and Jazzman was strung out much of the time. Or so rumour had it. I didn't see much of him.

For political groups it became a period of building alternative institutions. Much of our energy was spent planning: community meetings to plan seventy units of quality, low rent, integrated housing; community meetings to plan the opening of three free health centres, one run by the Young Lords in their church, one run by Concerned Citizens of Lincoln Park in John Leeds' church, one run by and in a settlement house in western Lincoln Park; Young Lords' meetings to plan a free breakfast for kids program to be held in the space they were trying to fix up to city code regulations for a free day care centre; meetings to plan how to turn the northeast corner of Armitage and Halsted from an empty lot with a sign into a real People's Park; meetings to plan the Puerto Rican cultural centre; meetings with groups from other neighbourhoods to plan how to make the protest against urban renewal city wide. There was much to do, but the passion of the period of protest was gone. How many freezing nights does it take to turn sodden snow into ice that can be walked upon?

Not that repression ceased. It was at its most brutal: Friends were being offed all around us. Yet as autumn yielded to winter, we too were growing cold. Perhaps we had become so accustomed to repression that it no longer aroused our emotions. Perhaps the grind of repression was smoothing the rough edges of our anger, levelling our emotions. It took the most extreme of acts, the machine-gunning of Fred Hampton in his bed, to arouse us again, and by then we had forgotten how to react.

Certainly I had become cold in my personal and political life. I found myself joking with the Red Squad pigs that followed me around. I went to every meeting possible, sometimes three in an evening, not because I was indispensable but because I dared not be idle. Working kept me from Priscilla and my frigid emotions.

It was Priscilla who suggested we split up. To my surprise I found I did not want to. A few months earlier, when we were still having continual disagreements and occasional fights, I kept planning to leave but never did. Now we seldom saw each other, and when together we spoke little. We didn't even make love very often, and when we did I caught myself thinking of other women, something which had never happened before. It was as obvious to me as to Priscilla that we should not be living together any more; still I did not want to move out. (I would have to be the one to move: Priscilla had rented the coach house before I came back from North Carolina and had decorated it and turned a room into her studio. She had lived and worked there; I had never done much more than eat, sleep and fuck.)

I had much work to do, I told Priscilla. There was no time to look for an apartment and move my stuff. If she liked I would sleep on the couch. She didn't like, not a bit. My offer provoked one last burst of anger from her: "You don't even want a woman any more. All you want is a goddamn cook and housekeeper. Get out!"

I didn't try to argue. I muttered something about being disgusted that she could attribute such motives to me and left. I slept in the office a few nights, and then a friend who had to be out of town for several months offered me the use of his apartment on Bissell south of Armitage, and there I stayed until I left Lincoln Park.

A late nineteenth century melodramatist would have known how to express what happened next: "When Dick left Priscilla, the abyss opened in front of him. He peered into the maw of the abyss and felt himself being drawn in." Interesting since I thought I had stopped loving Priscilla long before this. What would happen, I wondered, if I still loved her? I had read and thought much about insanity. In theory I knew there was a fine line between sanity and insanity. I had watched two friends crack up and tried unsuccessfully to help them. Yet it had never occurred to me that I could go crazy.

During the period between my breakup with Priscilla and my trial few other things occurred to me. All my time alone was spent thinking about my insanity and when it would become violent. When I was with people, I kept wondering why they acted normally towards me, seemed not to notice I was crazy. I knew I was nuts, why didn't they? (Or did they just pretend not to notice? Didn't that woman just wink at her friend? Perhaps they all know and just don't want to get stuck helping me. What are those people over there laughing at?)

I slept little because sleep brought all the nightmares of my boyhood. The Hound of the Baskervilles, whose story I read when I was ten or eleven and who chased me at night until I was fourteen, reappeared as soon as my eyes closed. If the dripping fangs woke me up when they caught me, I then had the choice of considering my insanity the rest of the night or returning to sleep and earlier and deadlier childhood nightmares, usually falling and crashing. I don't know how many airplanes I crashed in. (My mother always assured me planes were safe, but when we took one she always insured our lives with the quarter policies available in machines at the airport.)

My nightmares were so childish I might have relished them: surely the hound was preferable to the lake of Sal's blood which had so horrified me that I had fainted when I saw it in real life and which had often haunted my dreams before this time. But suddenly everything about my adult existence had become irrelevant. I could remember it, but I could not feel it. I could feel nothing but my insanity, had regressed to a child cowering in its shadow. I think I would have given anything during that short, crazy period to see a real adult horror, to be able to close my eyes and see the lake of blood. Insanity is crazy.

I sought out a group of radical therapists, ostensibly to involve them more in the community, a goal they desired, actually to be able to discuss madness. I was amazed that they never understood that I was asking about myself. (Or did they understand all too well?) I learned that radical therapists were no more perceptive than conservative ones, who were no more perceptive than ordinary folks. I'm sure Meg would have noticed if she wasn't busy pursuing her own problems. Perhaps my therapist friends respected my position in the radical community too much to suspect my insanity. Meg would not have made that mistake. In any case the therapists never invited me to any of their group sessions and I never asked directly. I'm thankful for that now. At the time I wasn't, but I did nothing but add their observations to my own and so increase the time I spent considering my insanity.

When I first moved away from Priscilla, I tried to keep working. Soon I found myself racing out of meetings as soon as they ended – previously the informal conversations afterward were more important to me than the meetings – so I would have more time to contemplate insanity. Then I began to leave in the middle of meetings, and finally I stopped going to meetings. Next I cut down on my time at the office and my visits to Jill and John and other friends.

In the end I almost stopped going to the office. It seems a measure of the burn out gripping the entire movement that no one commented on my slacking off. The therapists became my only friends. I did little but think and read: Freud, Jung, Adler, gestalt and existential psychology and, over and over, *Notes from the Underground* and *Oblomov*. Shortly before my trial I discovered *The Mass Psychology of Fascism*. I'm not sure whether Reich or the necessity to be sane during the trial saved me. I like to think it was the trial: it seems a fitting irony that the system's attempts at repression should provide my salvation. Just as they provided Jazzman's. Chicago's brutality drove us to the mountains.

THE WINTER'S SNOW IS MELTING in a gray drizzle. Chou En Lai is dead. He died two months ago, but I was reminded of him by a memorial program on the CBC, Canadian radio. There would never be one on American media. I admire Chou because he managed to be a revolutionary in spite of a middle class upbringing and extensive education. How does one shake off such heavy weights?

I had been in the middle of scores of illegal busts, beatings and murders by the Chicago police. I had seen tanks called out to deal with bottle-throwing black children in the south. I had seen Chicago police setting up barricades of squad cars with machine guns mounted on the hoods to confine a "riot" to the Cabrini-Green black ghetto, a riot that was never more than a rumour. Once when I was waiting in court for a charge against me to be dismissed, I had almost been fined for contempt for attempting to slip a note with our lawyer's and legal clinic's name and phone number to a black youth who had been unjustly jailed and didn't know he had a right to a lawyer.

Yet I believed I could not possibly be convicted of a crime because I had committed none. My friends were worried about my indictment. Not me: I was raised to respect American jurisprudence, had a good Jewish lawyer and wasn't about to let the evidence of my senses contradict my middle class upbringing. I was quite crazy by the time of my trial. I suppose it was a natural defense of a psyche which had reverted to childhood to revert to childhood illusions of security in an area where I needed a semblance of sanity. In Chicago that sort of logic easily passes for sanity, so no one noticed anything unusual about me.

I have notes from my trial. It went on for almost three weeks, and my lawyer had told me taking notes would make a good impression on the jury, would make me appear diligent and interested in everything that was said. Besides, taking notes took my mind off my insanity. So I took notes and tried to remember all the other theatrical advice my lawyer had given me for impressing the jury: "Always look serious, make as much eye contact with the jury as possible, dress neatly, look shocked and indignant at every lie you hear, invite your parents to court and embrace them when the jury is looking," etc., etc., etc. The main thing my notes express is first fascination, finally disgust at the game being played around and upon me.

Considering my childish state of mind, I suppose a game was appropriate. For it was nothing else: a contest between prosecutors and defense lawyers with the defendants and witnesses the chess pieces, now helpless pawns, now mighty queens, now mincing bishops, now powerful yet immobile kings, all always manipulated by the lawyers. While in chess only an occasional pawn can change its character and no piece can change colour, in court the character of the witnesses was an astonishingly inconsistent jigsaw of love and hate, honesty and depravity, schizophrenia, manic-depression and every other abnormality known to psychologists.

There were only the usual two colours, black and white, but the witnesses changed colour every time their questioner changed. The staid, unemotional, carefully observing attorney who happened to be in the CCC audience and humbly offered his recollections for the prosecution became, under defense cross-examination, a money lusting, chair hurling fiend who would tell any lie to protect his speculative real estate investments in Lincoln Park. The equally dignified attorney who had placed himself on the CCC stage to act as a peacemaker and be in position to observe what happened became, under prosecution cross-examination, a lawbreaking anarchist who deliberately sat on the stage to disrupt the meeting and, worse, was an acquaintance of mine and therefore someone who would tell any lie to protect his pal. This ludicrous attempt to convince the jury that all its pieces were white while all the other side's pieces were black was probably the least offensive aspect of the game.

The chess players, the opposing lawyers, had each read one book on the game. Each knew only one opening and one defense, and each held rigidly to that opening or defense no matter what the situation. None of them would have had a chance in a chess tournament, but in court, where the stakes were the lives of other people, their simplistic approach was the only one ever used. Before the trial each side had worked out an explanation of what had happened, and everything had to be jammed in to fit that explanation.

The defense explanation was that I was "just a man who came to a meeting," as my lawyer concluded her closing plea. I had come to the meeting because I was a good citizen interested in public affairs; I had remained in my seat except for two occasions, once to request that the speculator thugs in front of me stay in their seats and not provoke violence by charging the stage, once to comfort an injured child. The prosecution explanation depicted me as the sinister mastermind who had planned, then directed the entire riot. I had "stood prominently in the aisle waving (my) hands like an orchestra conductor conducting the whole disgusting, violent demonstration," according to the prosecutor. (Our lawyers always called him "prosecutor" except for occasional "slips" when they said "persecutor;" he called himself "state's attorney" or "attorney for the people of Illinois.")

Before the trial my lawyer asked me why I had tried to prevent the speculators from leaving their seats. I told her I thought they were cops and hoped to slow them down and make enough noise to warn the people on stage. "Forget that," she told me. "You wanted to preserve order in the meeting, no other reason. And nothing about even thinking of going up on stage."

So there I was, the apostle of order, shoved to the floor in the aisle trying to avoid the disruption of a Conservation Community Council meeting (whose meetings I had been disrupting for the previous year). It seemed an unnecessary stretch of facts and motives until I heard the prosecution account. It ignored my attempt to slow down the speculators, ignored the speculators completely, and pictured me in the aisle so I would be visible and could direct all the action. Fortunately the TV films showed there was far too much action to be directable, but although I was well away from all the violence, several prosecution witnesses had managed to notice me in the aisle motioning yet not one, not even the speculator who admitted shoving me, had noticed that I got there by being pushed to the floor.

Witnesses are carefully coached by their lawyers before testifying. The prosecution had to produce some such case since neither a single witness nor a single photograph – they must have had hundreds, they introduced about fifty into evidence – placed me near the mob I was accused of acting with. On the other hand we could not produce the one witness who knew everything I did, Priscilla. Were we to put her on the stand, the prosecution would bring out the fact that she and I had been living in sin and so both show that I was immoral and convince the jury that anything she said was a lie to protect her lover. It was especially strange since Priscilla and I had already split up. My lawyer asked her to attend the trial because her recollections might help the defense. It was the first time I had seen her in a month.

Cheating was a vital part of the game the lawyers were playing. Whenever possible they tried to nudge a piece onto a different square or make an illegal move, but their favourite tactic was to sneak a captured piece or a piece from an entirely different chess set onto the board. They constantly introduced irrelevant – therefore, they all knew – illegal evidence into the trial. They knew it would be ruled out of order by the judge, but they also knew the jurors would never be able to obey the judge's instruction to disregard it.

Since both sides were trying to advance a theory, not facts, all sorts of nonsense had to be implanted in the jurors' minds. Some of this was ridiculously trivial: The prosecution asked me if my short hair hadn't been longer at the time of the meeting (it wasn't but the hint that I was a hippie in disguise was not lost on the jury); when it came out during jury selection that a juror liked to bowl, my lawyer promptly inquired: "Would it prejudice you in my client's favour to learn he is a former city of Chicago high school bowling champion?" (It wouldn't, astonishingly, but the jury now knew I wasn't a hippie in disguise but an all-American boy.)

Some was fairly important: the prosecutor waving around a copy of the Lincoln Park *Press* and asking: "Are you the editor of this paper which calls policemen pigs?" (Not only was the question irrelevant, but I later checked the issue he was waving and found it didn't once use the word "pig." The prosecutor was too lazy and dishonest to read through the papers and dig up an issue in which we did call a cop "pig," just wanted to get a prejudicial sounding statement for the jury.) That one produced hysterics and a call for a mistrial from my lawyer. She was by far the best actor at the trial and that, I am sure, is what got me off. Actual guilt or innocence played little part in the legal game.

The lawyers did not think of the trial as a chess game: Their metaphors were of baseball. The first witness was the leadoff hitter; the one who did the damage the cleanup hitter; the lawyers pitched questions to them. The prosecution's leadoff and cleanup hitters were both Gang Intelligence Unit cops. To me the leadoff hitter was a knight, jumping onto the attack ahead of his pawns, setting things up for more powerful pieces to follow but inflicting little direct damage. Actually his main role had little to do with his testimony. He was also a coach.

The judge ruled that after completing his testimony he could remain in the courtroom. This insured that the game wouldn't be a fair one, for the cop didn't miss a minute of the trial and took careful notes to make sure his partner would not contradict any other witnesses. (Witnesses are not supposed to know of any other testimony.) Both cops were present every day of the trial. The Chicago Police Department paid them full time to sit around and try to convict us. By the time the cleanup hitter cop testified as the final prosecution witness, his coach knew and could instruct him in exactly what he should and should not say. The second cop was intended to be the all powerful queen who could command the now depleted board, but to my eyes he was the bullish rook charging the length of a vacant row but not mobile enough to protect all his flanks after the attack.

Before the cleanup hitter testified little had been said about me. The leadoff cop and two other witnesses, Milt Moore and Dick Steale, claimed I was in the aisle clapping and motioning; however, Moore had been seated on the opposite side of the auditorium from me while Steale was in the middle of the commotion on stage. I'm sure that Steale, especially, would have loved to convict me with a detailed lie, but the cross-examination made it apparent that neither LPCA leader was in a position to observe me, and even the little they did say seemed unlikely after my lawyer finished with them.

Frank Pender and several others, on the other hand, had been seated on my side of the hall yet failed to mention me in their testimony. My lawyer did not want to question any of these witnesses. She maintained that every non-mention was a point in my favour and that a question from her might enable them to make an adverse comment. But what John Leeds had once told me of Frank Pender persuaded me he wouldn't lie, so I insisted she question him. He had been sitting quite near me and replied that he had not noticed me do anything unusual.

The only other prosecution witness to mention me was the speculator who said I had urged him to remain in his seat and he had shoved me out of the way and gone up to the stage. My two co-defendants had at least been shown to be on the stage and in the middle of the action. So the cleanup cop's job was to get me. His description of the action made my lawyer furious (I assume because it was ganging up on her: the transparent professionalism of his testimony was especially evident to a pro like her, and in the legal game only the lawyers and judges were supposed to be pros) but made me rather proud.

He pictured me as I would have liked to be: a man of action, always in the right place at the right time, a leader who controlled masses with a single word or motion. I was all over the hall, conferring beforehand with every person who played any significant part in the melee, encouraging everyone on our side even, sinisterly, when I was silent and most of those on our side had their backs to me, perfectly directing a riot which, to anyone who had not observed my every move, appeared completely spontaneous. Other spectators and players could not testify against me because they could not see the pitches I was throwing. Only he, who knew of my evil genius and so had watched me closely, could follow the deceptive flight of the knuckleballs I was hurling with my feet while everyone else watched my empty hands.

Maybe I was lucky. But the prosecution was also hoping for a lot of luck in trying to get a conviction based on an almost one hundred per cent fiction. The cleanup witness said almost nothing about me which resembled my actions at that meeting, and there were almost a thousand people in attendance. It was Sam Jones' lawyer who called Alderman Krier to the stand (to testify that he had asked Sam to make a motion concerning People's Park and that was why Sam wanted the microphone). Only when I saw him on the stand did I remember my argument with him.

The cleanup cop had given a detailed description of me walking out of the hall with my arm around Joe (the other defendant) and then congratulating other "conspirators" outside the hall. So I whispered to my lawyer to ask the alderman whom he left the meeting with. He replied that he had walked up the aisle arguing with me and had argued continuously with me for at least ten minutes outside the hall. For once my lawyer didn't have to act: if she wasn't a Jew, I would have said her whole face lit up like a Christmas tree. "Have you ever met me or discussed this case with me before now?" "No, ma'am." "No further questions." Does the jury understand the significance, the rarity, of a witness who has not been coached?

The prosecutor made things even worse for his side by trying to link me with Krier. He asked the alderman if I had campaigned with him. (He assumed I must have supported Krier, an anti-machine alderman.) "No." "Did Vission's paper, the Lincoln Park *Press* support or oppose you in your campaign?" "It opposed me." The prosecutor quit asking questions.

It still took the jury over eight hours to reach a verdict. They weren't pleasant hours. The two cops followed us around – to earn their pay and make sure we didn't escape, I suppose. At a bar across from the courthouse they even tried to join us (the three defendants and our lawyers) at our table. I called the cleanup cop some names and he told me I should hope I was sent to jail because if I was on the street he would kill me. He didn't though: Too many lawyers had witnessed his threat.

▲ ▲ ▲

Historian: *I don't believe this. A cop threatened to off you in front of a whole table of lawyers?*

Novelist: *I didn't believe it either. I almost didn't use it. I was tempted to move the threat into the next chapter, make it the reason the narrator flees the city. It would work better there, but that wasn't the way it happened.*

Historian: *"What works in the novel goes in the novel."*

Novelist: *Caught. Now. But when I wrote it, I told it like it was. You're forcing me to admit that the novelist, at least the realistic novelist, is not as free as I like to brag I am.*

Historian: *A triumph for history. You couldn't write it the way it didn't happen. You wrote it the way it happened, not the way it would work best literarily.*

▲ ▲ ▲

I T TURNED OUT THE JURY was playing a game of its own. Joe, whom the prosecution had photos of standing on the meeting table with his fists clenched, was also being tried by the jury. (Sam Jones wanted no part of a "honky jury" and chose a bench trial. The judge acquitted him of the serious charge, mob action, but found him guilty of simple battery. Sam called him a honky, but his lawyer cooled him out before he got a contempt charge as well.) We later learned that a majority of the jury had begun by favouring conviction for both Joe and me, but eventually they worked out a compromise: Joe guilty, me innocent. Horsetrading is easier than thinking, and both sides on the jury won one decision; isn't that justice? A balanced verdict to go with the balanced indictment.

Not that I blame the jury: Twelve Einsteins couldn't have made an intelligent decision based on the nonsense presented as evidence at that trial. Only those intimately involved could understand the extent of the game being played with our lives. That's why the legal system keeps going: Few people get a chance to see how it really operates and those who do either get rich off it or are powerless victims of it. Some day a lawyer is going to begin to sing the praises of the American system of "justice" near me, and I'm going to puke in the self-serving bastard's face.

20.

THE VERDICT WAS HANDED DOWN at ten o'clock at night. I spent the rest of the night writing a story of the trial for the *Press*. I thought work might free my mind of the deadly game I had been playing for almost three weeks. I hoped that being forced to play that game had made me better, less crazy, and that work might complete the process. I was wrong, but I was right too. I was better because, although I wasn't better, I was prepared to do something about it – as I found out when I found out that I wasn't better.

For the next four days and nights I holed up in the office with Linda and Juan whenever they could join me. Juan was a Cuban refugee who had come to regret leaving his homeland but now couldn't get back, the latest and fastest of a long line of translators. We three put together the final edition of the Lincoln Park *Press*. I had begun to deliver the finished newspapers when I lost it, lost all control, went entirely crazy. I was in my car with stacks of undelivered papers in the back. I had just dropped off a batch at the Seminary Restaurant, down Lincoln Avenue from our office.

As I drove off a cop I didn't recognize greeted me by name. "How many babies have you billy clubbed today?" my mind screamed at him. I don't think I spoke out loud. Suddenly I knew I was nuts and dared not get out of the car in Chicago. I expected to crash, but death seemed preferable to being in Chicago. Somehow I got onto Lake Shore Drive, the Calumet Skyway, the Indiana Tollroad. The accelerator was floored, but fortunately the old Volkswagen couldn't go much over fifty. The tollgates scared the shit out of me. I think I set off the alarm once, but I was never stopped.

I examined my inner self. Driving a car wasn't the best or the right time to do it, but I had to do it. If I had to wait for the right time to do it, I wouldn't do it. I had been not doing it for months, waiting for others or for circumstances to do it for me. Sometimes you've got to do what you've got to do where you're at, even if where you're at is not where you would have chosen to do it if you could have chosen where and when to do it. When you're in the abyss, you're in it alone and you don't get to choose.

So I drove on. I don't remember seeing anything outside between a tollroad "oasis," where I gassed up and rolled in what passed for grass in that desert of the road, and the Canadian border. In Michigan the road was an interstate, straight and straightforward – not that I saw it until I drove it on the way back. On the way north what I was finally seeing – and sinking into – was my own insanity. Although I wasn't aware of any planning, I must have been prepared because I was carrying a lot more money than I usually did. I had paid for printing the newspaper in cash and never taken the excess out of my wallet.

As I drove I was watching a vision of myself on a slab. I was split in half, an open book. A thin line with some sort of hinge arrangement held the two halves together. (Maybe that line derived from ones on the highway, but I don't think so.) One side of me was red, healthy looking, with blood circulating nicely. The other side was green, the green of mould and dirty money. It too was moving but not with the constant flow of blood as on the healthy side.

The movement on the green side had no pattern. It was the random motion of millions of tiny worms and fast growing spores. The motion of this mass of microscopic vermin sent waves pulsing in every direction, crashing into each other, forming momentary miniature mountains which were immediately covered by new waves, new conflicts, new peaks, a restless ocean of slime beckoning me in for a dip. It was alive, all too alive, even if not the kind of life I thought I was seeking, even if it opposed the healthy looking red side of me. Was I really so dead this disgusting morass could attract me? Since I was attracted the answer was obvious.

I stared at the worms and spores, trying to discover purpose in their seething activity. Sometimes I thought they were trying to eat my heart, liver and other organs, but as soon as I reached this conclusion I realized that many, perhaps most of them, were ignoring these organs. Some of them were squirming aimlessly, some were even eating each other, while others were being born or at least newly emerging from the green slime around them. I managed to focus on one particularly fat worm in the act of assimilating – I could see no mouth – a smaller worm, which seemed to survive inside the larger one and caused it to convulse spasmodically. As it wriggled in opposing directions, a wave washed over it and it vomited forth dozens of tiny worms which in turn vomited still smaller ones until my eyes ceased to distinguish them and all seemed to dissolve into the squirm of green.

I was gazing at all this from the thin hingeline between my selves as if I were both the dissected creature and a whole being walking the line with a balancing pole, wondering how to close the hinged body, knowing it could not be done. This in addition to the me – or was it "it" – driving the car, but that self was of no interest. I only became aware of it once, at the "oasis."

As soon as I began driving again, I was back walking the hingeline and talking to myself: "So this is what my insanity looks like, and all this time I thought insanity was clear cut, sharp like a knife to sever mind from body. I believed theories about everyone being at least partially crazy yet never applied the ideas to myself. I have always been so damn reasonable. Even when I pictured myself as Lawrence's man of passion, it was the result of deciding logically that such a person benefitted the world more than the scientist."

I knew I could step off into the beckoning green mould and wallow. So I had to do it if only to learn if I could escape afterwards. I laughed at my desire for logical experimentation even as I felt the green ooze caressing, nibbling me and spitting out my pieces. It tickled and I laughed aloud as I drove. Or was I screaming? I knew I could rise back out of the mould, but I didn't know if I would. I speculated about whether I could become so fascinated by sensations of being devoured and regurgitated by creatures of my fantasy that I would never wish to do otherwise. Or whether at some point enough of me would be eaten so I would lack the strength to get out even if I chose to. Then I stepped out without choosing to and speculated about whether an instinct for self-preservation would not allow me to remain in too long. So I dove back in to spite the instinct.

That is what I wrote then. I wrote it (and a lot more) in a provincial park on Georgian Bay where I sheltered after the drive. It's not a very imaginative depiction of insanity. On the other hand, with a little more imagination I might have crashed the car and killed myself. Maybe I am writing now because my imagination simply wasn't up to conjuring an insanity hellish enough to make me crash.

All the way to Canada my mind wallowed in that slime. My only outside memory is of the "oasis." Then I climbed back into the car and into the muck and didn't stop again until Sault St. Marie. Once out of the United States I felt somewhat human and slightly saner. I pulled off the road. I think I slept a few hours, but if I did I dreamed the same dreams I had been dreaming when I was awake. Still, the stop seemed to enable me to drive more normally and look at the scenery outside. It was lovely, an infinitely finer shade of green than the one inside. Could it too become a part of me?

Eventually I followed a sign to the provincial park. I stayed inside the cold, cramped Volkswagen, venturing outside only for trips to the outhouse, for two nights and a day, sleeping and writing, but when I went out to pee during the second night, I saw the stars. I don't think I related them to the stars Jazzman had seen at Nippersink, but seeing them made it easier to get out of the car to better appreciate the dawn of the next day. During that day I gradually exchanged the green inside me for the green outside my car windows. Then I felt safe enough to walk in the woods.

Perhaps it was at Georgian Bay that I fell in love with my mountains although there are no real mountains around there. I don't know. I was too crazy to remember much of what I saw, only that I liked it, needed it. I haven't seen it since and know it cannot look much like these mountains. Yet when I first came into these mountains, I experienced a thrill of recognition: everything in me screamed that I had been here before and that before was at Georgian Bay. Perhaps it's simply that all wilderness looks the same to a city slicker. Perhaps I at least subconsciously remembered Jazzman and his stars and they led me to where I ended up both then and later. (As I write now I like to imagine Jazzman escaping toward western Canada at the very moment I was driving toward Georgian Bay.)

Maybe I was hallucinating some universal, primitive, group unconscious memory in Georgian Bay, and these mountains are another part of that memory. There are any number of explanations, so why make a big deal of it? I felt free in Georgian Bay and I feel free here. That is sufficient. I never felt free in Chicago. Except possibly during the big snow, when Chicago ceased to be Chicago for a few days.

Petty, personal, hypocritical justifications are the very smoke in the atmosphere of Chicago. In the clearer air of Georgian Bay I saw my parting argument to Priscilla for what it was, the last refuge of one who is wrong and cannot admit it even to himself. I laughed imagining myself pompously squeaking, "How can you understand me so little? How can you impute base motives to me?" It took a lot of kindness in Priscilla to keep from laughing her foghorn laugh. Now that I could laugh I could see how right she was to tell me to get out. I, with all my imagined strength, had become shamefully dependent on her and used her every way except fairly.

I resolved to remake myself, to become strong – again or for the first time? I wasn't sure – alone. Such a resolution seemed necessary at the time; that it stopped there shows that either my mountain air is much clearer than the air of Georgian Bay or that I didn't stay there long enough. For I returned to Chicago determined to treat Priscilla as a friend and political ally, nothing more. It was my ultimate cruelty to her, my ultimate delusion of myself.

At Georgian Bay I began to try to do what was just becoming fashionable in radical circles, to sort out the political and the personal. I bumbled badly, as I was bound to since I had to return to Chicago's smog. I tried to treat Priscilla politically, as just another member of Concerned Citizens of Lincoln Park, which broke her heart as hatred never could have. Yet while trying to remove the personal from my relations with Priscilla and bring her more fully into Concerned Citizens of Lincoln Park, I was trying to force the others in the organization to deal with the personal, to look inside themselves, to share their lives with each other.

This destroyed the organization. If I could not deal well with the frustrations seething inside myself, could not begin to understand my own needs for Priscilla or her feelings for me, how could I guess at the frustrations of others? What was I asking of Jill with her ten kids or Linda with her multiple existences as mother, secretary, student and activist when I asked them to pause in their lives, to take time to look within? Or of Bob, who had just learned that the woman he loved had been shipped to Greece to make sure he would never see her again, whose insides must have been an ocean of tears barely contained by his fragile shell of jokes and clowning? The political unity of Concerned Citizens of Lincoln Park had long been a shield to protect its members from their own selves as well as from Chicago. If only all of us could have got out of Chicago then and spared ourselves the death throes of our organization and neighbourhood.

I should have been able to figure out from my reaction to Georgian Bay that I could not feel alive in Chicago. But as soon as I began to feel alive, I went back to brag to others. It took Jazzman, invigorated by more than a year's escape from Chicago, to teach me I could escape. That part of me may never change. Even now, alone in my mountains, I am their student, not their explorer.

YESTERDAY MY WORLD was one of disintegration: wet ice crystals smudged with dirt, puddles, the early spring meltoff. Today all that ugliness is covered in a brief white beauty, an evanescent reminder of the winter which was needed and lovely in its rising, powerful at its peak, hateful and stagnant in its slow decline. An early spring snow is a transient glory; nevertheless, it is still glorious. Later, after the accumulation of winter is gone, the warm earth melts late, light snowfalls or couchgrass and knapweed poke through the thin layer which does survive.

April and May snows are insults to new life, disorganized rebellions against the future. This snow is different. It harmonizes although winter's best hour is long past. It covers ugliness before merging into it as it must. Tomorrow will be like yesterday, and soon after that will come the days of mud, the awful moment when all the desolation of last year becomes visible, before the first green shoots reassure us that even filth has its function, that corruption is but compost to feed new life. But for now I will try not to look ahead, will attempt to indulge my memory at least as long as the late March snow continues to indulge the winter in its last dreams of permanence.

WE ACCOMPLISHED SO MUCH so quickly in the early spring of 1970, yet my recollection blurs because everything vanished even more quickly. Jazzman was gone: He had crept quietly into the night without a farewell.

▲ ▲ ▲

Historian: *There was a farewell, but it didn't come at our last meeting. It came at the penultimate one.*
Novelist: *Oh my god, do you know what you just said? That's a magic word. Did you say it on purpose? Did that conversation really happen?*
Historian: *Which conversation? The one about your Ph.D. orals? Of course it did. It's one of the reasons I am where I am today.*
Novelist: *The question about the penultimate chapter of an obscure seventeenth century work of prose turned out to be the ultimate chapter in my career as a student and an academic.*
Historian: *And the opening chapter in mine.*
Novelist: *If I had answered that question …*

Historian: *Maybe even if you had failed the exam. It was the contradiction between failing the question and passing the exam that taught you what was wrong with academia.*

Novelist: *I wish there was a way to hug you over long distance telephone. You still catch on faster than I can think.*

Historian: *I'm not as fast as you keep saying I am. It took me over forty years to begin the second chapter in my career.*

Novelist: *For almost fifty years I have believed that our conversation happened only in my head, which did not rest solidly on my neck and shoulders in those days. I wanted to put it in my novel in the worst way, but I couldn't.*

Historian: *Why not?*

Novelist: *Because I didn't believe it happened. Given the condition I was in, I thought I was dreaming the farewell connection I wished we made.*

Historian: *Why should that stop you from including it? This is a novel!*

Novelist: *It felt too important, too unbelievable. The conversation in my mind was far out, but I was so far out of my mind that I was sure it was only in my mind. It couldn't be real. I mean I was entitled to wild imaginings, but readers were entitled not to have my wild imaginings foisted upon them. I simply couldn't do it.*

Historian: *Wait a minute. I seem to recall your telling me how unimaginative you were.*

Novelist: *Yes, when I was sane. But since I knew I was not sane at that time, every time I tried to tell myself it happened I ended up telling myself that even thinking it might have happened proved how crazy I was.*

Historian: *Maybe it has nothing to do with sanity or insanity. Maybe it has to do with truth. Maybe truth is not as easy to manipulate as you like to say you think.*

Novelist: *Wow! I have to think about that ... I became a novelist in a six student undergraduate seminar with the young Saul Bellow. Not that Saul seemed young to teenaged me, but I was so young it took me twelve more years to accumulate the life experience an unimaginative novelist needed to begin his first novel. And that life experience left me so crazy it took me another five years to start writing it.*

Historian: *We were both more than a little crazy. I ended up curing my craziness with the stars. You cured yours with the mountains.*

Novelist: *But if I wasn't completely crazy then, if that conversation in the car really happened, I have to add it.*

Historian: *We have to add it. We had it, not just you. It's important to me too. We had it in the car, but we had it because of the stars.*

Novelist: *You didn't want to get in the car. You just wanted to look at the stars. You acted stoned. That's why I thought you must have been on junk.*

Historian: *So you tried to act straight because you thought I was stoned? You weren't interested in my stars. That hurt. You just wanted to get back in the car and drive to the city.*

Novelist: *I had orders to get you back as soon as possible, and I had been looking at those stars since I was a boy.*

Historian: *But I spent my life in the city. I never saw anything like that. The only stars I knew anything about were movie stars. There were millions of stars in the sky, and the Milky Way was clearer than a three D cinemascope movie. I almost got religion looking at them.*

Novelist: *I didn't know what to do. You weren't acting like you. The only junkies I knew anything about were in books.*

Historian: *I'm sure I acted strange. I had just started using again. I wasn't completely hooked. In fact I was trying to use the time I was out there to kick. That's why I couldn't sleep. I spent both nights walking around looking at the stars.*

Novelist: *I was strained too, just as strange as you. Maybe stranger. All kinds of crazy crap going on in my head.*

Historian: *The time after Fred's murder was a terrible time. And getting in the car that night made it worse for me. It turned off the stars. I made you stop. I said I needed to piss. Anything to get out of the car. But the place you stopped wasn't as good as your parents' house. It wasn't as dark. The stars were still there, but they weren't as good. I was losing them.*

Novelist: *After you got back in the car, you didn't say a word for a long, long time. I thought you were somewhere else, and after a while I thought I was somewhere else too. That's why I thought the conversation never happened. I thought I was driving the car and dreaming words I wanted to hear. I'm surprised we didn't crash.*

Historian: *I was lost in the stars. Do you know there's a song by that name?*

Novelist: *By Kurt Weil, Brecht's collaborator.*

Historian: *Good, we're together now. I was lost for a long time. Finally I said: "That is one strange place. All those big, empty houses, and in Lincoln Park my people are being forced out of their homes. Often there are two or even three families living in an apartment that was crowded when there was one family. It pissed me off – until I saw the stars. I spent both nights awake, lost in the stars." So I asked you: "What is the word for an animal who stays awake all night?"*

Novelist: *"Nocturnal. You were nocturnal."*

Historian: *"Right. Except I couldn't sleep in the day either. What's the word for that?"*

Novelist: *That's when I cracked up. I couldn't believe you really asked that question. That's another reason why I didn't believe the conversation was real. You asked about my other magic word. When I finally stopped laughing I explained: "Do you know that I once studied for a Ph.D.? I completed all my coursework. Then on my oral exam a professor asked me: 'What is the key word in the penultimate chapter of Sir Thomas Browne's* Hydrotaphia *or* Urn Burial*?' The key word is the word you just asked me, 'diurnal.'"*

Historian: *I was in bad shape, but not so bad that I couldn't join your laughter. Then I said: "I didn't know you had such a high class education. That's why you have so many books."*

Novelist: *"I'm not proud of my education. That professor's question taught me how useless it was. That's why I quit school and started working with people, not books."*

Historian: *I was out of it in the car. I needed the stars and I needed to sleep. It took me a while to digest that. Then I surprised myself by saying: "It doesn't look like our revolution is going to happen. If it doesn't, one day I'm going to go back to school, study in a college, maybe get a Ph.D. myself. I'd like to learn all your fancy words and ideas."*

Novelist: *That idea seemed unreal, not you, another reason for thinking the connection was in my head alone. Taking final exams at an age when you should be collecting social security is not my idea of fun. When I created Jazzman I gave him the love of nature I saw in your appreciation of the stars. So he ended up in the mountains, not the university.*

Historian: *And writing in the mountains you couldn't put our conversation in because it felt unreal, out of place, fictional. You refused to manipulate truth ... Unknowingly you created a history, not a novel. A novel history, not a historical novel.*

Novelist: *I never finished my novel, never wrote a proper conclusion. I wanted to end on an optimistic note. I wanted so badly to end well, but I could not end well in fiction what in fact ended so badly.*

Historian: *But maybe by ending without a conclusion you imply it is not over. History never is. Novels and people end. History doesn't.*

Novelist: *Maybe ... After the Tiananmen Massacre ended another chapter of my life in 1989, I bought a t-shirt that said: "You cannot massacre an idea."*

▲ ▲ ▲

MEG WAS GONE: Her needs took her away. Lots of farewells from her, strategy session after strategy session, some with what was left of the group, some alone with me, about what the Citizens should do in her absence. She didn't want to leave, she fought against leaving, but with Jazzman gone it was a fight she couldn't win. She – all of us – had been through too much hate to reject a chance at love. Dear, damned Meg, never had one of your endearments looked so much like damnation to me. You needed to get away from Chicago as much as I did, but your mountains had legs. I should have said "almost all of us." Priscilla was gone from my life although she remained in her coach house and even became more active in Concerned Citizens of Lincoln Park than she had been when we lived together. We often worked alongside one another, pretending love had mellowed into friendship.

I had returned from Georgian Bay with a transitory illusion of well being and power. I had begun to understand some of our errors and confused this glimmer of understanding with light. I was relieved to feel sane again yet so aware of the insanity I had come through that my thoughts centred on personal salvation, my own – but more important since I had almost convinced myself that mine had been achieved, that I was no longer crazy – and that of others.

I began to notice people who had long worked with me but had remained in the background because they were just ordinary folks: Linda, Bob, Chuck and others. I assumed the movement in Lincoln Park must have been as destructive of their mental health as it had been of mine, and what we needed was to become friends. We began to play charades at our meetings and held a weekend retreat at a Wisconsin farm owned by one of my radical therapist friends. Things seemed less intense, yet while we appeared to be accomplishing many of our goals, we were actually disintegrating rapidly.

Even the cops seemed to sense this and hassled us far less than in 1969. Probably this was not the result of a shrewd decision to let us fall apart on our own but of the murder of Fred Hampton. Although the assassination shattered the radical movement in Chicago, its immediate consequence was an upsurge of liberal resentment which shackled the police temporarily. While radical organizations were quietly collapsing, the liberals were loudly condemning Hanrahan and his raiders. Eventually even Mayor Daley was forced to desert Hanrahan, and long before that happened the cops were forced to slacken the vigour of their political repression. People like me were allowed to fade into their mountains instead of being buried in coffins or jails. I suppose I should be grateful.

So we set up and helped and encouraged others to set up free community alternative institutions designed to give poor people a few of the rights they can seldom afford in a society based on money: the legal office and clinic, the medical clinics, a strengthened welfare rights group, a breakfast program for kids, a day care centre, a free school. One project failed but only after a series of successes which threatened to revitalize the Lincoln Park movement.

OUR MAIN FOCUS HAD ALWAYS BEEN HOUSING. This was necessarily so because urban renewal and real estate speculation were destroying our neighbourhood, driving poor people out in droves. Most of our struggles aimed at slowing this process, keeping poor people around. The ultimate goal of all our alternative institutions was to create an environment in which poor people could survive with dignity and for which they would fight. One object of all our marches, demonstrations and festivals was to proclaim as loudly as possible that Lincoln Park was our community, that we controlled the streets and would not slink away silently, that wealthy people would not be able to purchase suburban stillness based on poor people's removal.

However, the fact was that people were being pushed out, and although we might slow the pushers down, we could not hope to stop them and push them back unless we provided new housing for our people. So a coalition had formed for the occupation of McCormick, a coalition of Latin, black and poor white groups, the Poor Peoples' Coalition.

Its main purpose was to use the seed money and expertise pledged by the seminary to plan and construct low-rent, occupant-controlled housing.

The Coalition hired the young architect who had already worked with us on People's Park. He sympathized with our goals and agreed to meet with and be guided by the kind of people who would be living in the apartments he planned. It was this architect who invited Buckminster Fuller to the community and helped secure his aid and advice. The meeting with Fuller was the first of a series of open meetings at which poor people, especially those with large families, spoke out about their housing problems and needs. The architect listened, asked questions, responded with his ideas and, if they seemed acceptable, incorporated them into the plan.

For example, there was an ongoing discussion about porches. Jill began it. She and many other people at the meetings had grown up in the country and lovingly remembered their old front porches. Obviously, front porches were impracticable in a seventy unit, three storied structure. Besides, who wanted to look out onto Larrabee Street? The architect suggested rear balconies. The audience was sceptical: Balconies were narrow, confining, unsafe.

The architect researched the matter and returned to the next meeting with a plan for ten foot wide balconies with high railings to protect playing children. The size satisfied people, but they still disliked leaving children on them unsupervised. So the architect rearranged all floor plans to insure that all balconies were adjacent to the kitchen and connected through a glass wall. This meant a small child on the balcony would be visible to an adult in the kitchen, the most commonly used room during the day. The final plan called for continuous wide balconies separated by doors so there could be either privacy or visiting.

So the process went and it was an exciting process. One seldom sees professionals and ordinary folks interacting as equals in the professional's field of specialty. Certainly both sides learned a lot. So did I: It was a glimpse of how people can cooperate, how a society can be structured without class differences based on education.

By late 1969 we had blueprints and could embark on getting the apartments built. This involved two tactics, one secret, the other public. Secret negotiations were held with the Chicago Housing Authority, the agency which runs all Chicago's housing projects. This was necessary because we intended to build good quality housing. Our units would not be cheap. Without a sizeable subsidy we would have to charge rents too high for the people we wanted as tenants to afford, and the CHA was the only agency with the power and finances to grant such a subsidy. We had to be careful though because the last thing we wanted was CHA control of our housing, or even involvement in its management. We wanted nothing from them but cash.

Ordinarily we would have had no chance of achieving such terms, but the Authority was in a desperate situation as a result of the locally famous Austin Decision. In the mid-Sixties federal judge Austin had ruled that the CHA's practice of constructing public housing only in black neighbourhoods was discriminatory. Therefore, he ruled, public housing must be built in white neighbourhoods before any more could be built in the black ghettos. Since public housing was federally financed, it could not be segregated, and none of Chicago's segregated white areas wanted integrated housing. The Daley machine was not about to alienate either realtors, who made huge profits from Chicago's near total segregation, or the base of its votes, a base which had long been nurtured on racial hatred.

As a result no new public housing of any kind had been constructed in Chicago for years, and Austin and the federal government were pressuring the CHA to build some. Our plan was perfect for the CHA, especially since we were stipulating that the units would be approximately one-third black, one-third Latin and one-third white. We would do the building, and they could take the credit with the federal government while avoiding most of the local blame. They had never subsidized housing without controlling it before and certainly did not like the idea, but they were desperate.

Seventy units was small enough not to seem too threatening yet large enough to boast of to the federal government and Austin's court. At our third secret meeting the CHA director and commissioners signed an agreement drawn up by our lawyers. They agreed to subsidize seventy units while granting full management rights to the tenants and the Poor Peoples' Coalition. Suddenly our plan was economically feasible.

Now we had to get it approved, first by our old enemies on the Conservation Community Council and then by the Department of Urban Renewal, which meant Mayor Daley himself. The CCC turned out to be relatively easy. It hadn't attempted to meet since the police-packed fall meeting which followed the People's Park skirmish. When we requested a meeting, the Council was overjoyed since this marked the first time we had ever acknowledged its right to exist. (We had debated making the contact for this very reason; we didn't believe it had the right to exist with its unrepresentative membership, but there seemed no other way to get our housing approved.)

We packed the Urban Renewal Building Hall, sang songs of our own composition about Lincoln Park and charmed our enemies into a thirteen to two vote to approve giving us one large and three small parcels of land on Larrabee Street despite the fact that their neighbourhood renewal plan called for only eighteen low-income housing units in the entire area between Larrabee and Halsted. Only Dick Steale and one of his allies on the right wing of the Lincoln Park Conservation Association voted against us.

The Department of Urban Renewal Board was less easily influenced. Editorials in three of Chicago's daily newspapers – the *Tribune* remained silent – praised and endorsed our plan and pointed out that no Conservation Community Council recommendation had ever been rejected by the city. However, we knew that Dick Steale and his friends had made several trips to the mayor's office. Some people claimed he had been granted an audience by Hizzoner himself.

The public meeting at City Hall had to be moved into the City Council Chambers, the only room large enough to accommodate the hundreds of people who came to support the Coalition plan. We spent hours in corridors being switched from one place to another and signing up on official lists of people who desired to speak at the "public hearing," but the meeting itself was the shortest one since the CCC meeting that didn't take place in January, 1969. We had barely settled into our seats when Lyle Hoel, Mayor Daley's director of urban renewal, announced that in view of the large attendance he would not call for individual public statements but would ask members of the audience to express their preference by standing to show which plan (three firms as well as the Poor Folks' Coalition had submitted bids) people favoured.

The entire audience (except Dick Steale and a few friends) rose to support the Coalition plan, and as we did so with a prolonged shuffling of feet and bumping of chairs, the commissioners conducted a quick and unanimous vote giving the land to a commercial developer to construct fancy townhouses. The vote must have taken all of five seconds.

Bob was the first among us to catch on to what had just happened. Chuck, who usually anticipated and restrained Bob's wilder impulses, was a second late this time. As Bob vaulted the gallery railing, Chuck snatched at him but missed. Chuck started after him but lacked Bob's agility, and Priscilla was able to pull him back. Others then held on until he, like the rest of us, realized there was nothing we could do but watch. Six months earlier we might have reacted otherwise, but now our only possible role seemed to be that of stunned spectators.

At Bob's first movement the doors on either side of the front of the council chambers banged open and dozens of cops charged in. All motion converged on the centre of the stage where Lyle Hoel stood at a microphone with the commissioners seated behind him. With his usual flair Bob chose the most spectacular if not the most rapid route. He leapt monkeylike from green felt covered aldermanic table to table, dove off the final table toward Lyle Hoel's throat, was intercepted in midair by a bevy of cops, dragged – screaming "down with urban renewal, down with Mayor Daley" – from the chambers, heaved into the back of a paddy wagon, and driven around Chicago for two hours while cops took turns beating him with fists, clubs, rubber hoses and his own heavy belt buckle.

Sometime during the excitement of Bob's wild rush the meeting must have been adjourned, for when we turned our heads back from the side door through which Bob was being carried, Hoel and the commissioners had vanished. Their entire precisely choreographed performance could not have taken more than a minute. The cops had been prepared for a lot more action than poor Bob was able to provide.

It took us over six hours to retrieve Bob, who looked worse than Larrabee Street when the police finally released him. As he limped painfully toward me, he tottered and I caught him. He threw his arms around me and said: "Sorry, Dick, I stuccumbled."

"No," I told him. "You stood tall. We stuccumbled."

He had to spend several days in the hospital recovering and undergoing examinations for internal injuries. His only consolation was that he was never prosecuted. Our lawyers worked out a typical Chicago deal: Bob agreed not to press charges against the cops who beat him (none of whom he could positively identify anyhow since they had removed all nameplates and badges, and he was in no shape to recognize anything after a few minutes in the paddy wagon) if the city dropped charges against him.

THIS IS THE FIRST TIME I've written in a week, and I know I won't have time to write of the way Concerned Citizens of Lincoln Park and I squished and squelched, rotted, melted away, dissolved, evaporated. Like a deep winter's snow in the spring. I look out my window. It's happening as I write. I did not want to end like that. The night before I was to leave Lincoln Park I filled a bottle with gasoline, plugged it with a gasoline soaked rag and crept into the alley behind 2100 Bissell Street. The remodelling was almost complete, but for now the block was black, deserted, peopleless. I lit my rag, hurled my parting gift into Jazzman's former residence and ran, ran, ran two blocks down the alley to my apartment, where I lay panting on my bed, waiting to hear the sirens. They never came. Without Fred Hampton all our Molotov cocktails were duds.

NOW I KNOW THE SEASONS, have seen the full year go by in my mountains. The year has taught me that I did not come here to escape Chicago by writing about it but to live. The life promised to me on Bissell Street more than ten years ago, the life which remained incomplete as long as I remained in Chicago, has been given to me in the mountains of British Columbia, given to me by Jazzman, who lived on Bissell Street and is back in Chicago now, although Bissell Street as he knew it no longer exists. What was it like for him that spring, summer and fall of 1970, when he lived in these mountains and made himself strong enough to face Chicago and jail again? How could he have gone back? I can't imagine it.

Maybe that is what I will write of next winter. Maybe writing about it can teach me to understand it. Writing, learning the lessons of Chicago, is a part of the cycle of life, a small part. The past must always be part of the present if we are to reach the future without repeating ourselves and our mistakes endlessly. But living and being now are far more important, especially when spring nears. So I become impatient with the cycle, want it to spin more quickly into spring so I can be outside working, sowing, not inside writing. Perhaps next spring I will be more fully a part of the cycle, will not become restless, will write relentlessly until the moment it is time to stop and go out to prepare for planting. Or perhaps I will understand that impatience is another part of the cycle. Or that my mountains do not care what or if I write.

A HOT SPRING SUN is shining on the last of the winter's snow. By tomorrow the last smudges will be gone down here. Even in the mountains it is melting fast. The river is rising; streams are roaring; everywhere rivulets race down the mountainside, along the roads, into ditches, into each other and the creeks and rivers. Yesterday I drove up the Slocan Valley with a friend, and her three-year-old daughter, Revolutionary Hope, assured me: "The Little Slocan flows into the big Slocan, the Slocan flows into the Kootenay, the Kootenay flows into the Columbia and the Columbia flows into the Pacific Ocean."

EPILOGUES: 2018

Disturbing the Dust:
Making Do Fifty Years Late(r)

Novelist's Epilogue: Now and Then

THE NOVEL HAS ENDED. *It began as a novel of contemporary life, but time has changed it into the historical novel you, reader, have just finished. If a historical novel, a tale of two countries, a tale of a flat American city of the 1960s viewed from the mountains of Canada in the 1970s was all you sought, stop here. If the audacity of the novelist stepping out of the pages of his novel to address you disgusts you, read no farther. The novel ended as novels occasionally do, with the sort of symbol novelists love, with Hope, Revolutionary Hope, the words of a child: from the mouths of babes ...*

In fact, in the world of fact, not fiction, I loved that baby. She was my daughter, now grown to be a mother herself, the mother of my grandchildren, and she was really named Revolutionary Hope, is still called Revi. She was born in Chicago, the great blessing of the bleak years after I abandoned Lincoln Park and before I escaped the city, and was a beautiful baby with a head of ringlets as blond and bright as the moon. Now the ringlets have straightened and the hair is dyed red, the colour of revolution. Except that in the United States, where she now lives after growing up in Canada, red is the colour of the Republican Party. "All's changed, changed utterly." But despite the colour, there's no beauty in the terror that has been born.

The terror was there when I was young, but it was sometimes tinged by beauty although the world was mainly black and white despite Revi's ringlets and our attempts to splash around a bit of red. Black lives mattered. Leaders like Malcolm X and Fred Hampton were what J. Edgar Hoover, the boss of the FBI, christened "black messiahs." Jailing them could only enhance their reputations, so they had to be assassinated. In Chicago the terror of Fred Hampton's assassination haunted us. Back then we who had chanted "I am a revolutionary" with Fred were left in despair by our leader's murder. We walked the streets of Chicago and talked the talk of revolutionaries out of habit yet were imprisoned in that despair, each alone, each trying to devise a "jailbreak," as the Weathermen called it. Mine took me to the mountains of British Columbia, where I became a novelist. That was then.

Today Lincoln Park, the urban-renewed version built on the rubble of the one I loved, is the wealthiest neighbourhood in Chicago, one of the wealthiest in the world. I have never seen it and hope I never will. I refuse even to look at pictures of it. The diverse Lincoln Park I fell in love with more than fifty years ago and wrote of more than forty years ago is long dead, but Cha Cha and I are not. Stumbling through the internet I stumble upon an interview of Cha Cha Jimenez (not Jazzman Morales, which he became in my novel) by a Winnipeg radio station. He went to jail, so his jailbreak was more literal than mine. More than forty years after he got out and I last saw him, he is still inviting all and sundry to revolt. Fred often said: "You can kill a revolutionary, but you can't kill the revolution." Fred was wrong: His murder killed our revolution. Nevertheless, although you can kill a revolution, you can't kill revolutionary hope. I stumble on until I locate Cha Cha, email him, talk to him on the telephone. At age sixty five the boy I knew as an eighth grade dropout, the kid who lived in the present for the future, has become a graduate student of history.

Today too many black lives matter as commodities to be warehoused in prisons, used to make a profit for capitalist masters. In my youth jail scared the hell out of a middle class kid like me, but to a ghetto kid like Cha Cha it was almost a vacation, a place to get himself together, a hermitage in which to kick, strengthen and plan. It had not changed much since the Seventeenth Century:

> Stone walls do not a prison make,
> Nor iron bars a cage;
> Minds innocent and quiet take
> That for an hermitage.
> If I have freedom in my love,
> And in my soul am free,
> Angels alone that soar above,
> Enjoy such liberty.

Inmates worked in the prisons of my youth, but at least the ostensible purpose of their labour was rehabilitation for them, not profit for the stock-holders of the prison.

I am a novelist who writes mainly from experience, not imagination. My experience – the experience of a middle class white kid who had the privilege of living in a world not his own and participating in a movement to overthrow the tyranny of his own class and race – gave me material for a great novel. I dropped out to write it, might as well have gone underground so isolated from my former world was I, but my lack of imagination prevented my novel from attaining greatness.

Because of my lack of imagination I often end up attributing to characters unlike me many of my own characteristics. If time could let me reimagine my main character, a historian who once was a kid I knew well but could not imagine well when I knew him, might that reinvigorate the novel I wrote more than forty years ago, a novel I cannot rewrite because an old man could never recapture the youthful spirit in which it was written? The lover of mountains I became when I got to British Columbia invented Jazzman. Might the arthritic unable to climb them I am today reinvent him? But what good would that do? How can reimagining a character I can't change reinvigorate a novel I can't revise?

Time is the crime: It stole the identity of my novel, twisted it into a history being used in a historian's thesis; it mugged the firebrand author, who awoke a burnt out ash in a world he hardly recognized, a full blown police state complete with slavery and run by a psychopath. Even if I can't change my novel – you can't change history, or at least you shouldn't – might the brave new world time has awakened me into let me add to what I cannot finish, splash my bucket of water onto our burning world? And might that reinvigorate me?

When I reached the Slocan Valley in 1975, I heard stories of Weather Underground stalwarts who had been there five years earlier – at one time half the FBI's "Ten Most Wanted List" had resided in the Valley. I asked if a blond haired, blue eyed Puerto Rican had been there too. Nobody remembered one, but everybody said there might have been one. Those had been overfull days in which no one fully comprehended what was happening and who was there, only that too much was happening and too many people were around to know – or remember. That was enough for me – and Jazzman. With my defective imagination I imagined Jazzman underground in the Slocan Valley, attributed to him falling in love with the mountains I fell in love with five years later.

Now that I know the truth, namely that Cha Cha never got near my mountains, was underground in a farmhouse near Tomah, Wisconsin, can I reimagine him, perhaps in love with the stars he first saw in Nippersink (not far from Tomah) where I had loved them as a boy? Can the old man I am today reinvent Cha Cha – and Jazzman: Aren't Cha Cha's stars Jazzman's mountains? – perhaps as the poet I wanted to be long ago, not the revolutionary I became or the novelist I am? Thinking about time can drive you crazy. But if there is one thing crazy people do not lack, it is imagination.

On my last trip to Chicago, a trip I undertook mainly to show my Chinese wife where I grew up (but not Lincoln Park, never Lincoln Park), I was able to remeet Bernardine Dohrn, the leader of the Weathermen, who had emerged from underground. She had not been in the Slocan Valley, but most of her comrades had. She told me a little about being underground. If I had heard her tale thirteen or fourteen years earlier, my novel might have been better. Could I have rewritten it or written its projected third part then? I'll never know because that was 1989 and I had a huge Chinese novel, a novel that grew into three, to write. I could not think about my earlier novel until I finished that one. I wrote, rewrote and revised it for a quarter of a century. It seems to be finished now (although if time grants me even more time, perhaps I can rework that one too). Time holds me grey and dying; can I sing in my chains like the sea?

"Police state" is a term you don't hear much anymore. In my youth it was regularly applied to communist governments like the Soviet Union and China. One seldom hears it now for a simple reason: The United States today imprisons more people and a much higher percentage of its population than Russia, China or any other government in the world. I could cite statistics, but others have done that and I am a novelist, not a statistician or a social scientist. I am a novelist who writes mainly from experience, and the worst experience of my life was the murder of my friend and our leader, Fred Hampton. I was with him at a meeting at Black Panther Headquarters the night of December 3, 1969. O'Neal, the FBI infiltrator, was at the meeting too and must have drugged Fred sometime after the meeting ended.

In one of my novels I attempted to imagine a scene in which Fred, influenced by an appeal for equality I made at the meeting, refuses the drink O'Neal brings him and stays at headquarters writing all night instead of going home to sleep. If only it had happened that way. Alas, a few hours after we said right on and good night, the most alive person I have ever known was dead. Time, which has managed to make the historical novel which I began writing over forty years ago into a novel history, cannot make a fiction of Fred's survival fact. It cannot bring him back, but by reminding us what he stood for – revolution, equality – perhaps it can help make what he stood for as possible as it seemed to me when he stood for it.

I did little after his murder. I must do more now because it's no surprise to me that the country whose state police (the FBI) planned the assassination of its opposition's most charismatic leader is now the world's greatest police state. You can even buy stocks in its gulag.

Instead of fighting to right one country gone wrong, I opted to write to make a better world. My British Columbia mountains gave me the peace I needed, but what I wrote was often "Part Three," a fictional conclusion of my first novel, this novel, based on my experience in the 1960s. I wrote many "Part Threes" at many different times. In all those attempts to conclude my novel I returned to Chicago and the struggle. None of them were any good: How could I, safe in Canada, living in peace, believe in the bloody fiction I felt compelled to write? I had escaped; the world had not. In fact my revolutionary hope took me not south but west, to the East, to China, where I thought to fashion a new life under socialism. Deng Xiaoping betrayed that revolution, but by the time he did I had a Chinese wife and enough experience to write three Chinese novels.

Most of those experiences were good, but one was horror at passing a long line of high stone walls with watchtowers, prisons along what at that time was a little used railway spur in the desert of Qinghai. Good or bad, keeping my body in Canada and my mind in China enabled me to continue ignoring what was happening in the United States. What was happening was complex: The military-industrial complex a Republican president and former general had warned against grew so potent it spawned a child, the prison-industrial complex. Is it my lack of imagination or is the reality really unimaginable to one of my generation, at least one who escaped, who was acquitted at his trial but who might as well have been convicted and gone underground so long ago?

Time does not always heal, but it always alters. Although I think about Fred's assassination less often than I did, when I do it still hurts. And time has altered me from a novelist with too little imagination into a historian with too much imagination, for the novel I set out to write to right history has turned out to be a history that needs somehow to help unwrite a reality so unreal it feels like fiction to me, who has been out of it: The United States has reinstituted slavery. It turns out that the Constitution does not prohibit slavery – so long as the slave is a convicted felon. So pass laws making possession of white powders and green weeds a felony and, presto: more slaves than there were during Slavery. And capitalism knows just what to do with them: private prisons to exploit the new slaves for private profit, post Victorian workhouses to replace antebellum plantations.

The great grandchildren of the slaves freed a century and a half ago are being herded into prisons and made to work under conditions often worse than those of their ancestors. For the police state operates only in the ghettoes. Indeed, I witnessed a demarcation: "I had seen Chicago police setting up barricades of squad cars with machine guns mounted on the hoods to contain a 'riot' to the Cabrini-Green black ghetto, a riot that was never more than a rumour." I am quoting myself, from Chapter Nineteen of this novel. What I saw in the summer of 1969 had been an occasion for laughter, for I had been in Cabrini that day and knew the "riot" the cops were attempting to contain had never been more than a rumour.

By the time I wrote about the incident, seven years after I saw it, I was apprehensive but still did not fully understand what I had seen. That barricade was the police saying that the law applied differently inside the ghetto and outside it. It was a transition in the evolution of the police state. In 1969 the police would let blacks smash and burn the ghetto, but not leave it. I suppose that is the definition and rationale of a ghetto. If the law, especially the drug laws, of the police state was enforced today in white or even middle class black or integrated neighbourhoods the way it is in the black and brown ghettoes, there would be revolution, genuine red revolution, not the red versus blue games they play down there, not just the occasional rebellion we now see.

Newfangled laws reinforce the police state. Police officers are rewarded by being allowed legally to confiscate money and property of those they arrest – they often did that in my day, but on a smaller scale and it wasn't legal then – while police departments are rewarded with the military equipment and technology which enable them to enforce a true police state. They have more – and far more sophisticated – weapons of control than the guns I witnessed on the hoods of their cars in 1969.

How dare the country with the largest prison population in the world boast of its freedom, call itself a democracy and criticize other countries for human rights violations? The simple fact is that a decent society does not use its wealth to build prisons and weapons. It uses it to wipe out poverty and build good housing, schools and hospitals for all its people. When gross inequality ceases to exist and all citizens are well housed, fed and educated, there will be little crime, little need for repressive police and jails.

I thought I had found such a country in China. When I was there, the cops did not carry guns and people hardly believed me when I told them that in Chicago police were ordered to carry guns even when off duty. In those days China was not rich, but neither were any of its people. Every capable adult had a job, and the best paid workers, including the leaders of workplaces and government, earned perhaps three or four times what a beginning worker did. Housing was basic, but it and health care, education and employment were guaranteed to everyone.

That was why the line of prisons I encountered in Qinghai caused me such distress: I wanted socialism to be based on freedom, not jails. Nevertheless, the United States today imprisons almost fifty per cent more people than China even though China has four times its population. Is slavery freedom? I was in China in 1984 – the year, not the novel. It feels to me like Americans today are in 1984 – the novel, not the year. Could Orwell have created a better exemplar of doublethink than Donald Trump? Indeed, when Trump and his minions began talking about alternative facts and fake news, Orwell's 1984 rose to the top of Amazon's best seller list. When the real world turns fictional, the realistic novelist turns factual.

I went to China in 1983 and was there for most of the Eighties. Mainly they were good years for me. I fell in love in Shanghai, married and expected to live the rest of my life in China. I wrote no novels but kept extensive journals because I knew I would one day write novels about China. The day came sooner and more suddenly than I expected. On June 4, 1989 my wife and I were in British Columbia. I wanted to show the woman I loved the mountains I loved before we returned to flat Shanghai and our future. Except when Deng Xiaoping sent tanks and troops in to crush the Tiananmen demonstrations, Canada became our future. For Deng the way in (to wealth) was out: opening China to the rest of the world (especially the United States, which he had visited with great fanfare in 1979). He, like Zhou Enlai and Zhu De, had been in Europe and joined the Chinese Communist Party there during the 1920s. Mao Zedong had never been out of China before the success of the revolution in 1949, and his ideas were rooted in Chinese culture. For Mao the way out (of poverty) was in, to Chinese self-sufficiency.

All's changed, but perhaps not utterly. What happened in the United States in 1968 and 1969 predicted what is happening today. Time always alters but seldom randomly: Time future is contained in time past. So what we do today can determine our future. If we do not change the direction in which we are heading, the world will end up where we are heading. Seventy years ago Orwell saw where we were heading, and although we may not have arrived there as soon as he feared, we have not changed direction.

My generation, inspired in part by 1984, attempted to change that direction fifty years ago. I like to think that our movement – rainbow children of the Sixties on a raft headed into a maelstrom which the best of us did not survive – moved Orwell's clock back so we are not yet in the hopeless world of Winston Smith. I like to hope there is still hope. Fred Hampton used to say: "The only solution is revolution." I share with Fred a love of words and poetry. "The ballot or the bullet?" Malcolm X, another lover of words, used to ask. Probably it will take both and more. Just as it will take more than better words and poetry to get us there. The way out is in. But the way in to a world of equality, a world with little need for prisons or police, the world we have to try to reach to save our species and our planet, is first to get our sisters and brothers out. It is time for a quiet Canadian survivor of the catastrophe to the south to shout out. It is time an old writer's words speak to the present, not the past he cannot escape. Remember Fred Hampton! Remember the Bastille!

Historian's Epilogue: Then and When

I READ MY FIRST BOOK IN JAIL. I was already eighteen and a junkie. The Catholic priest at Cook County Jail gave me The Seven Storey Mountain *by Thomas Merton. I didn't tell the priest I never read a whole book before, and this one was almost five hundred pages long. But I had time. I had* nothing but time. I was doing time.

I learned a lot reading that book. Not what the priest hoped I would learn but what I needed. Although the priest would not like what I learned, maybe he would be proud that I ended up in a university. The first thing I learned from the book was that I could read it. In school I had been classified as "educable mentally handicapped." That was the school's way of calling me stupid. I knew I was not stupid, but no way was I going to let the teachers know what I knew. I hated school. I hated the way Puerto Rican and black kids were made to feel stupid. I quit school as soon as I could.

The second thing I learned from The Seven Storey Mountain *was that I liked reading it. That was a discovery. In school I had learned to hate reading because I hated school. In jail* The Seven Storey Mountain *taught me I was wrong. Almost everything I learned in school was wrong, but I didn't know that until I finally read a book. I learned a lot more in jail than I did in school.*

The most important thing I learned reading that book was contemplation. I didn't even know the word when Merton started talking about it. Once I found out what the word meant, I contemplated contemplation. I don't think my love of words came from Merton. One of the reasons I was willing to read his book was the title. I wanted to find out what those funny words were all about. So I loved words even before I read his book, but reading his book strengthened my love.

It is a passion I have to be careful about. It can lead me into junk. When I am high I sometimes try to write poetry. Usually it is bad poetry. More like a child playing with words, like what I just wrote, "contemplated contemplation." Those words and these thoughts came to me in the hole. In the hole I learned I can get high on hope, not dope. By contemplating. But as I said I have to be careful. When I was young, I thought dope might improve my contemplation and inspire me to write good poetry. Really I was not much like Merton. He was educated. I was not. But we both wanted out of the world we were in. Junk was my way out, religion was his. My god was junk, his junk was God. Going into a monastery seemed to me like going to jail. And in his monastery you could not even talk. You might as well be in the hole.

As I contemplated contemplation in my hole, I figured out that he must have figured out most of what he wrote in the book by contemplating in his hole. I figured that out about him and a lot about myself in the hole of Cook County Jail. When I got out of jail, my head was in a much better space because I read Merton's book and taught myself to contemplate. I had contemplated a new me, a new organization, and a new world. The me was not a junkie. The organization was not a gang or a social club. The world was one without prisons and police. All negative, all things that were not. I would have to make them positive. I wasn't sure how to do that. I just knew I had to change. Everything. Contemplating was only a beginning. I had to do some doing.

I did.

Until I didn't.

I got out of jail at the right time. Right before the big political Convention. Protesters were coming from all over the country and they were gathering in Lincoln Park. The park, not the hood. Though they had to sleep in the hood when they got driven out of the park. If they slept. I didn't do anything at the demonstrations, but I went and watched. Heavy shit. The pigs were beating the hippies with big clubs, bigger than their nightsticks. They were not bothering to bust them, only beating them. Busting them would waste time. It would mean they couldn't beat as many heads. The Young Lords used to beat up hippies in Old Town. But that was because we couldn't beat the pigs. I thought the pigs only beat on brown and black kids. The hippies were almost all white. Most of them ran when the pigs came at them. But some of them fought back. White kids were fighting the pigs. I learned something new. And later the first night I learned I wasn't the only one learning. I met two of the other guys. They were watching too. Every night a few more of us went and watched. For once we were on the sidelines, not in the middle of the action.

It turned out that some of the guys knew more than I did. They knew two local radicals who were with the protesters. A dude and a girl. Both white, but they both called cops pigs. The right words made the first connection. I ended up getting the dude's books and the girl's passion. We met them the last night of the Convention, when the action had shifted downtown.

We first met at our hangout, the corner of Halstead and Dickens across from the hot dog stand. The guys talked with them and I listened. We wanted to have our own demonstration, a Puerto Rican march. But the hood was still stinking of tear gas and swarming with pigs. So some of us went along to where the dude lived. He didn't live far from where I lived. I did some talking there. The dude did not look like the hippies who were fighting in the park. He had short hair. He needed a shave, but he did not have a beard. What he did have were books. I never saw so many books in one place. His house was a library. I used it like one for the next months. He fed me political books, but I asked for books of poetry too. That surprised him, but he had plenty of both. I did lots of reading before I did much doing.

I did for most of 1969. That's history. It's in the dude's book. He calls it a novel. He can't end it because it hasn't ended yet. History doesn't. TV sports announcers like to say: "When the going gets tough the tough get going." I thought I was tough, and I knew the going would never get tougher than it got after Fred's assassination. Yet I was going nowhere. I couldn't do any more or anymore. I needed to contemplate. Contemplating in the hole at Cook County Jail had taught me that the way out is in. I thought I was thinking after Fred's murder, but what I thought was that if I could go deeper in, I could get farther out. Too much was going on around me and inside me. I couldn't contemplate. And Lovin' Charlie had some dynamite junk. I got deeper in all right. I ended up underground, and then I had to go back and do time in jail to kick.

Back in the hole my head cleared. But by the time I did my time and got out the times had changed. So when I tried to do something, it was electoral politics, not revolution. That was not the sort of thing I was good at doing. It was the sort of thing Mayor Washington was good at doing. Then he died too. The times and leaders kept changing, and every change made every thing worse. At least I was able to get out. They keep prisoners in longer now. They give them time to work, not contemplate. What you learn in jail these days is hate. Of everything. Of everyone including yourself. No more seven storey mountains.

I wanted to be a poet. Like Fred. I became a historian so I could go back to the good times, the times when I was doing, not doing time. The time with Fred. Poetry is dangerous. It led me to dope and Fred to death. History is about time, but it is also like poetry. Without being too deep. When you understand history, it fits together like a poem. I can even hear it rhyme. If "time present and time past are both perhaps present in time future and time future contained in time past," we need to study history to find out where we're going fast.

Ignorance is not strength. A government based on its military might make an empire but never a democracy. A state based on police and prisons can make a police state, never a democracy. Capitalism can make rich capitalists, never democracy. Those are lessons history teaches. I have learned them. Now. I certainly did not learn them in my first round of school. I was taught to be ignorant. Then. Fortunately I managed to learn enough in jail and life to go back to school and study history. Most ghetto kids don't get a second chance. And even fewer will get one with today's jails. History also teaches that when the imperial capitalist police state makes as much inequality as this one does, the unequal revolt. That's what I was doing in 1969. History is now. I'm still doing it.

I loved Fred Hampton. Everyone who knew him loved him. I am proud I worked closely with him all through 1969. His murder changed me forever. I have a photo of Fred and me laughing together. It was taken at the first demonstration we were on together, a March march to the Wicker Park Welfare Office. It started to snow and I said: "Apropos of the Wet Snow." He replied: "I am a sick man. I am a spiteful man." We had both been reading Dostoyevsky's Notes from Underground. *Two uneducated ghetto kids laughing about literature. Our friendship was full of coincidences like that.*

"I'll meet you underground. We'll both end up there," Fred said, and we laughed some more. We did not meet underground. When I was underground, Fred was under ground. We met in the sky. Under beautiful Wisconsin stars that you couldn't see in a city, I remembered Fred. I contemplated Fred. I even consulted Fred about what I should do. I always saw Fred in the stars at night. It made me think about where we might be.

Once I got to know him in 1969, I consulted Fred whenever I could. Consulting him may have saved my life. I left Orlando's party in Bridgeport early to consult Fred, so I wasn't around when the shooting started. I was the kind of kid who would have shoved himself in front of the pig's gun. For me the way out is in. Fred never worried about ins and outs. He just did. What needed to be done. He loved words so he loved to talk. But he was doing when he was talking. His words always said: "Do." He said what to do, and he did what he said. He said: "You can kill a revolutionary, but you can't kill the revolution." He was right, but his followers didn't follow his words. We made him wrong. After the revolutionary was killed, we didn't do. None of us did. All of us did nothing. Other friends' murders angered me. They made me fight back. Fred's murder immobilized me. It was intended to. It didn't just happen. It was obviously planned. Damn O'Neal.

It's easy to think the dead could do what you didn't, but I have faith in Fred. Obama couldn't even beat Bobby Rush in an election. The voters in Bobby's district remember Fred and return his former lieutenant to Congress every two years. Imagine what might happen if Fred was alive. History would be different. Anyone who knew Fred knows that. The novelist's novel completes my thesis project. When the history of what happened has happened, the historian is free to turn to a history of what did not happen. The way out is in.

Nelson Mandela inspired a revolution from inside prison. If Fred had not been assassinated at the end of 1969, he probably would have been put back in Menard Prison in 1970. At an even younger age than Mandela went in but with a shorter sentence at a different time. I like to think of Fred as starting the revolution that could not be killed when he was in but making it when he got out. Because I went in and got out a little later.

Fred was a real poet who didn't know it. Words just came to him. I was a poet who knew it but thought I couldn't do it without dope. It took time to teach me.

> Time present is not time past,
> Pretending it is gets us nowhere fast.
> But if all time is infernally present,
> What you did matters as little as what you didn't.
> History is now, history is me,
> What I make of myself makes history.
> History is now, history is Fred,
> Can remembering dead Fred make the future red?
> Why not? It's worth a try.
> The tyranny of time we must defy.

But once I learned, I was a historian. No dope. I contemplate or read books to find words. They poured out of Fred like wine coming directly from crushed grapes. His mind instantly fermented and mellowed his words. Fred never did dope. He didn't need it. The FBI had to drug him to kill him. The pigs didn't have to kill me. They could chill me with junk. It was damn good junk. I was a damn fool. Doing dope is not doing. Doing time is not doing. If I did like Fred instead of being done, history might be different.

THEY JAILED FRED IN 1970. That was their big mistake. Their jails were not ready for Fred, but he was ready for jail. Outside he gave himself too many duties and was too much loved by too many people to have time to write a book. Inside he wrote the book which became the bible of our movement. He came out like I did. Stronger than he went in. And he came out with a plan. "The only solution is revolution," he announced to the friends waiting for him at his release. They all knew that. Then he went on: "Liberty was the battle cry of the first American Revolution. Equality will be the battle cry of the New American Revolution."

He had organized Menard Prison. By the time he came out, he had planted roots for an organization of revolutionary prisoners which would grow without him and spread from jail to jail. I know. I helped spread it. The prison grapevine is an awesome plant. It spreads far beyond its roots. Inmates with no idea of its roots share its fruits. I knew its roots and its fruits. The sweetest of Fred's fruits was his book, Beyond Liberty, which he wrote in Menard. It picks up where John Stuart Mill left off. To liberty it adds equality and camaraderie ("fraternity" sounds too male), the goals of the French Revolution. "Complete equality cannot be imposed, but inequality can and must be opposed," Fred wrote.

UNDER THE STARS Fred and I discussed revolution. We met, just as Fred said we would, at the farmhouse near Tomah, where I was underground. Jail had hardened Fred. He and his new book seemed less poetic, more professional than the old Fred. Yet if anything even more simple. Everything he said and wrote was clear and easy to understand. Almost like Lenin but with writing that flared into slogans of fire. "The way to get rid of government of the rich, by the rich, for the rich is to get rid of the rich." "Once there are no more rich there will be no more poor." Speaking of the law, he asked a simple two word question: "Whose law?" I told him my slogan: "The way out is in." "The way out is to bring others in," he told me. "Jailbirds are on our side. A few chirps and they're singing our song."

Inside, our old song had to be freedom. What else could a prisoner ask for? Yet every prisoner understood the new song, equality. Without the rich and their laws, there would be little crime, little need for prisons. "You would have to be nuts to steal from or attack your equals if there were no unequals," they said. Former country clubs, not prisons, could be used to educate and rehabilitate mentally deficient and defective "nuts."

FRED'S WORDS CONVINCED ME. I had been thinking about contacting our lawyers and serving my time so I could get out from underground. When I told Fred what I intended to do, he wrapped his arms around me in one of his famous bear hugs that lifted me off the ground. We talked it over. We made plans for my time in and my time out. In I reinforced and extended the organizing Fred had done. Out I began working directly with Fred. That was great. The Panthers were no longer only black and the Young Lords were no longer only brown.

I found and recruited my two honky friends, the girl and the dude from Lincoln Park. The girl was married to a radical Christian pastor, a friend of my murdered friend Bruce Johnson. So they and their friends expanded our new movement. The dude was underground in Canada. I went there. The place he was living was beautiful in a freaky way. It was full of hippies and mountains. I could understand why Jazzman loved it, but the mountains were so close they scared me. During the day. Then at night the dude took me to a dark place and showed me the stars. The sky was not as wide as it was in Wisconsin, but the stars were just as bright. Maybe brighter. He didn't want to return. He wanted me to stay there. I had to sing all of our songs to lure him back.

THE MOVEMENT WAS COMING TOGETHER. Bringing all its parts together was the key to making the revolution. Fred was the leader who could bring it all together. He was loved. Except by the ruling class, which hated him because he would not join them by running for office. He reshaped American politics by declining to play them. He called the high stakes game politics had become an "electatrocity" and refused to sit at the table. In the 60s "the pigs," mainly the police who terrorized the ghettoes, had been the main enemy. To make a revolution we had to move up the food chain. To the pig farmers, the politicians, and to the owners of the pig farms, the big corporations. "It's not up to the politicians" became one of our main slogans. We scrawled it on posters with the words "up," "the" and "politicians" written in red.

The message was especially effective among lower ranks of a bloated military sent by the politicians to fight and die in yet another corporate sponsored war. In speeches Fred usually added to the slogan: "It's not up to the politicians because the politicians are not up to it." Or "it's not up to the politicians because so and so (a politician in the news, usually the president) is up to no good." Attacking what he was not always led Fred to what he was, his old rap that we all joined: "I AM A REVOLUTIONARY."

FRED AND MORE AND MORE OTHERS preached equality, race and culture in the ghettoes; equality, class and culture in working class white and mixed communities; liberty, equality, camaraderie in prisons and the military. When we brought all the cultures together, our movement came together the way it didn't in the 60s. But it took time. Time and the idiocy of their last and least popular war. Time and hunger strikes in the jails, worker and student strikes on the outside. They struck to support our march on DC. We marched to support their strikes. Although we chanted "power to the people," few of us people understood our power as we faced the domestic wing of the army guarding the White House. Fred would later say: "When an army of poor people with a head of rich people needs to shoot itself, it does not do it in the foot."

THE REVOLUTION WAS PLANNED. For a second march on Washington. A march which, even within this history which did not happen, did not happen. Shakespeare knew that sometimes history makes Hamlets, not vice versa. When the time is right, a consummation devoutly to be wished consummates. If the time had not been right the first time, we would have proceeded according to plan.

A SEA OF PROTESTERS chanting anti-government slogans and calling on the troops to join them faced soldiers guarding the White House. Our ranks stretched farther than the eye could see, but we were unarmed civilians facing armed, trained soldiers. "Fire," shouted a commander. A shot rang out and the commander fell. "Who else wants us to shoot unarmed sisters and brothers?" asked the new unknown soldier. Silence. We surged forward to embrace our soldier comrades. Other shots were fired. Other commanders and a few friends fell. But the New American Revolution was surprisingly bloodless. The mob ruled.

The president and Congress were shocked and frightened at being betrayed by the army they had poured trillions into. Most of the Congress resigned. Big celebrations and bigger meetings. We opened the jails to let prisoners out and the president and his most unrepentant followers in. Revolution had revolved our world. Country clubbers occupied the jails and jailbirds studied in the country clubs. In big meetings held when every jail was opened, ex-cons had elected members in need of further education. The clubs seemed like graduate school, not punishment, and therefore worked well. Even politicians could graduate into them.

There was a glut of prisons. We turned a few penitentiaries into museums and urban renewed most jails. Whenever possible former inmates were employed in the wrecking and, later, construction crews. We had made, remade and unmade history. Mob rule, the rule of the many, not the rules of a few, turned out to be a great improvement over bought elections between two people few people gave a damn about. And as more and more people become more and more educated, it will become a better and better thing.

AT FIRST THE NEW GOVERNMENT CHANGED OFTEN. Fred knew many people and accepted volunteers with only an occasional question. "Revolutionary enthusiasm is more important than knowledge," he confided to me. "Knowledge can be taught, and the enthusiastic will learn." (It was the philosophy that led Fred to trust O'Neal, but in this world murderous FBI infiltrators did not happen. Little wonder this world did not happen.) The revolutionary enthusiasm of those days was contagious and overpowering. Of course there were problems. We solved and resolved them in mass meetings open to all. Defenders of the old order could speak but usually were quickly shouted down.

WHEN WE FINALLY MADE THE REVOLUTION, we kids of the 60s were older than we could imagine becoming in the days when one of our slogans was "never trust anyone over thirty." Bringing the cultures together brought the races and the ages together. Into the one human race, a united revolutionary culture with many subcultures. Participatory democracy. The New American Revolution was just one part of the world revolution. A late part but a vital part because the United States led the capitalist world.

As our American movement came together, it divided and weakened the old Amerikan government. That encouraged revolutions all over the world. And every revolution swelled the wind of revolution sweeping the globe. Momentum built. The dominoes the capitalists feared were finally falling. One of the last to fall was China, where it had all started in the previous century.

WE LEARN BY DOING, but we learn by writing too. If I could have read Fred's book, the fruits might have ripened sooner in me. Unfortunately Fred never got to write his book. I never wrote a whole book either, but I contemplated one. That's how I became a historian. What I just learned from writing is that time messes with us. The novelist and the historian connected before the novelist was a novelist or the historian was a historian. The world seemed simpler then. Because we were. It took time and contemplation to become what we became. And time made contemplation complicated. The novelist wrote a history, the historian wrote a fiction. He wrote what happened fifty years ago. I wrote what didn't happen. But shit happens. O'Neal happened. In a history of what didn't happen, shit didn't happen either. My shitless history is still too simple. Simplistic. A fairy tale, not a novel. Still, the novelist and the historian reconnected by writing. The moral of my fairy tale is the same as his history: Revolutionary hope is not as easily assassinated as people. Write on. Make writing do what doing didn't. It is time to defy time and resurrect our martyred black messiahs. Fred lives! The Bastille fell!

About the Author

I became a novelist as a teenager in a seminar with Saul Bellow, but when I quit school to write the great American novel, I discovered I lacked imagination. It took me many years of living to compensate for this lack, but eventually I acquired enough experience to write six novels. *The Foundations of Kindness* is the first – and last – of them. Most of it was written in 1975-6. The logues (prologue, dialogues, epilogues) were added between 2014 and 2018. After leaving Chicago I lived thirty-five years in the West Kootenays of British Columbia and six years in China. I presently live in the Victoria area of Vancouver Island.

Printed in November 2019
by Gauvin Press,
Gatineau, Québec